Mal and Chad

Stephen McCranie

The BIGGEST, BESTEST TIME EVER!

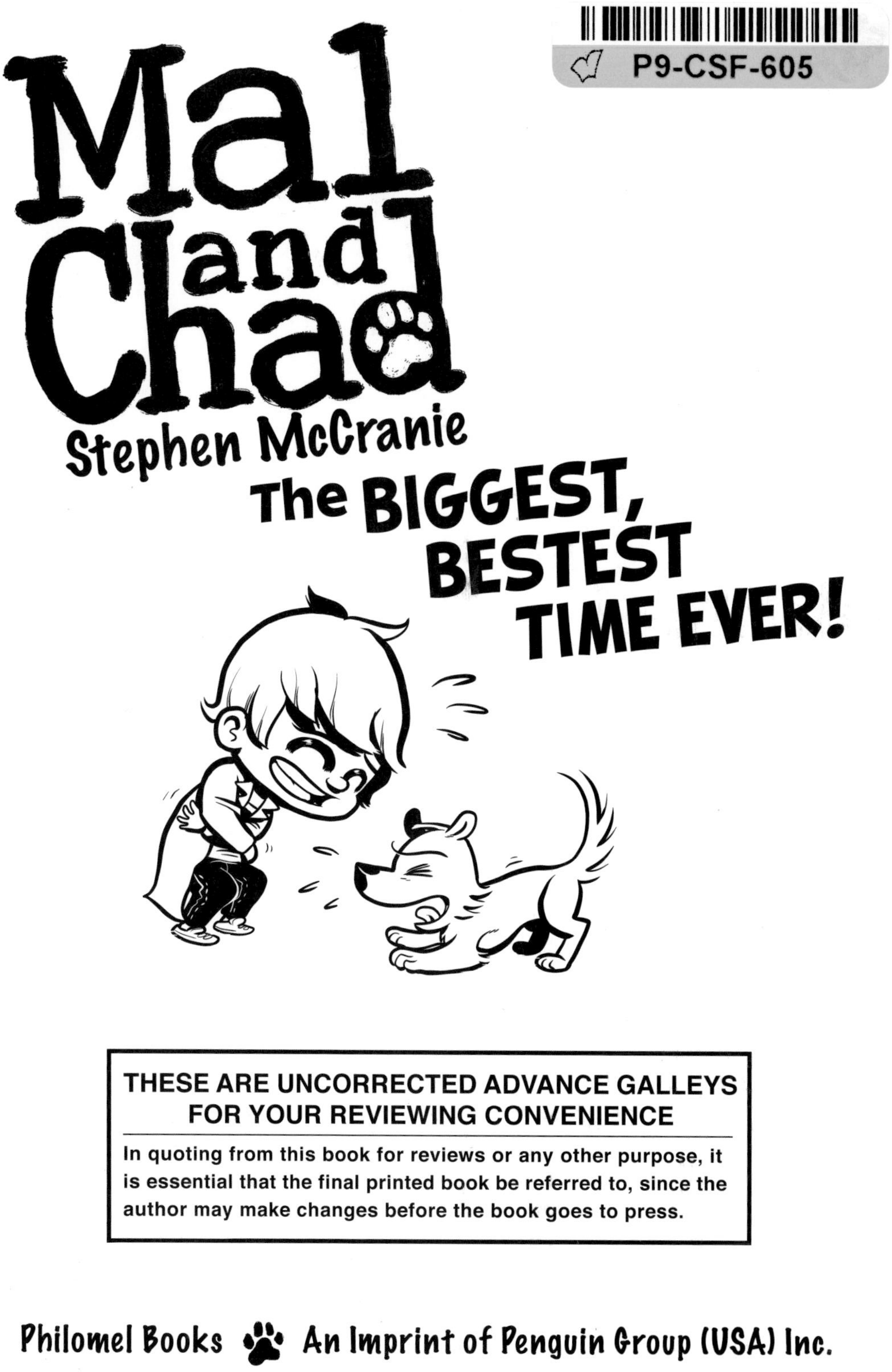

THESE ARE UNCORRECTED ADVANCE GALLEYS FOR YOUR REVIEWING CONVENIENCE

In quoting from this book for reviews or any other purpose, it is essential that the final printed book be referred to, since the author may make changes before the book goes to press.

Philomel Books · An Imprint of Penguin Group (USA) Inc.

For my dad.

PHILOMEL BOOKS

A division of Penguin Young Readers Group.

Published by The Penguin Group. Penguin Group (USA) Inc., 375 Hudson Street, New York, NY 10014, U.S.A. Penguin Group (Canada), 90 Eglinton Avenue East, Suite 700, Toronto, Ontario M4P 2Y3, Canada (a division of Pearson Penguin Canada Inc.). Penguin Books Ltd, 80 Strand, London WC2R 0RL, England. Penguin Ireland, 25 St. Stephen's Green, Dublin 2, Ireland (a division of Penguin Books Ltd). Penguin Group (Australia), 250 Camberwell Road, Camberwell, Victoria 3124, Australia (a division of Pearson Australia Group Pty Ltd). Penguin Books India Pvt Ltd, 11 Community Centre, Panchsheel Park, New Delhi—110 017, India. Penguin Group (NZ), 67 Apollo Drive, Rosedale, North Shore 0632, New Zealand (a division of Pearson New Zealand Ltd). Penguin Books (South Africa) (Pty) Ltd, 24 Sturdee Avenue, Rosebank, Johannesburg 2196, South Africa. Penguin Books Ltd, Registered Offices: 80 Strand, London WC2R 0RL, England.

Published simultaneously in Canada.

Printed in the United States of America.

Edited by Michael Green.

Designed by Richard Amari.

Library of Congress Cataloging-in-Publication Data is available upon request.

ISBN 978-0-399-25221-1

1 3 5 7 9 10 8 6 4 2

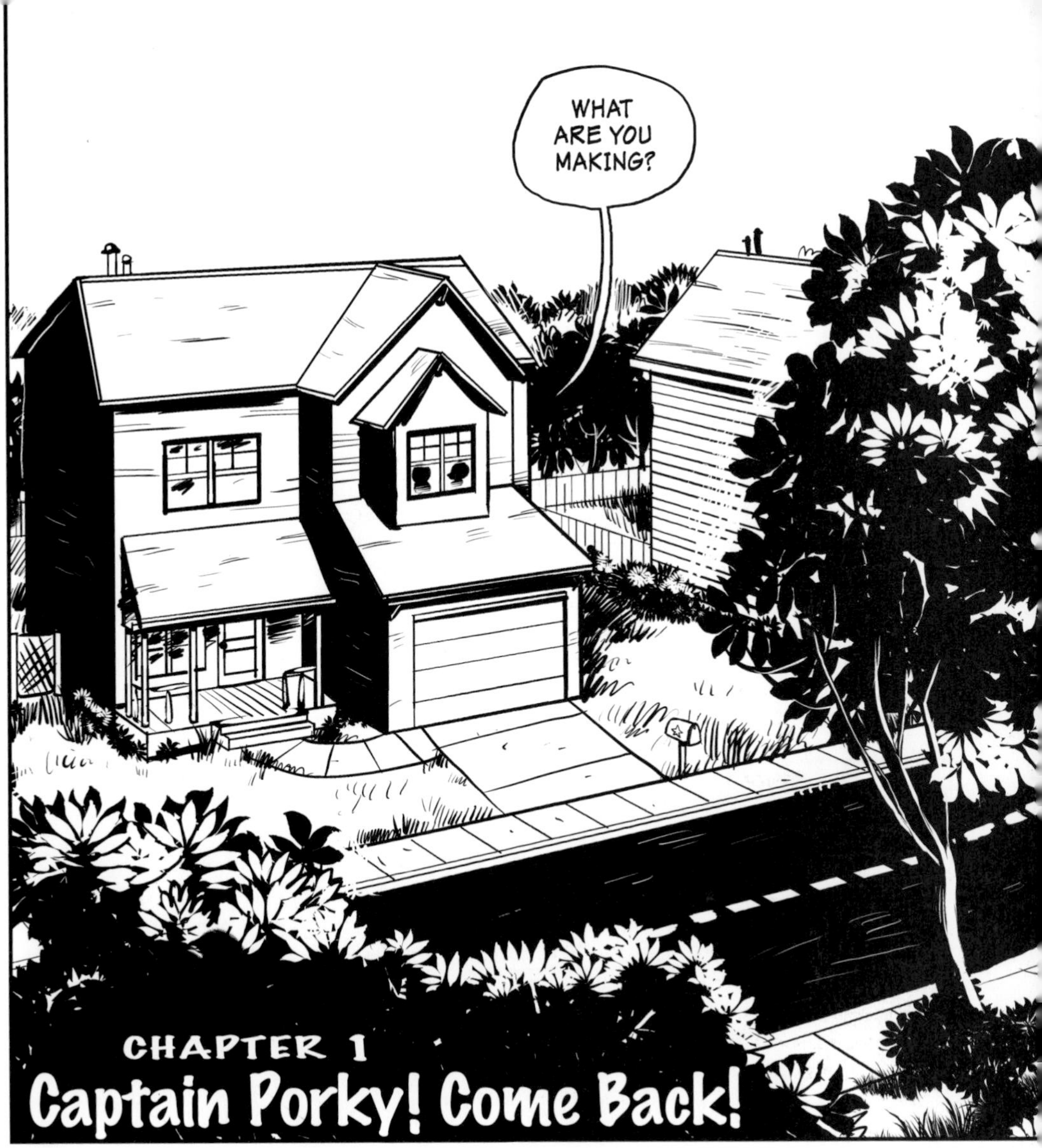
WHAT ARE YOU MAKING?
CHAPTER 1
Captain Porky! Come Back!

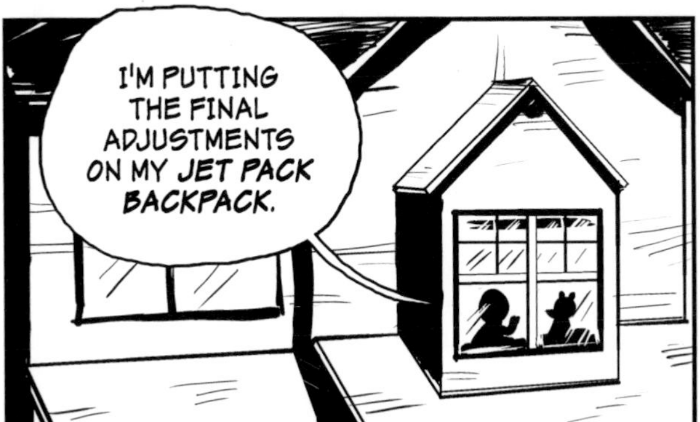
I'M PUTTING THE FINAL ADJUSTMENTS ON MY JET PACK BACKPACK.

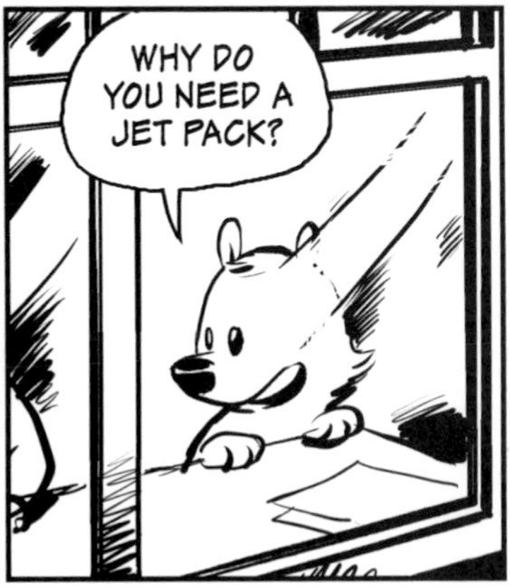
WHY DO YOU NEED A JET PACK?

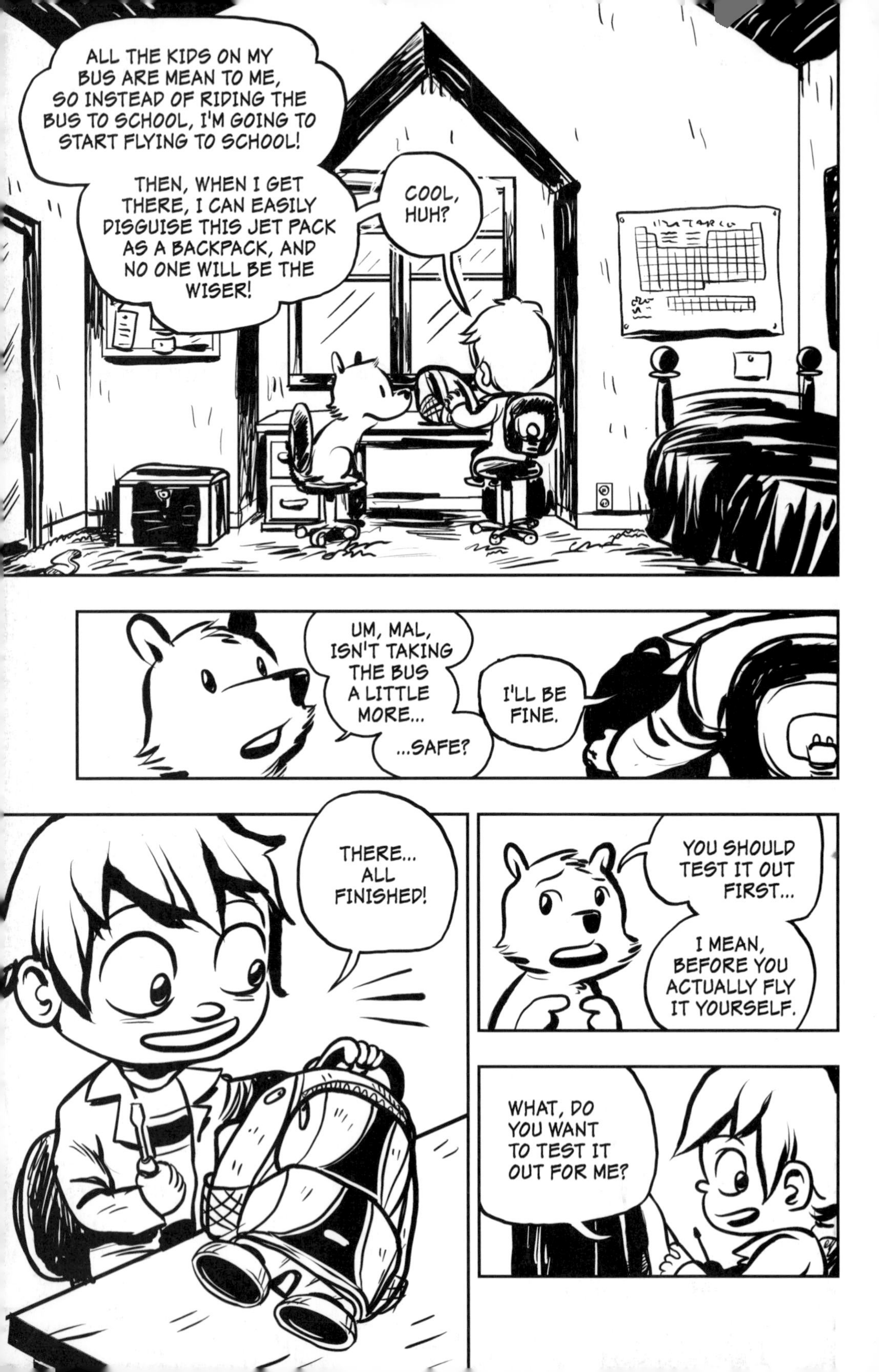
ALL THE KIDS ON MY BUS ARE MEAN TO ME, SO INSTEAD OF RIDING THE BUS TO SCHOOL, I'M GOING TO START FLYING TO SCHOOL!
THEN, WHEN I GET THERE, I CAN EASILY DISGUISE THIS JET PACK AS A BACKPACK, AND NO ONE WILL BE THE WISER!
COOL, HUH?
UM, MAL, ISN'T TAKING THE BUS A LITTLE MORE...
...SAFE?
I'LL BE FINE.
THERE... ALL FINISHED!
YOU SHOULD TEST IT OUT FIRST...
I MEAN, BEFORE YOU ACTUALLY FLY IT YOURSELF.
WHAT, DO YOU WANT TO TEST IT OUT FOR ME?

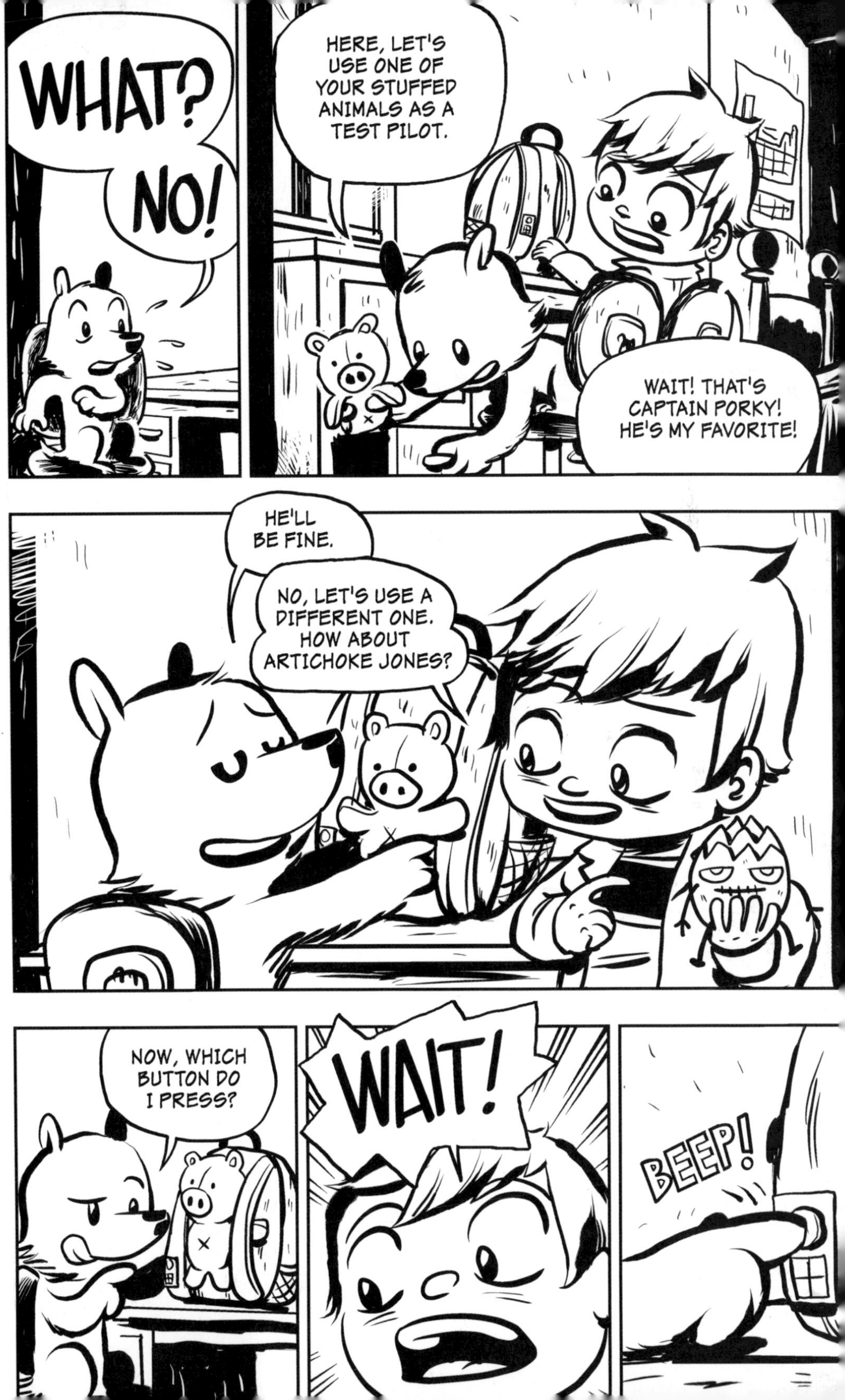
WHAT?
NO!
HERE, LET'S USE ONE OF YOUR STUFFED ANIMALS AS A TEST PILOT.
WAIT! THAT'S CAPTAIN PORKY! HE'S MY FAVORITE!
HE'LL BE FINE.
NO, LET'S USE A DIFFERENT ONE. HOW ABOUT ARTICHOKE JONES?
NOW, WHICH BUTTON DO I PRESS?
WAIT!
BEEP!

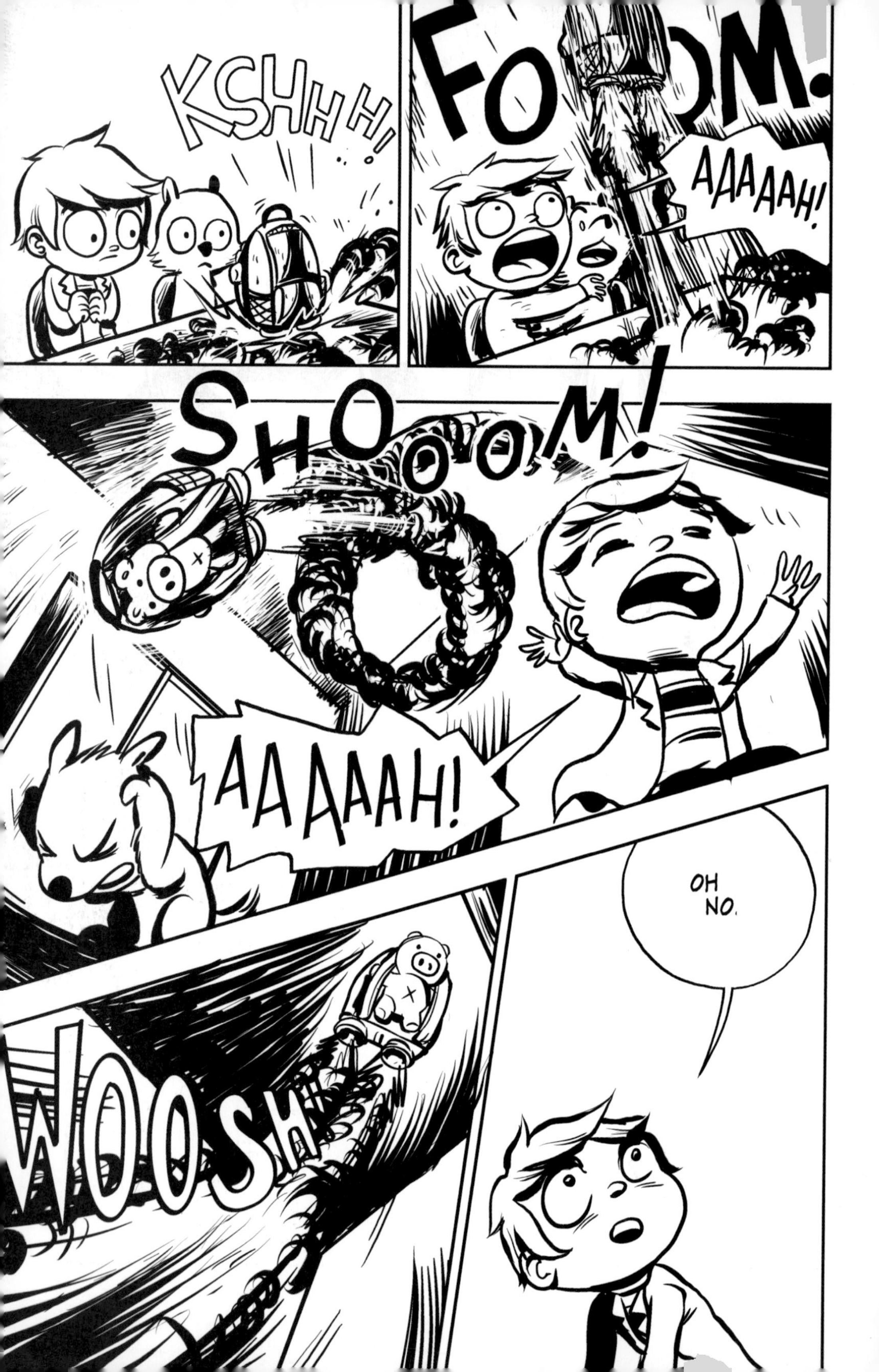
KSHHHH!
FOOM!
AAAAAH!
SHOOOOOM!
AAAAAH!
WOOSH!
OH NO.

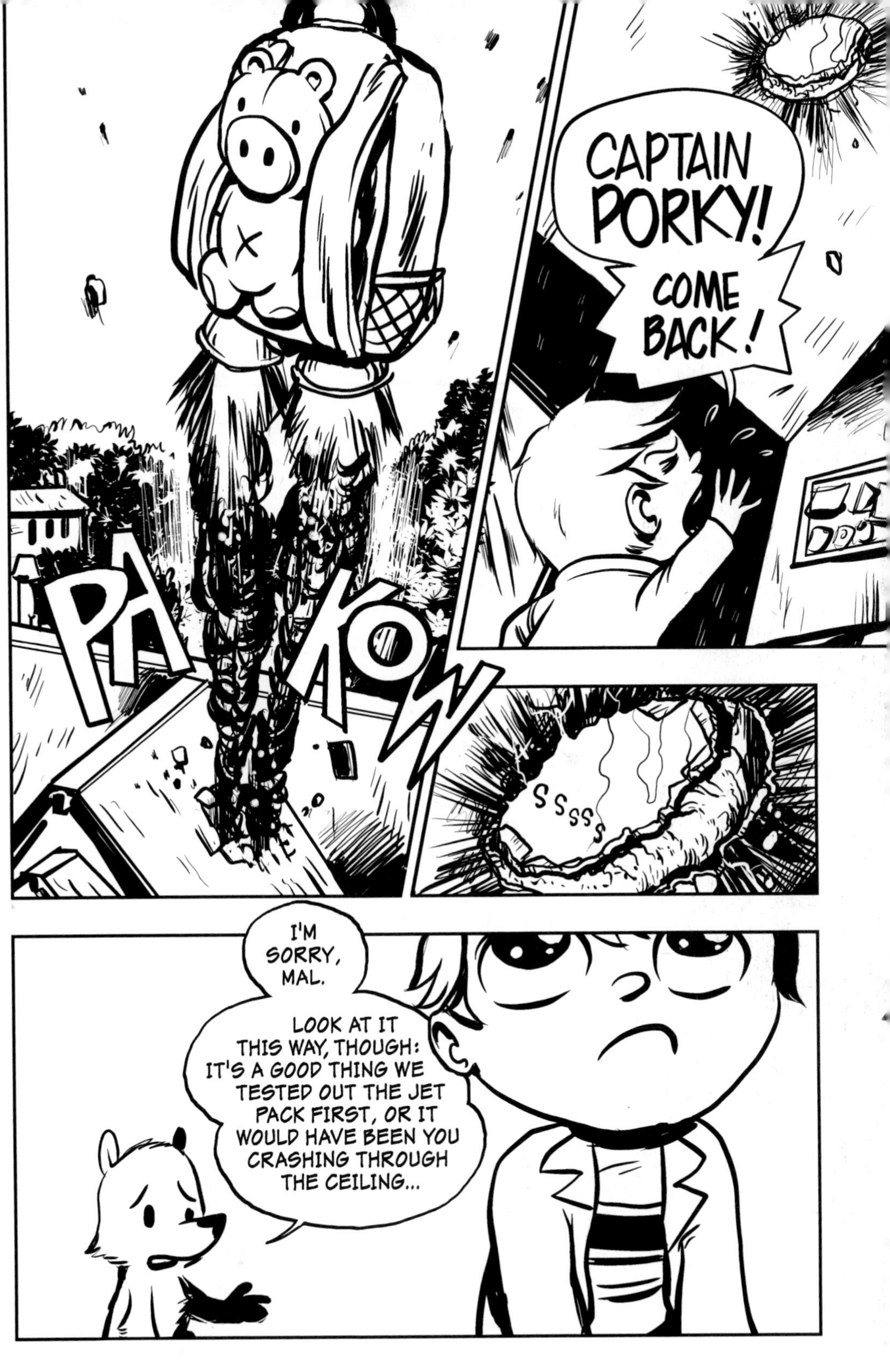
PA-KOW
CAPTAIN PORKY!
COME BACK!
SSSSS
I'M SORRY, MAL.
LOOK AT IT THIS WAY, THOUGH: IT'S A GOOD THING WE TESTED OUT THE JET PACK FIRST, OR IT WOULD HAVE BEEN YOU CRASHING THROUGH THE CEILING...

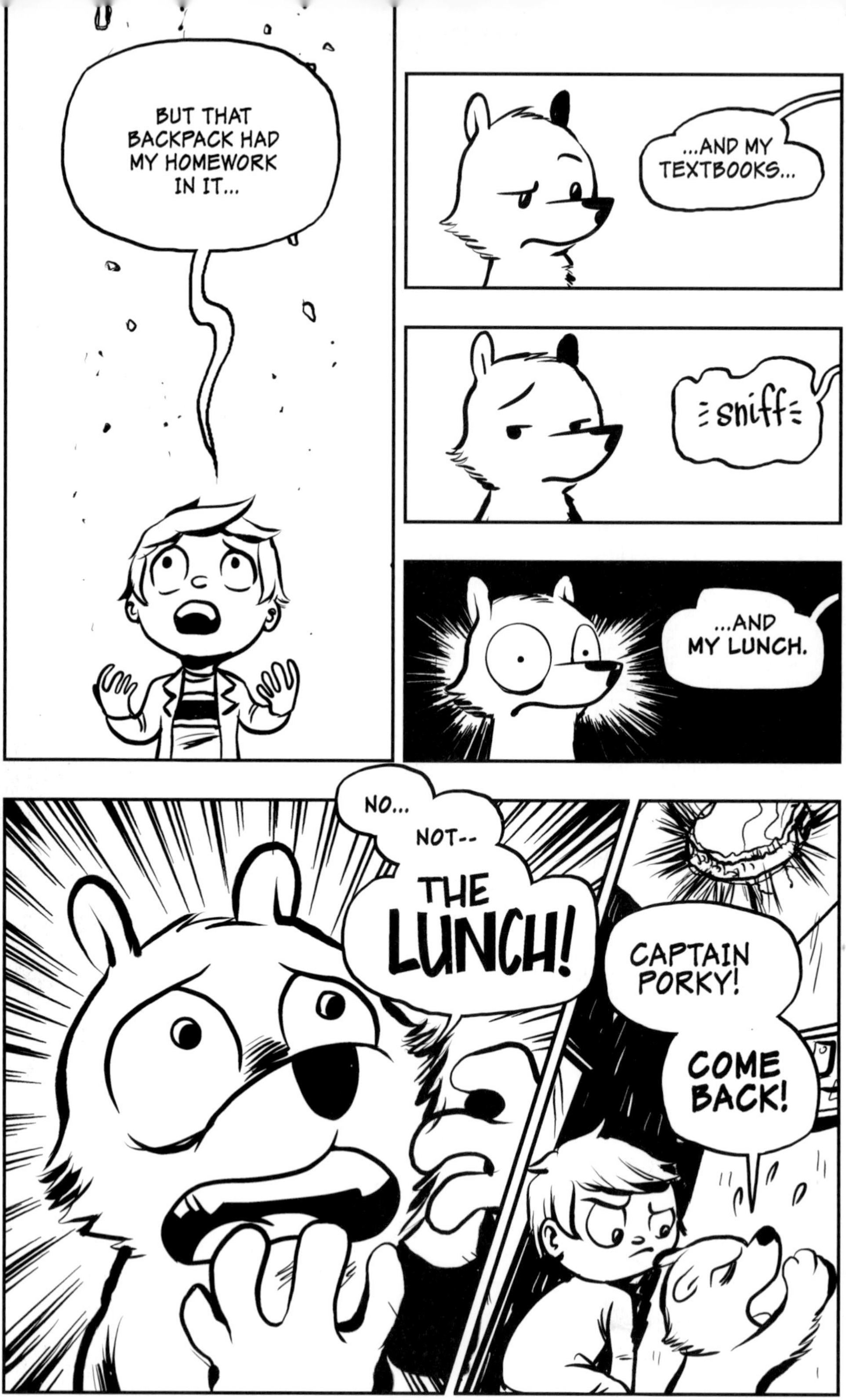
BUT THAT BACKPACK HAD MY HOMEWORK IN IT...
...AND MY TEXTBOOKS...
sniff
...AND MY LUNCH.
NO... NOT--
THE LUNCH!
CAPTAIN PORKY!
COME BACK!

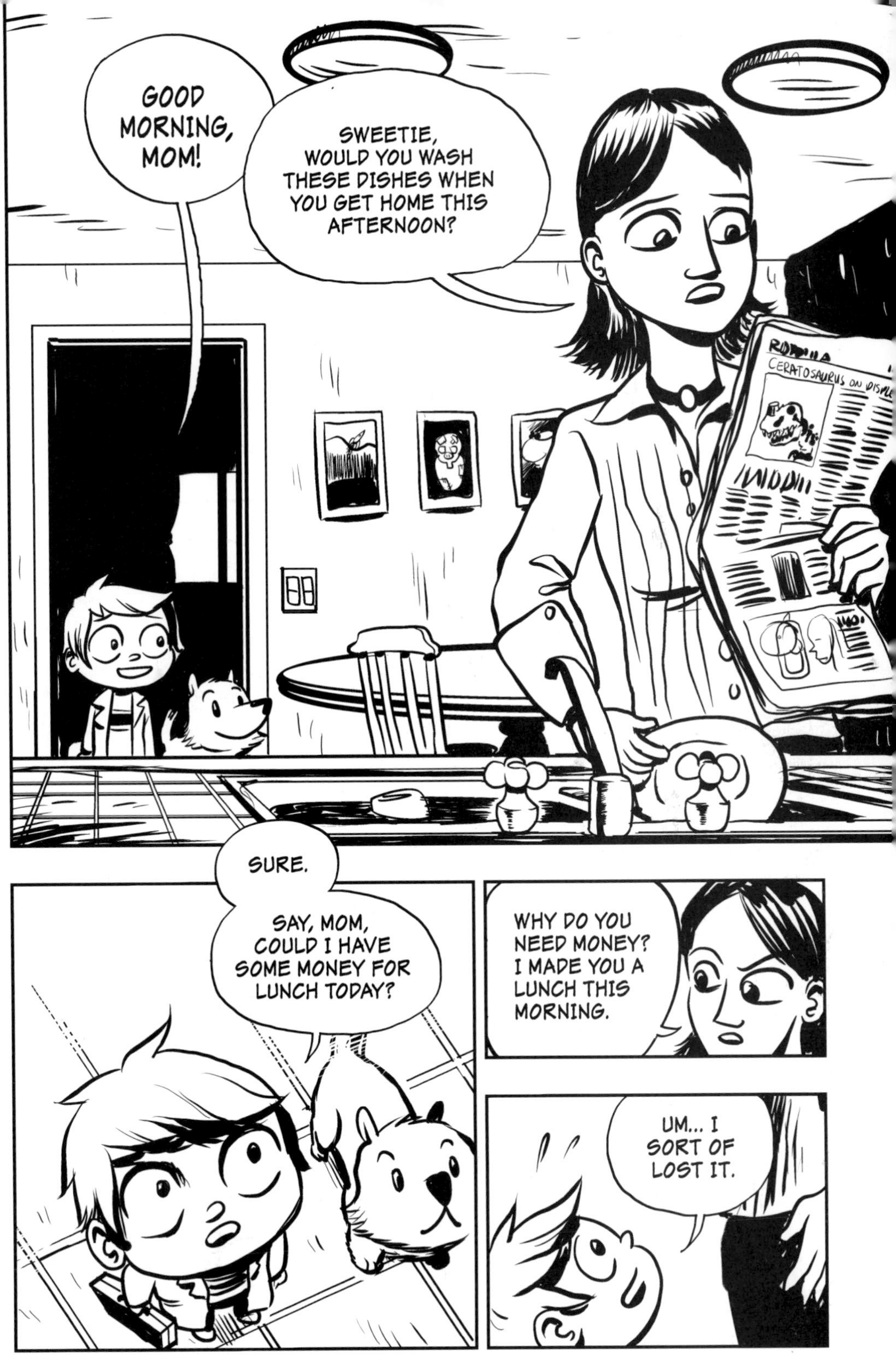
GOOD MORNING, MOM!
SWEETIE, WOULD YOU WASH THESE DISHES WHEN YOU GET HOME THIS AFTERNOON?
CERATOSAURUS ON DISPLA
SURE.
SAY, MOM, COULD I HAVE SOME MONEY FOR LUNCH TODAY?
WHY DO YOU NEED MONEY? I MADE YOU A LUNCH THIS MORNING.
UM... I SORT OF LOST IT.

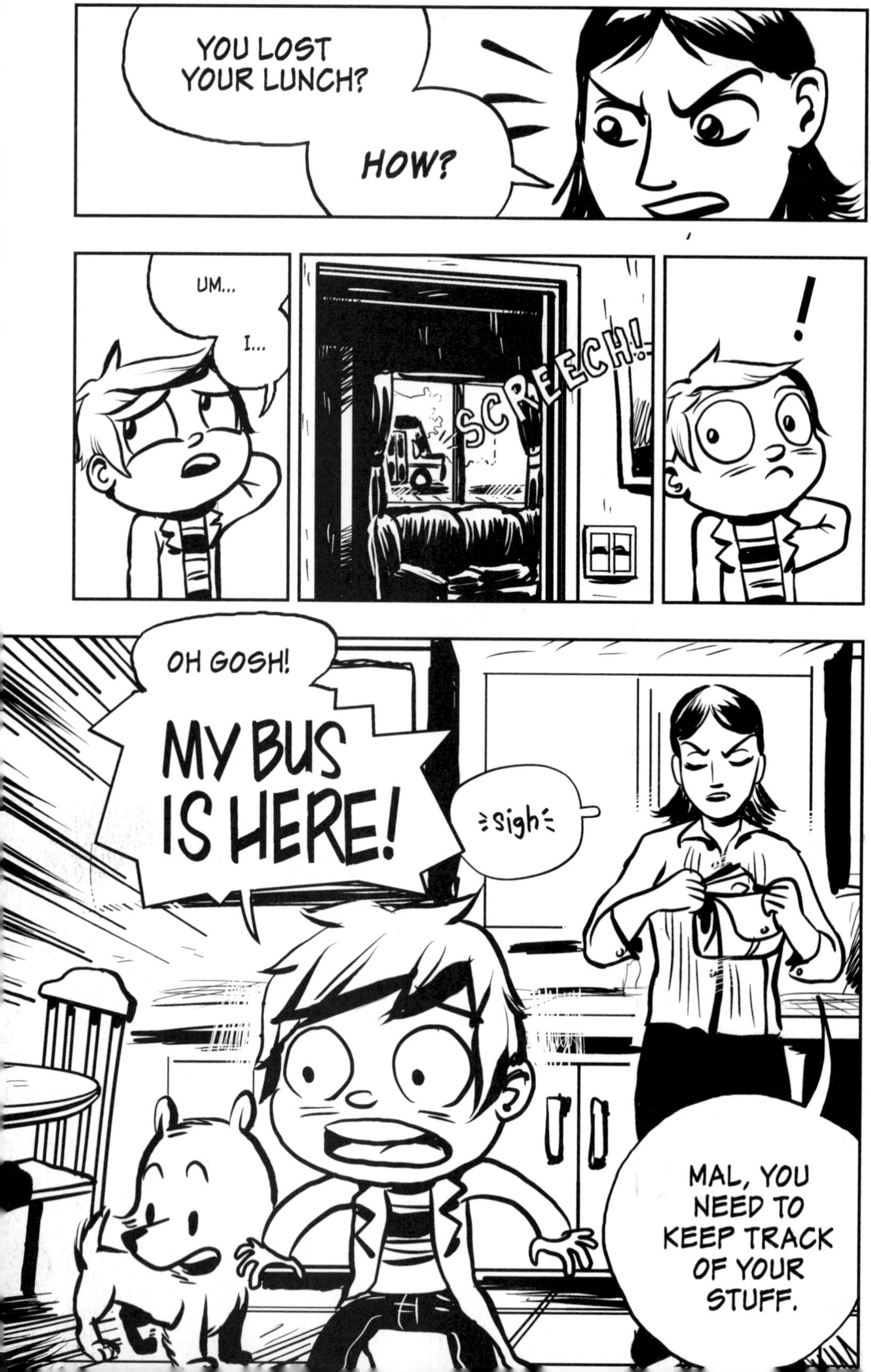
YOU LOST YOUR LUNCH?
HOW?
UM...
I...
SCREECH!
!
OH GOSH!
MY BUS IS HERE!
sigh
MAL, YOU NEED TO KEEP TRACK OF YOUR STUFF.

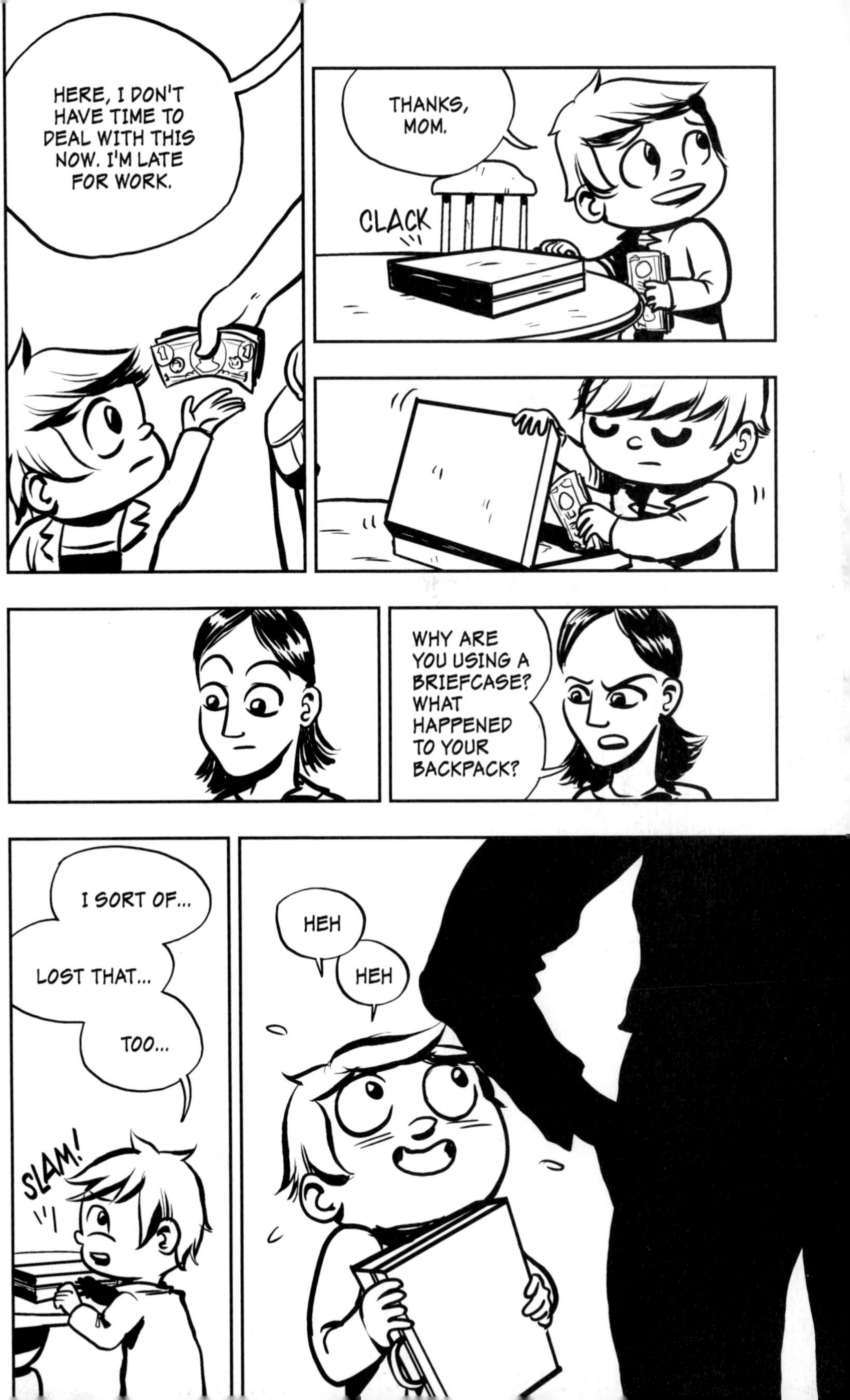
HERE, I DON'T HAVE TIME TO DEAL WITH THIS NOW. I'M LATE FOR WORK.
THANKS, MOM.
CLACK
WHY ARE YOU USING A BRIEFCASE? WHAT HAPPENED TO YOUR BACKPACK?
I SORT OF...
LOST THAT...
TOO...
SLAM!
HEH
HEH

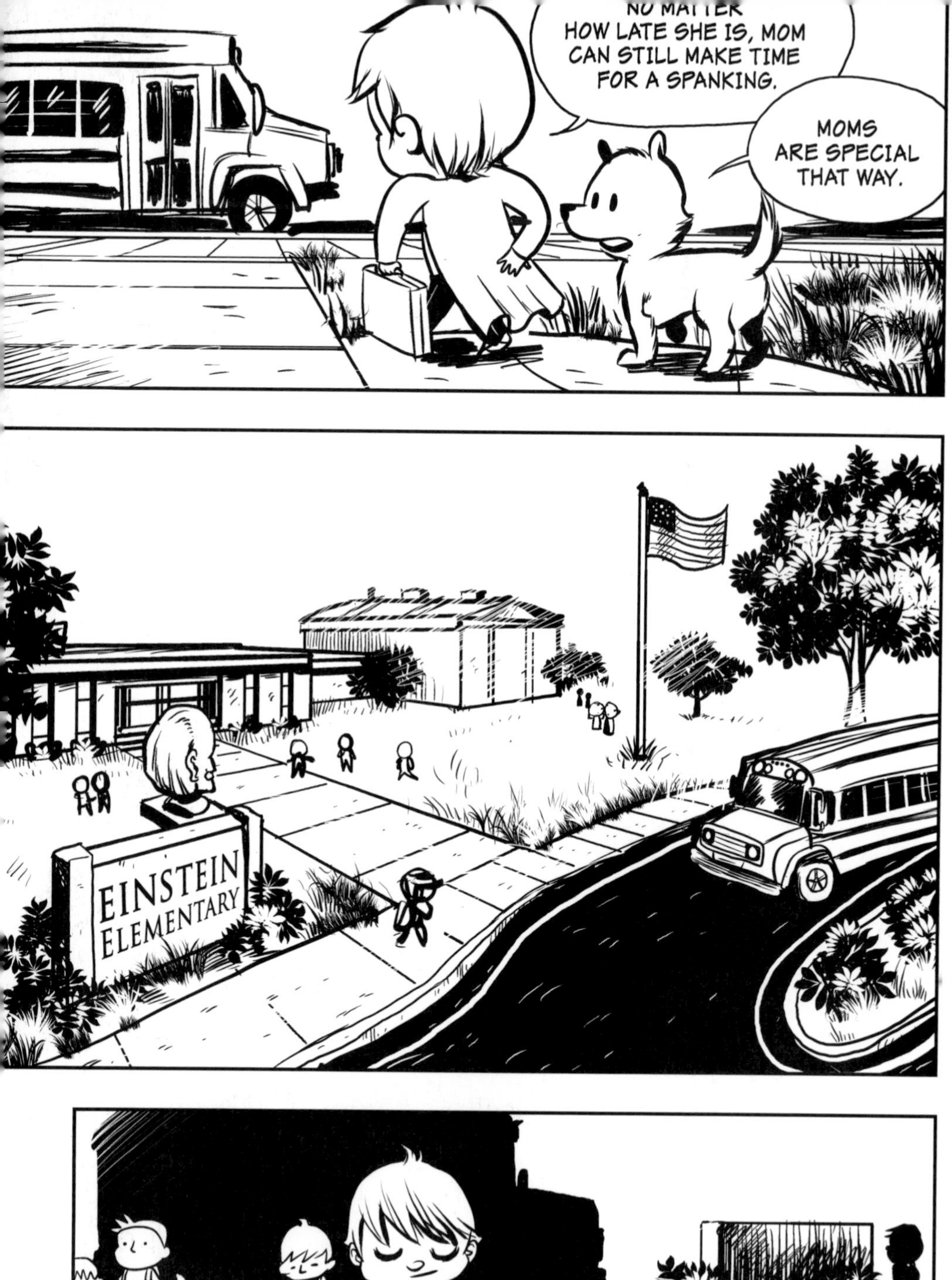
NO MATTER HOW LATE SHE IS, MOM CAN STILL MAKE TIME FOR A SPANKING.
MOMS ARE SPECIAL THAT WAY.
EINSTEIN ELEMENTARY

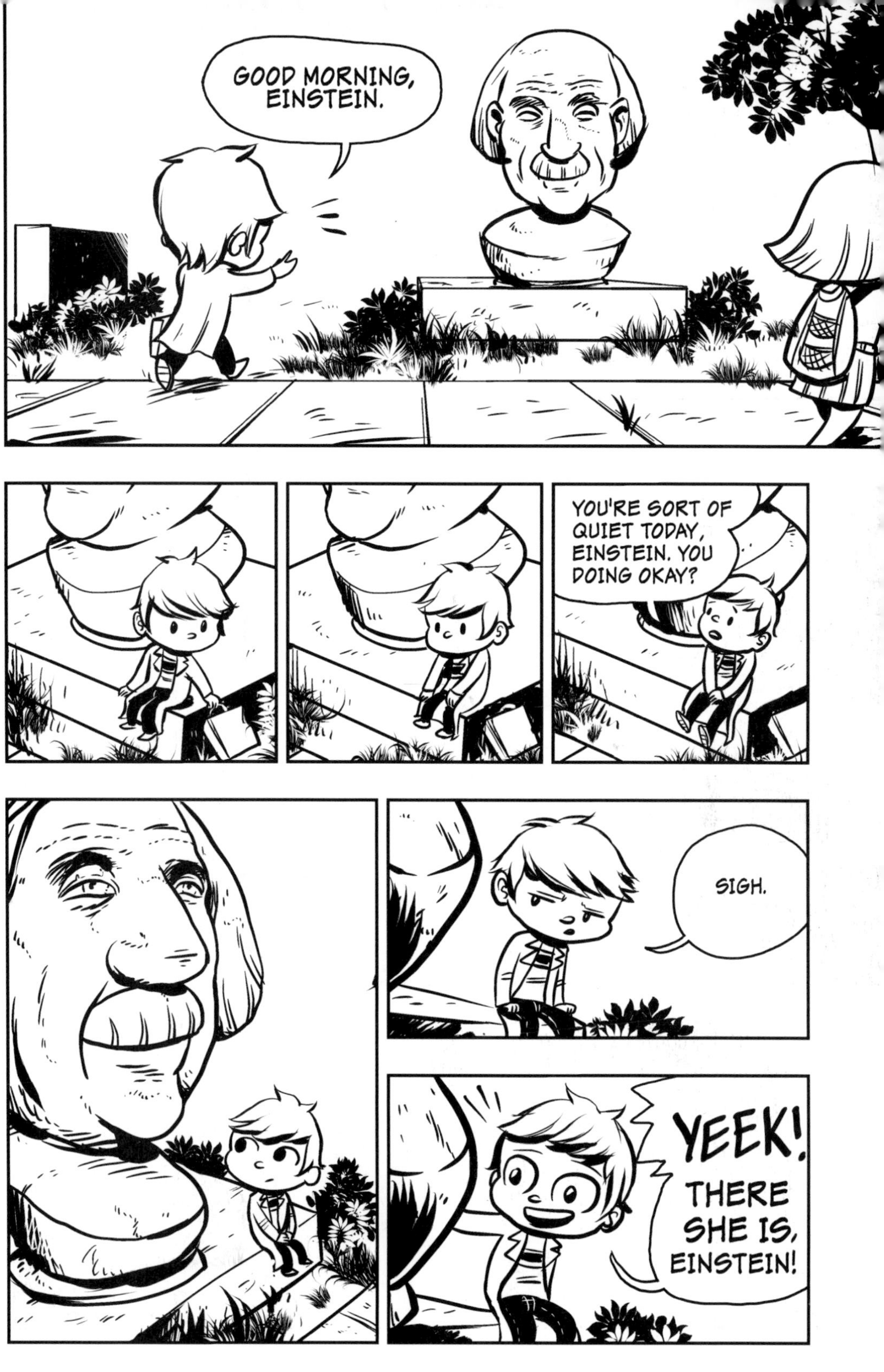
GOOD MORNING, EINSTEIN.
YOU'RE SORT OF QUIET TODAY, EINSTEIN. YOU DOING OKAY?
SIGH.
YEEK! THERE SHE IS, EINSTEIN!

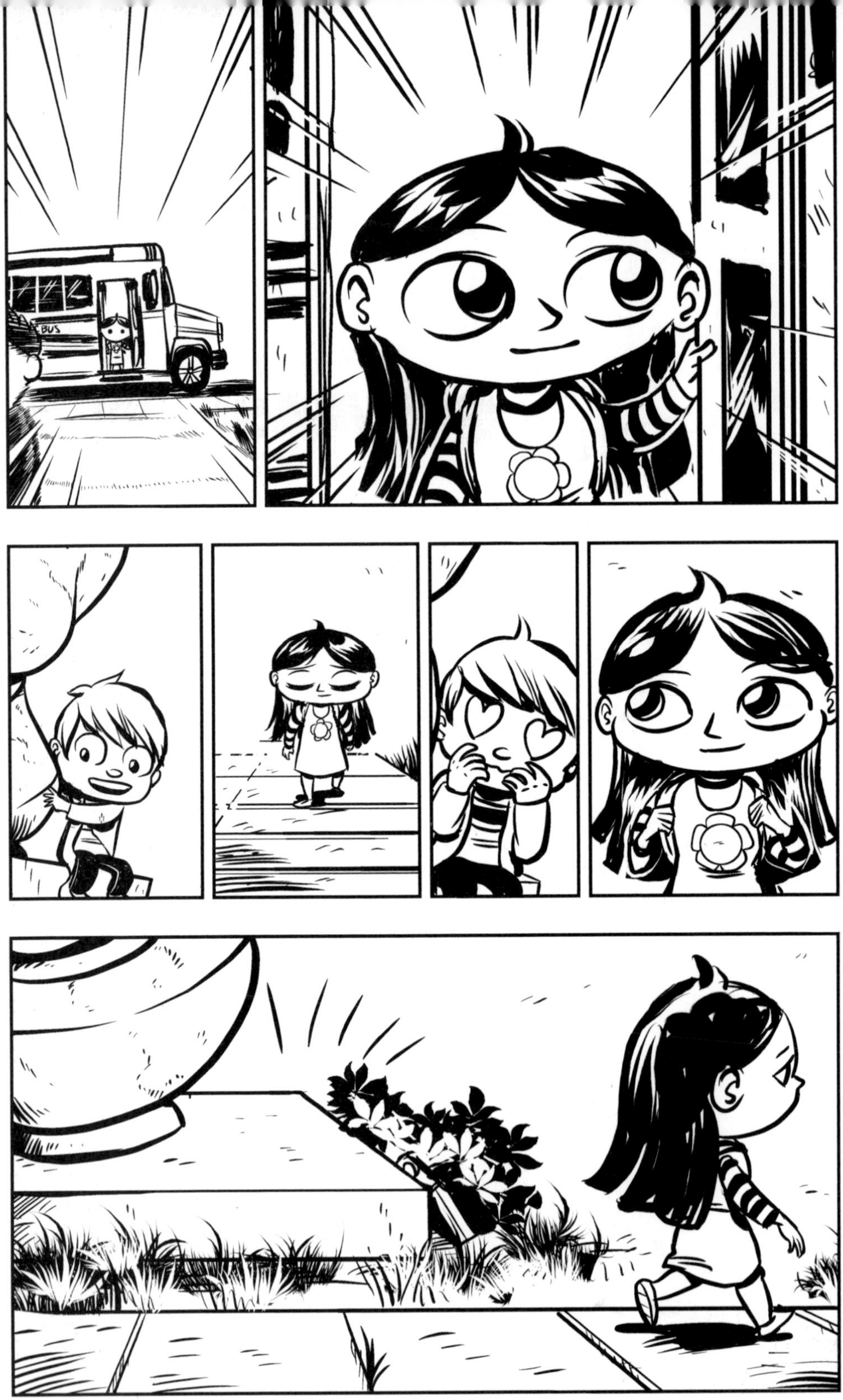
BUS

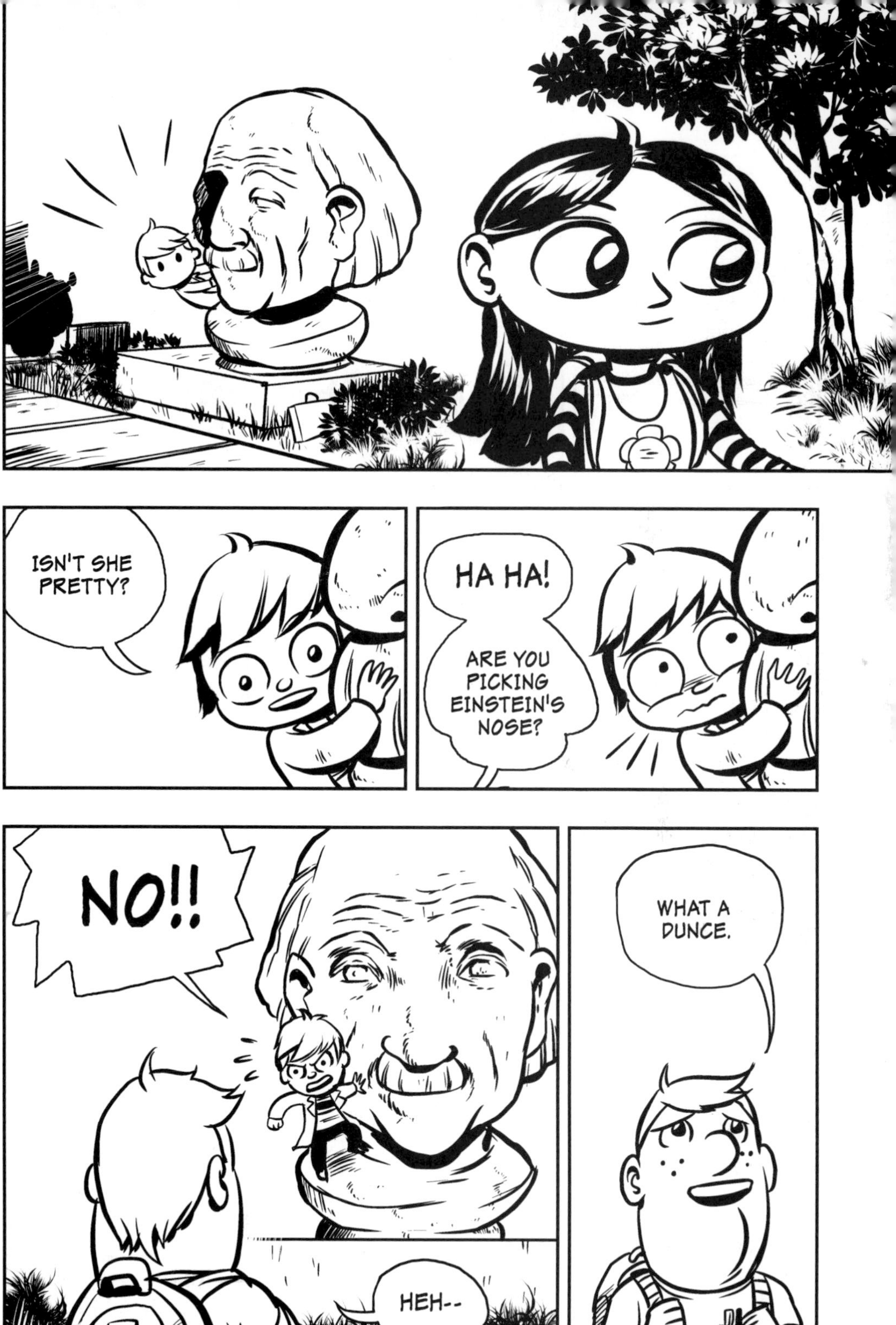

ISN'T SHE PRETTY?
HA HA!
ARE YOU PICKING EINSTEIN'S NOSE?
NO!!
HEH--
WHAT A DUNCE.

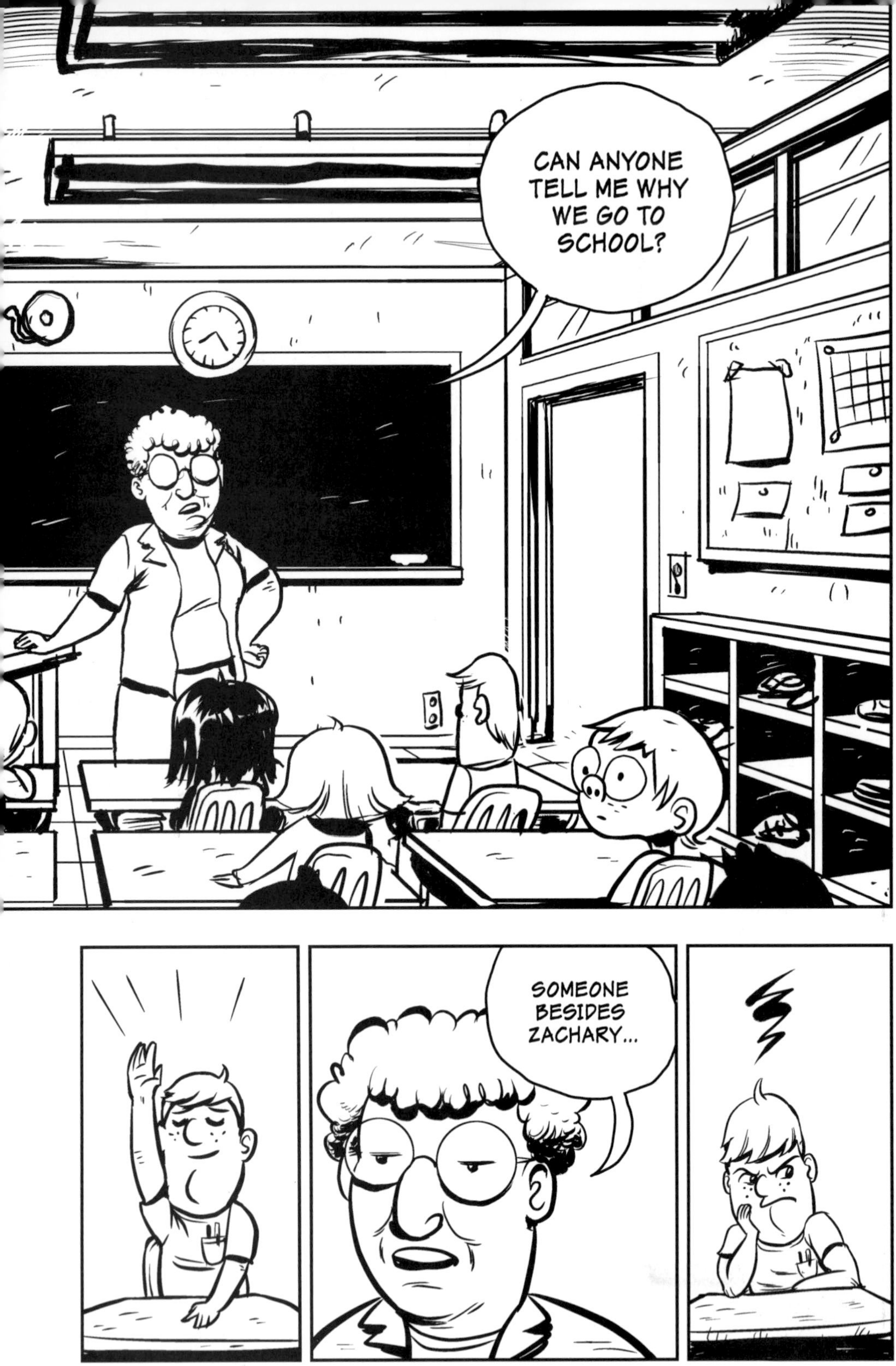
CAN ANYONE TELL ME WHY WE GO TO SCHOOL?
SOMEONE BESIDES ZACHARY...

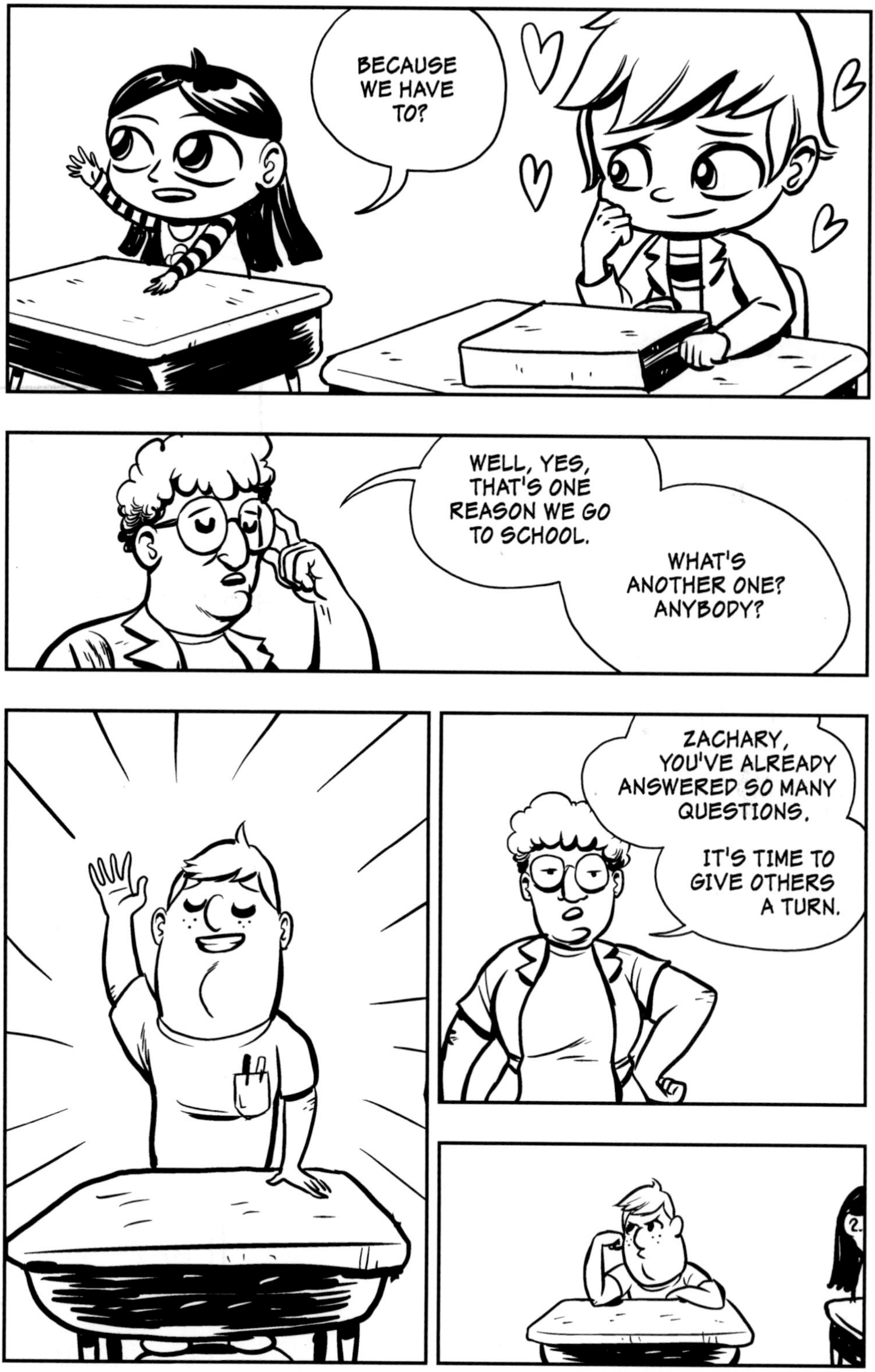
BECAUSE WE HAVE TO?
WELL, YES, THAT'S ONE REASON WE GO TO SCHOOL.
WHAT'S ANOTHER ONE? ANYBODY?
ZACHARY, YOU'VE ALREADY ANSWERED SO MANY QUESTIONS.
IT'S TIME TO GIVE OTHERS A TURN.

MAL?

I SUPPOSE THE MAIN PURPOSE OF GOING TO SCHOOL IS TO GAIN SPECIALIZED KNOWLEDGE IN ORDER TO ENABLE ONE TO SECURE MORE PROFITABLE OR DESIRED OCCUPATIONS.

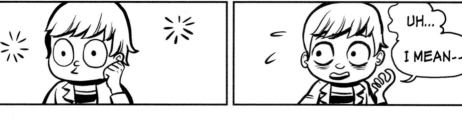

UH....

I MEAN--

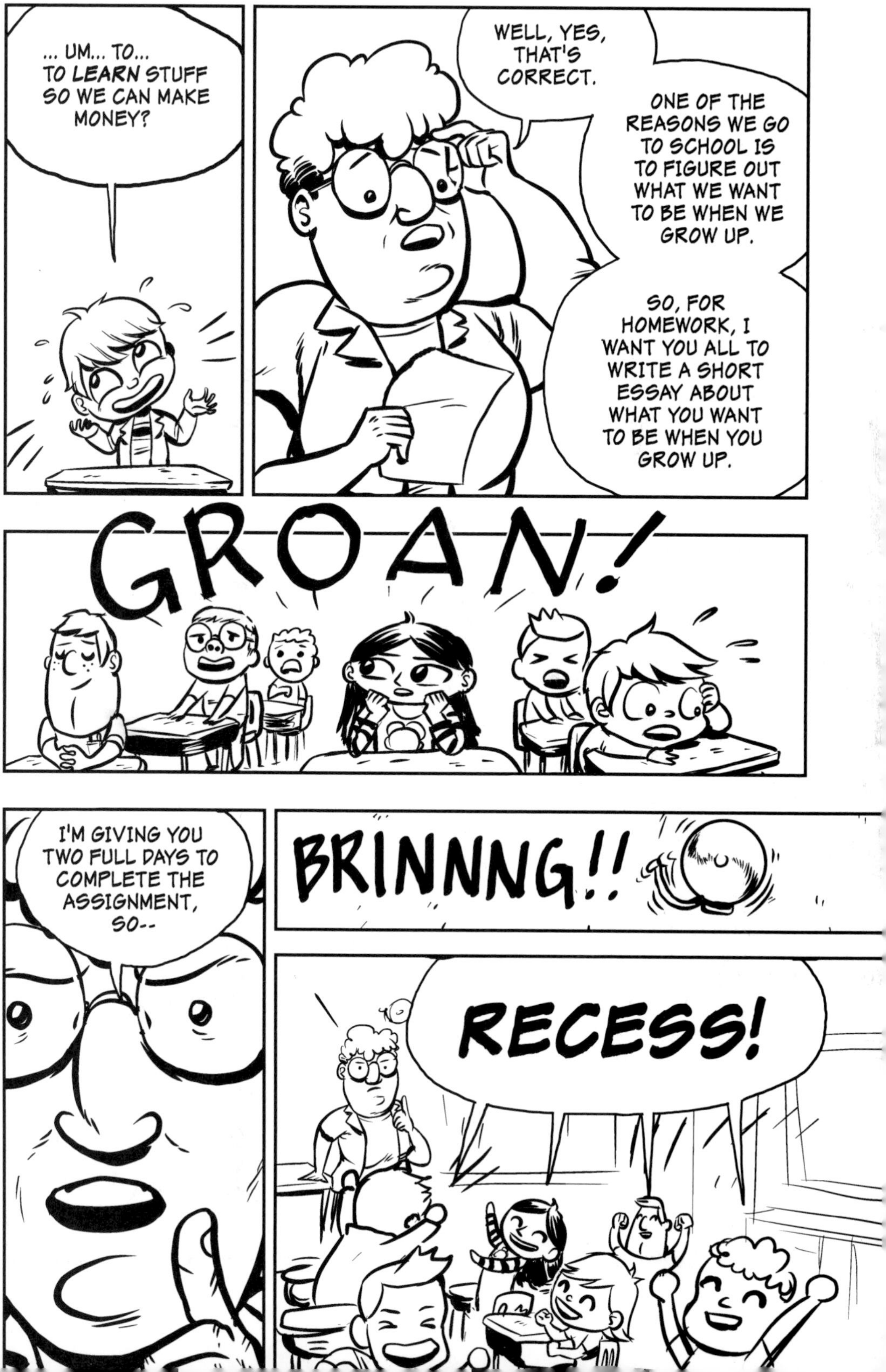
... UM... TO... TO **LEARN** STUFF SO WE CAN MAKE MONEY?
WELL, YES, THAT'S CORRECT.
ONE OF THE REASONS WE GO TO SCHOOL IS TO FIGURE OUT WHAT WE WANT TO BE WHEN WE GROW UP.
SO, FOR HOMEWORK, I WANT YOU ALL TO WRITE A SHORT ESSAY ABOUT WHAT YOU WANT TO BE WHEN YOU GROW UP.
GROAN!
I'M GIVING YOU TWO FULL DAYS TO COMPLETE THE ASSIGNMENT, SO--
BRINNNG!!
RECESS!

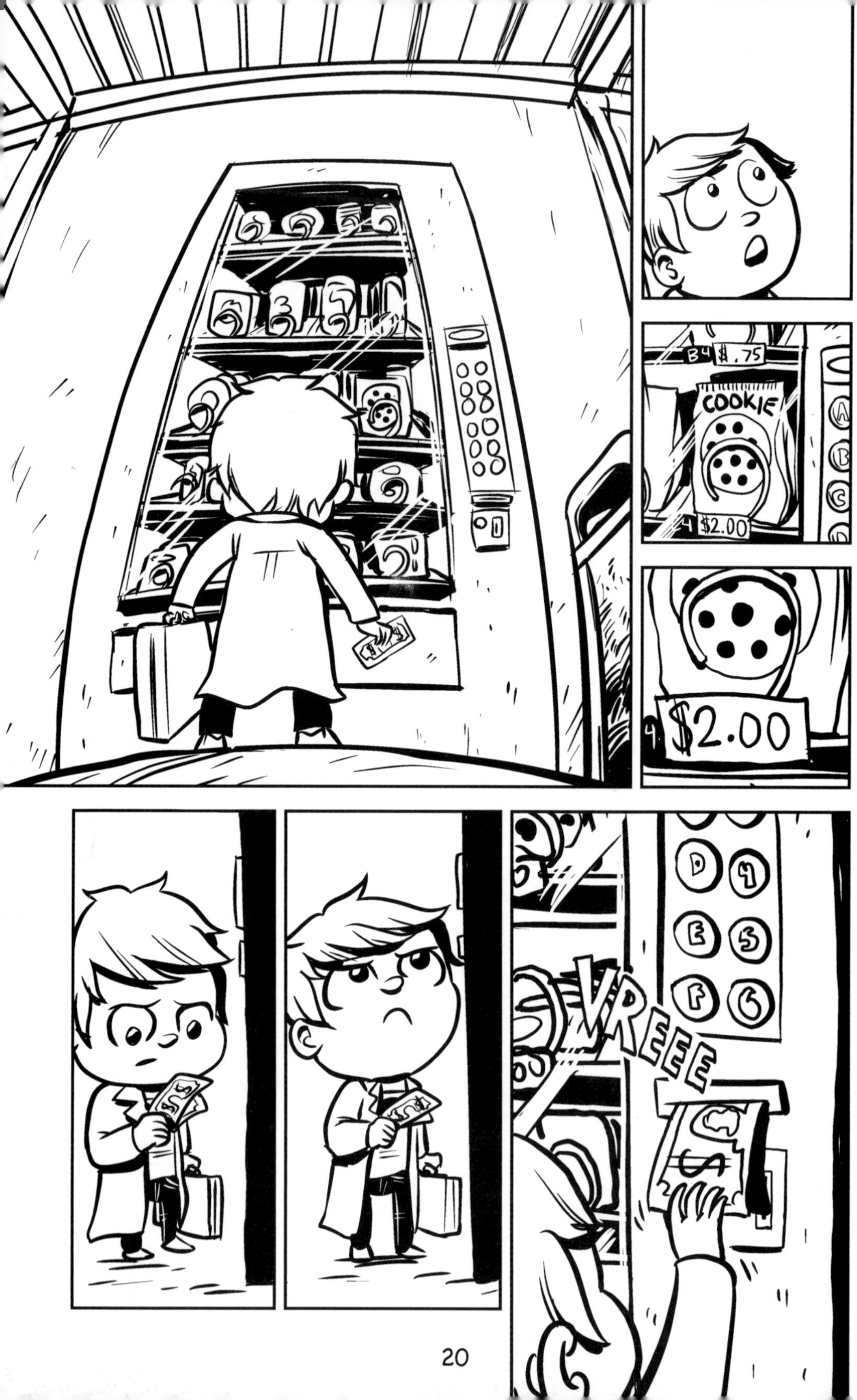
B4 $.75
COOKIE
4 $2.00
4 $2.00
VREEE

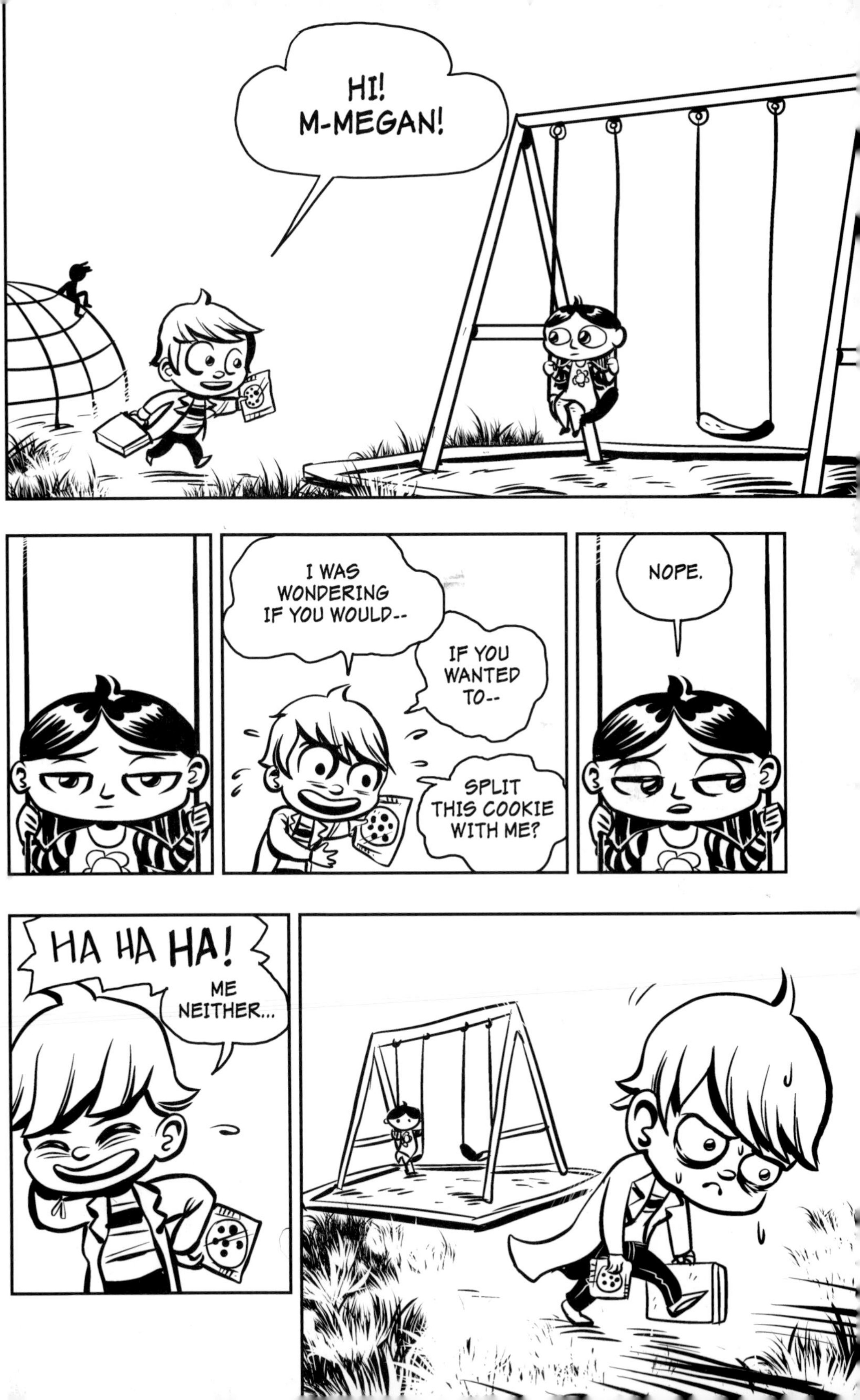
HI!
M-MEGAN!
I WAS WONDERING IF YOU WOULD--
IF YOU WANTED TO--
SPLIT THIS COOKIE WITH ME?
NOPE.
HA HA HA!
ME NEITHER...

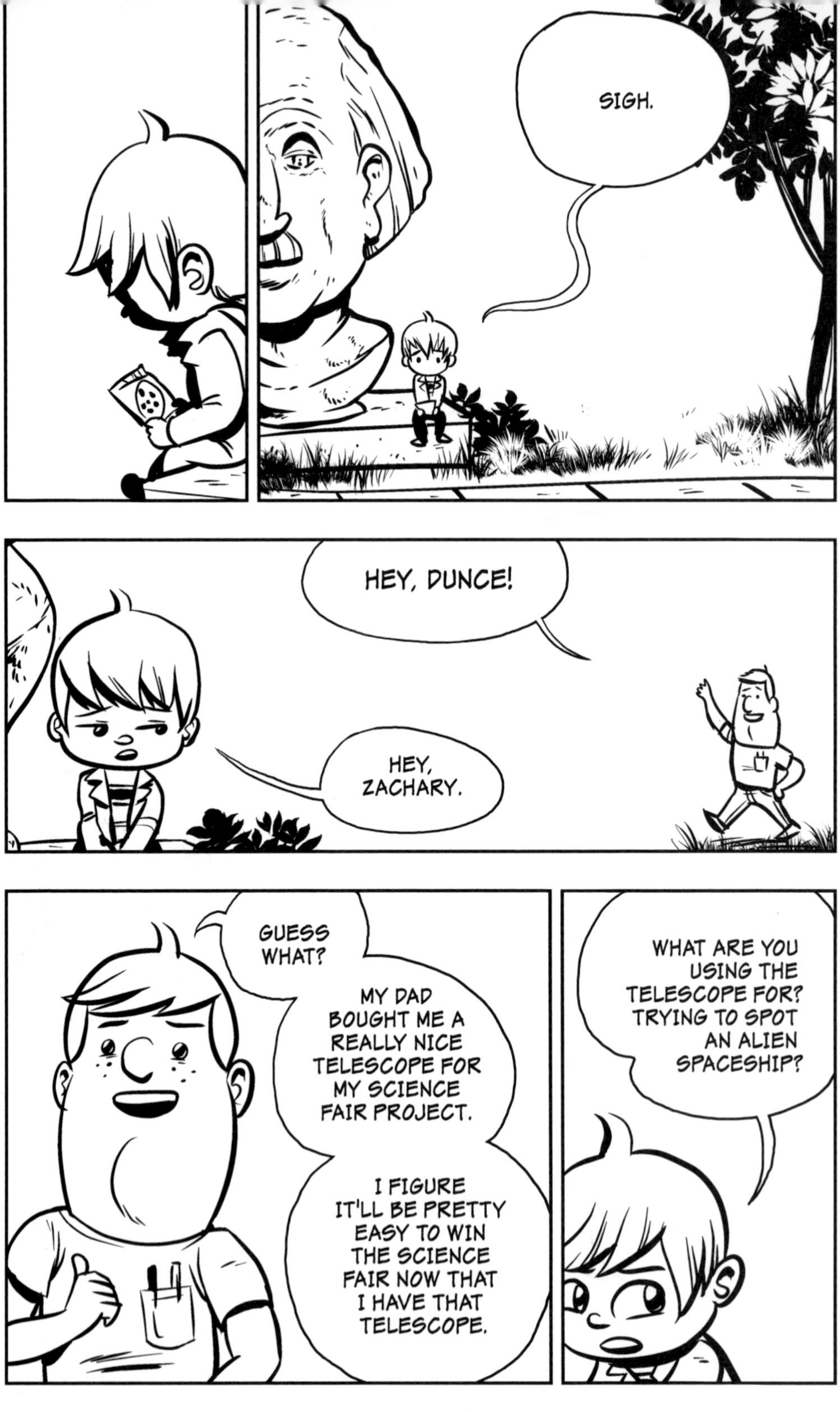
SIGH.
HEY, DUNCE!
HEY, ZACHARY.
GUESS WHAT?
MY DAD BOUGHT ME A REALLY NICE TELESCOPE FOR MY SCIENCE FAIR PROJECT.
I FIGURE IT'LL BE PRETTY EASY TO WIN THE SCIENCE FAIR NOW THAT I HAVE THAT TELESCOPE.
WHAT ARE YOU USING THE TELESCOPE FOR? TRYING TO SPOT AN ALIEN SPACESHIP?

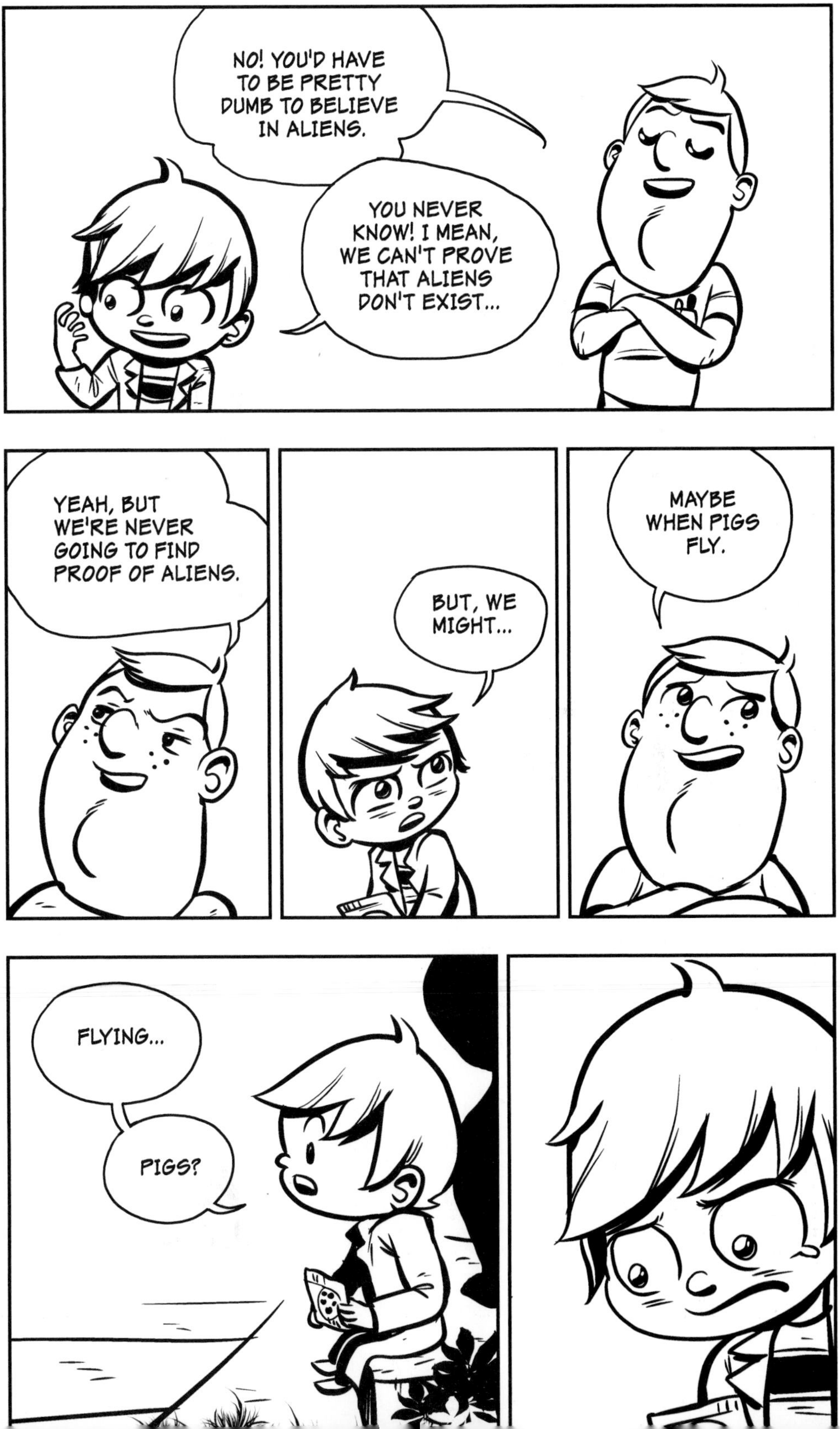
NO! YOU'D HAVE TO BE PRETTY DUMB TO BELIEVE IN ALIENS.
YOU NEVER KNOW! I MEAN, WE CAN'T PROVE THAT ALIENS DON'T EXIST...
YEAH, BUT WE'RE NEVER GOING TO FIND PROOF OF ALIENS.
BUT, WE MIGHT...
MAYBE WHEN PIGS FLY.
FLYING...
PIGS?

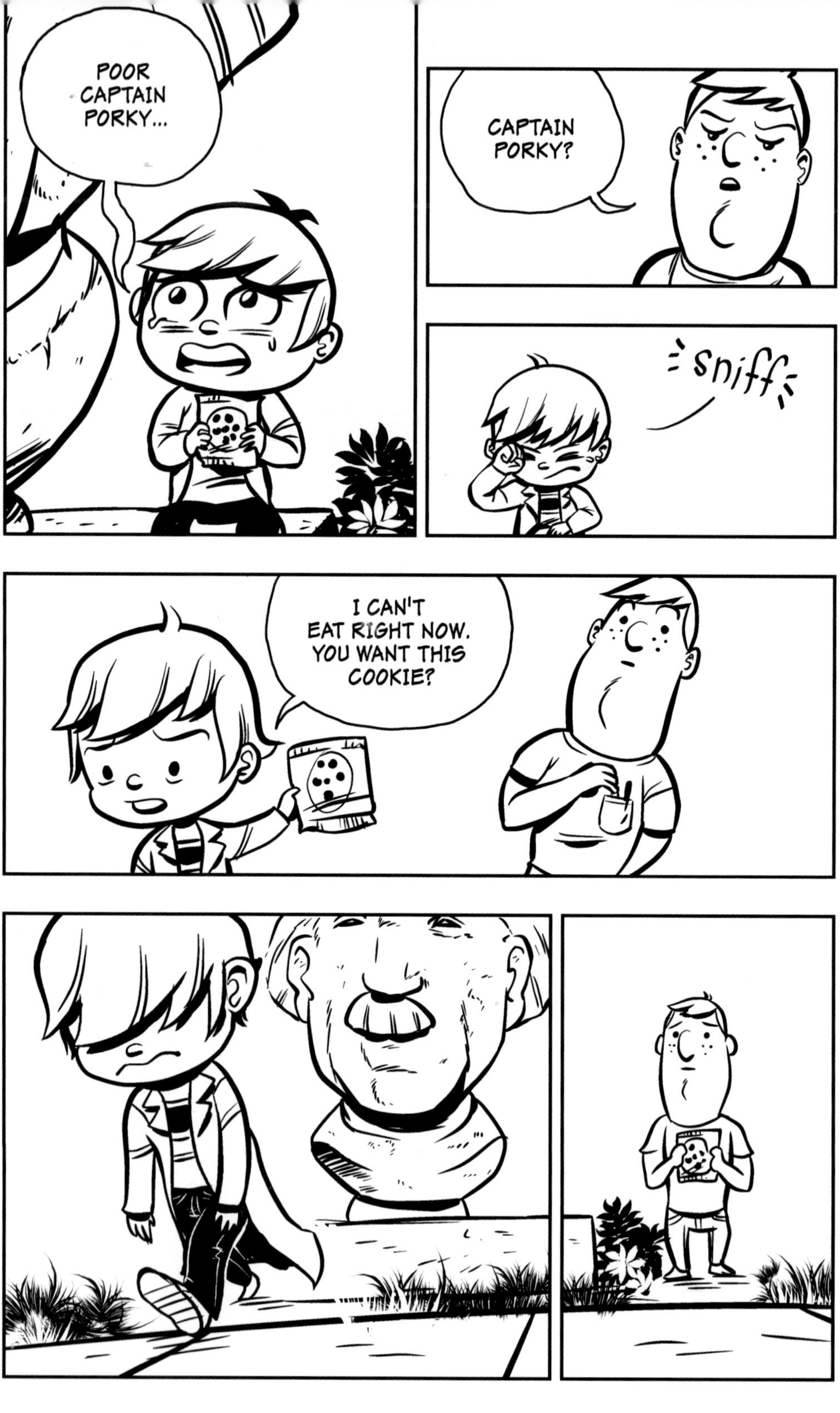
POOR CAPTAIN PORKY...
CAPTAIN PORKY?
sniff
I CAN'T EAT RIGHT NOW. YOU WANT THIS COOKIE?

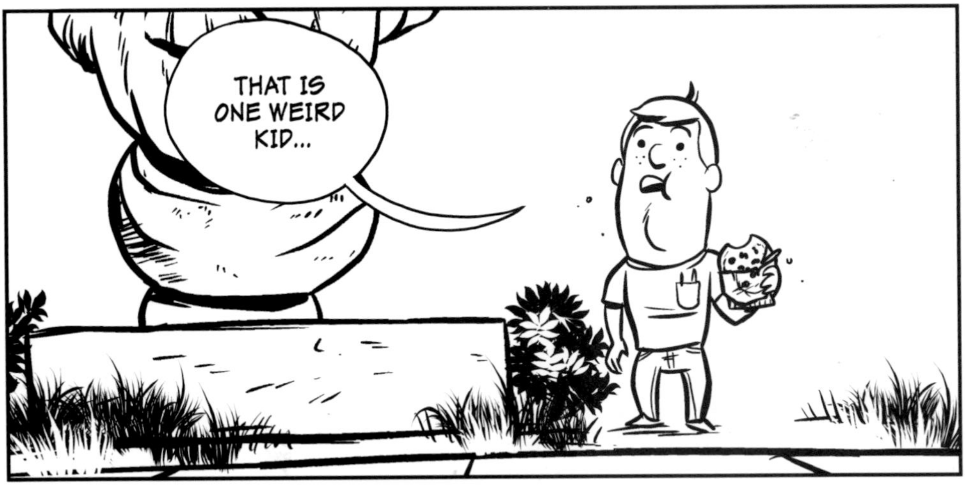
THAT IS ONE WEIRD KID...

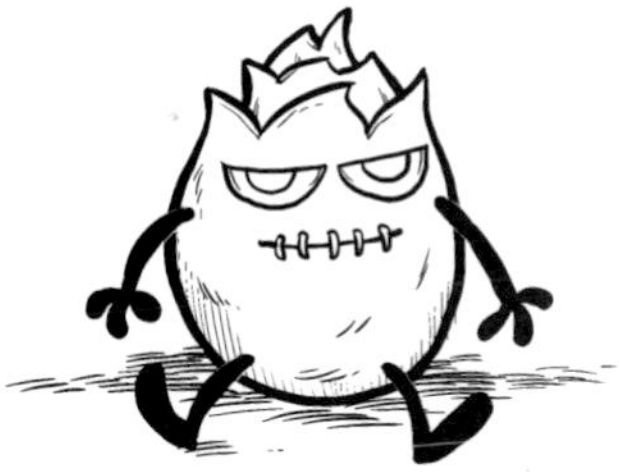

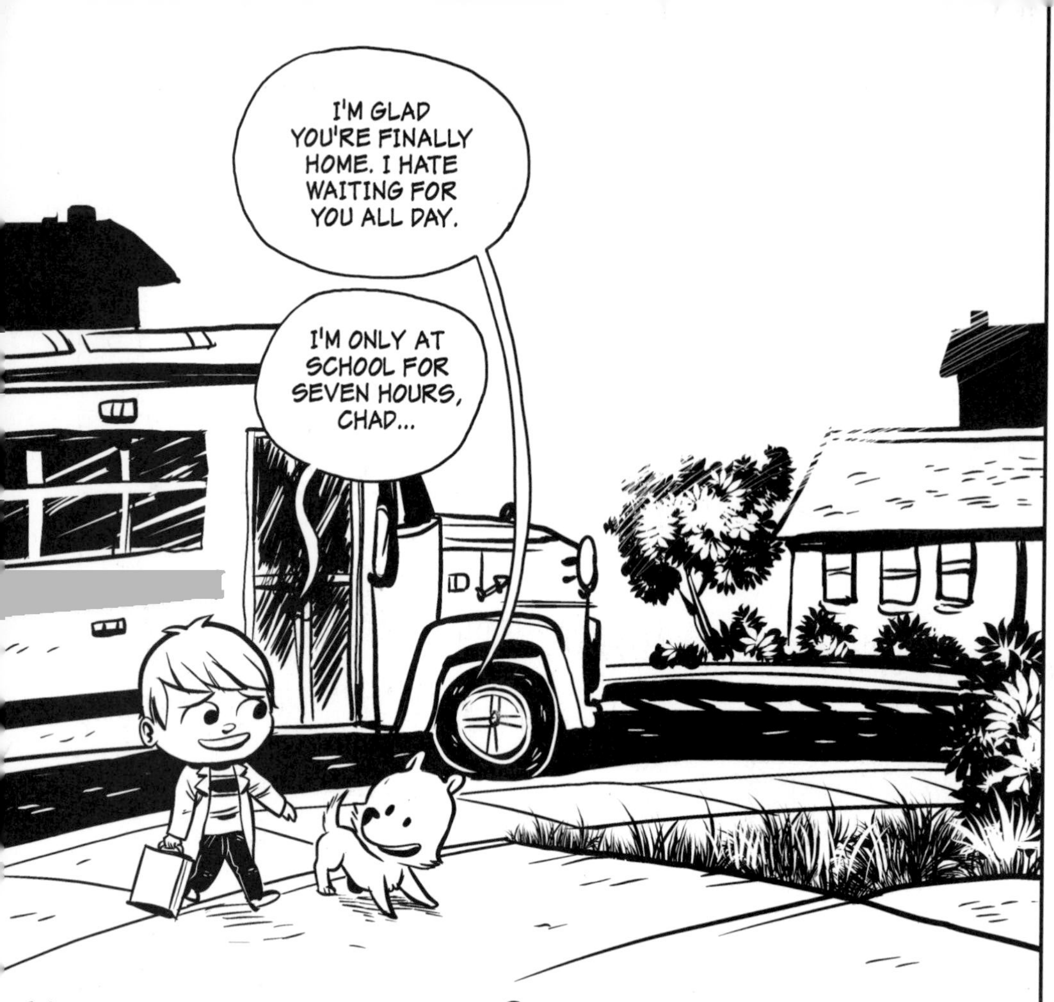
I'M GLAD YOU'RE FINALLY HOME. I HATE WAITING FOR YOU ALL DAY.
I'M ONLY AT SCHOOL FOR SEVEN HOURS, CHAD...

CHAPTER 2

Don't Be Such A Cry-Puppy!

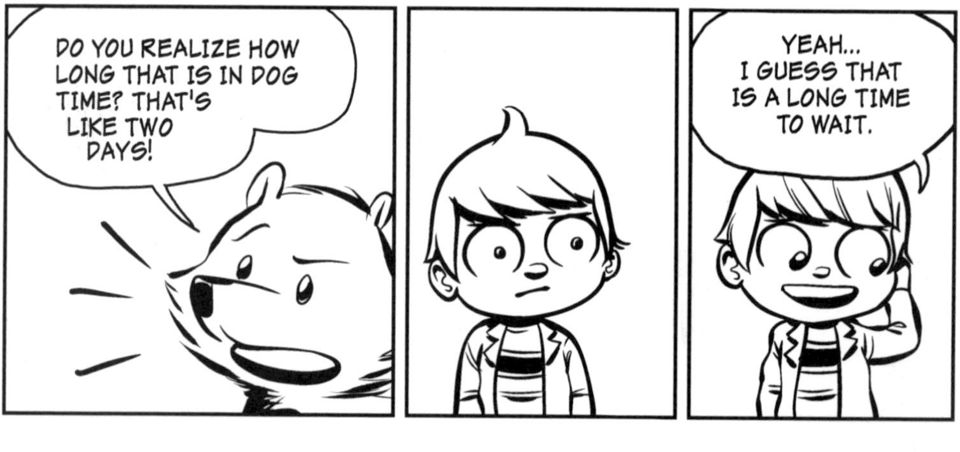
DO YOU REALIZE HOW LONG THAT IS IN DOG TIME? THAT'S LIKE TWO DAYS!
YEAH... I GUESS THAT IS A LONG TIME TO WAIT.

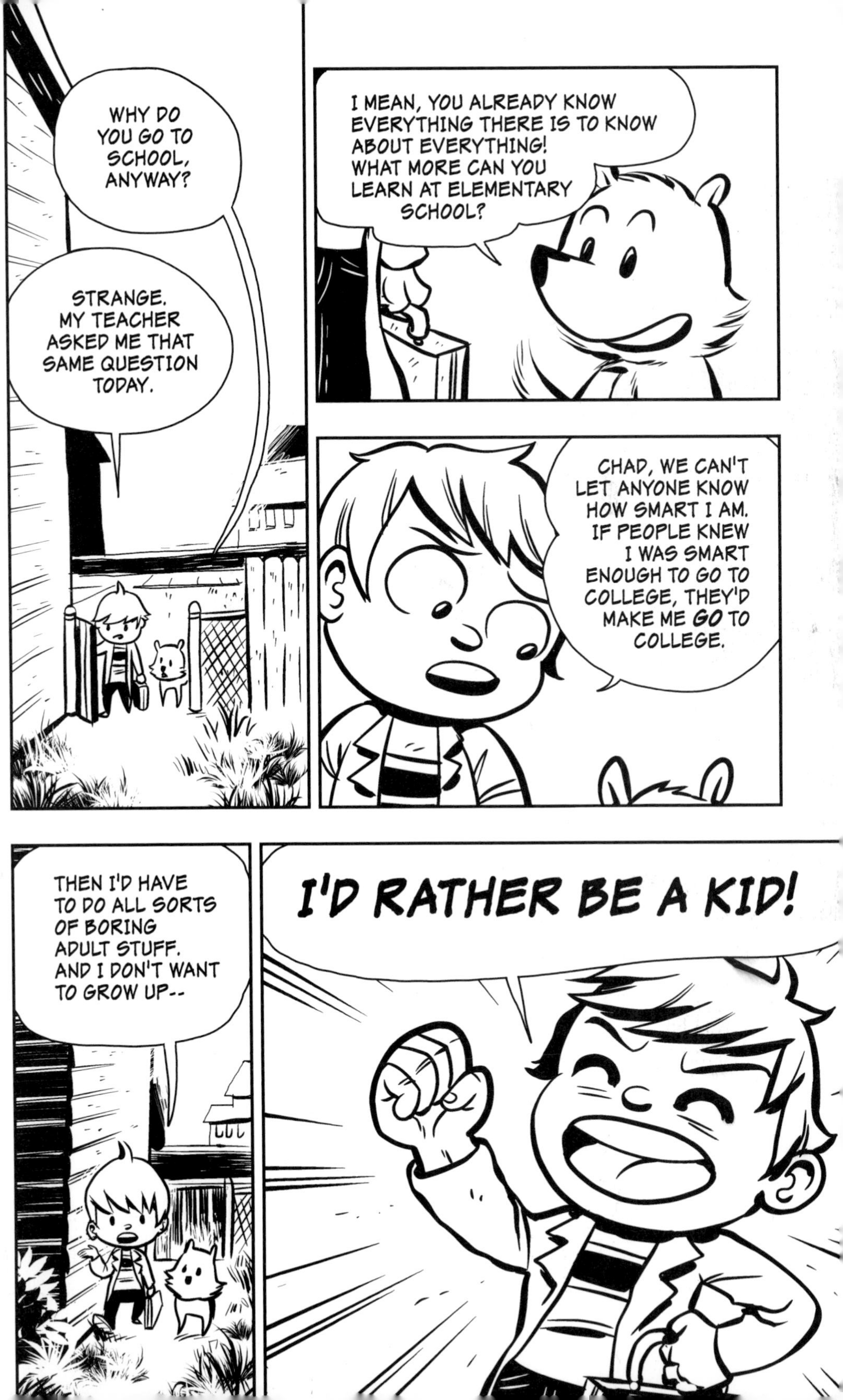
WHY DO YOU GO TO SCHOOL, ANYWAY?
STRANGE. MY TEACHER ASKED ME THAT SAME QUESTION TODAY.
I MEAN, YOU ALREADY KNOW EVERYTHING THERE IS TO KNOW ABOUT EVERYTHING! WHAT MORE CAN YOU LEARN AT ELEMENTARY SCHOOL?
CHAD, WE CAN'T LET ANYONE KNOW HOW SMART I AM. IF PEOPLE KNEW I WAS SMART ENOUGH TO GO TO COLLEGE, THEY'D MAKE ME *GO* TO COLLEGE.
THEN I'D HAVE TO DO ALL SORTS OF BORING ADULT STUFF. AND I DON'T WANT TO GROW UP--
I'D RATHER BE A KID!

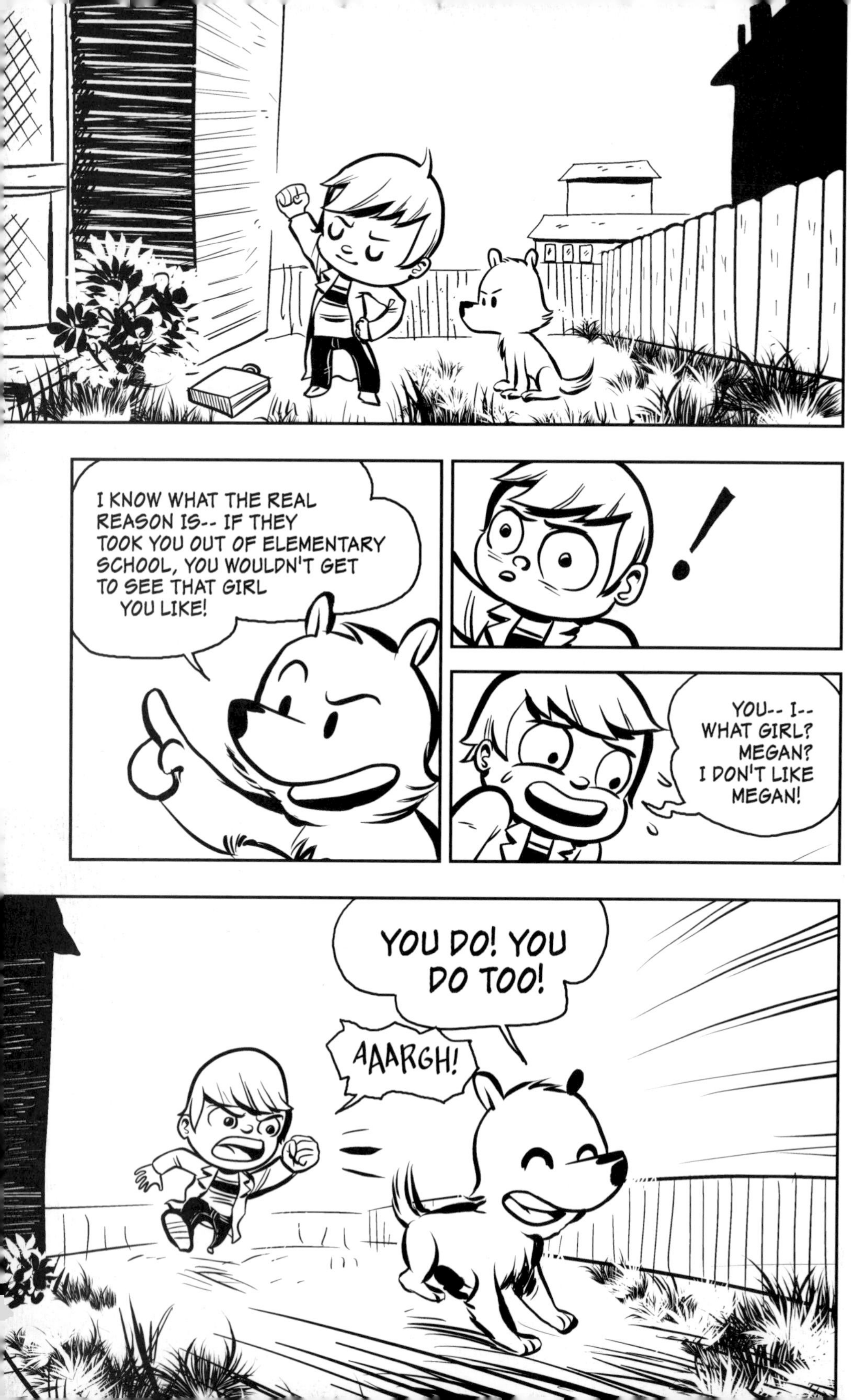
I KNOW WHAT THE REAL REASON IS-- IF THEY TOOK YOU OUT OF ELEMENTARY SCHOOL, YOU WOULDN'T GET TO SEE THAT GIRL YOU LIKE!
!
YOU-- I-- WHAT GIRL? MEGAN? I DON'T LIKE MEGAN!
YOU DO! YOU DO TOO!
AAARGH!

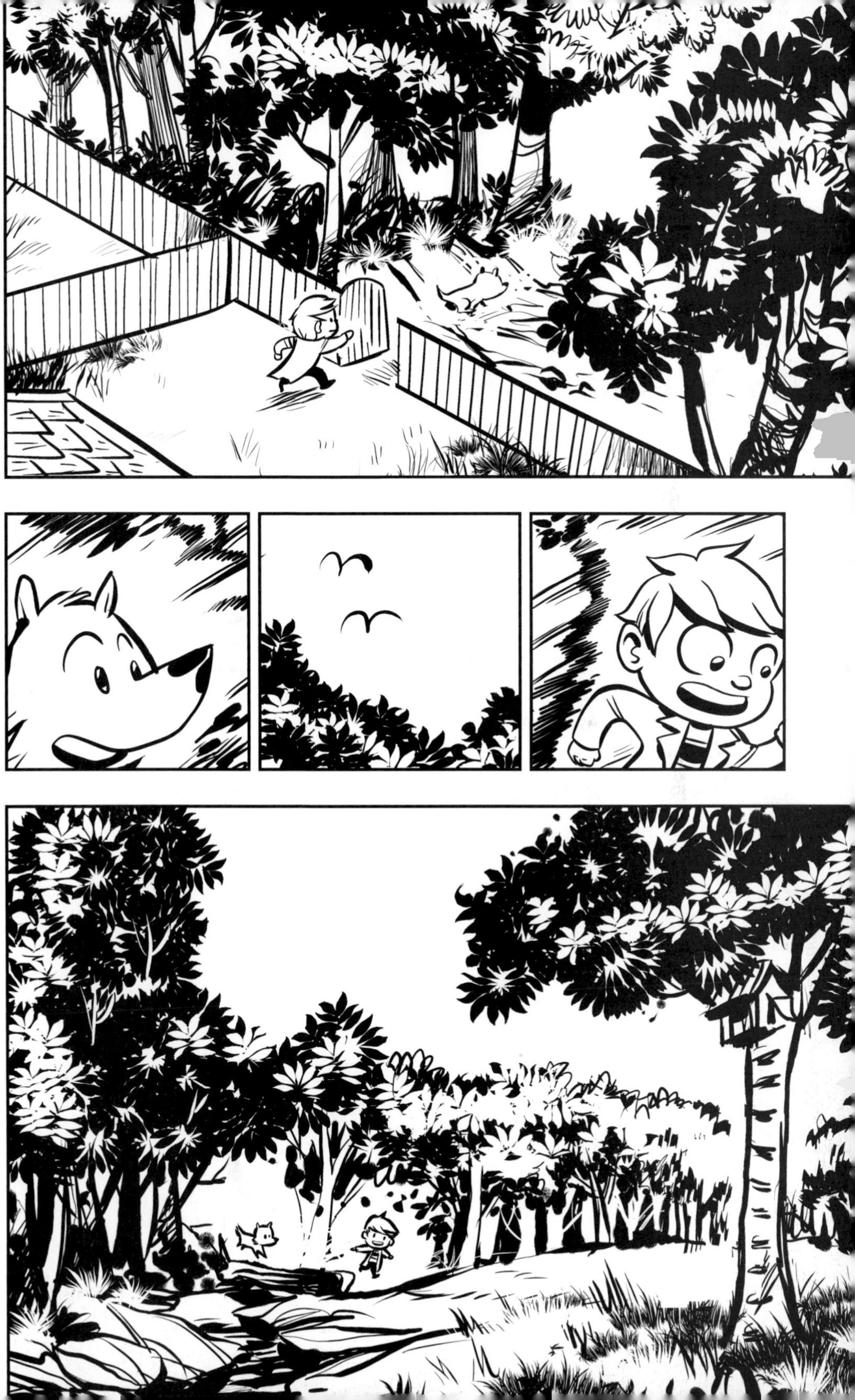

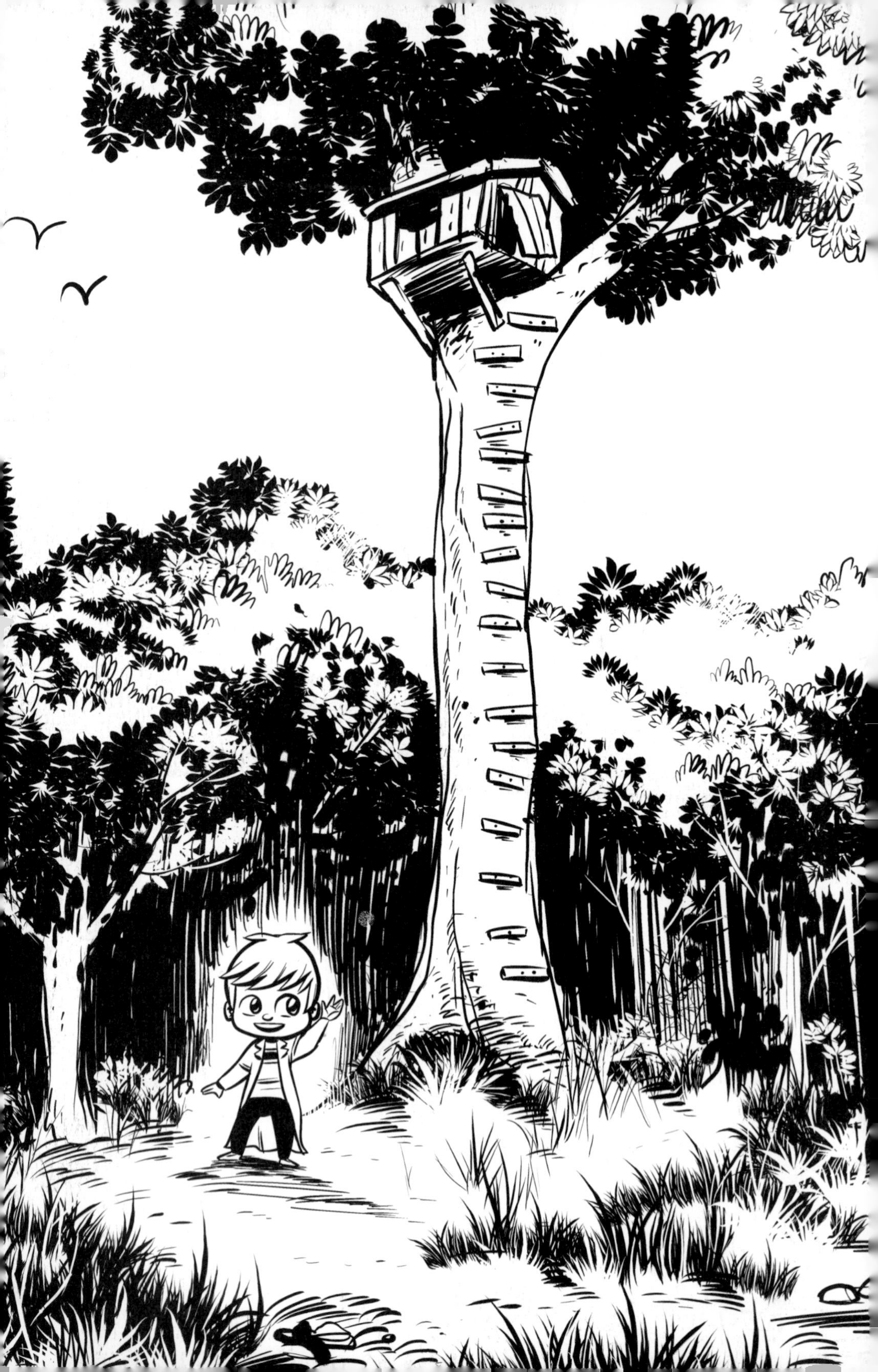

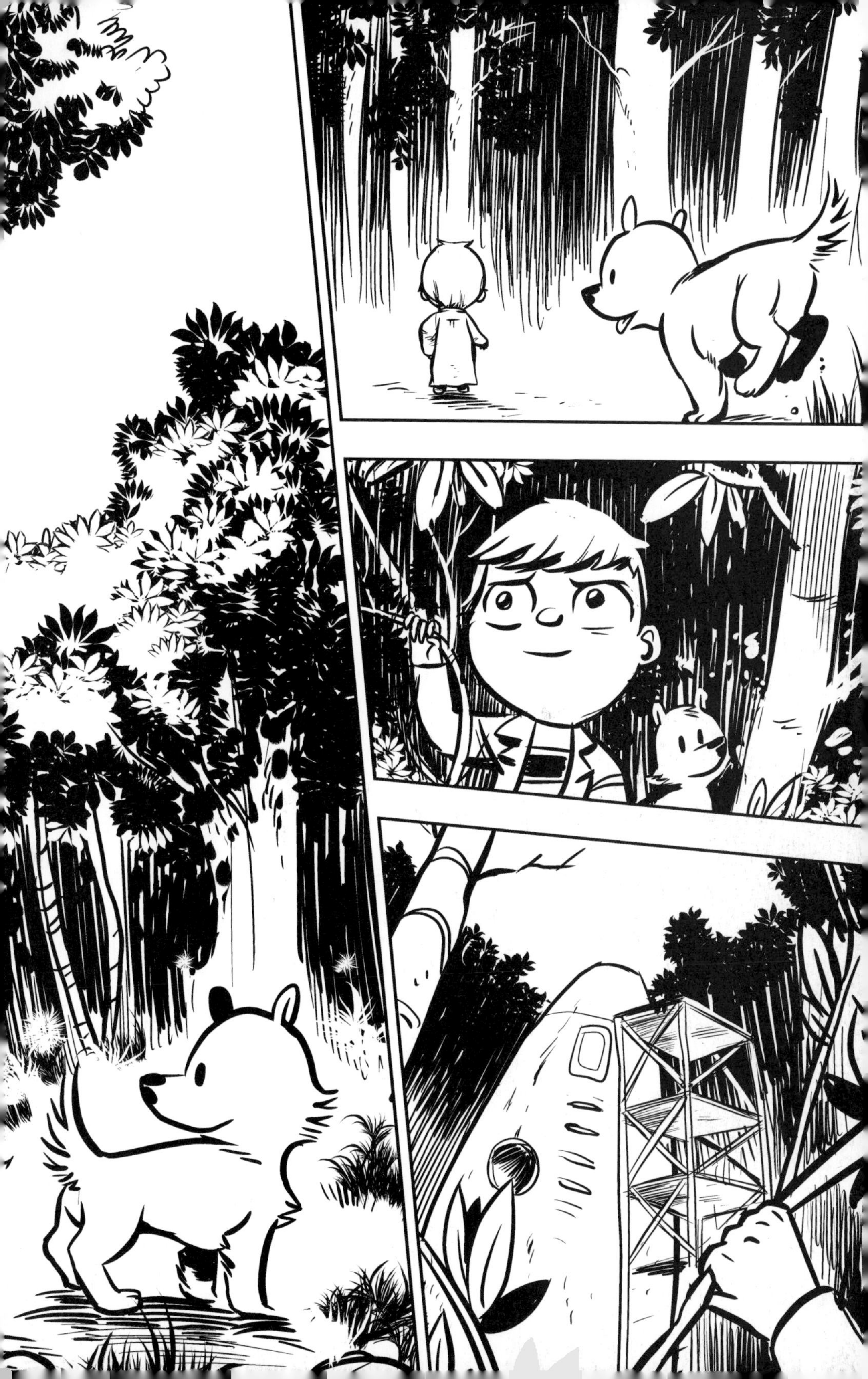

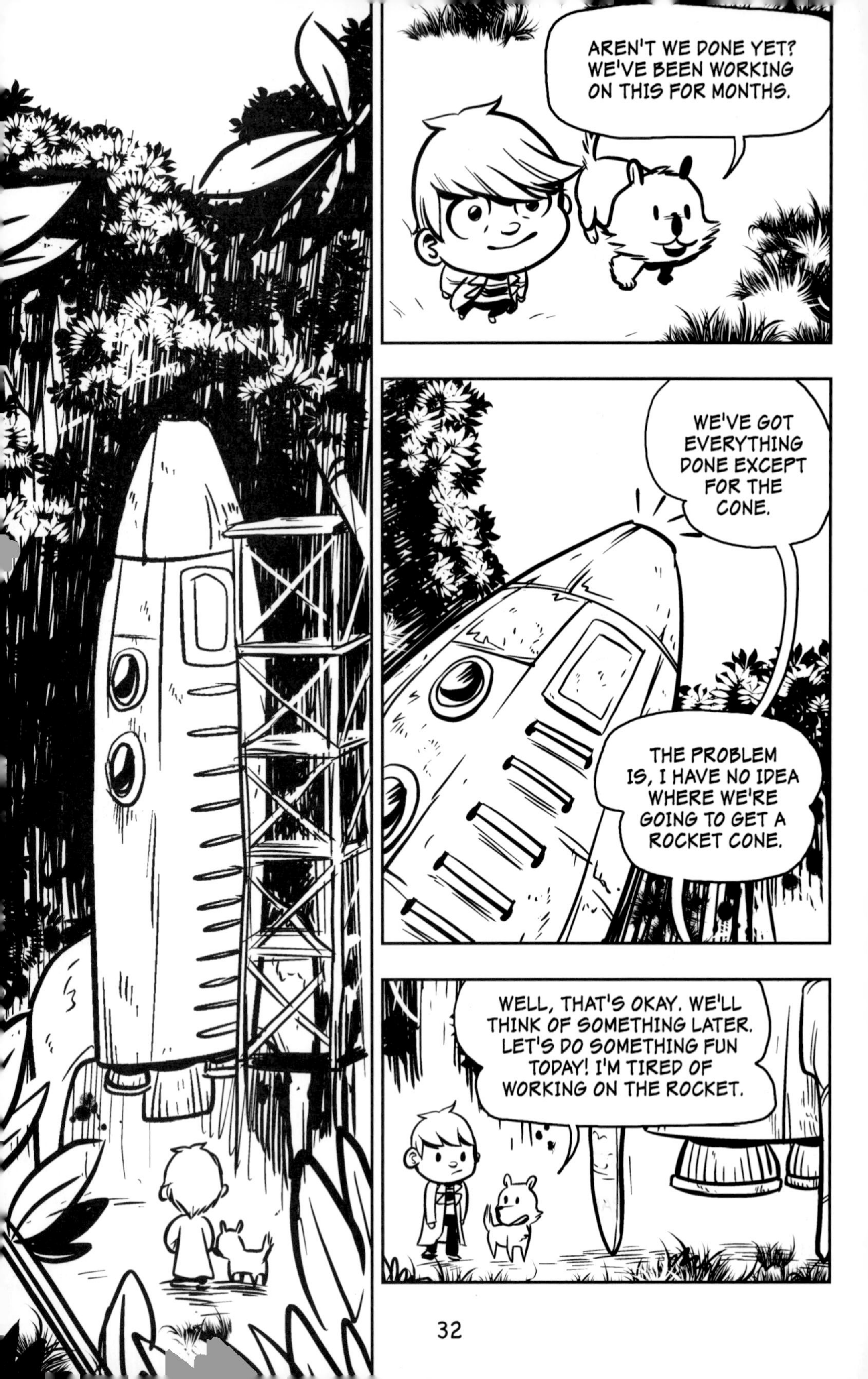
AREN'T WE DONE YET? WE'VE BEEN WORKING ON THIS FOR MONTHS.
WE'VE GOT EVERYTHING DONE EXCEPT FOR THE CONE.
THE PROBLEM IS, I HAVE NO IDEA WHERE WE'RE GOING TO GET A ROCKET CONE.
WELL, THAT'S OKAY. WE'LL THINK OF SOMETHING LATER. LET'S DO SOMETHING FUN TODAY! I'M TIRED OF WORKING ON THE ROCKET.

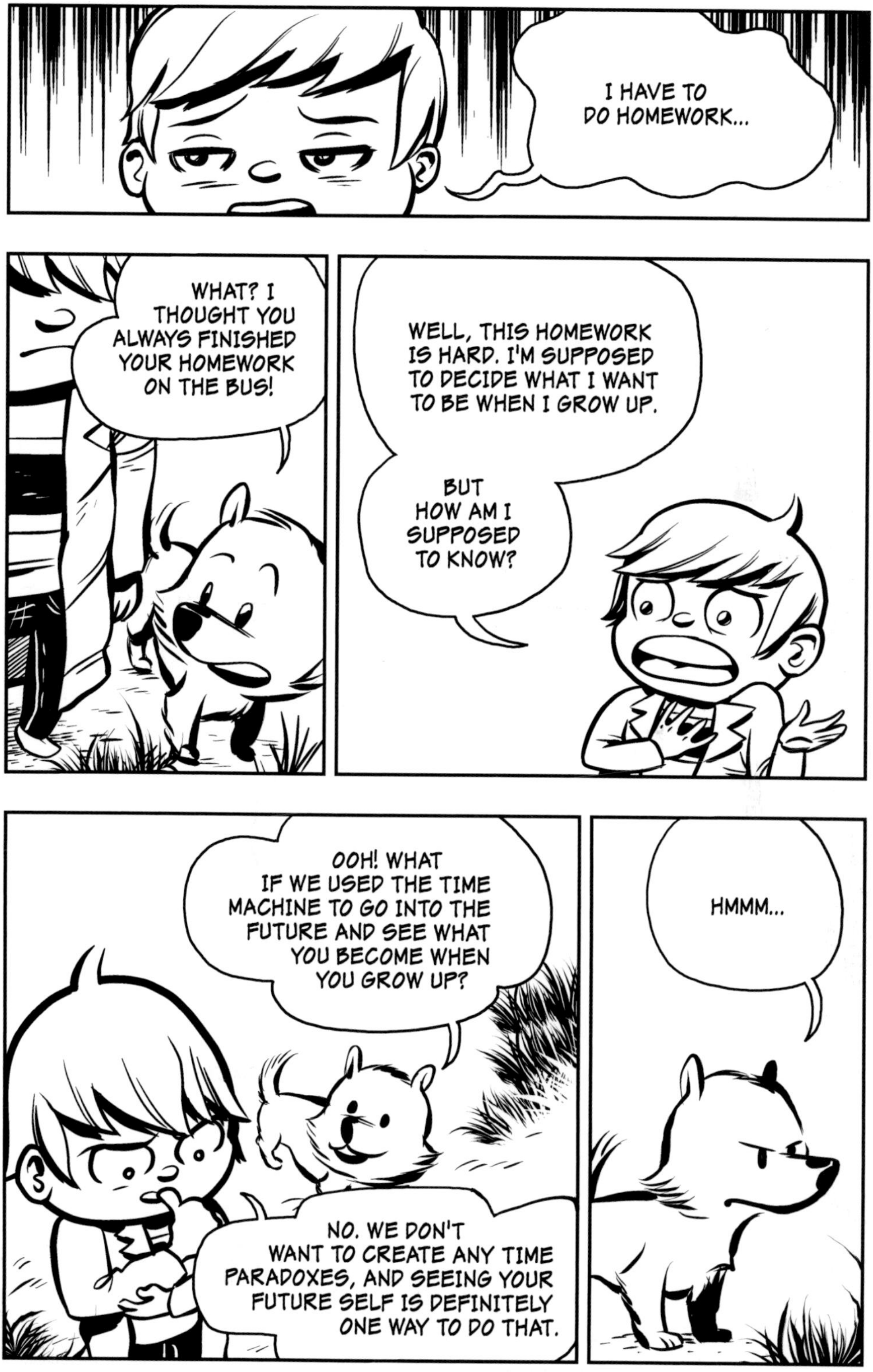
I HAVE TO DO HOMEWORK...
WHAT? I THOUGHT YOU ALWAYS FINISHED YOUR HOMEWORK ON THE BUS!
WELL, THIS HOMEWORK IS HARD. I'M SUPPOSED TO DECIDE WHAT I WANT TO BE WHEN I GROW UP.
BUT HOW AM I SUPPOSED TO KNOW?
OOH! WHAT IF WE USED THE TIME MACHINE TO GO INTO THE FUTURE AND SEE WHAT YOU BECOME WHEN YOU GROW UP?
NO. WE DON'T WANT TO CREATE ANY TIME PARADOXES, AND SEEING YOUR FUTURE SELF IS DEFINITELY ONE WAY TO DO THAT.
HMMM...

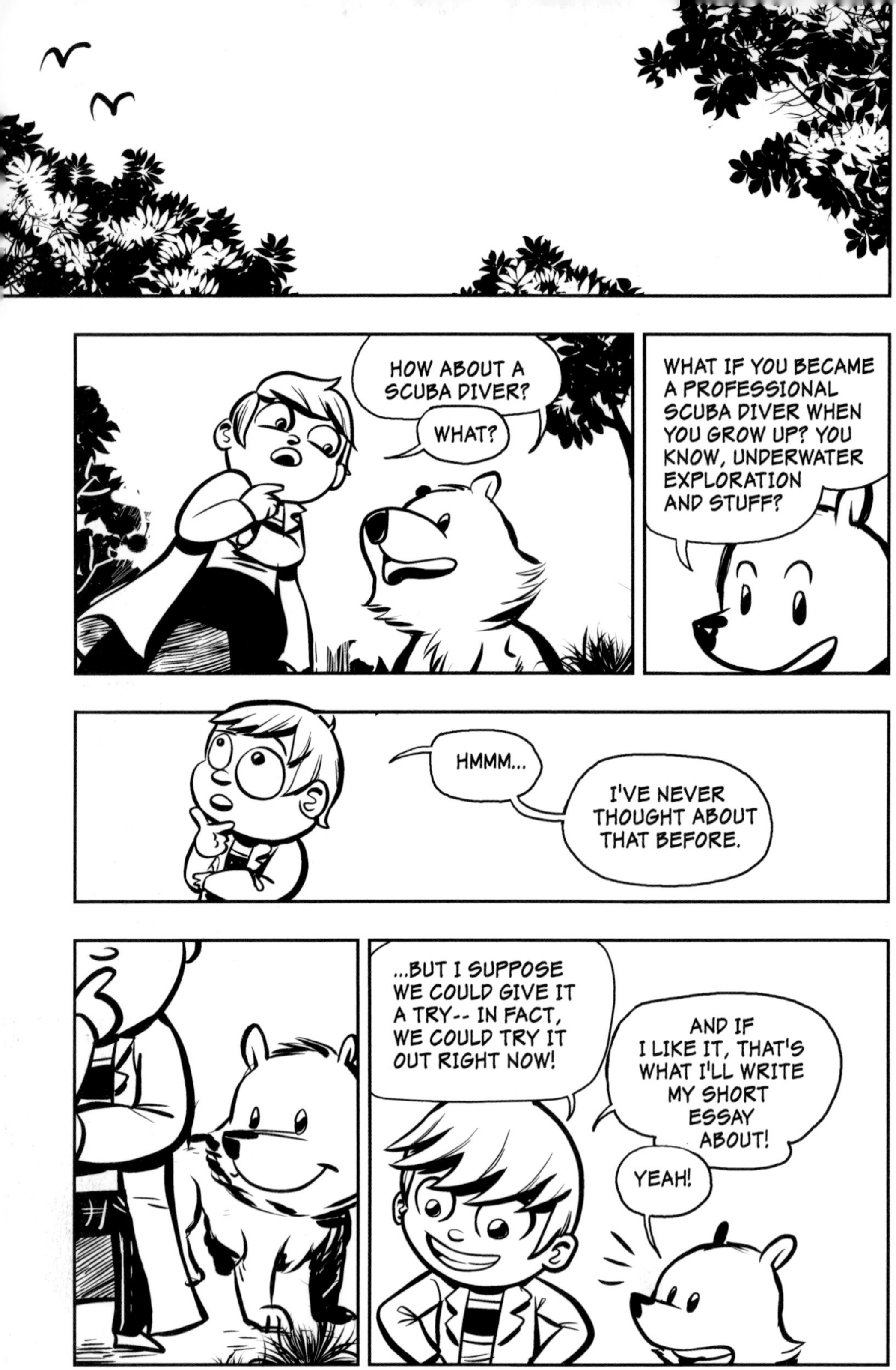
HOW ABOUT A SCUBA DIVER?
WHAT?
WHAT IF YOU BECAME A PROFESSIONAL SCUBA DIVER WHEN YOU GROW UP? YOU KNOW, UNDERWATER EXPLORATION AND STUFF?
HMMM...
I'VE NEVER THOUGHT ABOUT THAT BEFORE.
...BUT I SUPPOSE WE COULD GIVE IT A TRY-- IN FACT, WE COULD TRY IT OUT RIGHT NOW!
AND IF I LIKE IT, THAT'S WHAT I'LL WRITE MY SHORT ESSAY ABOUT!
YEAH!

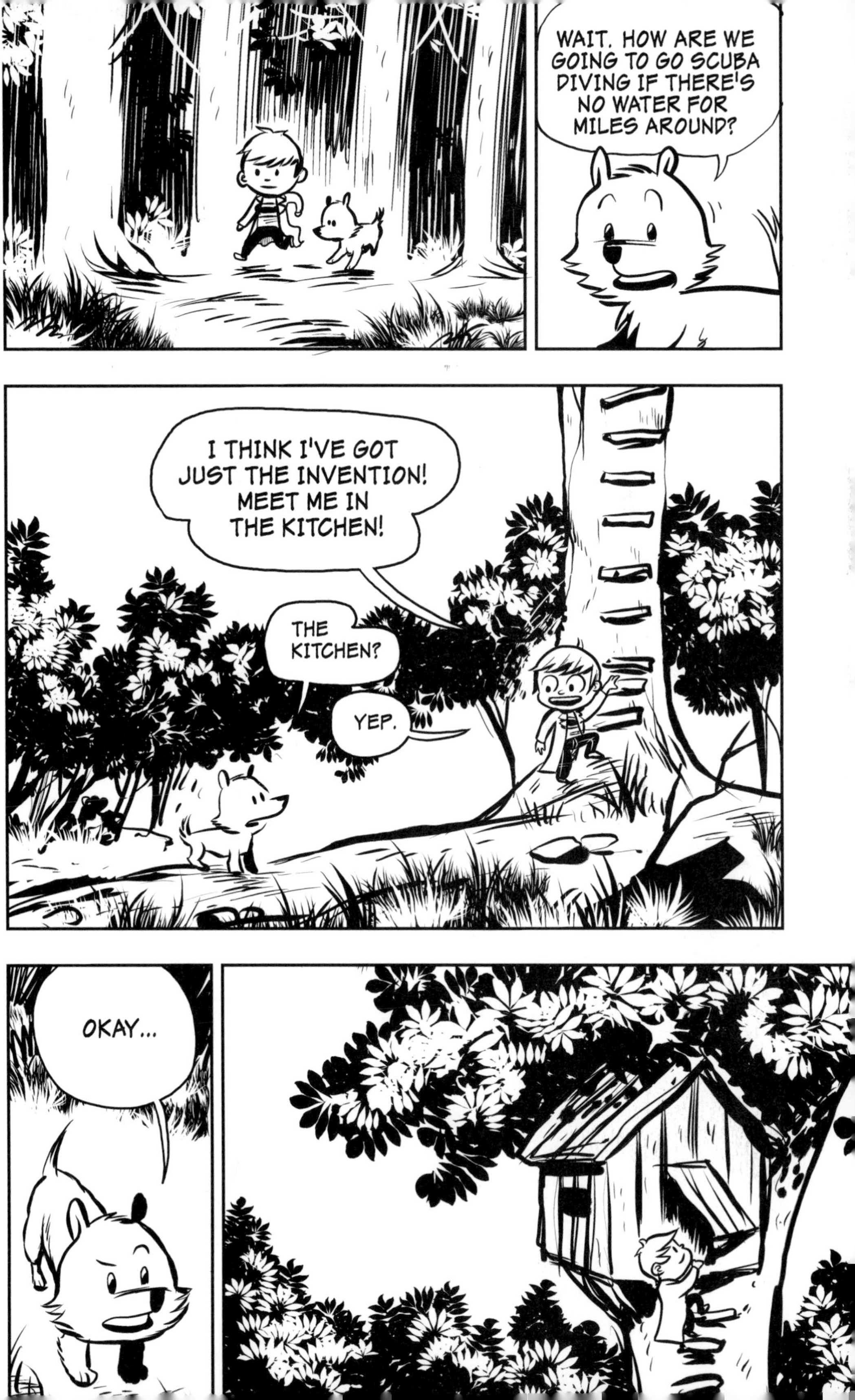
WAIT. HOW ARE WE GOING TO GO SCUBA DIVING IF THERE'S NO WATER FOR MILES AROUND?
I THINK I'VE GOT JUST THE INVENTION! MEET ME IN THE KITCHEN!
THE KITCHEN?
YEP.
OKAY...

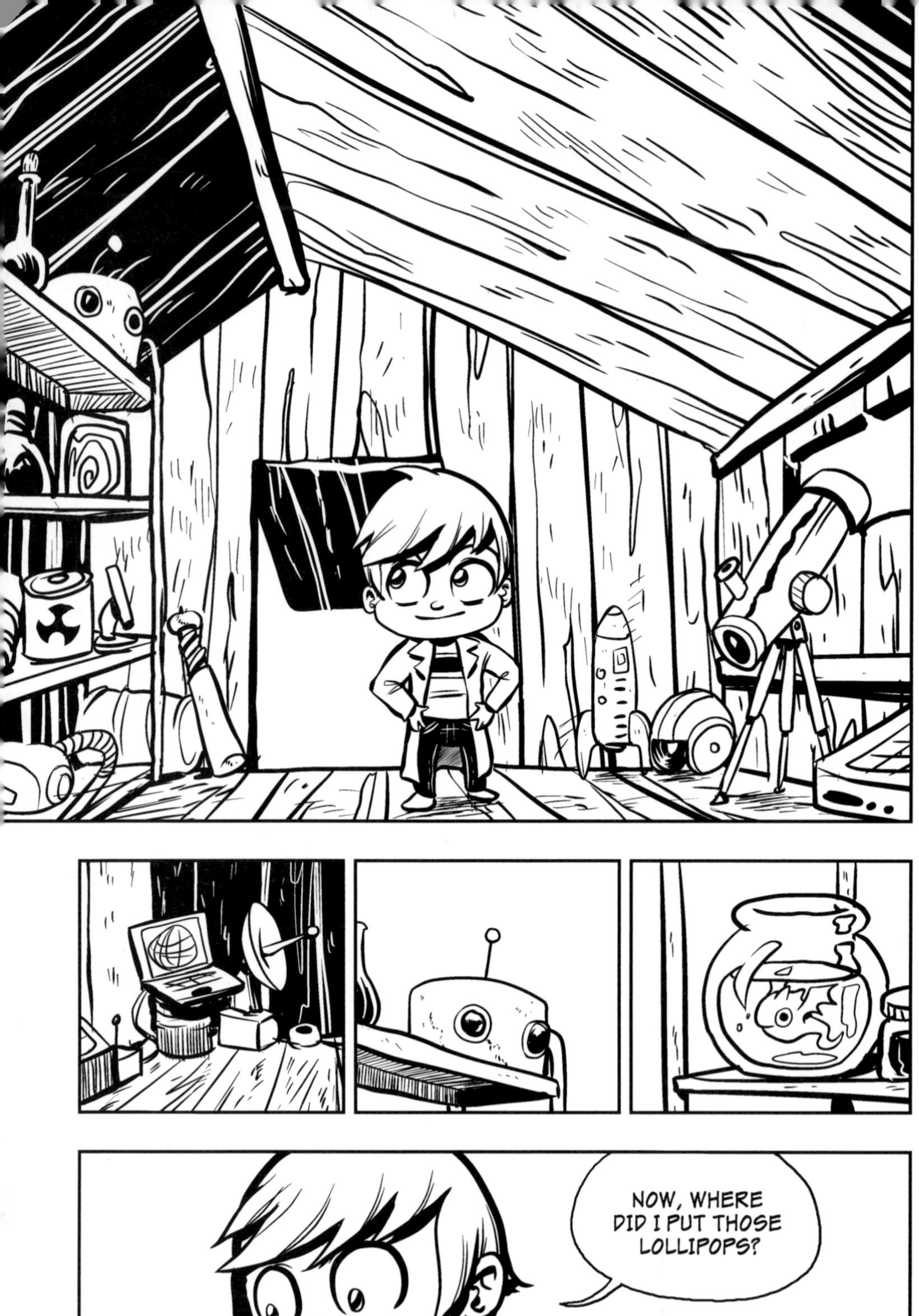
NOW, WHERE DID I PUT THOSE LOLLIPOPS?

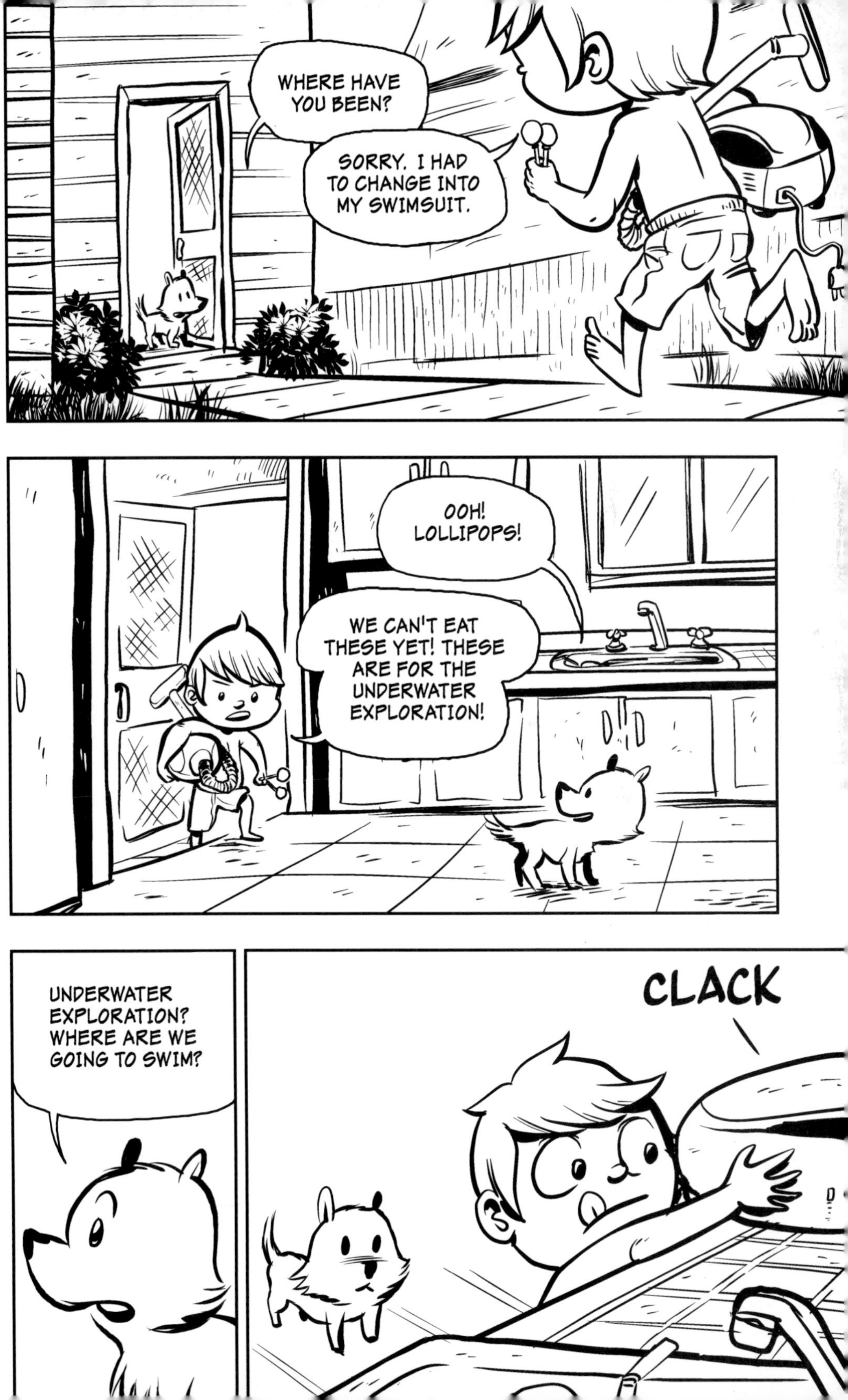
WHERE HAVE YOU BEEN?
SORRY. I HAD TO CHANGE INTO MY SWIMSUIT.
OOH! LOLLIPOPS!
WE CAN'T EAT THESE YET! THESE ARE FOR THE UNDERWATER EXPLORATION!
UNDERWATER EXPLORATION? WHERE ARE WE GOING TO SWIM?
CLACK

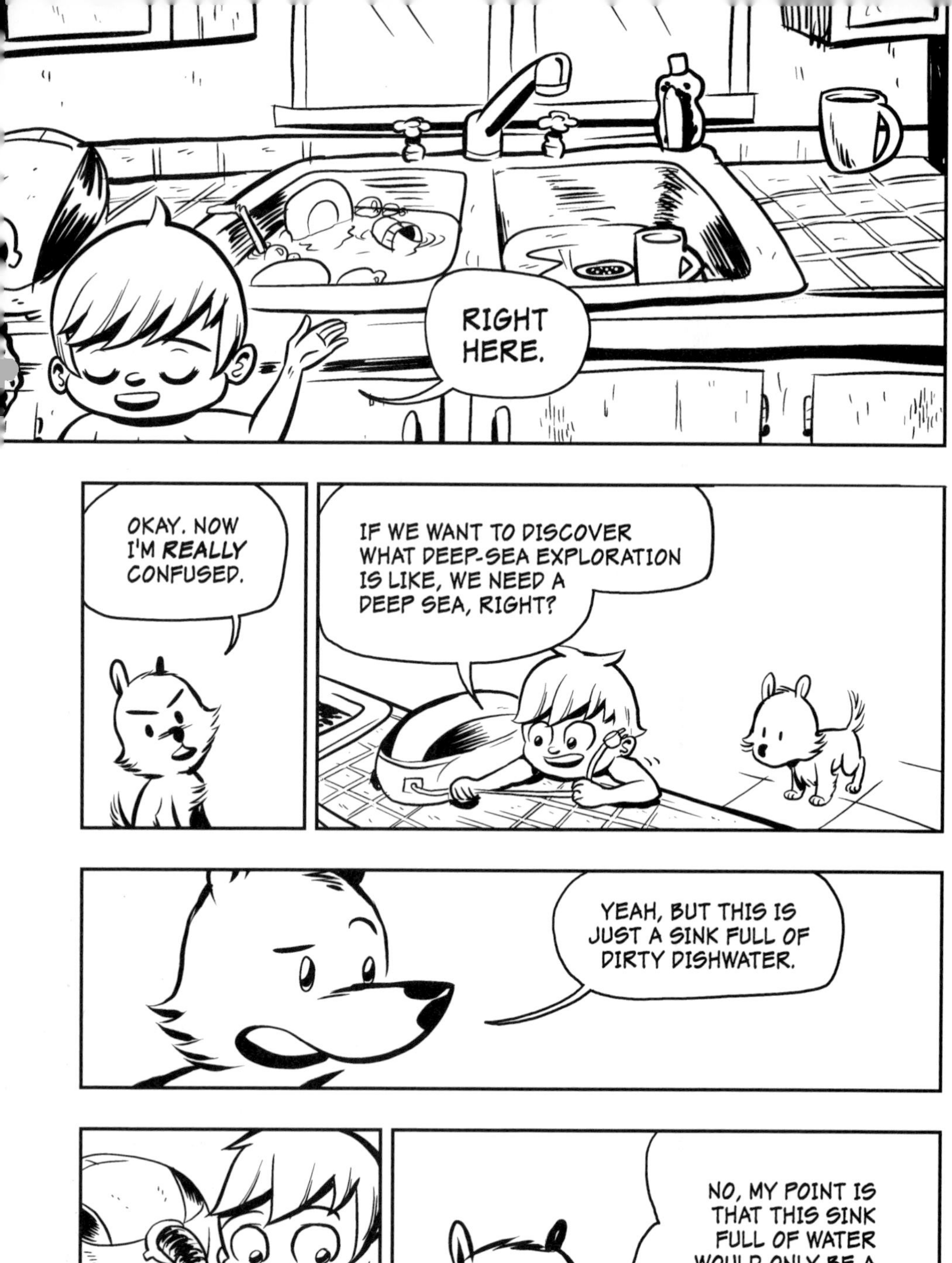
RIGHT HERE.
OKAY. NOW I'M REALLY CONFUSED.
IF WE WANT TO DISCOVER WHAT DEEP-SEA EXPLORATION IS LIKE, WE NEED A DEEP SEA, RIGHT?
YEAH, BUT THIS IS JUST A SINK FULL OF DIRTY DISHWATER.
THIS WATER IS PROBABLY CLEANER THAN OCEAN WATER.
NO, MY POINT IS THAT THIS SINK FULL OF WATER WOULD ONLY BE A DEEP SEA TO SOMEONE WHO IS ABOUT HALF AN INCH TALL...

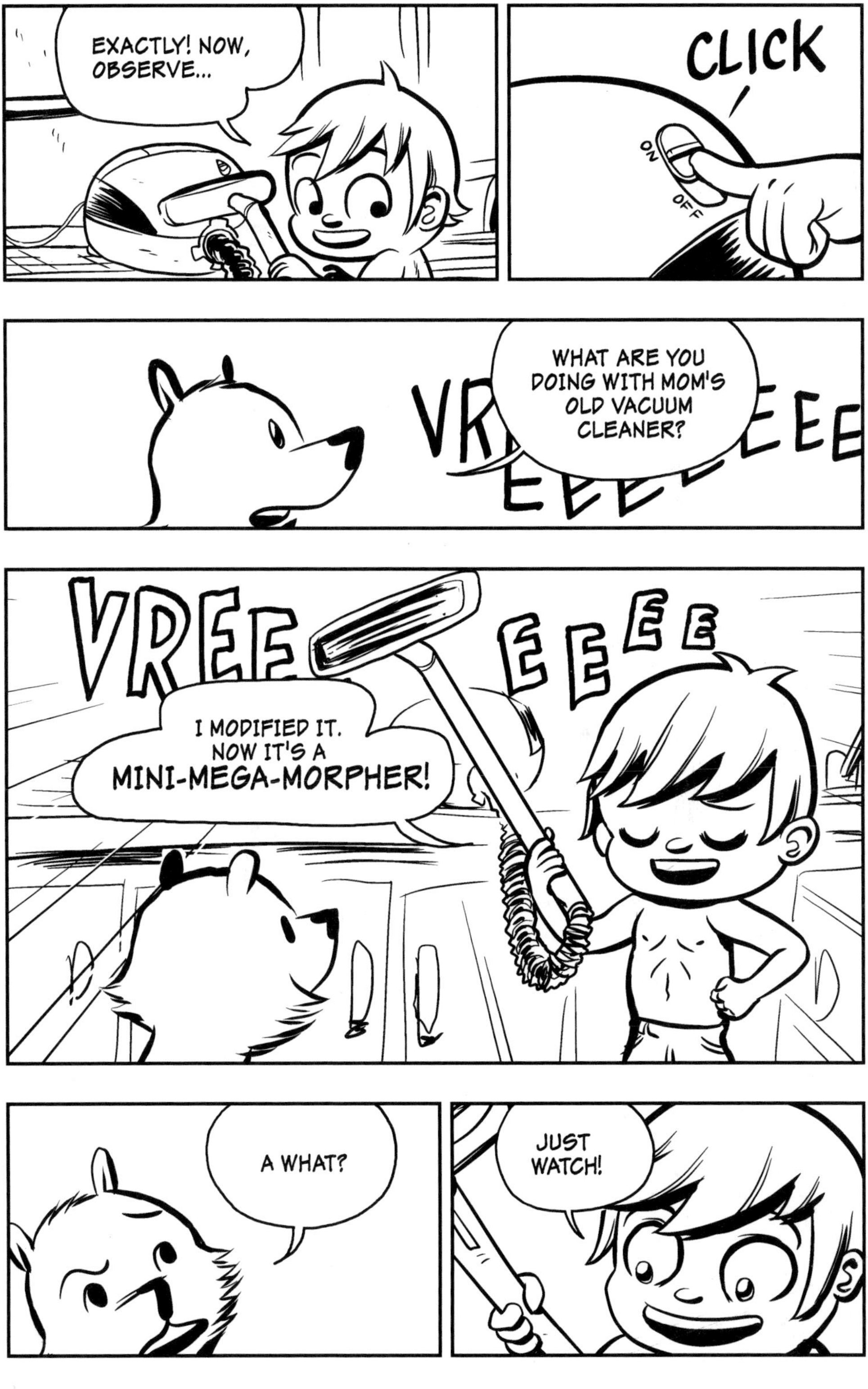
EXACTLY! NOW, OBSERVE...
CLICK
ON
OFF
VREEEEEEEEE
WHAT ARE YOU DOING WITH MOM'S OLD VACUUM CLEANER?
VREEEEEE
I MODIFIED IT. NOW IT'S A MINI-MEGA-MORPHER!
A WHAT?
JUST WATCH!

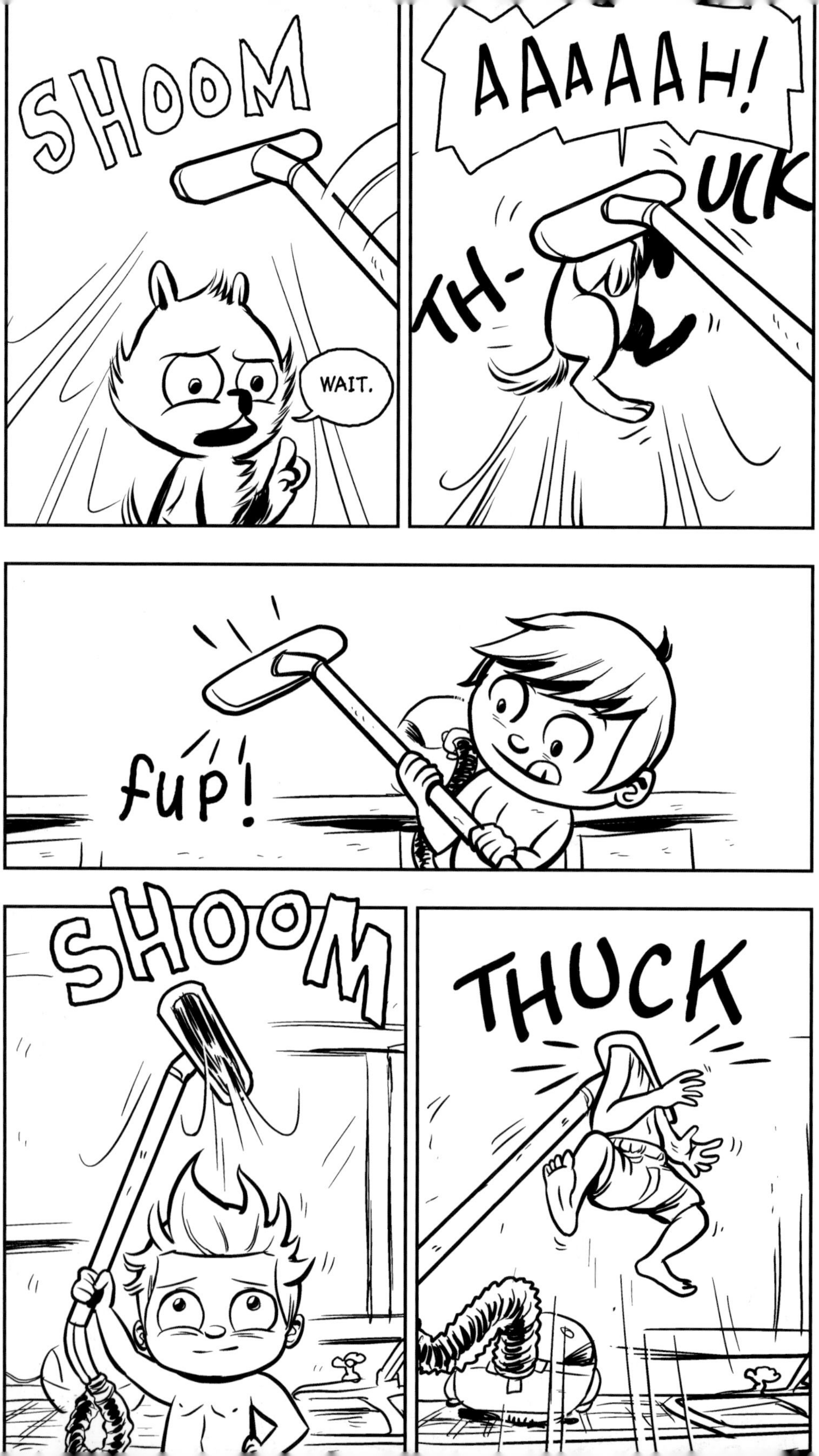
SHOOM
WAIT.
AAAAAH!
TH-
UCK
fup!
SHOOM
THUCK

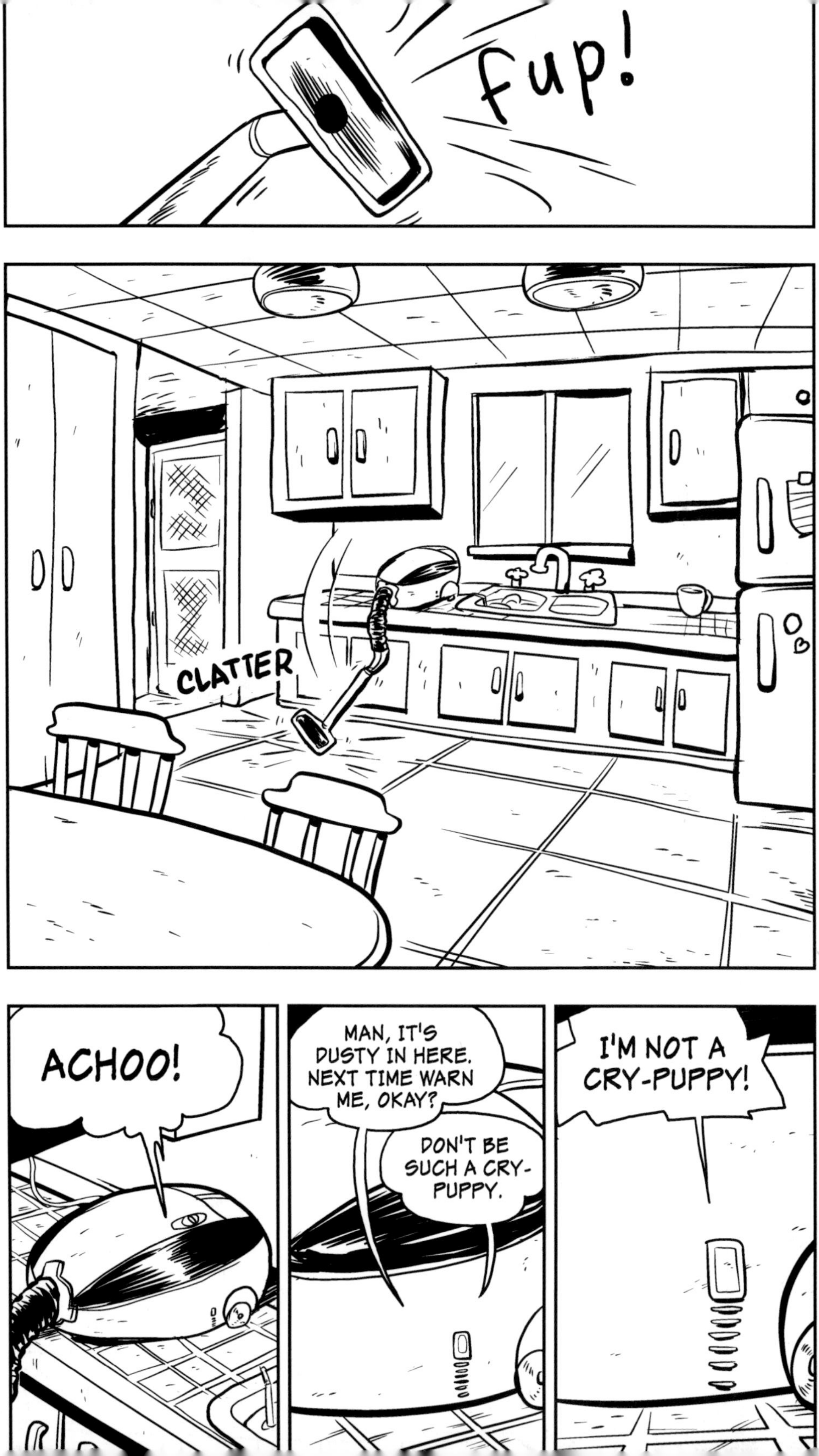

FUP!
CLATTER
ACHOO!
MAN, IT'S DUSTY IN HERE. NEXT TIME WARN ME, OKAY?
DON'T BE SUCH A CRY-PUPPY.
I'M NOT A CRY-PUPPY!

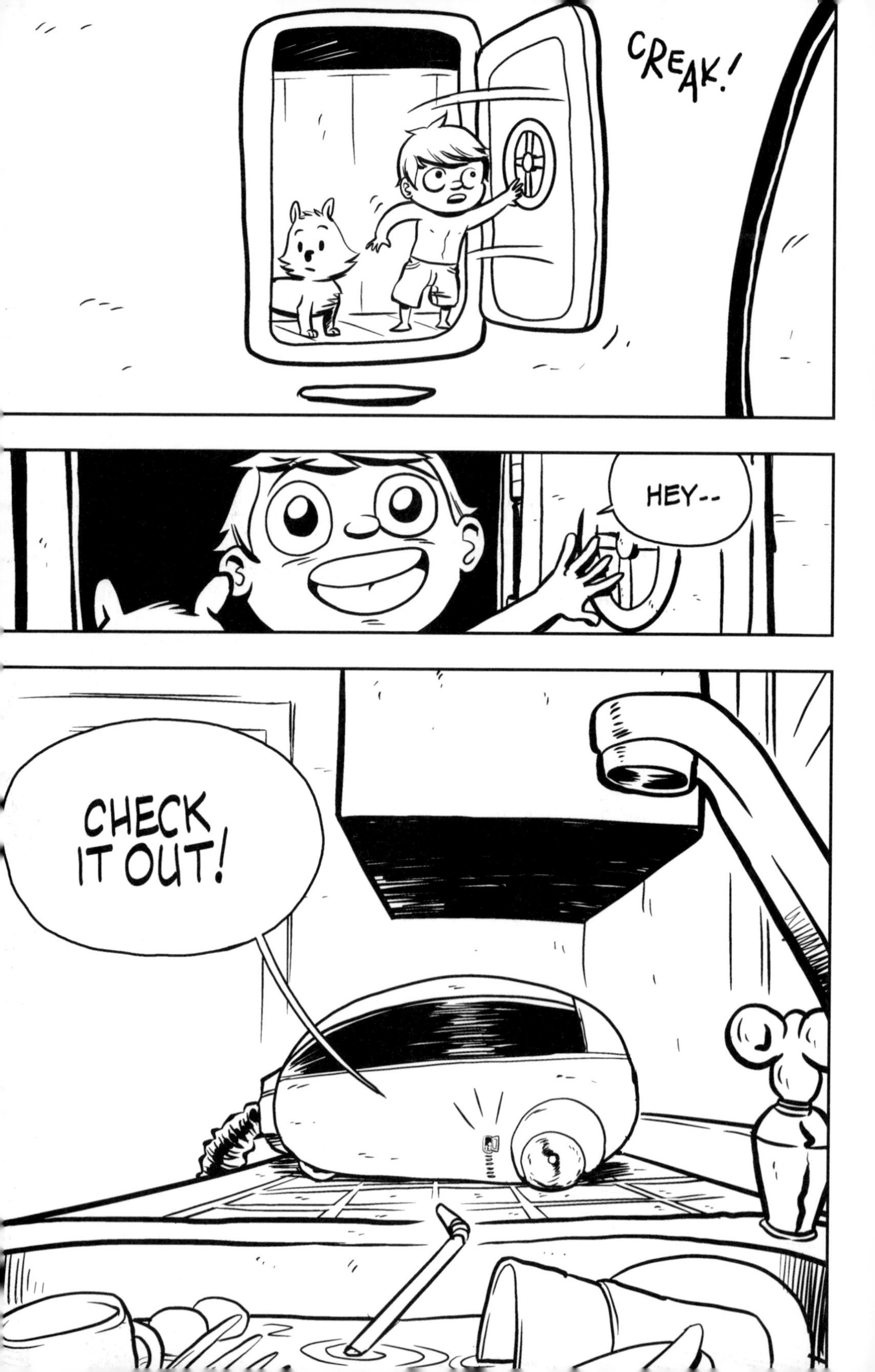
CREAK!
HEY--
CHECK IT OUT!

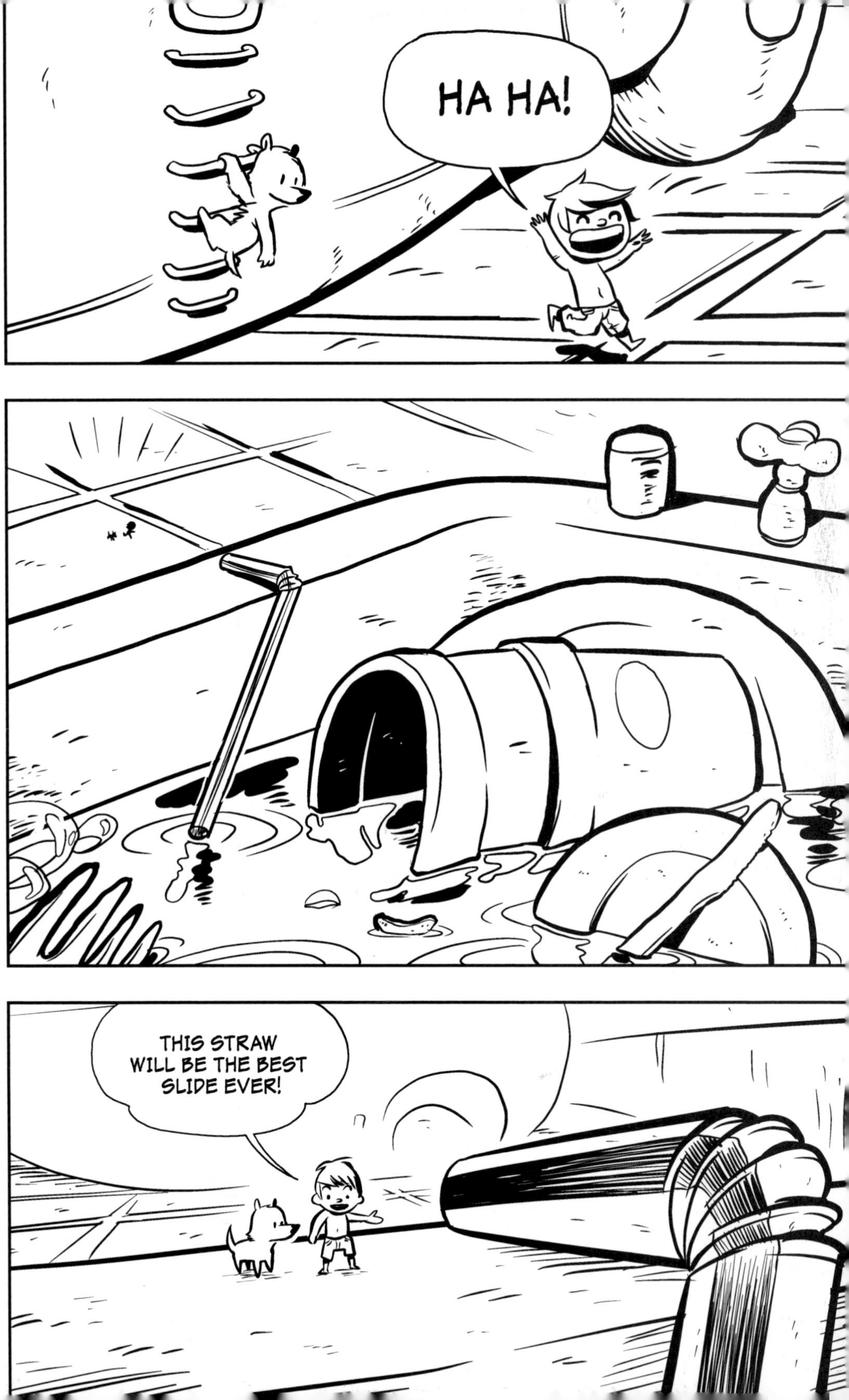
HA HA!
THIS STRAW WILL BE THE BEST SLIDE EVER!

SORRY, BUT I'M TIRED OF GETTING SUCKED THROUGH TUBES.

COME ON! IT'LL BE LIKE A WATERSLIDE!

WHAT IF WE, UM...

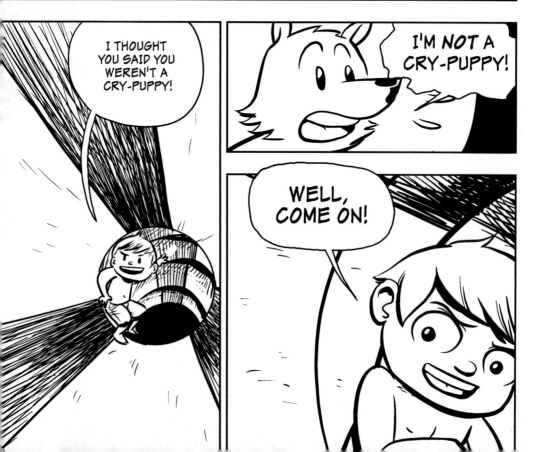

I THOUGHT YOU SAID YOU WEREN'T A CRY-PUPPY!

I'M NOT A CRY-PUPPY!

WELL, COME ON!

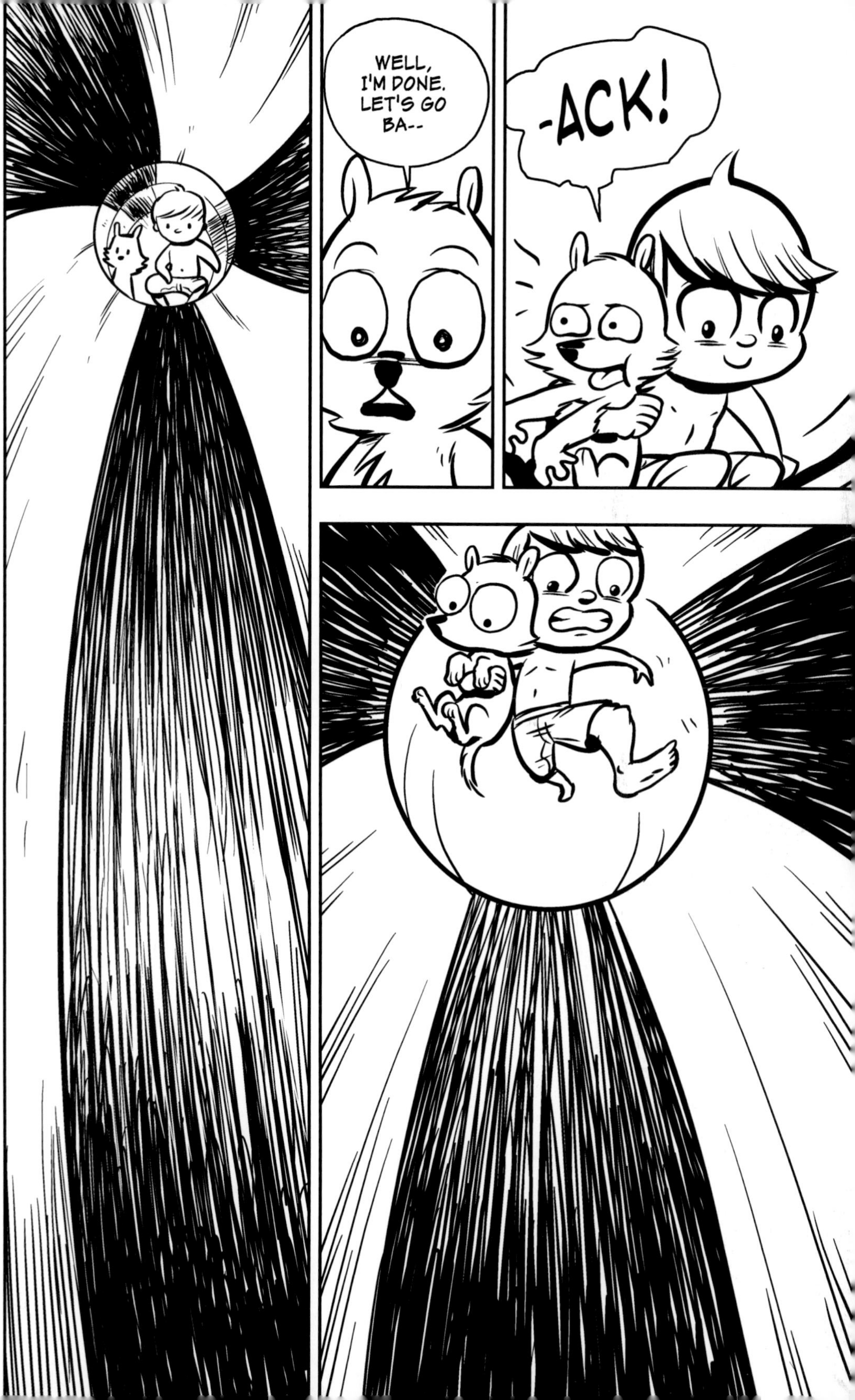
WELL, I'M DONE. LET'S GO BA--
-ACK!

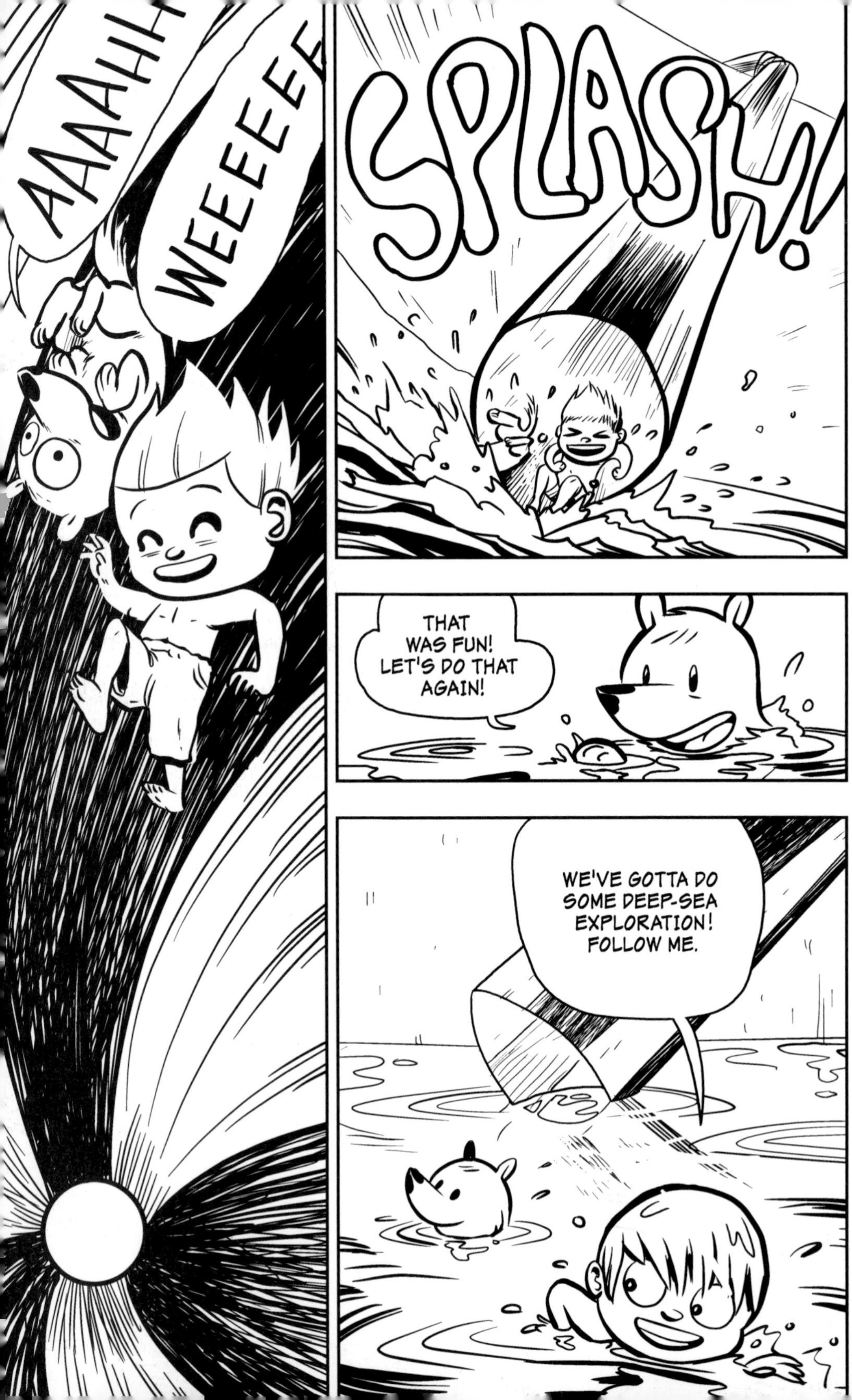

AAAAHH
WEEEEEEE
SPLASH!
THAT WAS FUN! LET'S DO THAT AGAIN!
WE'VE GOTTA DO SOME DEEP-SEA EXPLORATION! FOLLOW ME.

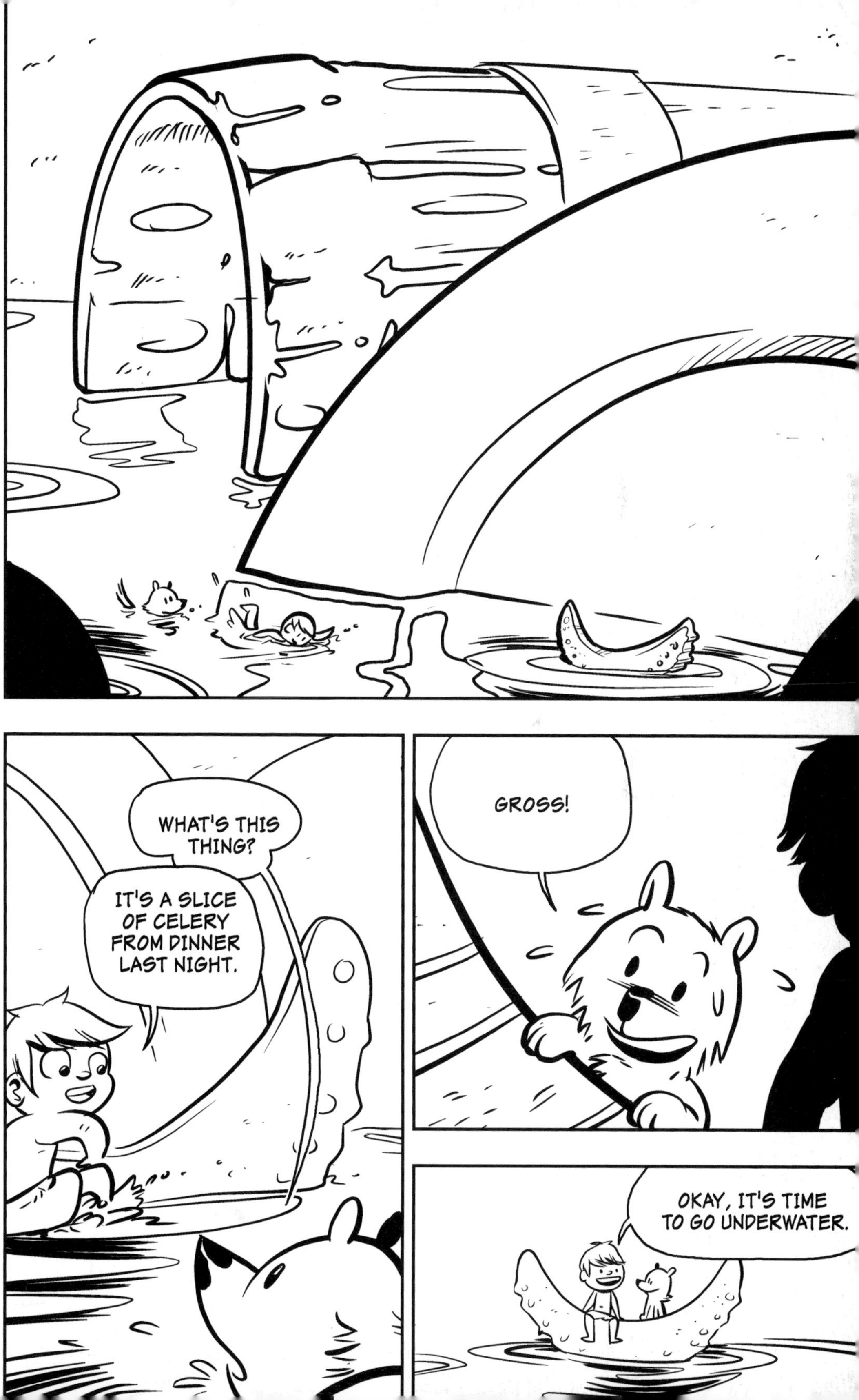
WHAT'S THIS THING?
IT'S A SLICE OF CELERY FROM DINNER LAST NIGHT.
GROSS!
OKAY, IT'S TIME TO GO UNDERWATER.

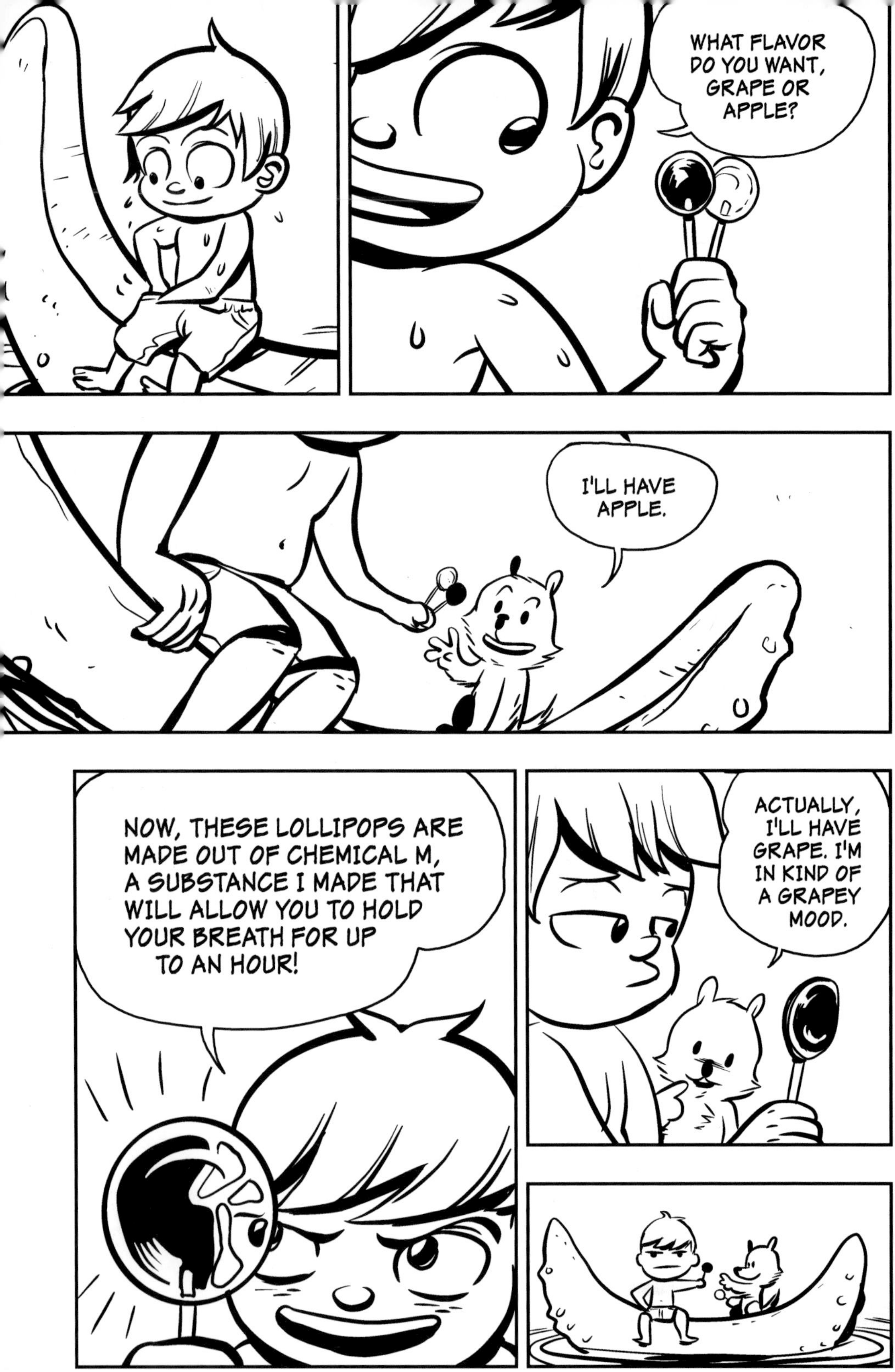
WHAT FLAVOR DO YOU WANT, GRAPE OR APPLE?
I'LL HAVE APPLE.
NOW, THESE LOLLIPOPS ARE MADE OUT OF CHEMICAL M, A SUBSTANCE I MADE THAT WILL ALLOW YOU TO HOLD YOUR BREATH FOR UP TO AN HOUR!
ACTUALLY, I'LL HAVE GRAPE. I'M IN KIND OF A GRAPEY MOOD.

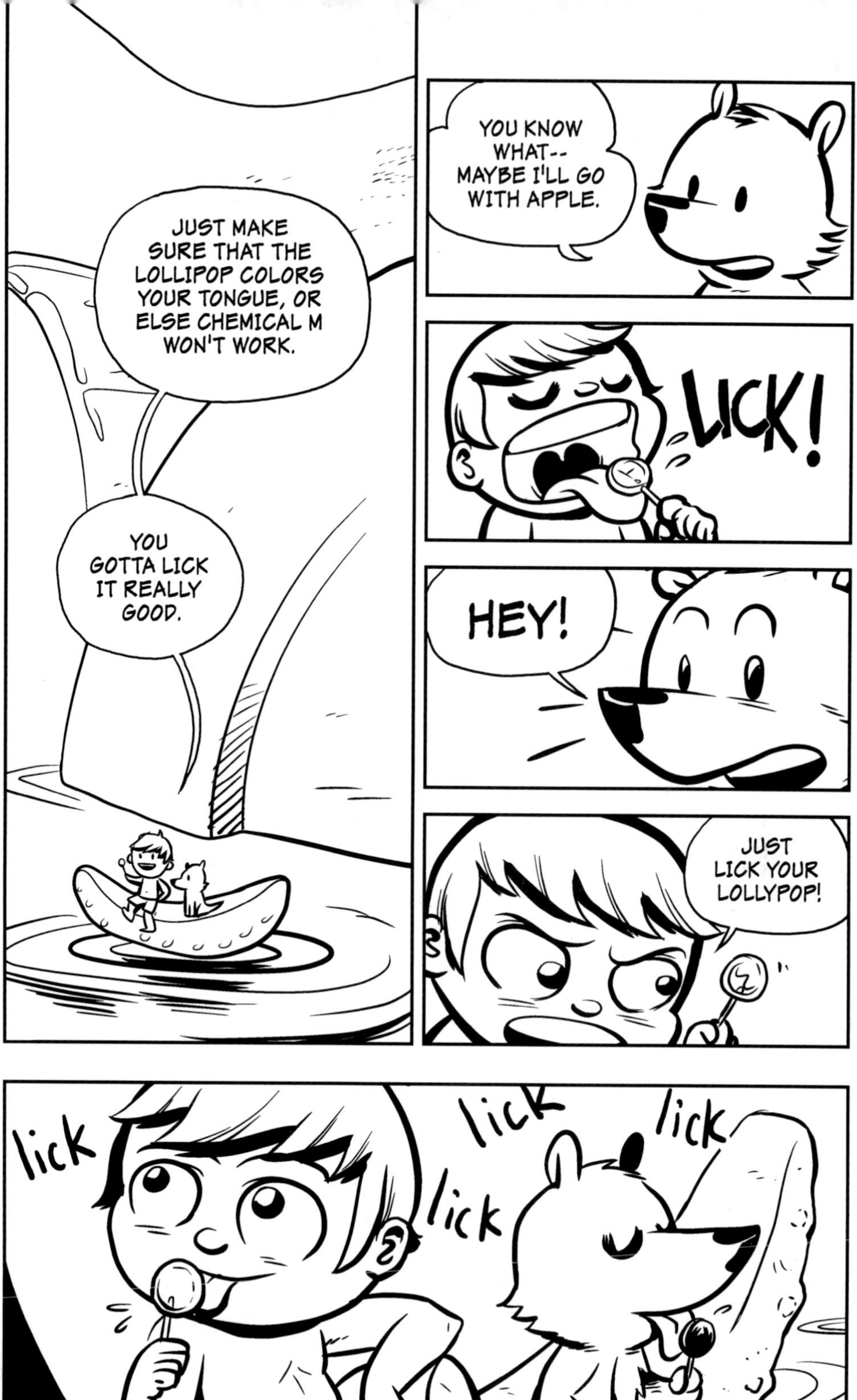
JUST MAKE SURE THAT THE LOLLIPOP COLORS YOUR TONGUE, OR ELSE CHEMICAL M WON'T WORK.
YOU GOTTA LICK IT REALLY GOOD.
YOU KNOW WHAT-- MAYBE I'LL GO WITH APPLE.
LICK!
HEY!
JUST LICK YOUR LOLLYPOP!
lick
lick
lick
lick

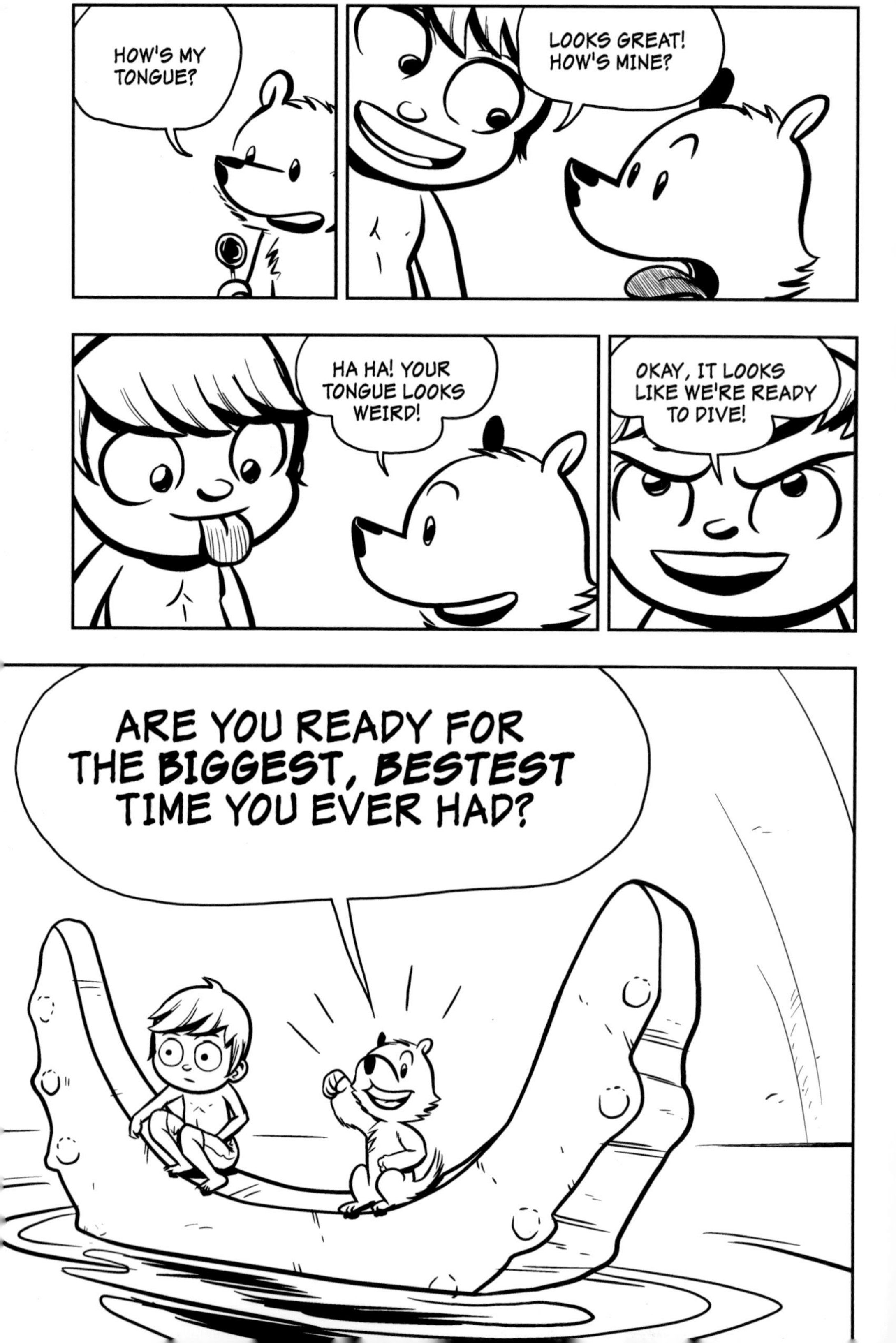
HOW'S MY TONGUE?
LOOKS GREAT! HOW'S MINE?
HA HA! YOUR TONGUE LOOKS WEIRD!
OKAY, IT LOOKS LIKE WE'RE READY TO DIVE!
ARE YOU READY FOR THE BIGGEST, BESTEST TIME YOU EVER HAD?

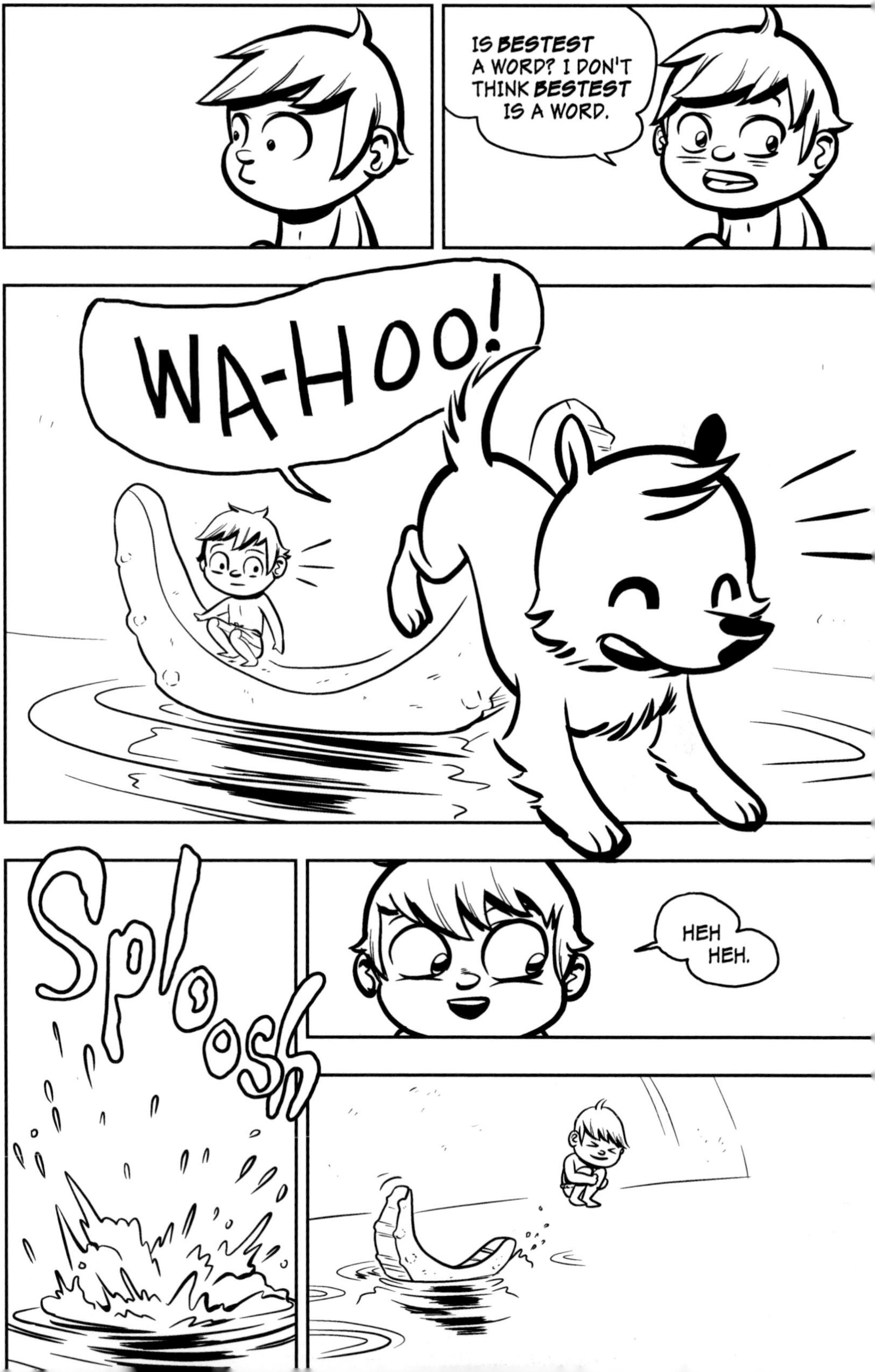
IS BESTEST A WORD? I DON'T THINK BESTEST IS A WORD.
WA-HOO!
Sploosh
HEH HEH.

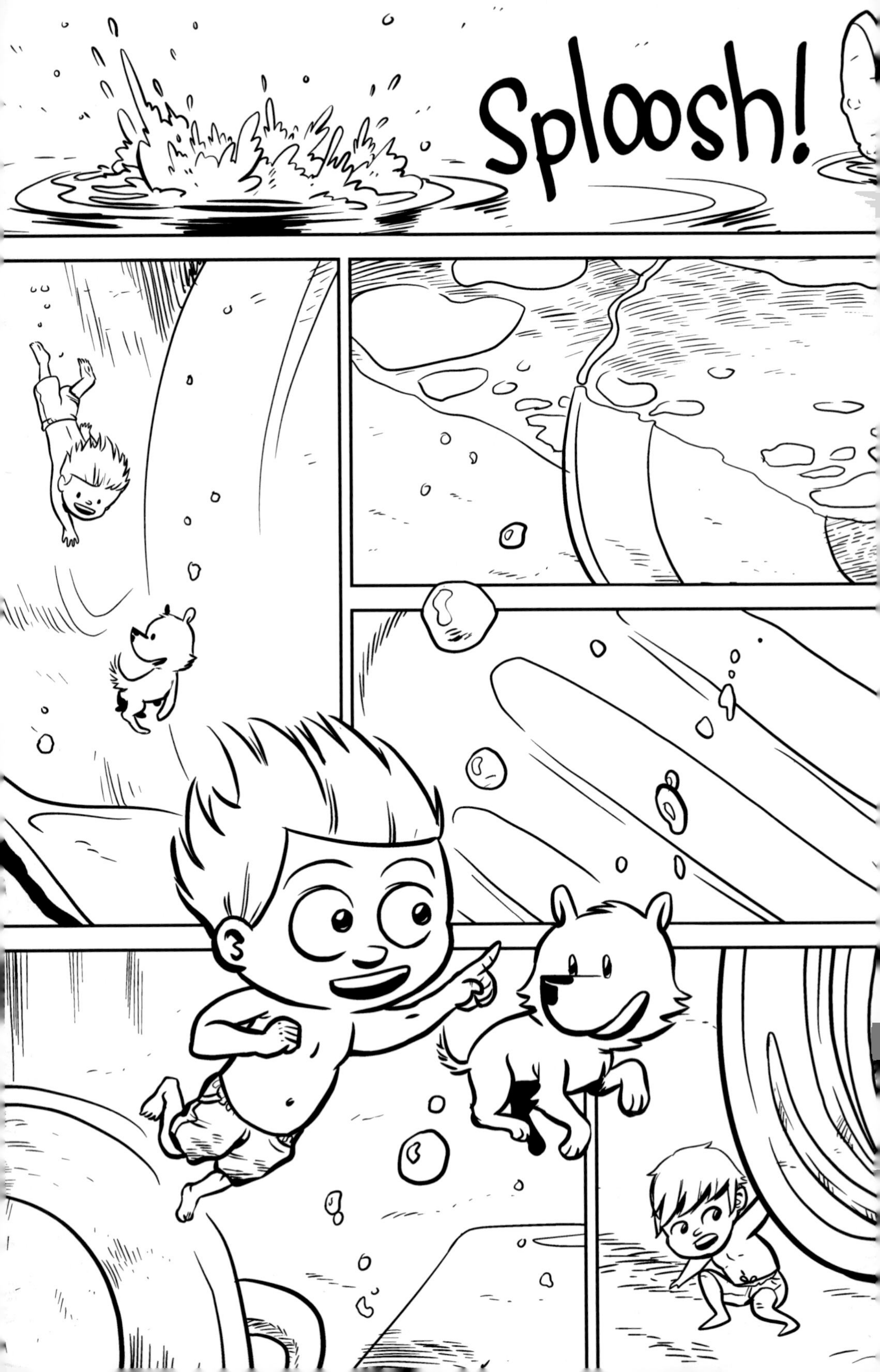
Sploosh!

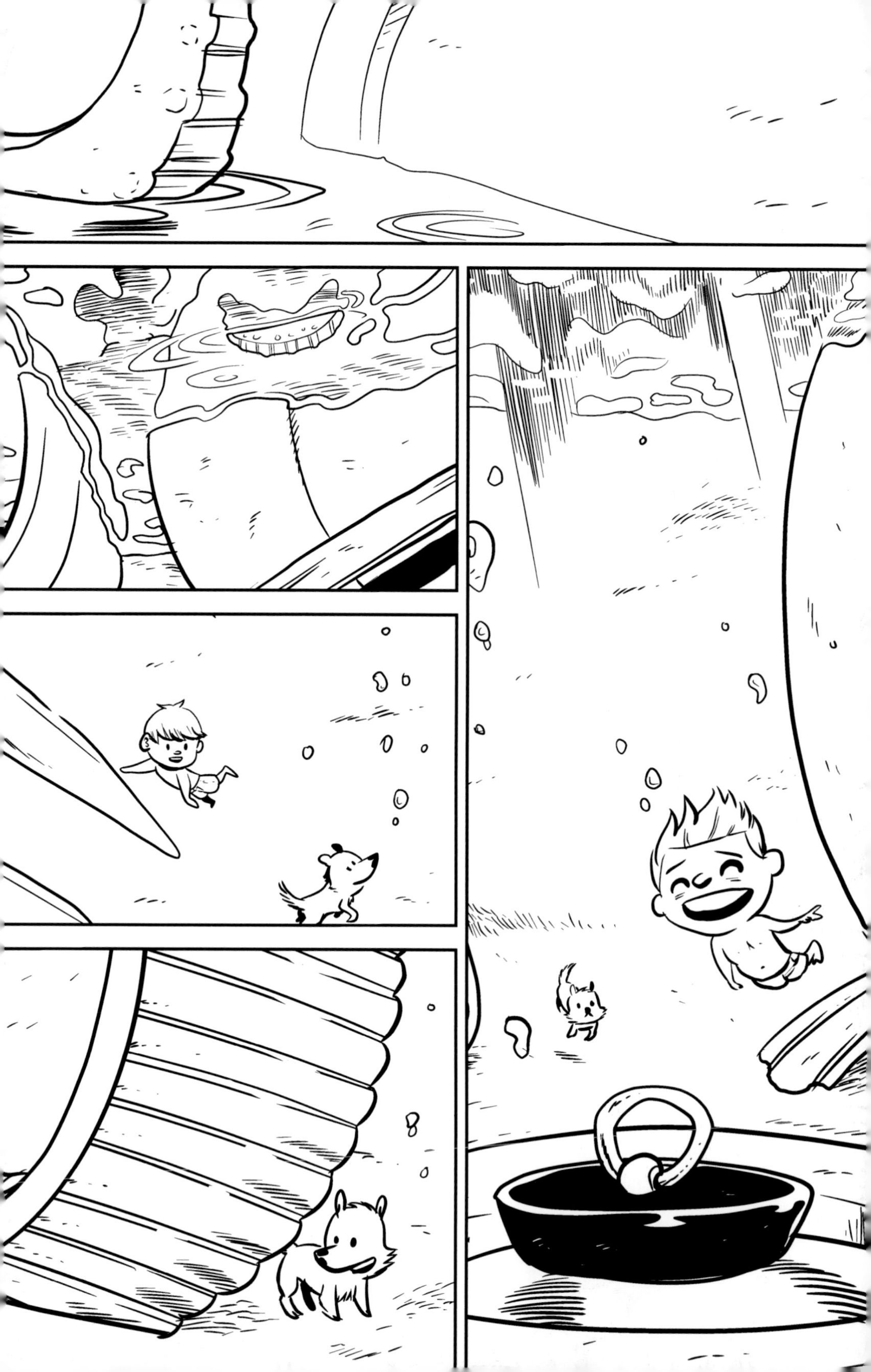

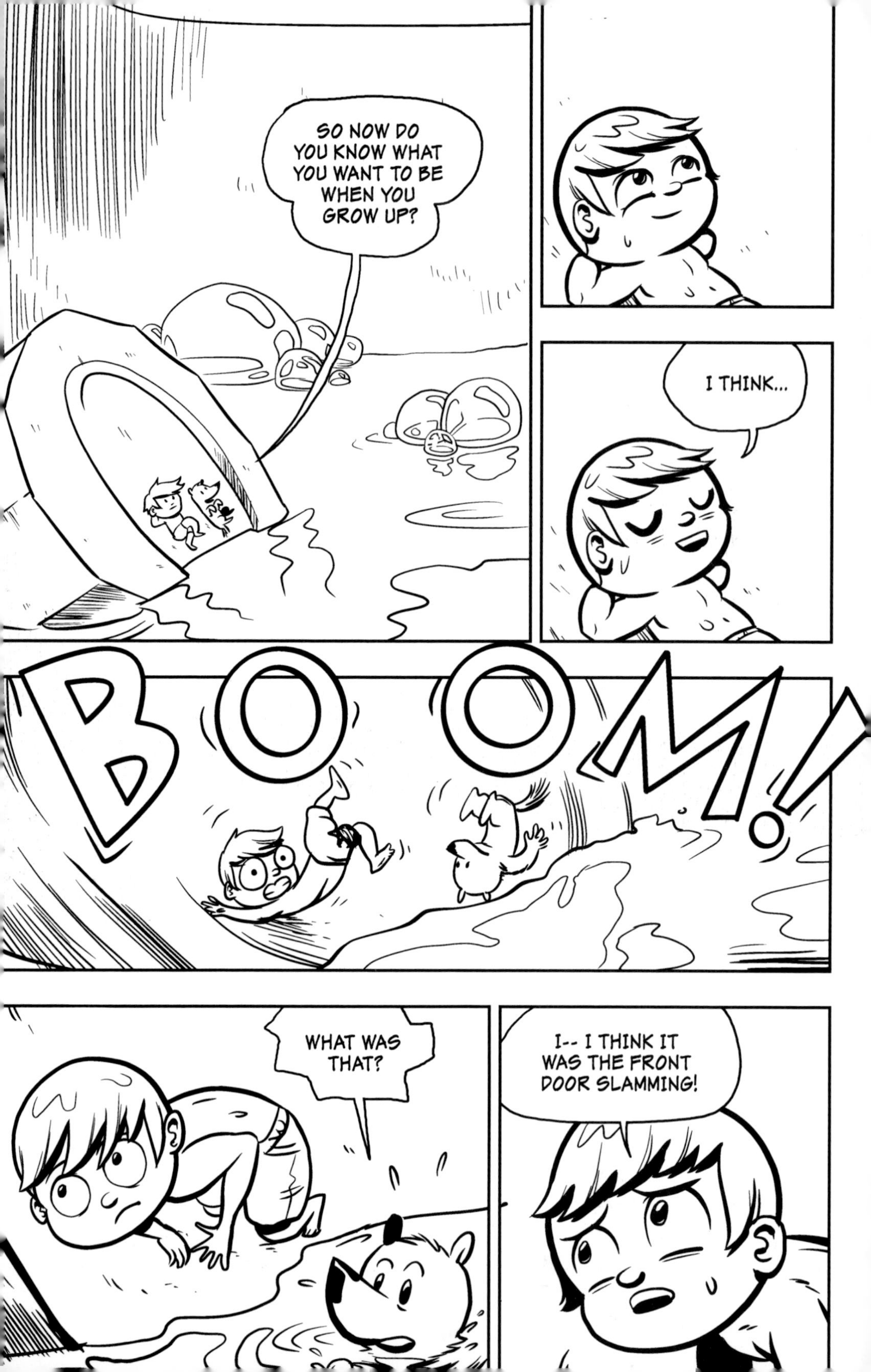
SO NOW DO YOU KNOW WHAT YOU WANT TO BE WHEN YOU GROW UP?
I THINK...
BOOM!
WHAT WAS THAT?
I-- I THINK IT WAS THE FRONT DOOR SLAMMING!

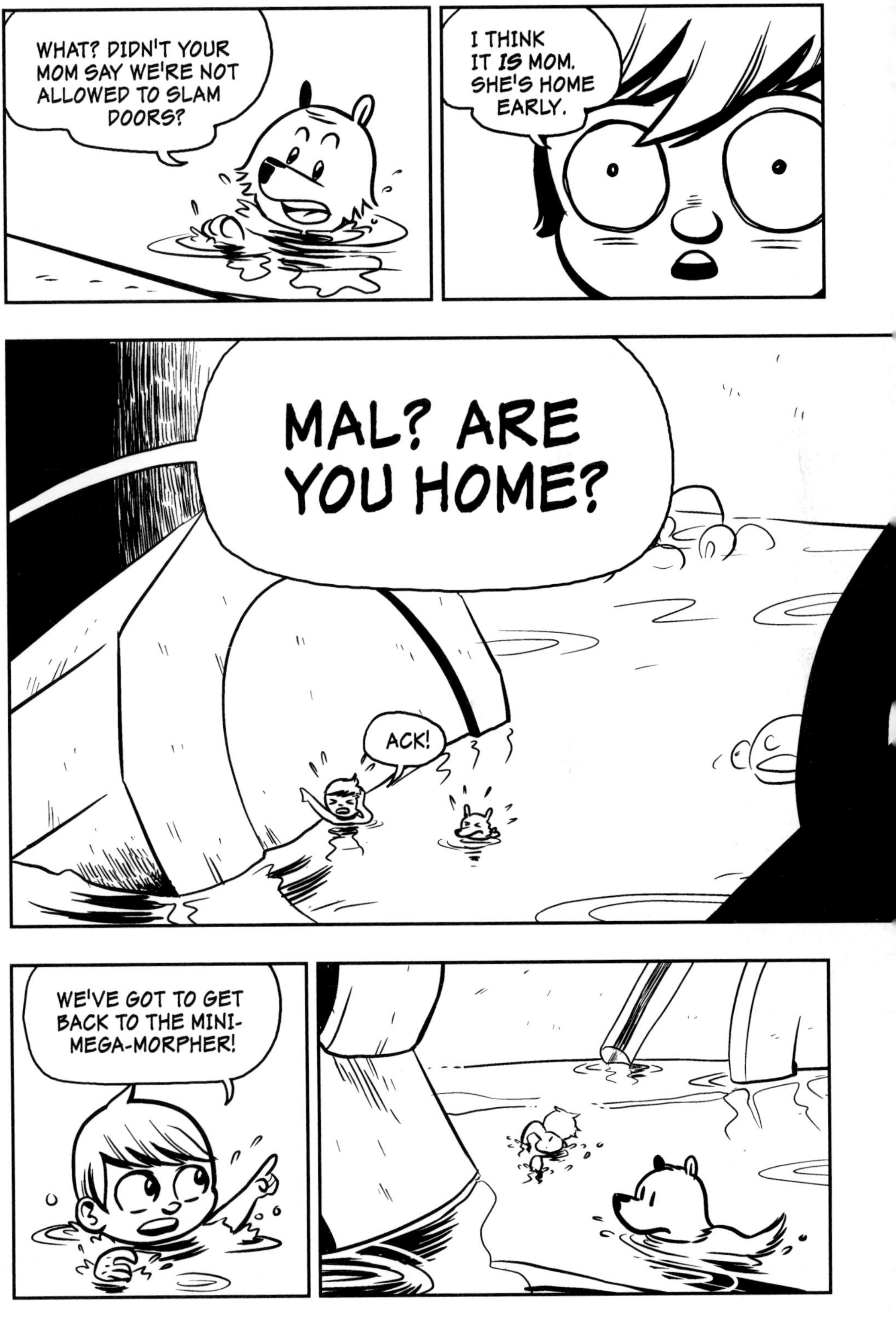
WHAT? DIDN'T YOUR MOM SAY WE'RE NOT ALLOWED TO SLAM DOORS?
I THINK IT *IS* MOM. SHE'S HOME EARLY.
MAL? ARE YOU HOME?
ACK!
WE'VE GOT TO GET BACK TO THE MINI-MEGA-MORPHER!

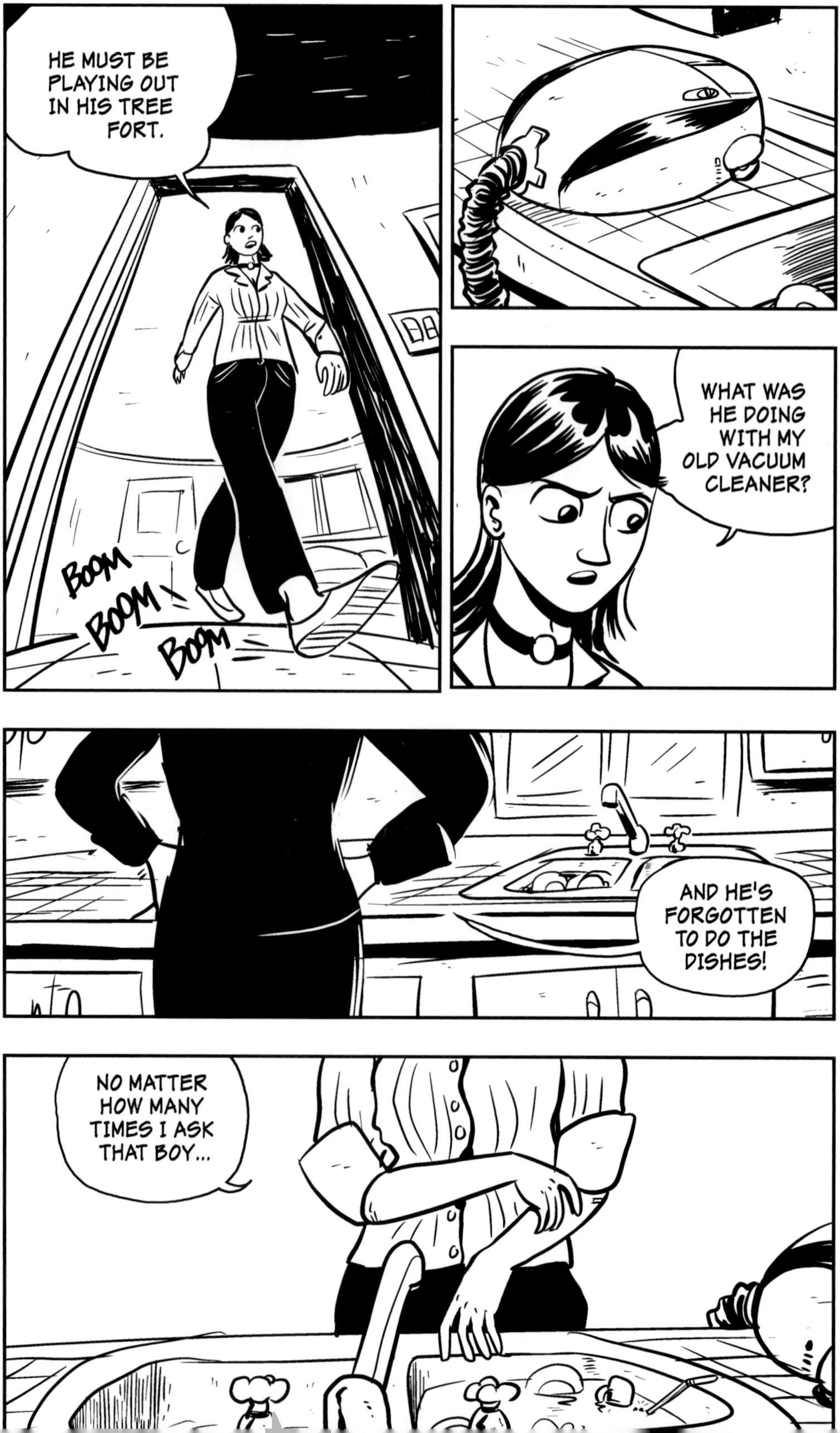
HE MUST BE PLAYING OUT IN HIS TREE FORT.
BOOM BOOM BOOM
WHAT WAS HE DOING WITH MY OLD VACUUM CLEANER?
AND HE'S FORGOTTEN TO DO THE DISHES!
NO MATTER HOW MANY TIMES I ASK THAT BOY...

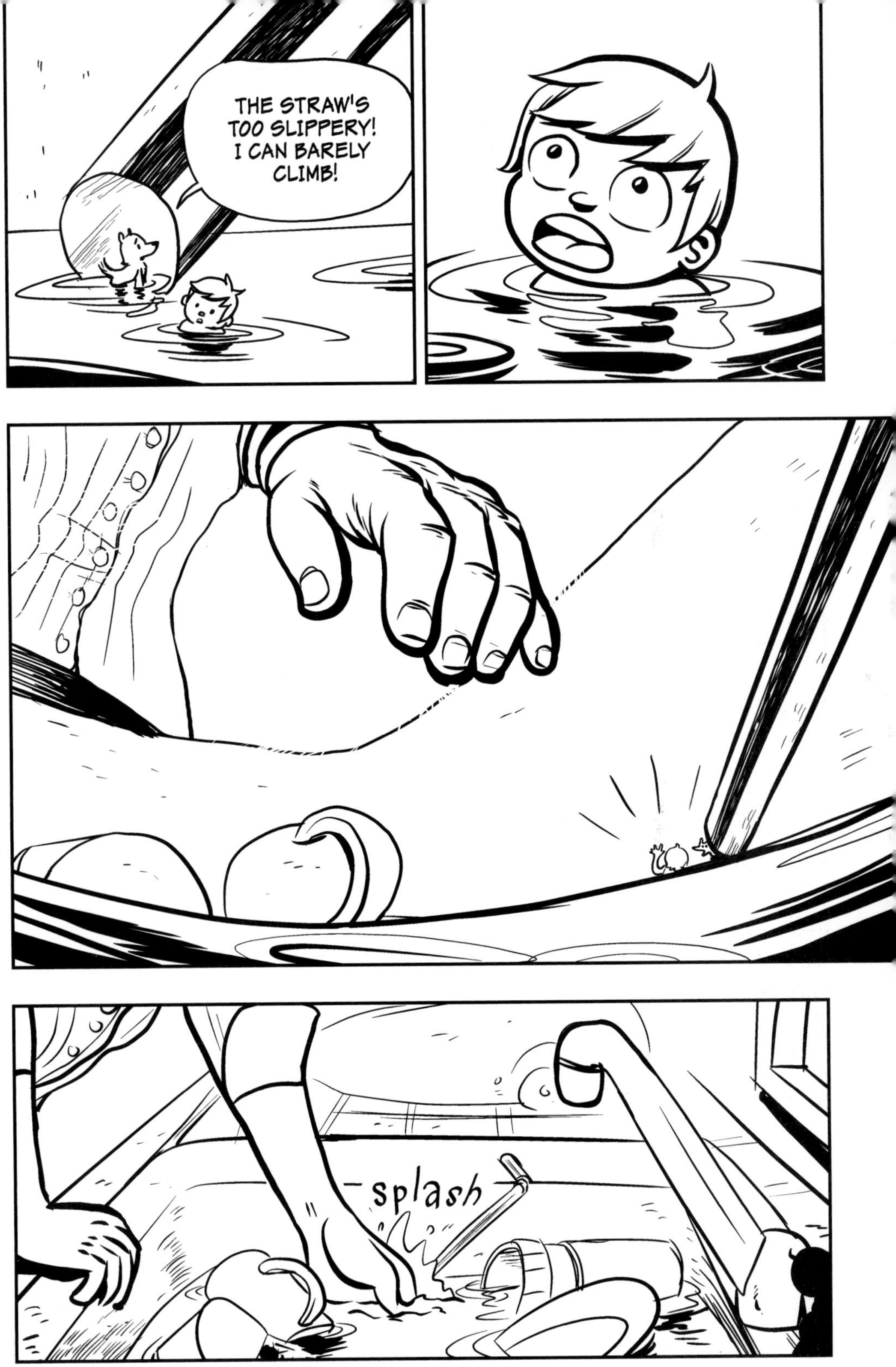
THE STRAW'S TOO SLIPPERY! I CAN BARELY CLIMB!
splash

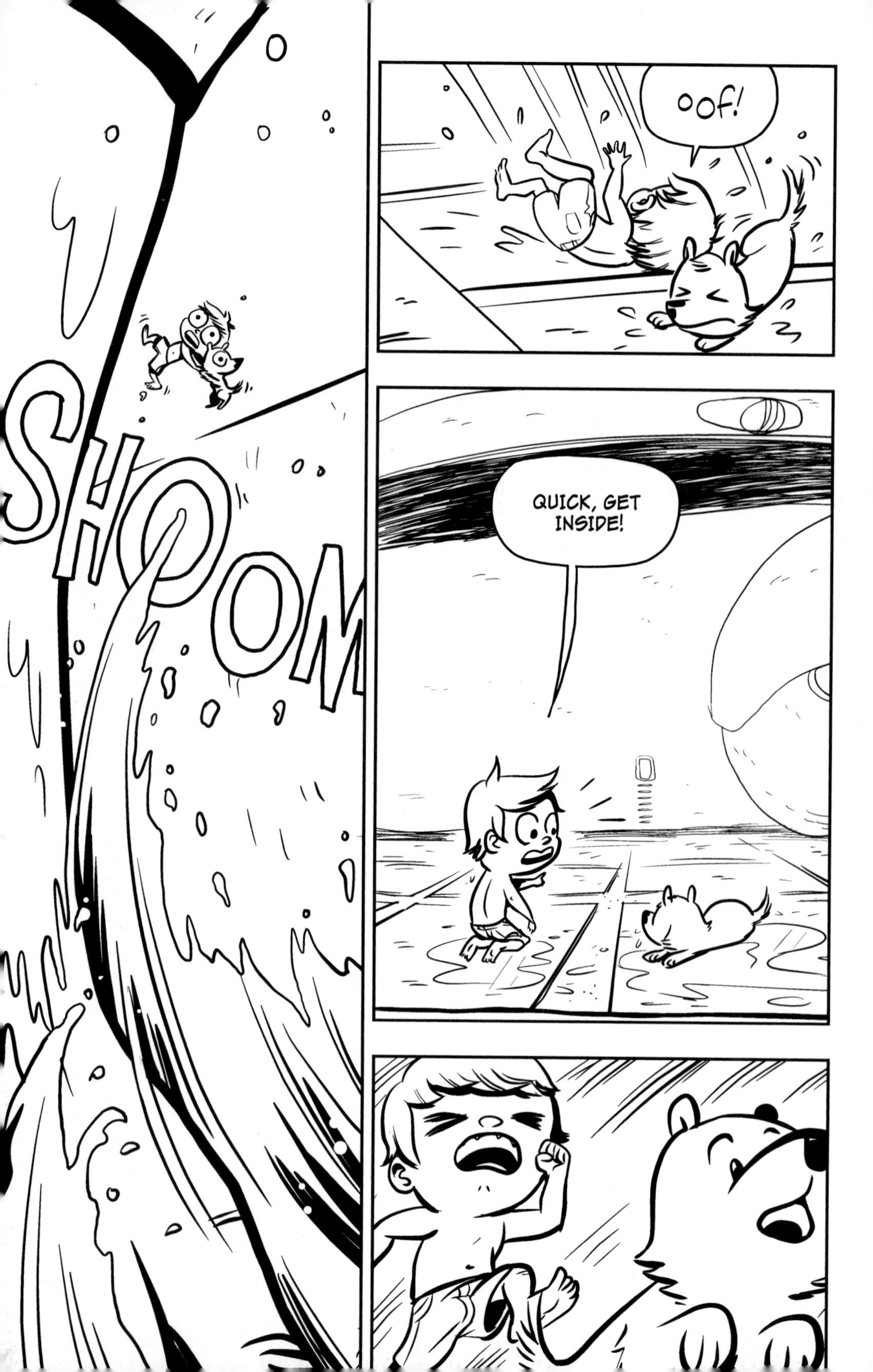
SHOOM
OOF!
QUICK, GET INSIDE!

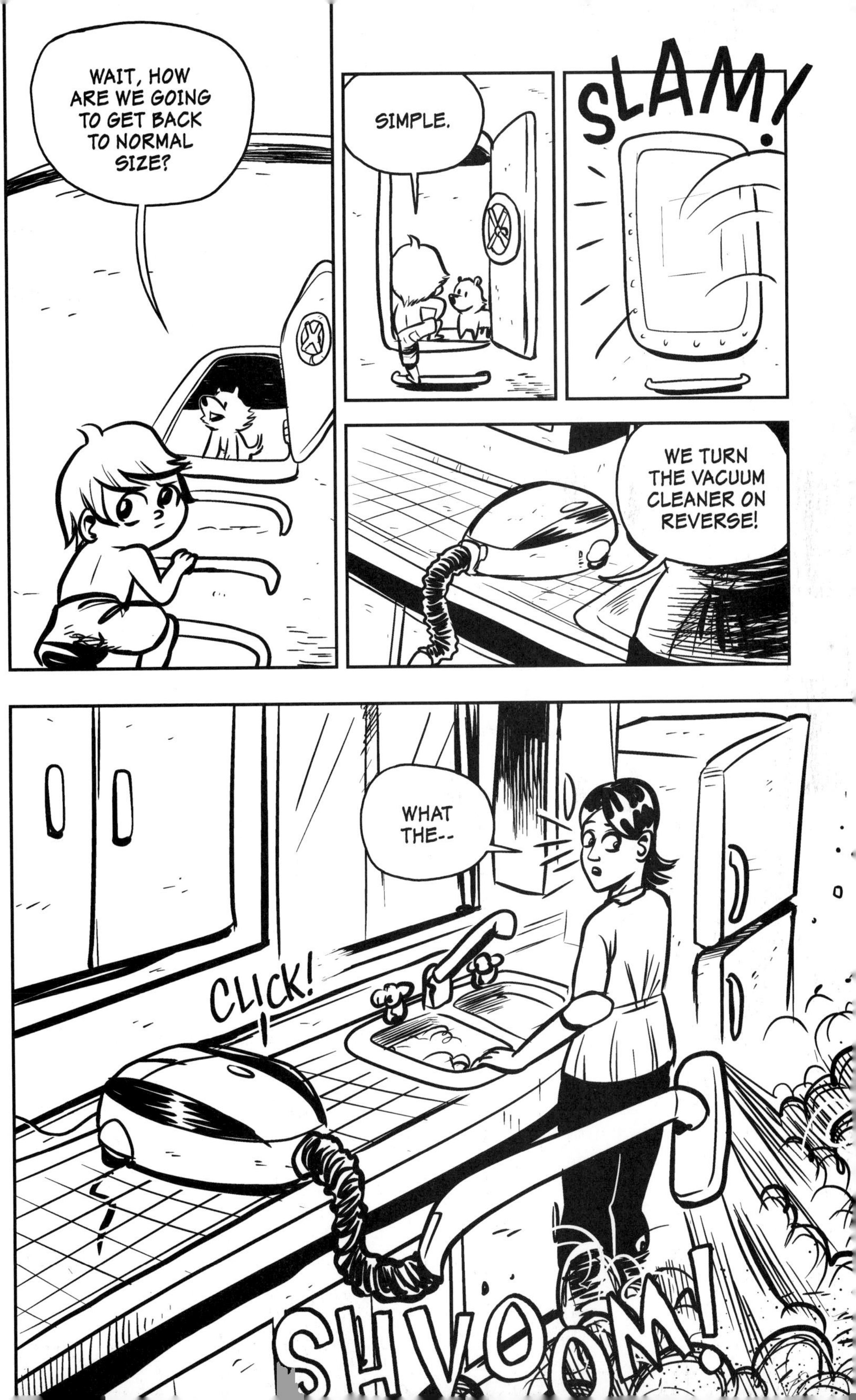
WAIT, HOW ARE WE GOING TO GET BACK TO NORMAL SIZE?
SIMPLE.
SLAM!
WE TURN THE VACUUM CLEANER ON REVERSE!
WHAT THE--
CLICK!
SHVOOM!

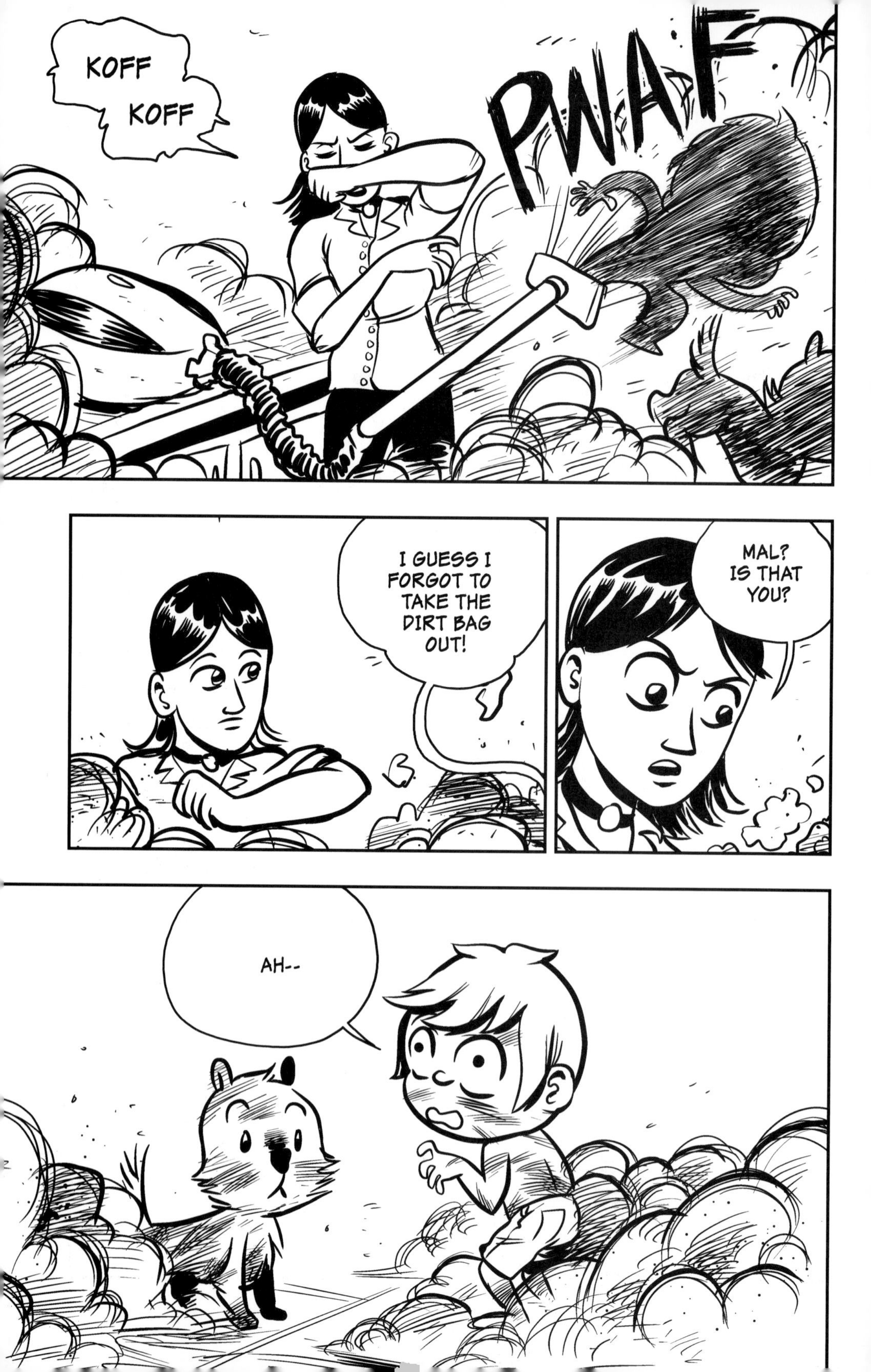
KOFF KOFF
PWAF
I GUESS I FORGOT TO TAKE THE DIRT BAG OUT!
MAL? IS THAT YOU?
AH--

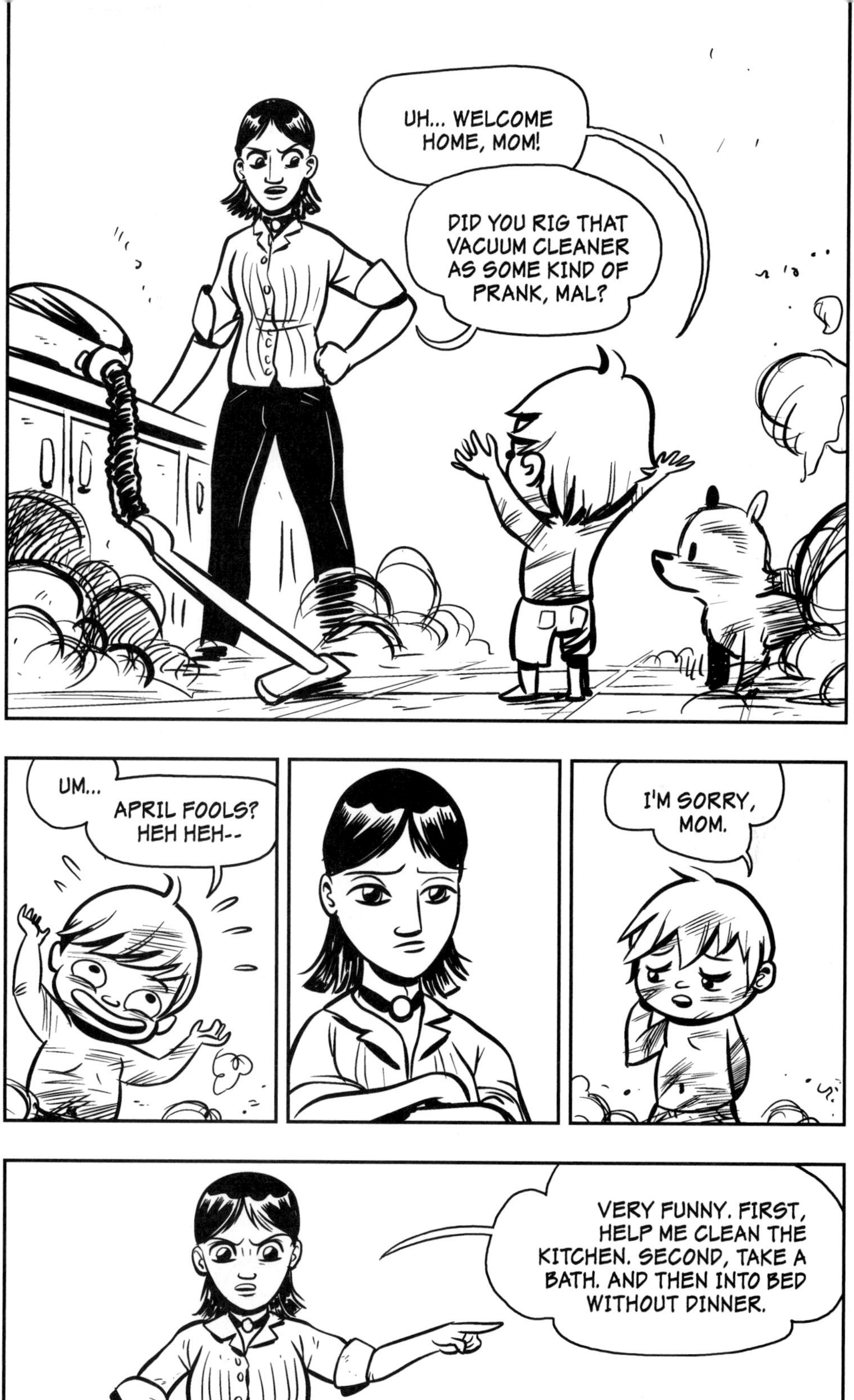
UH... WELCOME HOME, MOM!
DID YOU RIG THAT VACUUM CLEANER AS SOME KIND OF PRANK, MAL?
UM...
APRIL FOOLS? HEH HEH--
I'M SORRY, MOM.
VERY FUNNY. FIRST, HELP ME CLEAN THE KITCHEN. SECOND, TAKE A BATH. AND THEN INTO BED WITHOUT DINNER.

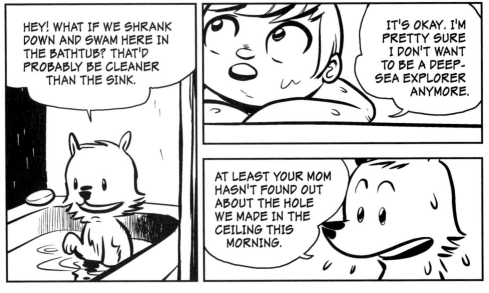

HEY! WHAT IF WE SHRANK DOWN AND SWAM HERE IN THE BATHTUB? THAT'D PROBABLY BE CLEANER THAN THE SINK.

IT'S OKAY. I'M PRETTY SURE I DON'T WANT TO BE A DEEP-SEA EXPLORER ANYMORE.

AT LEAST YOUR MOM HASN'T FOUND OUT ABOUT THE HOLE WE MADE IN THE CEILING THIS MORNING.

MAL! WHY DID YOU PUT A POSTER ON YOUR CEILING?

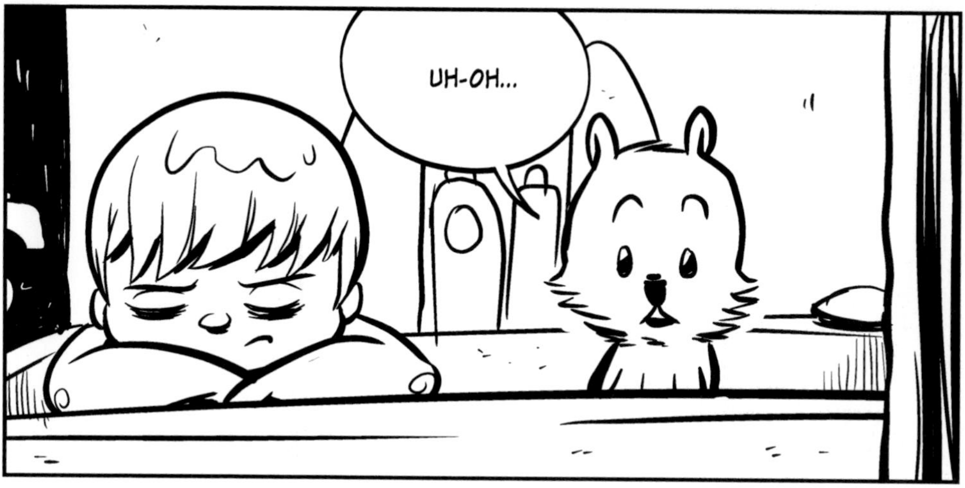
UH-OH...

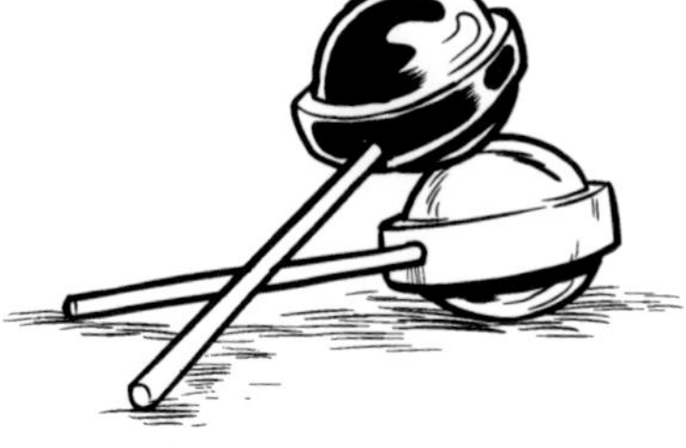

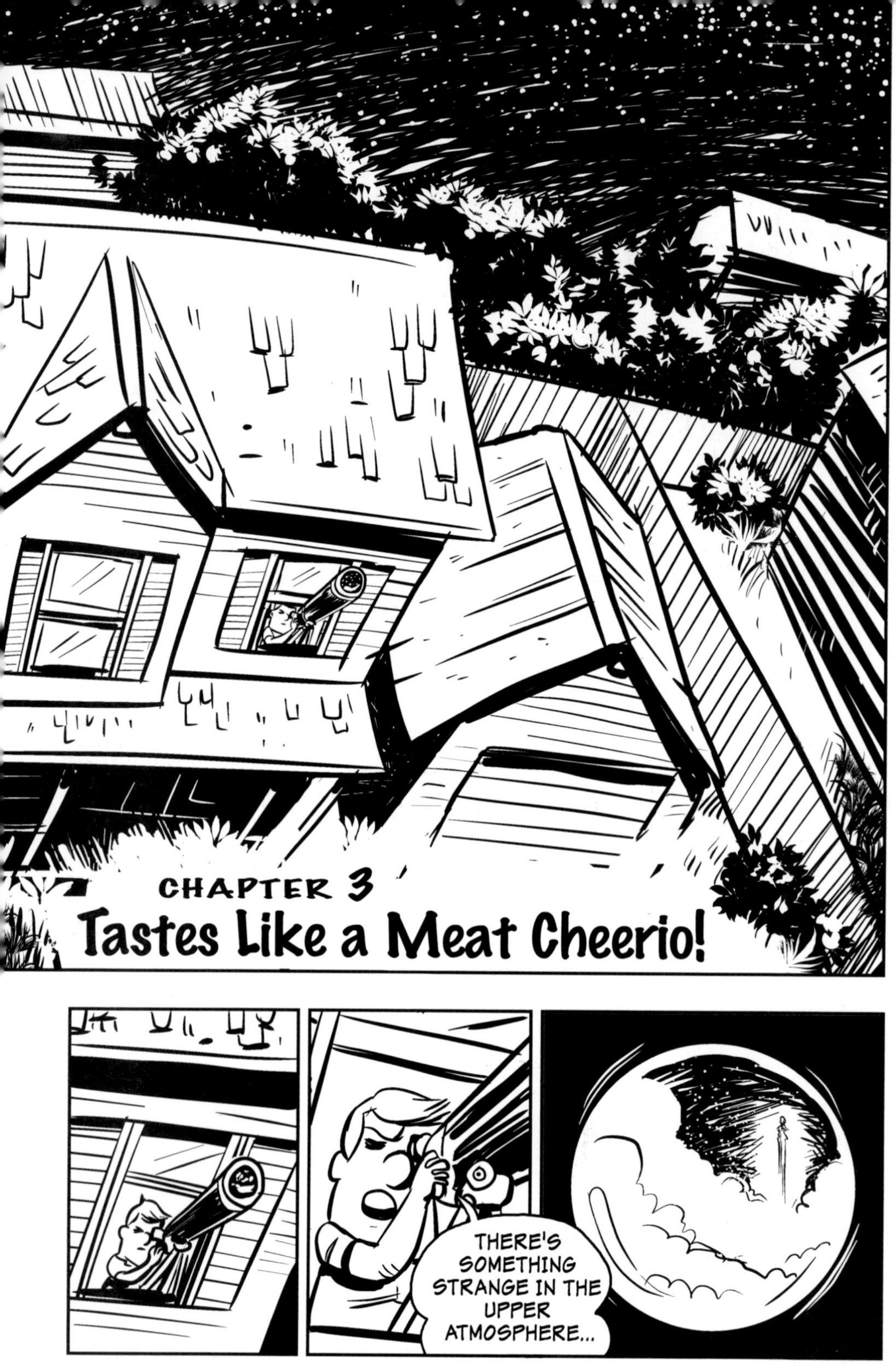
CHAPTER 3
Tastes Like a Meat Cheerio!
THERE'S SOMETHING STRANGE IN THE UPPER ATMOSPHERE...

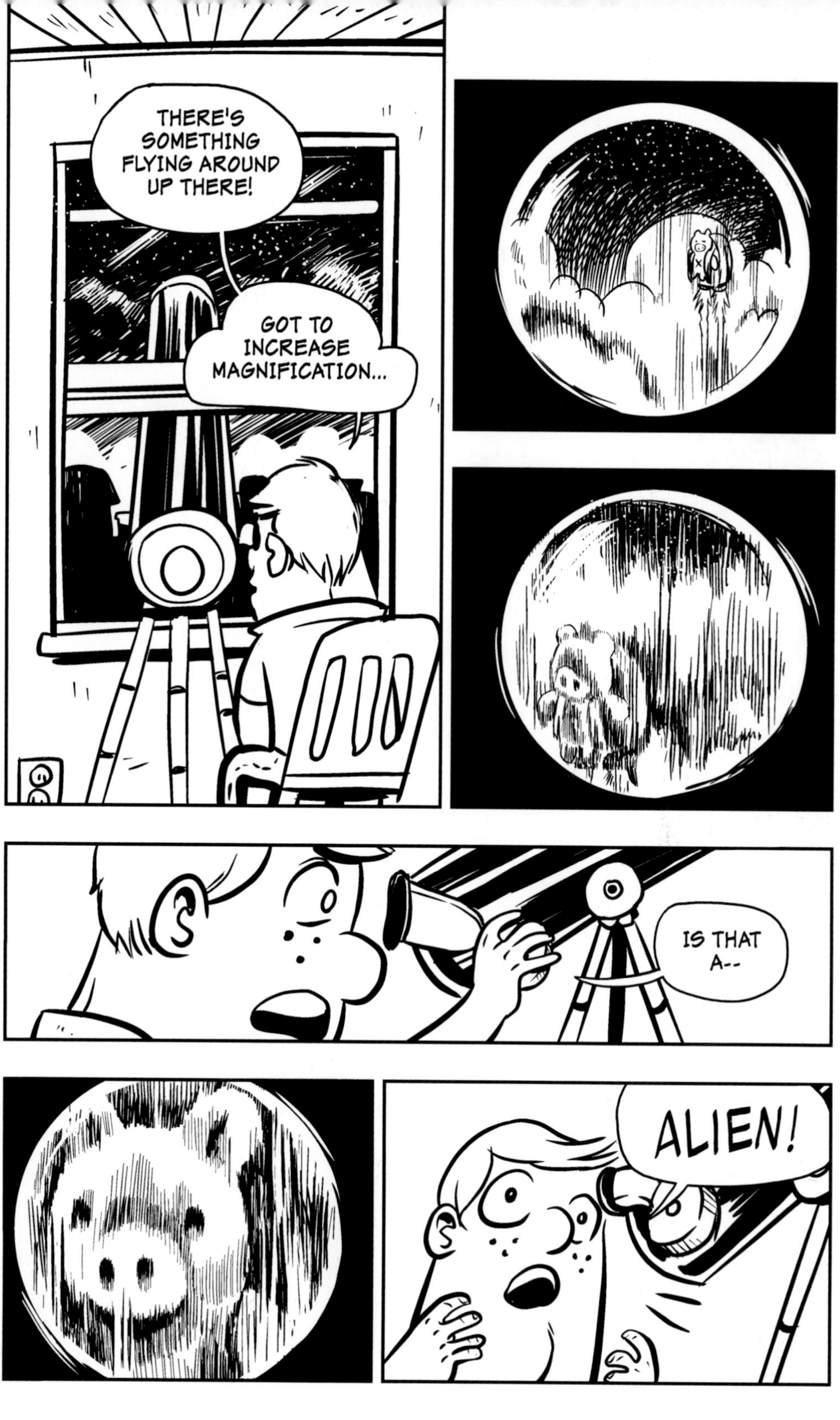
THERE'S SOMETHING FLYING AROUND UP THERE!
GOT TO INCREASE MAGNIFICATION...
IS THAT A--
ALIEN!

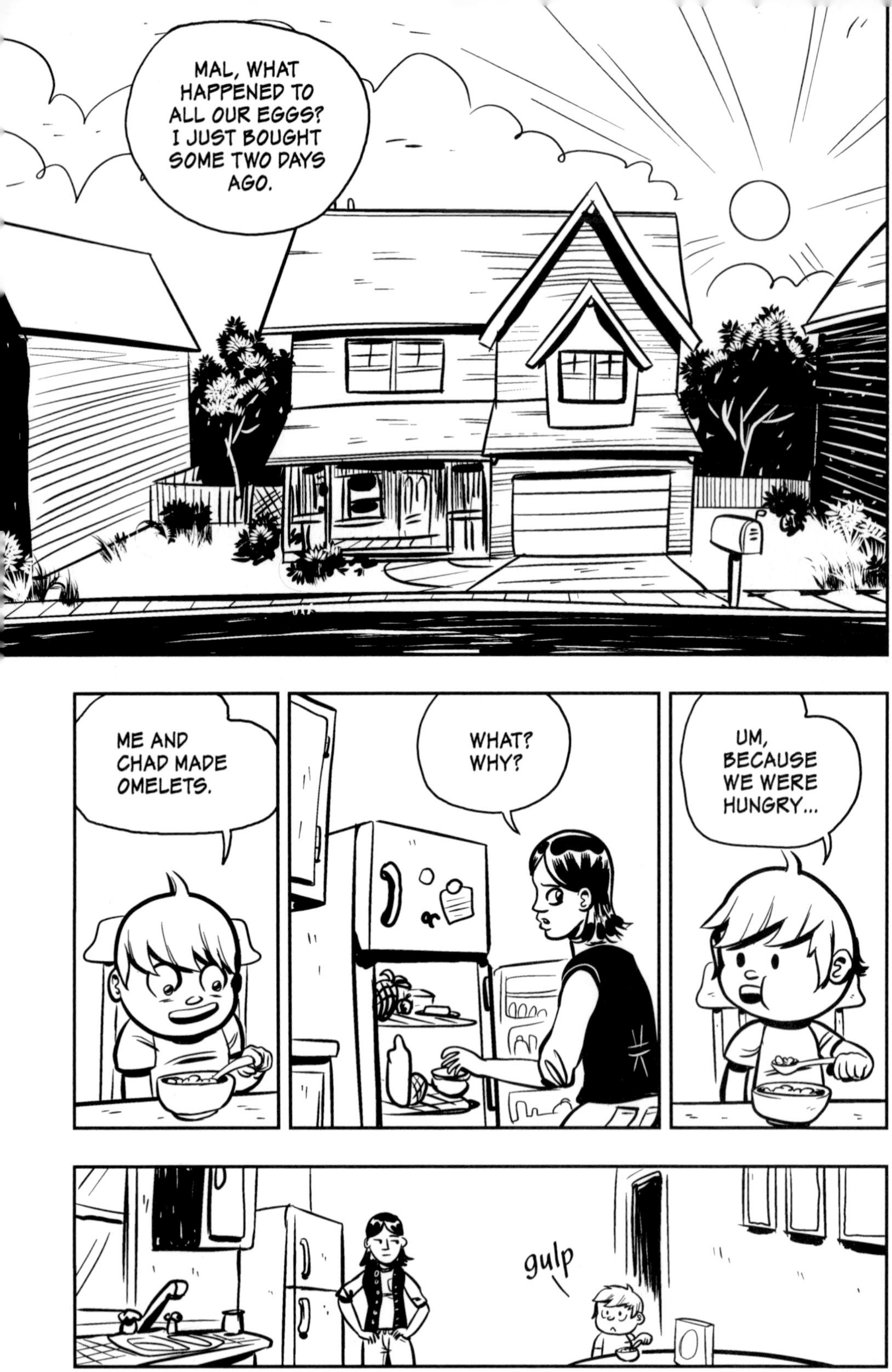
MAL, WHAT HAPPENED TO ALL OUR EGGS? I JUST BOUGHT SOME TWO DAYS AGO.
ME AND CHAD MADE OMELETS.
WHAT? WHY?
UM, BECAUSE WE WERE HUNGRY...
gulp

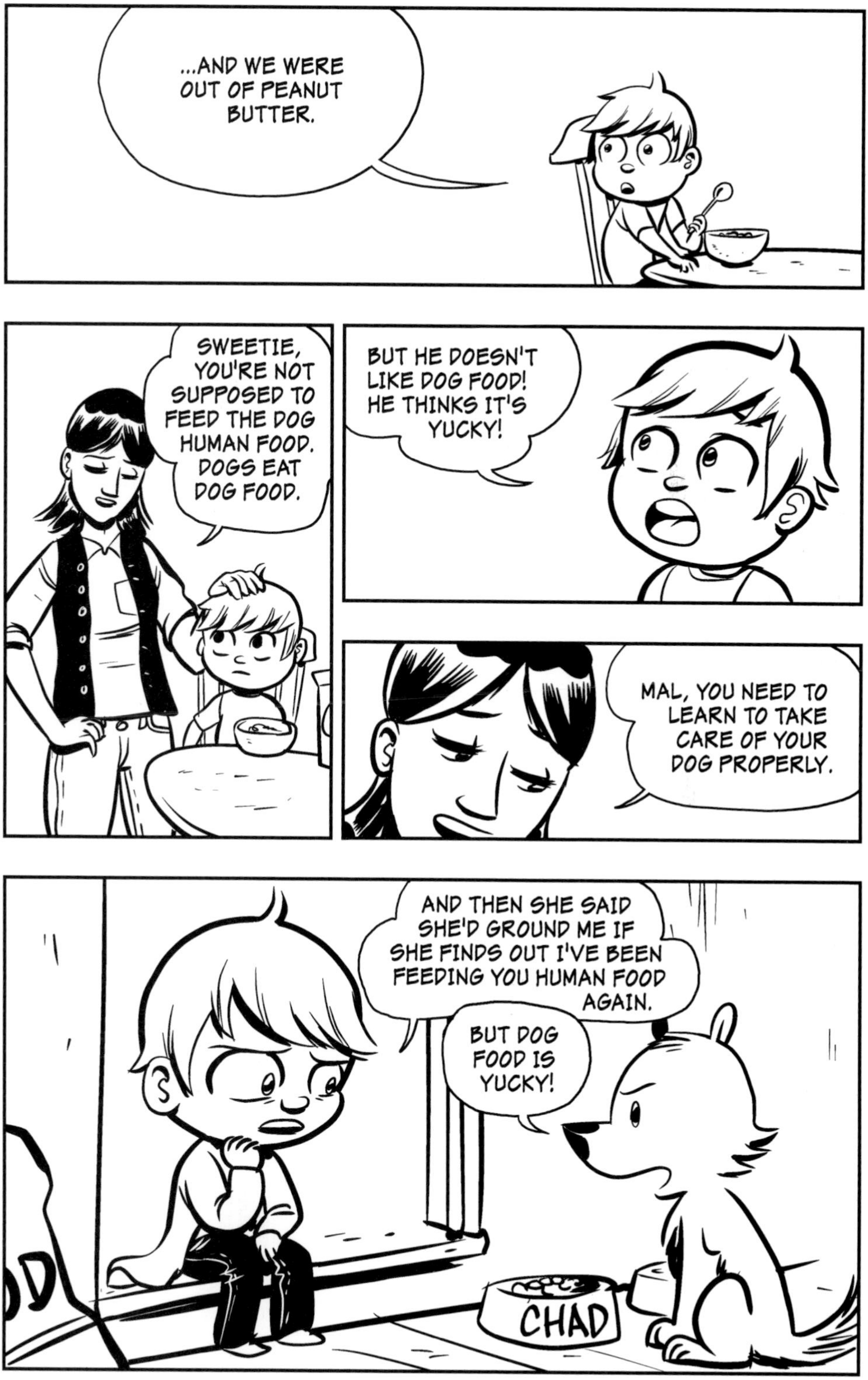
...AND WE WERE OUT OF PEANUT BUTTER.
SWEETIE, YOU'RE NOT SUPPOSED TO FEED THE DOG HUMAN FOOD. DOGS EAT DOG FOOD.
BUT HE DOESN'T LIKE DOG FOOD! HE THINKS IT'S YUCKY!
MAL, YOU NEED TO LEARN TO TAKE CARE OF YOUR DOG PROPERLY.
AND THEN SHE SAID SHE'D GROUND ME IF SHE FINDS OUT I'VE BEEN FEEDING YOU HUMAN FOOD AGAIN.
BUT DOG FOOD IS YUCKY!
CHAD

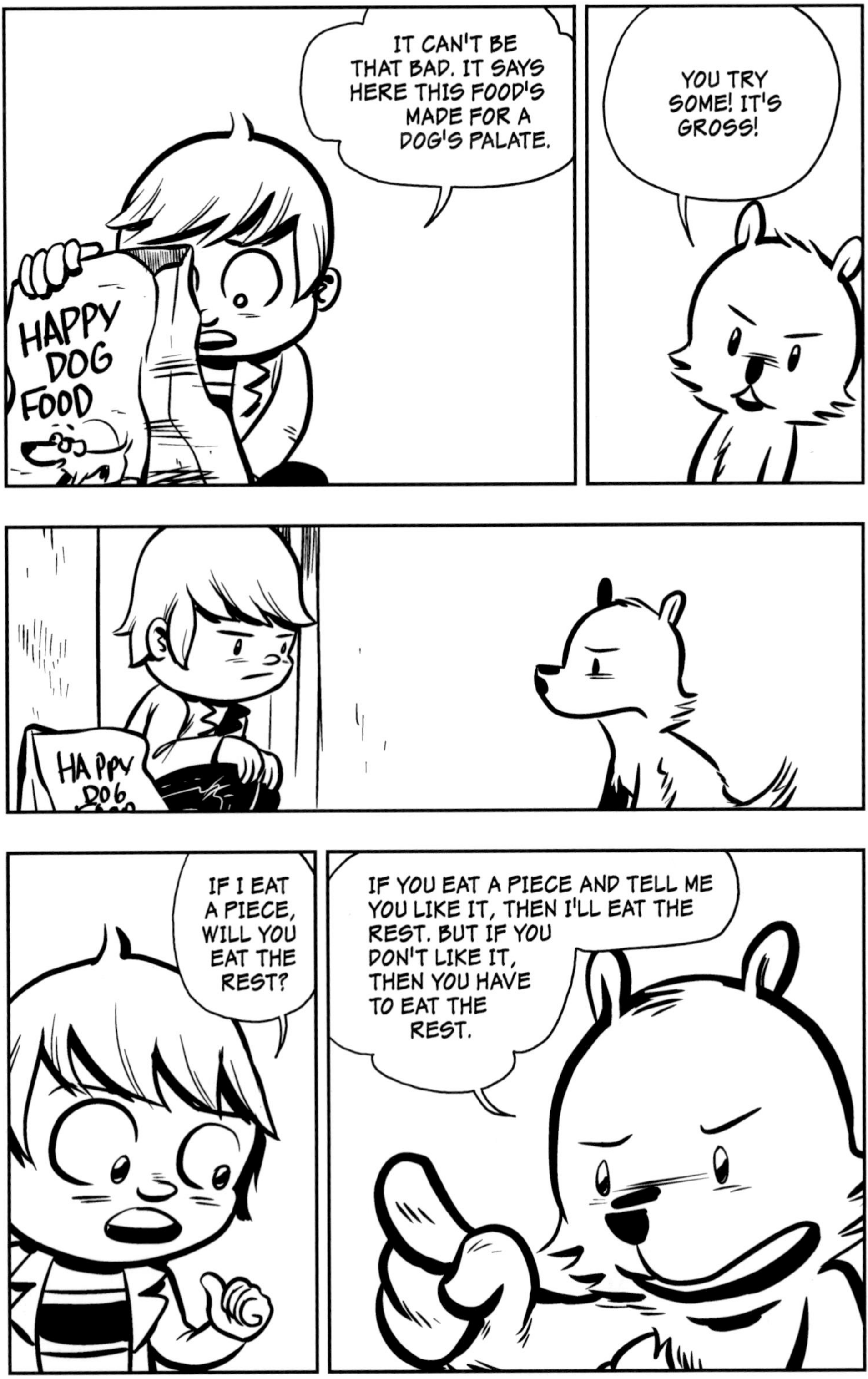
IT CAN'T BE THAT BAD. IT SAYS HERE THIS FOOD'S MADE FOR A DOG'S PALATE.
HAPPY DOG FOOD
YOU TRY SOME! IT'S GROSS!
HAPPY DOG
IF I EAT A PIECE, WILL YOU EAT THE REST?
IF YOU EAT A PIECE AND TELL ME YOU LIKE IT, THEN I'LL EAT THE REST. BUT IF YOU DON'T LIKE IT, THEN YOU HAVE TO EAT THE REST.

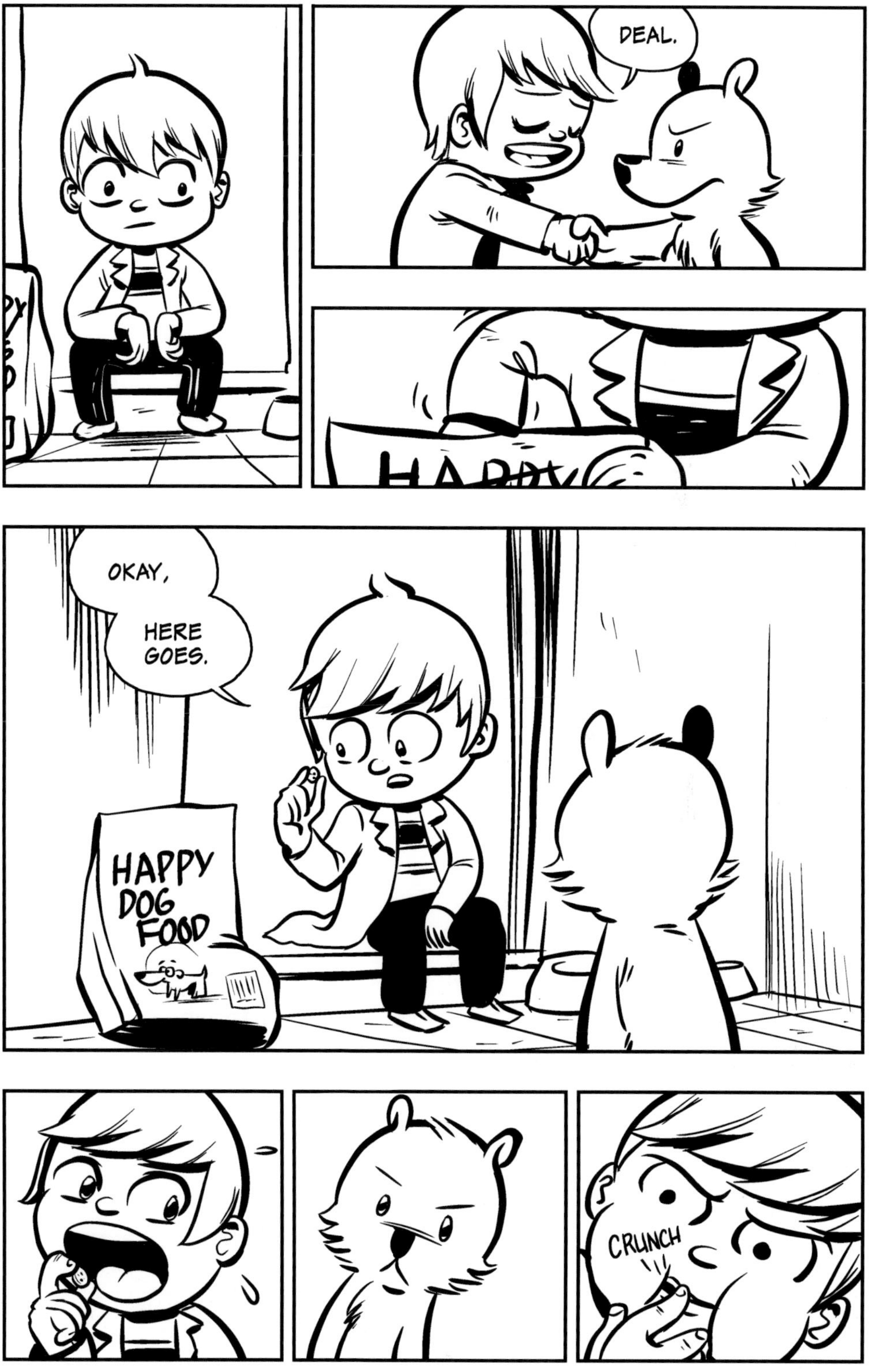
DEAL.
HAPPY
OKAY,
HERE GOES.
HAPPY DOG FOOD
CRUNCH

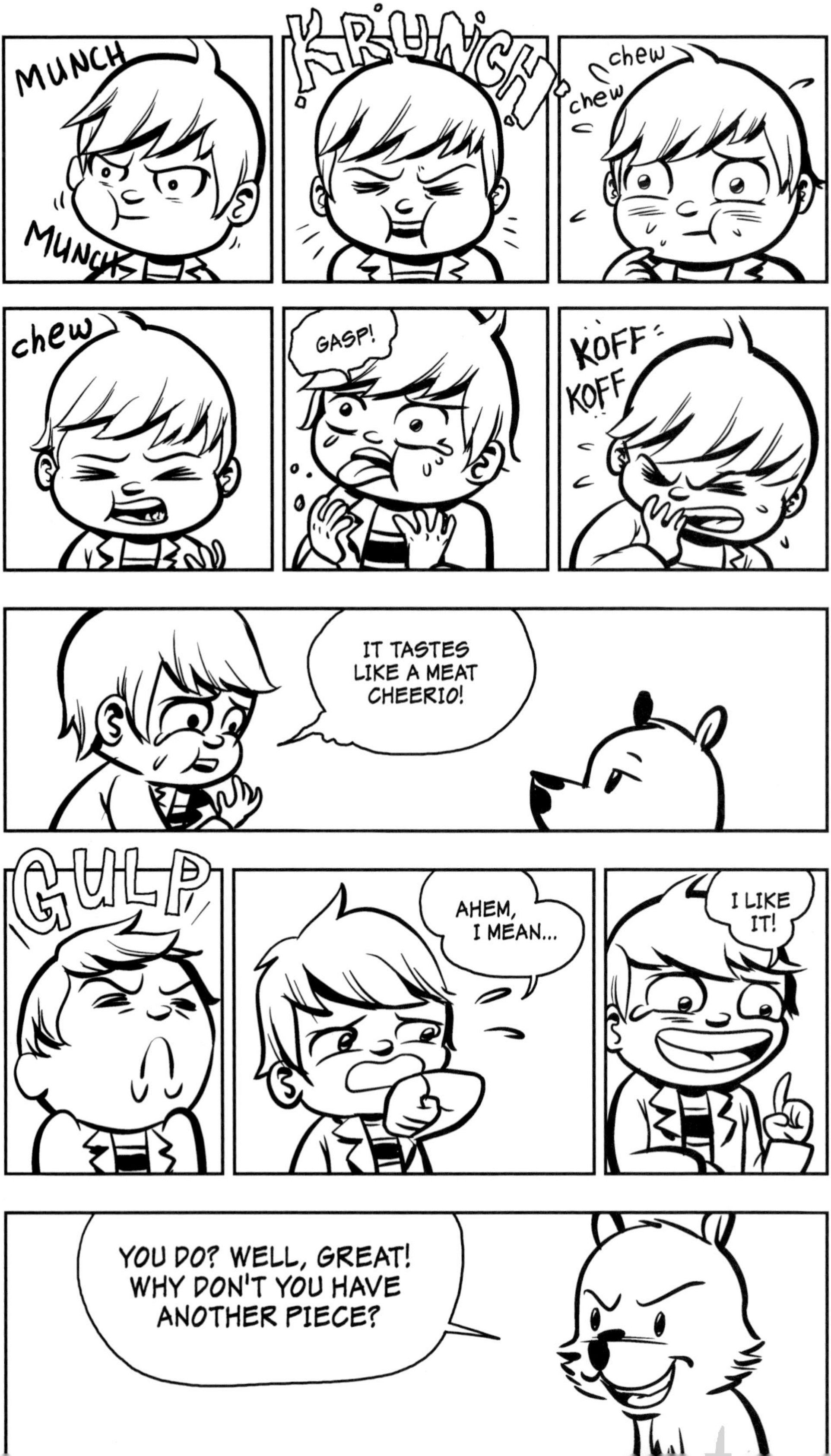
MUNCH
MUNCH
KRUNCH
chew
chew
chew
GASP!
KOFF
KOFF
IT TASTES LIKE A MEAT CHEERIO!
GULP
AHEM, I MEAN...
I LIKE IT!
YOU DO? WELL, GREAT! WHY DON'T YOU HAVE ANOTHER PIECE?

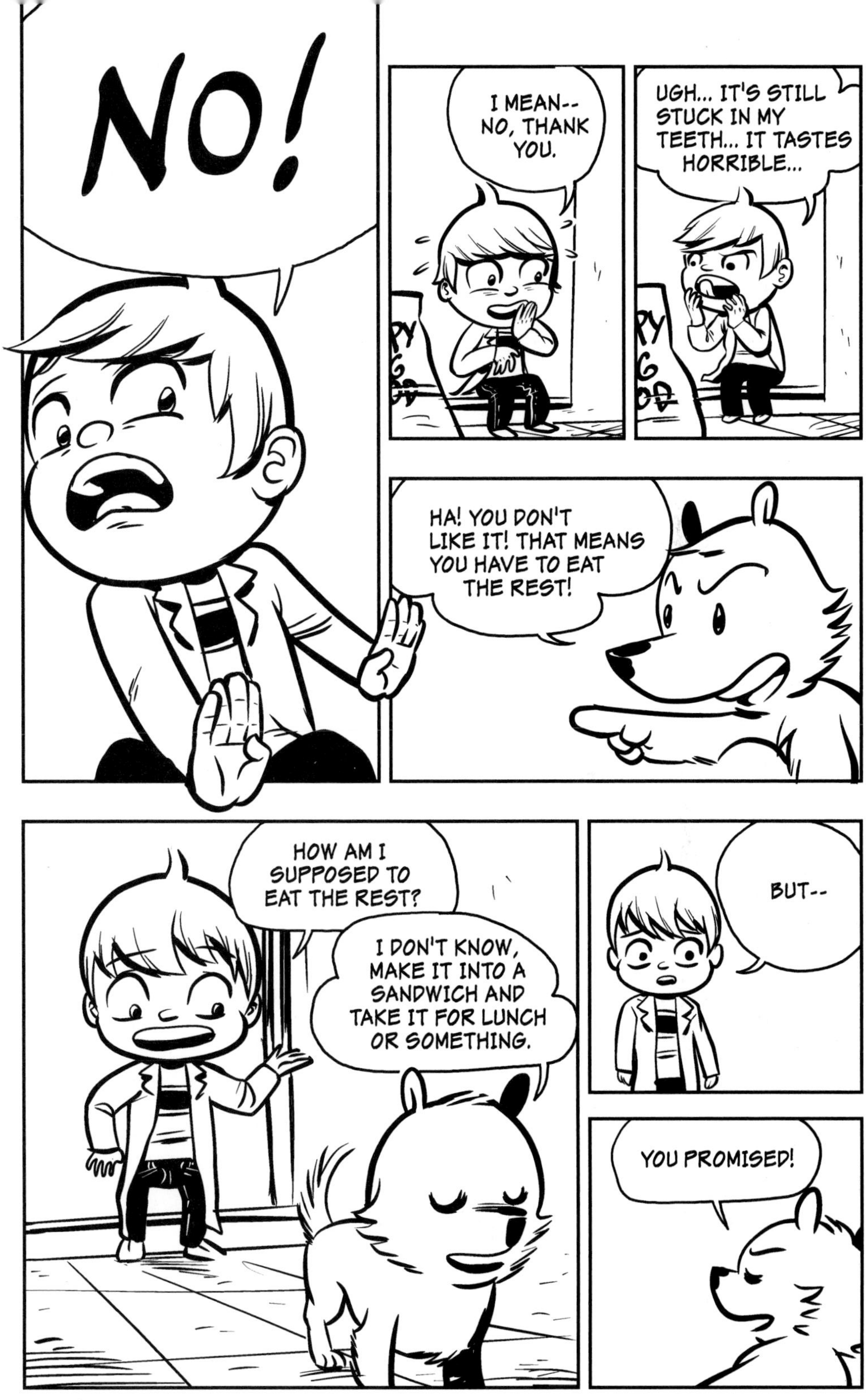
NO!
I MEAN-- NO, THANK YOU.
UGH... IT'S STILL STUCK IN MY TEETH... IT TASTES HORRIBLE...
HA! YOU DON'T LIKE IT! THAT MEANS YOU HAVE TO EAT THE REST!
HOW AM I SUPPOSED TO EAT THE REST?
I DON'T KNOW, MAKE IT INTO A SANDWICH AND TAKE IT FOR LUNCH OR SOMETHING.
BUT--
YOU PROMISED!

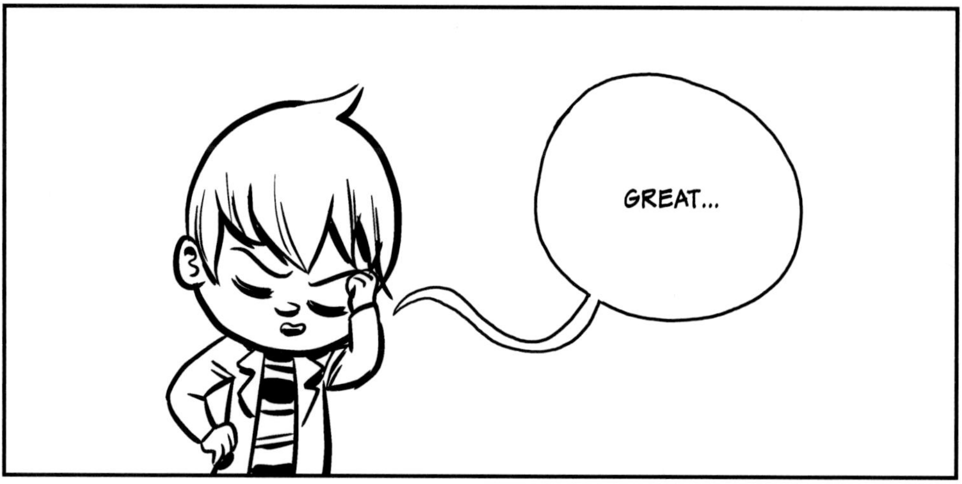
GREAT...

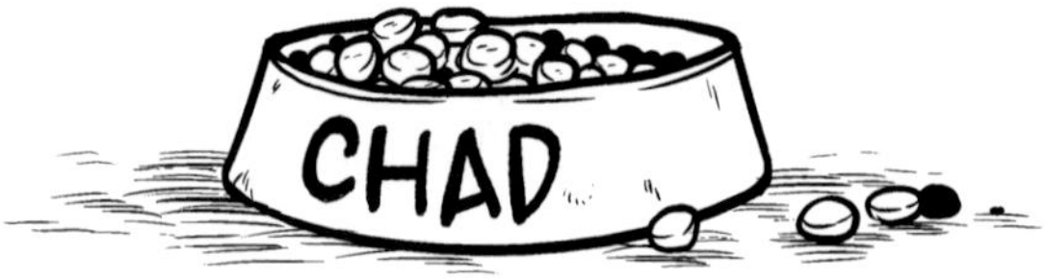
CHAD

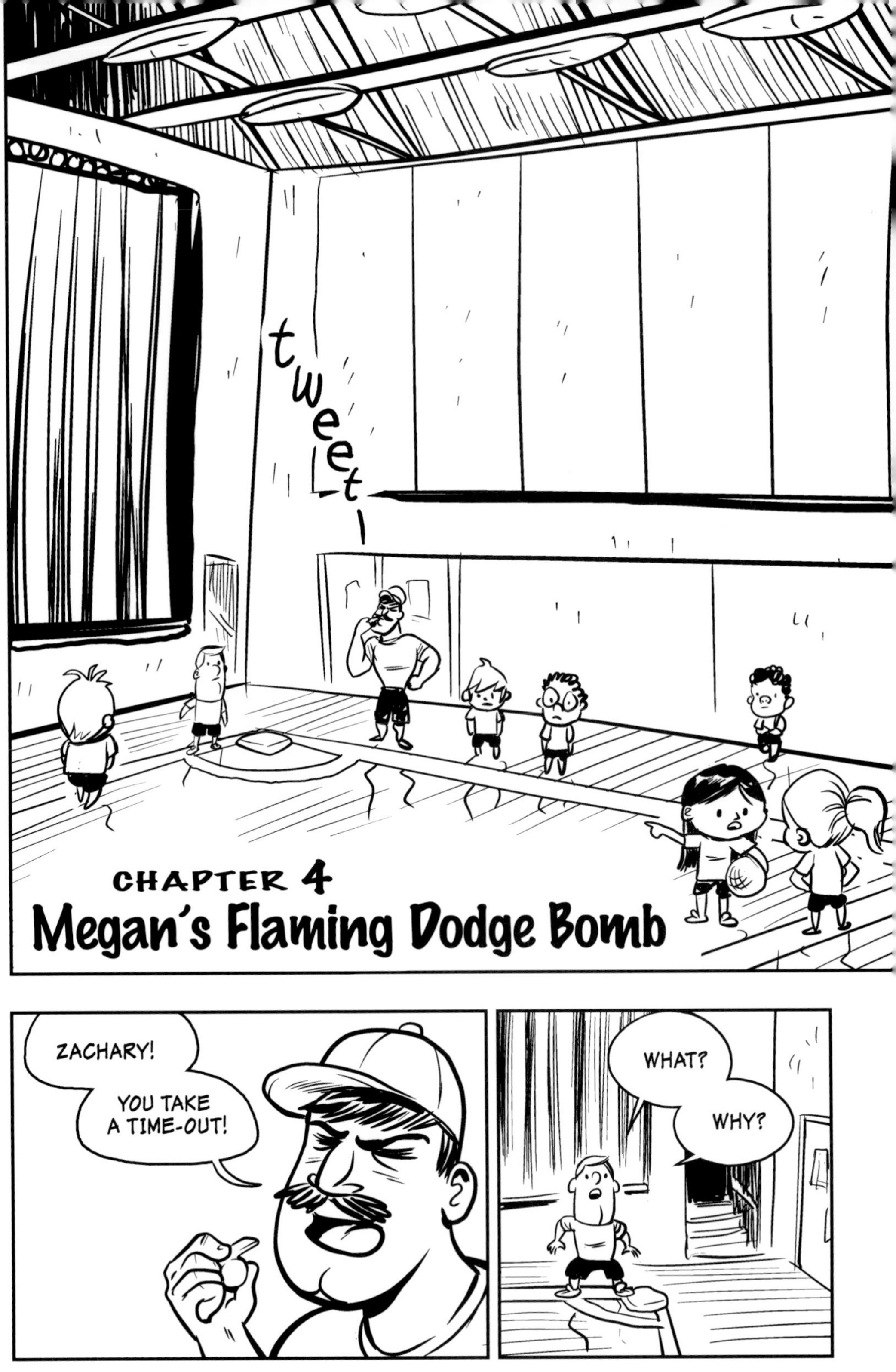
tweet!
CHAPTER 4
Megan's Flaming Dodge Bomb
ZACHARY!
YOU TAKE A TIME-OUT!
WHAT?
WHY?

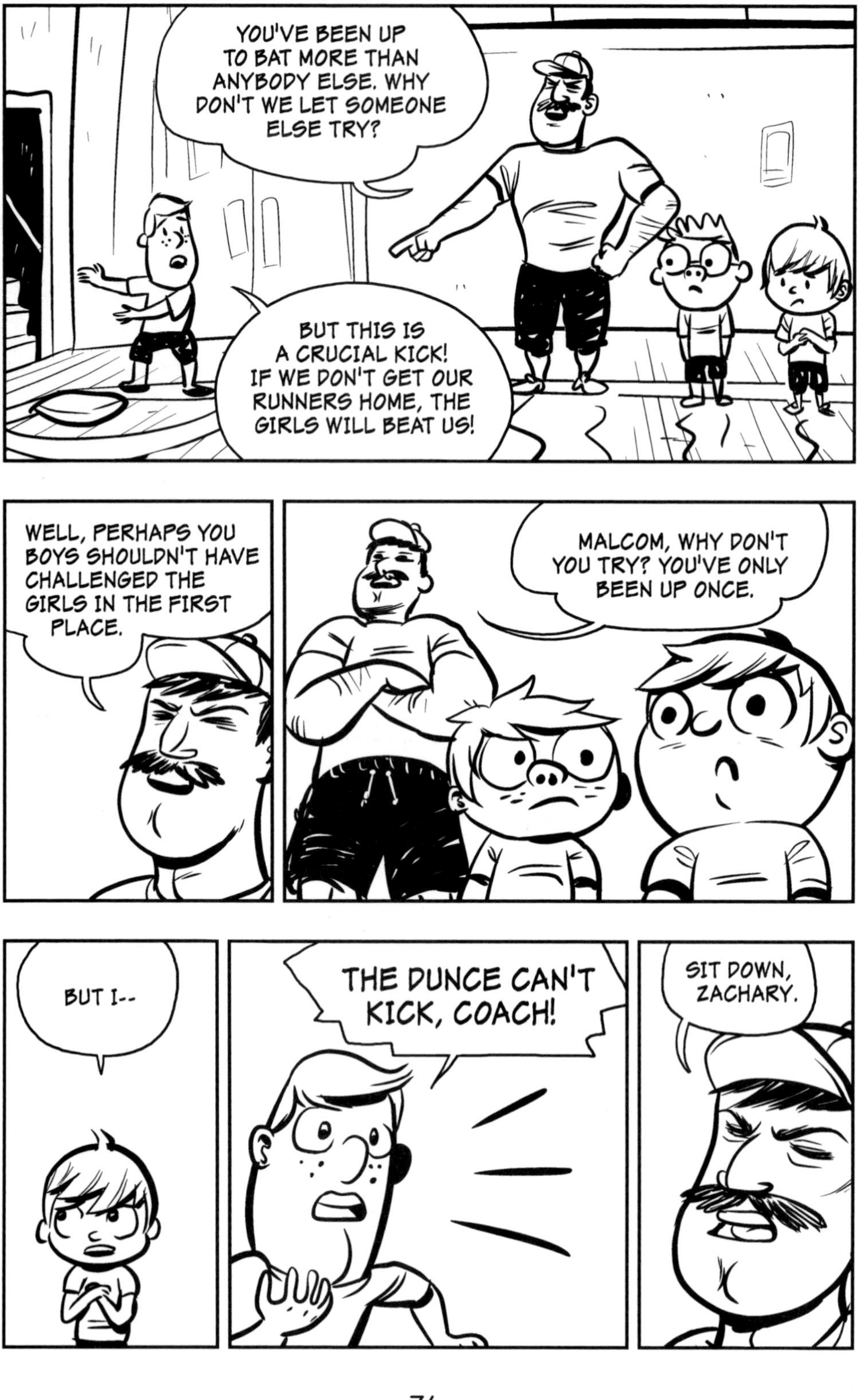
YOU'VE BEEN UP TO BAT MORE THAN ANYBODY ELSE. WHY DON'T WE LET SOMEONE ELSE TRY?
BUT THIS IS A CRUCIAL KICK! IF WE DON'T GET OUR RUNNERS HOME, THE GIRLS WILL BEAT US!
WELL, PERHAPS YOU BOYS SHOULDN'T HAVE CHALLENGED THE GIRLS IN THE FIRST PLACE.
MALCOM, WHY DON'T YOU TRY? YOU'VE ONLY BEEN UP ONCE.
BUT I--
THE DUNCE CAN'T KICK, COACH!
SIT DOWN, ZACHARY.

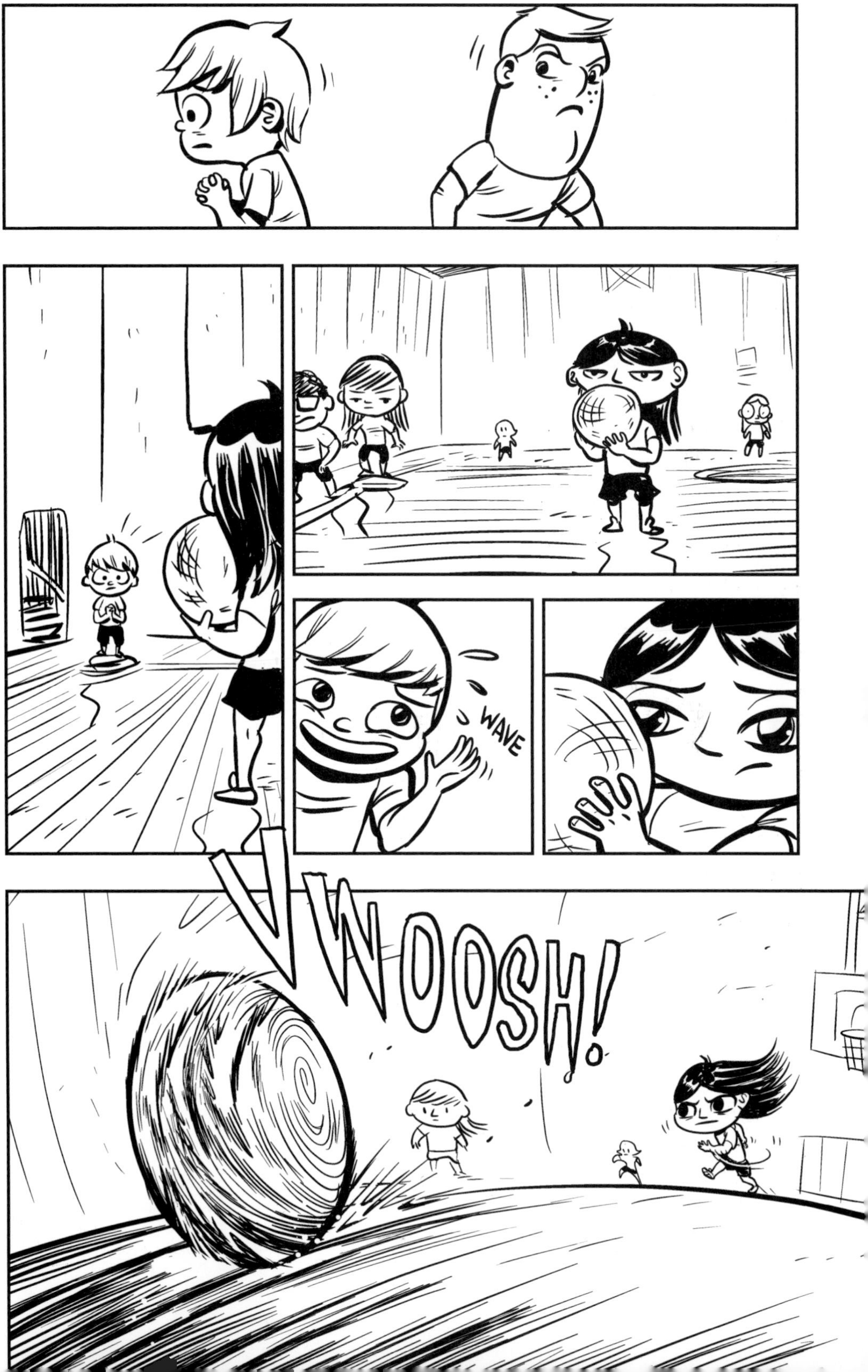
WAVE
WHOOSH!

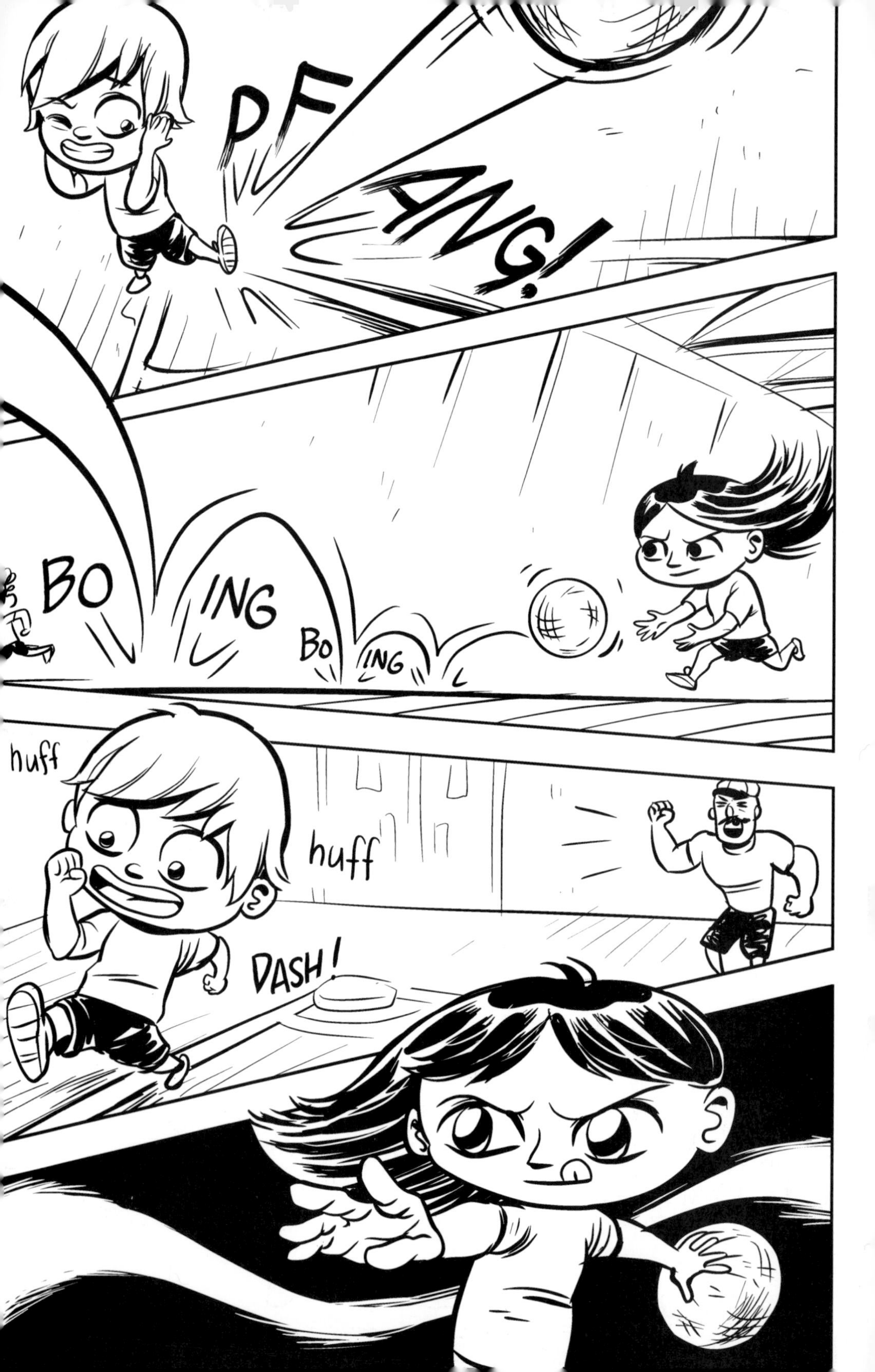

PF
ANG!
BO
ING
Bo
ING
huff
huff
DASH!

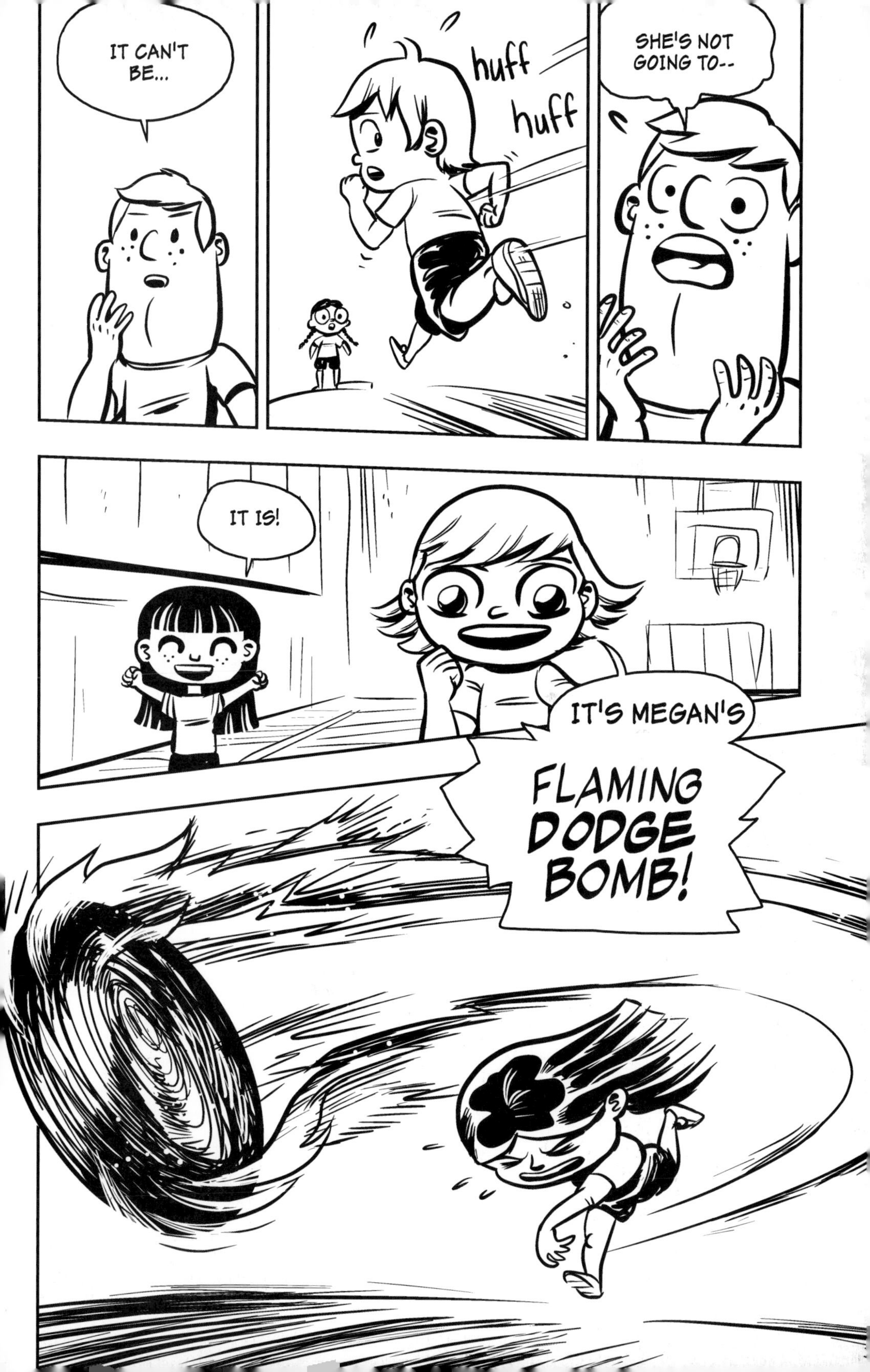
IT CAN'T BE...
huff
huff
SHE'S NOT GOING TO--
IT IS!
IT'S MEGAN'S
FLAMING DODGE BOMB!

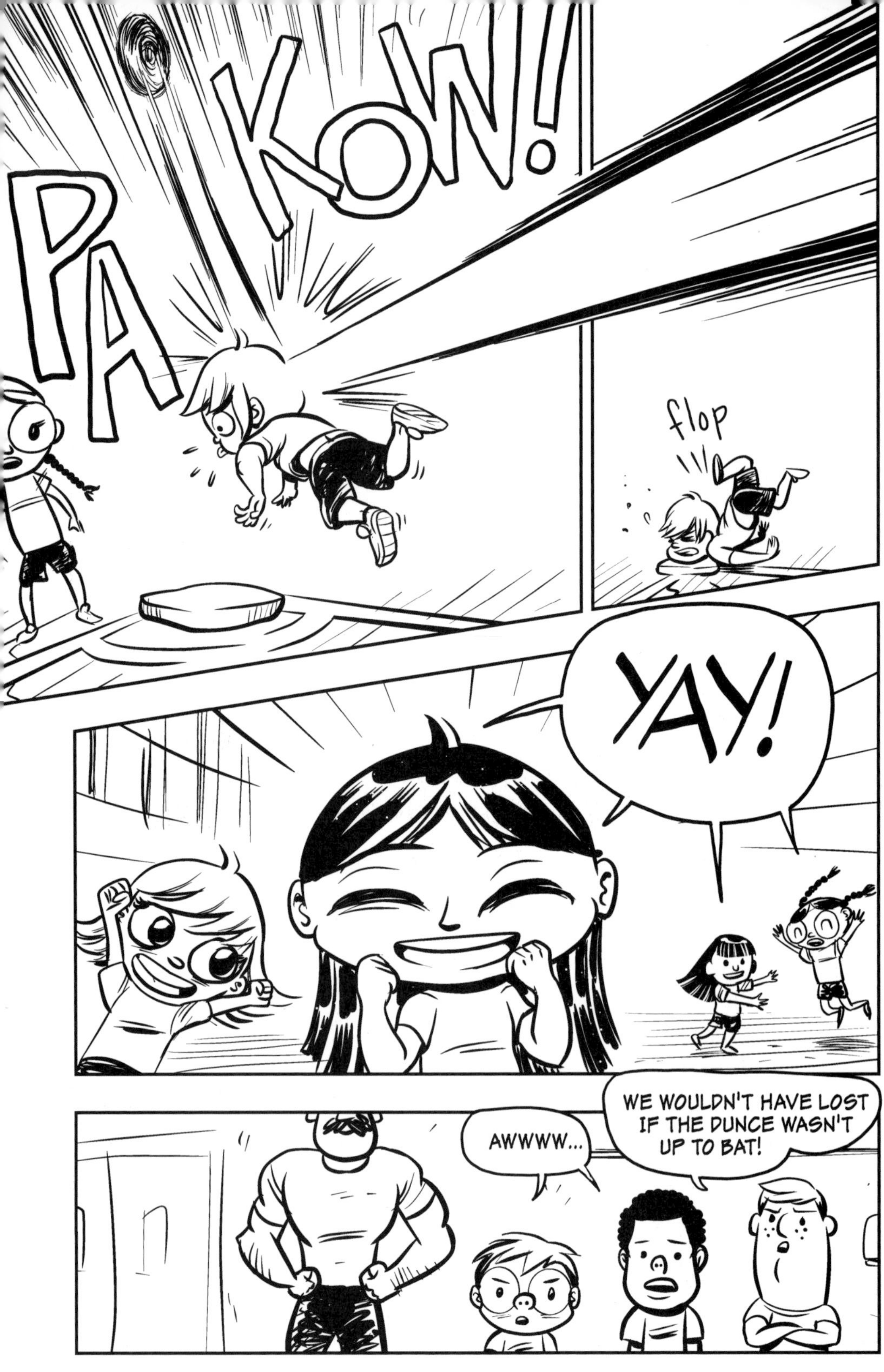
PA
KOW!
flop
YAY!
AWWWW...
WE WOULDN'T HAVE LOST IF THE DUNCE WASN'T UP TO BAT!

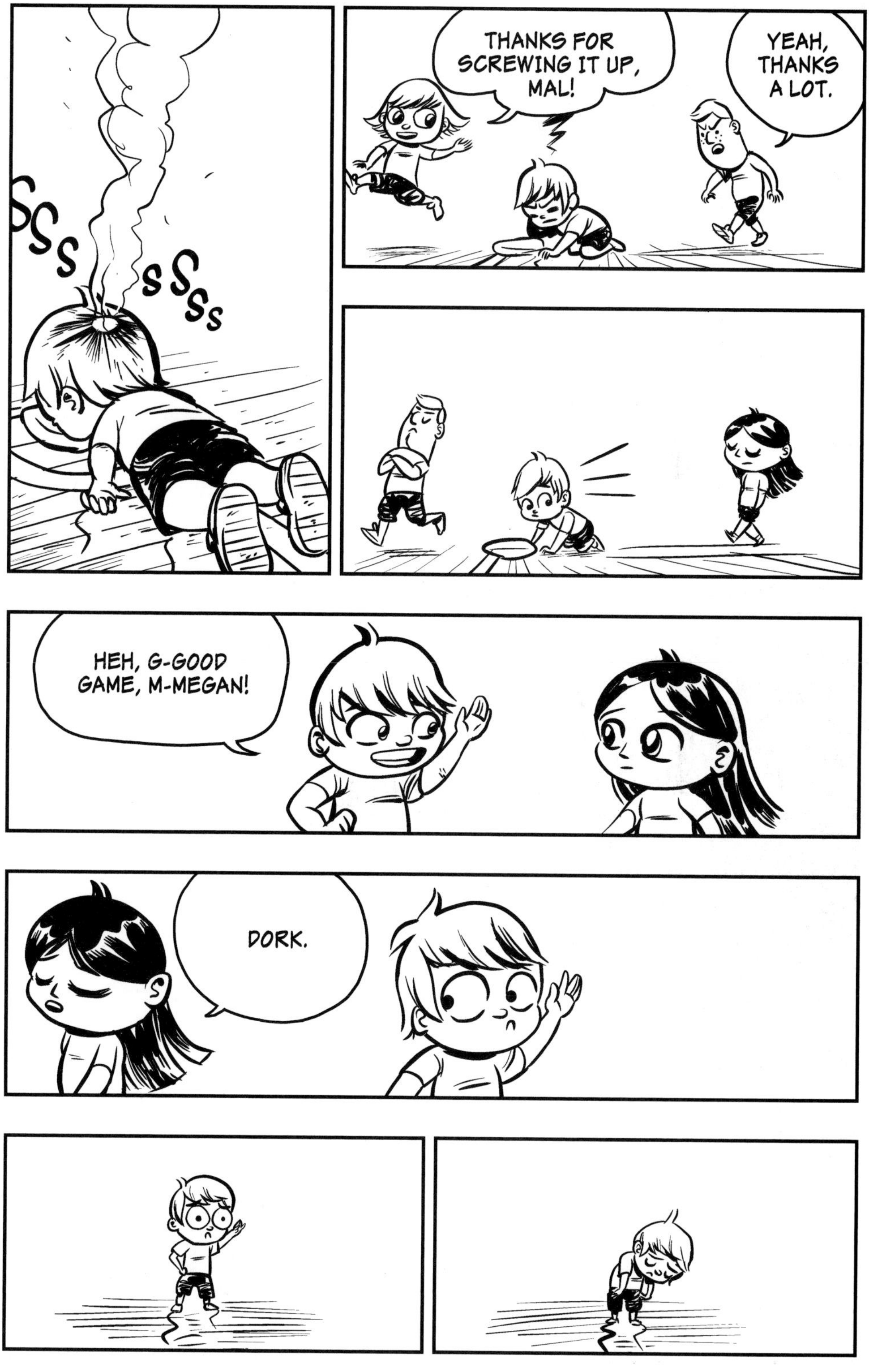
SSSS
SSSS
THANKS FOR SCREWING IT UP, MAL!
YEAH, THANKS A LOT.
HEH, G-GOOD GAME, M-MEGAN!
DORK.

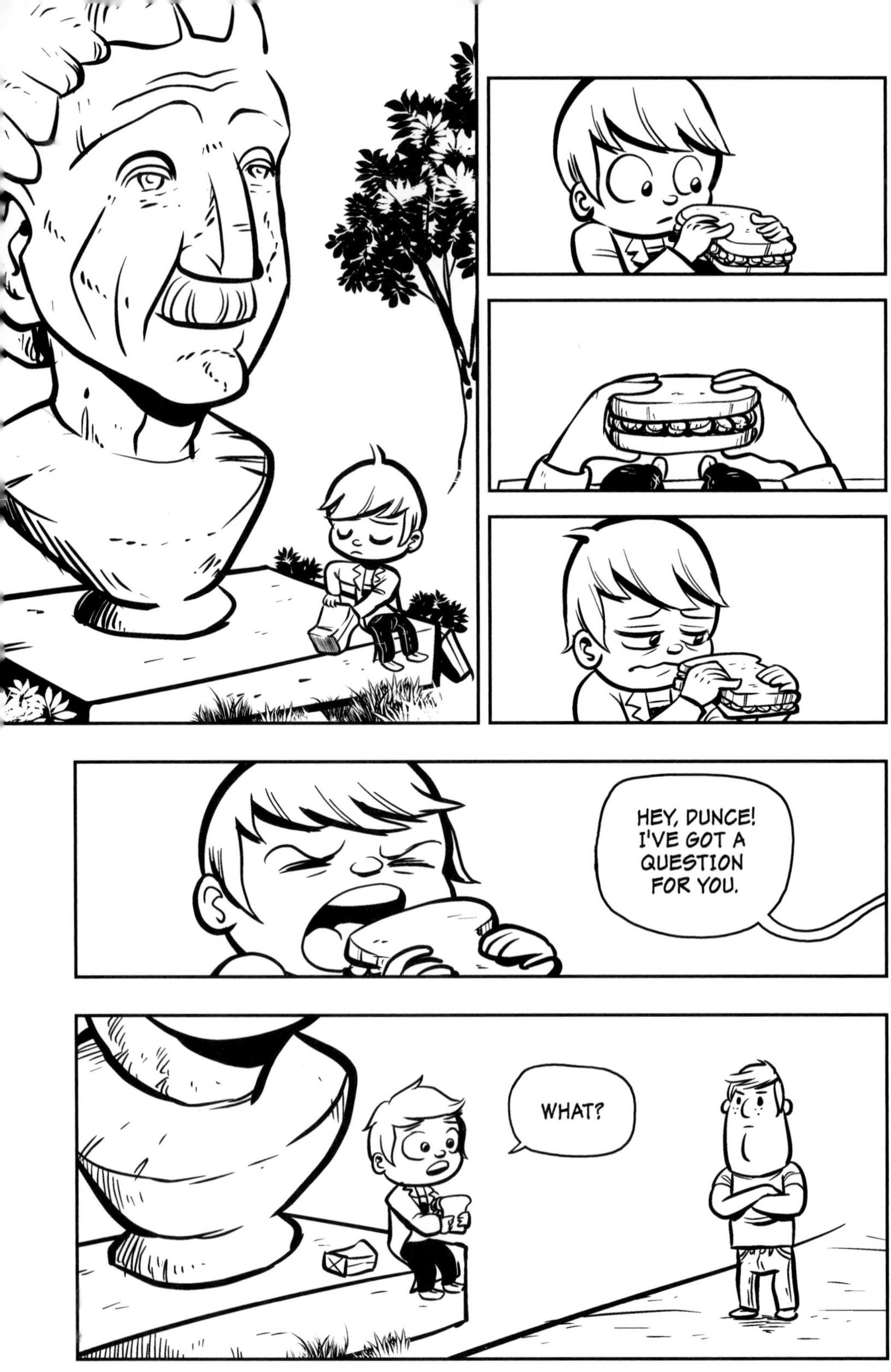
HEY, DUNCE! I'VE GOT A QUESTION FOR YOU.
WHAT?

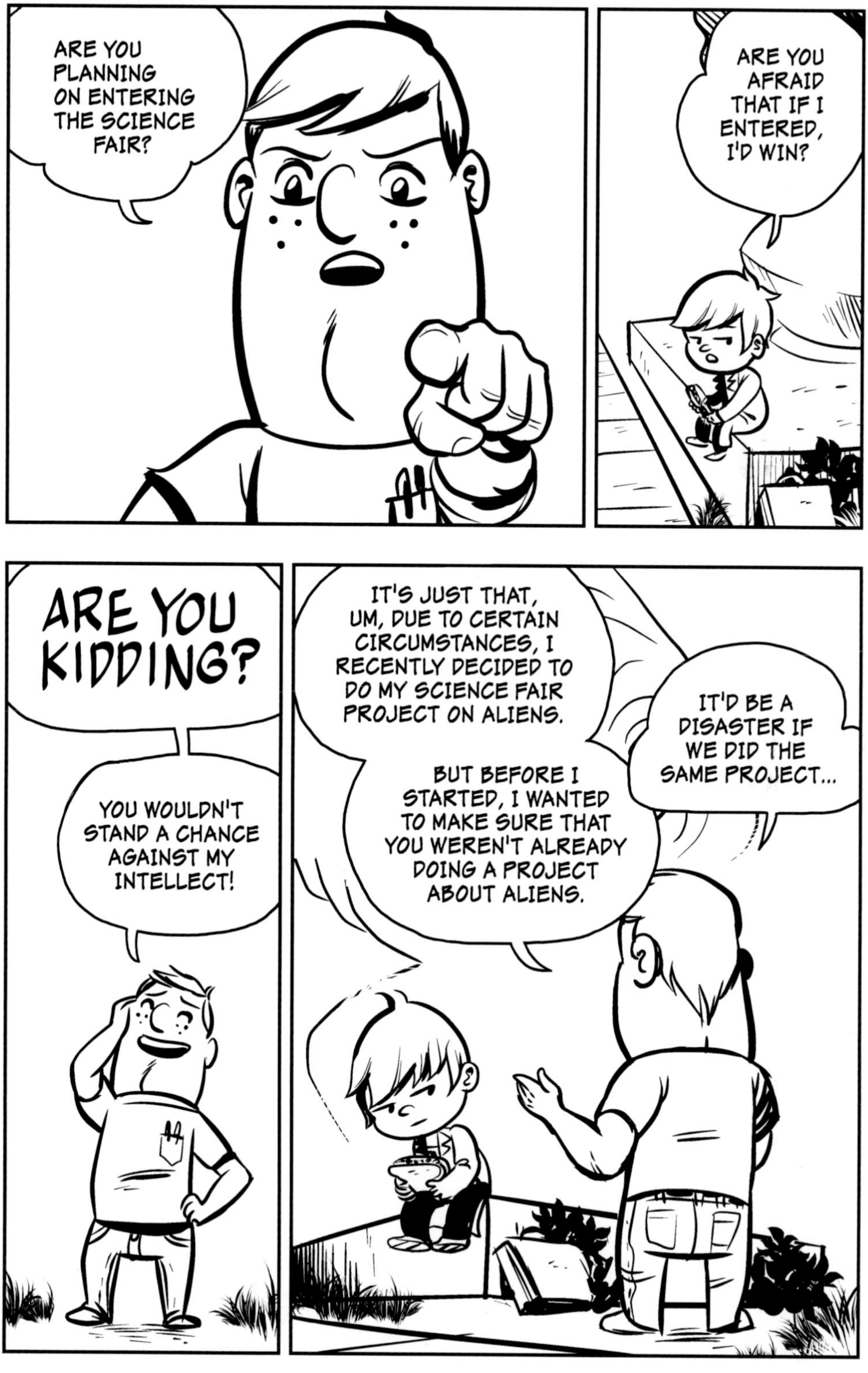
ARE YOU PLANNING ON ENTERING THE SCIENCE FAIR?
ARE YOU AFRAID THAT IF I ENTERED, I'D WIN?
ARE YOU KIDDING?
YOU WOULDN'T STAND A CHANCE AGAINST MY INTELLECT!
IT'S JUST THAT, UM, DUE TO CERTAIN CIRCUMSTANCES, I RECENTLY DECIDED TO DO MY SCIENCE FAIR PROJECT ON ALIENS.
BUT BEFORE I STARTED, I WANTED TO MAKE SURE THAT YOU WEREN'T ALREADY DOING A PROJECT ABOUT ALIENS.
IT'D BE A DISASTER IF WE DID THE SAME PROJECT...

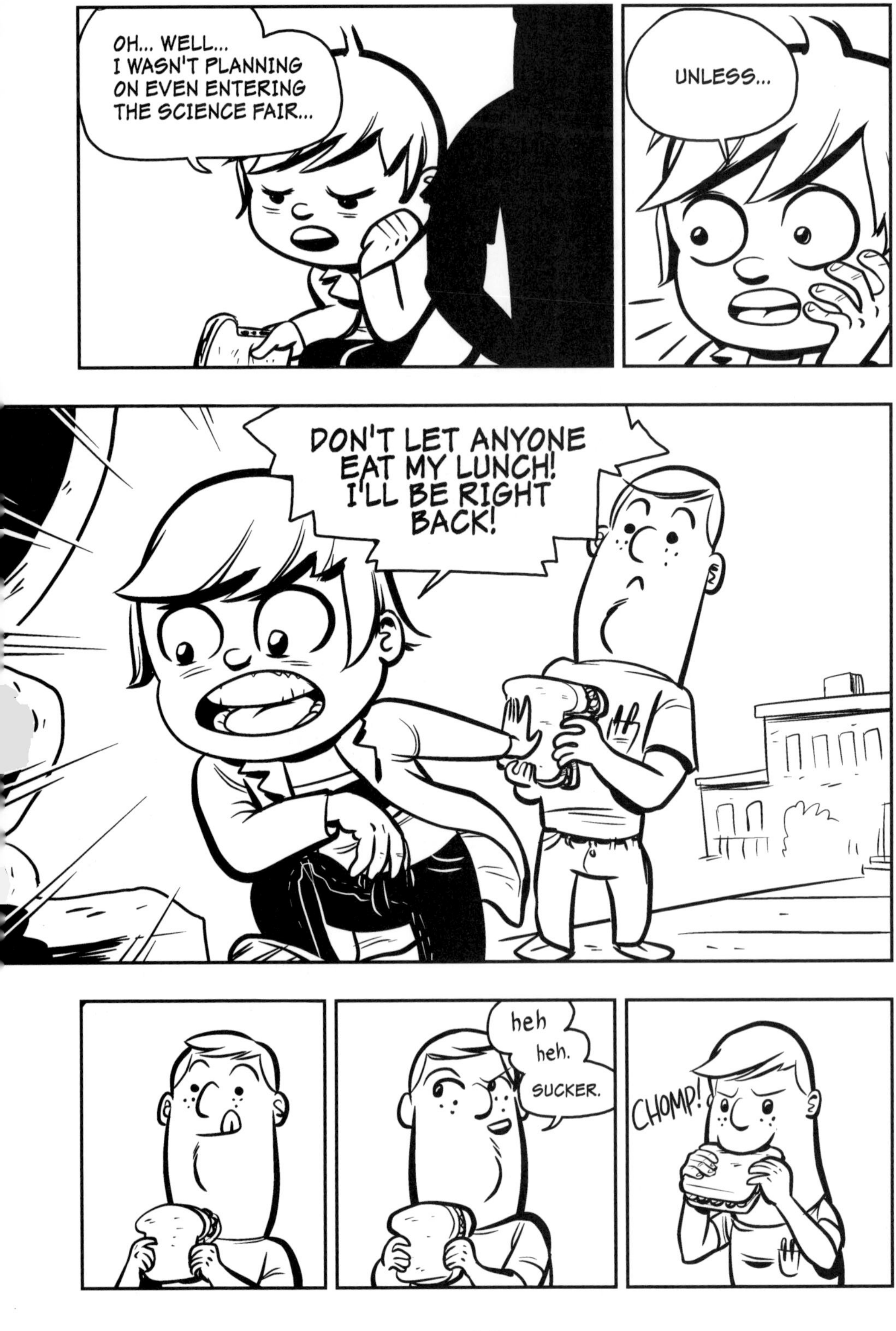
OH... WELL... I WASN'T PLANNING ON EVEN ENTERING THE SCIENCE FAIR...
UNLESS...
DON'T LET ANYONE EAT MY LUNCH! I'LL BE RIGHT BACK!
heh
heh.
SUCKER.
CHOMP!

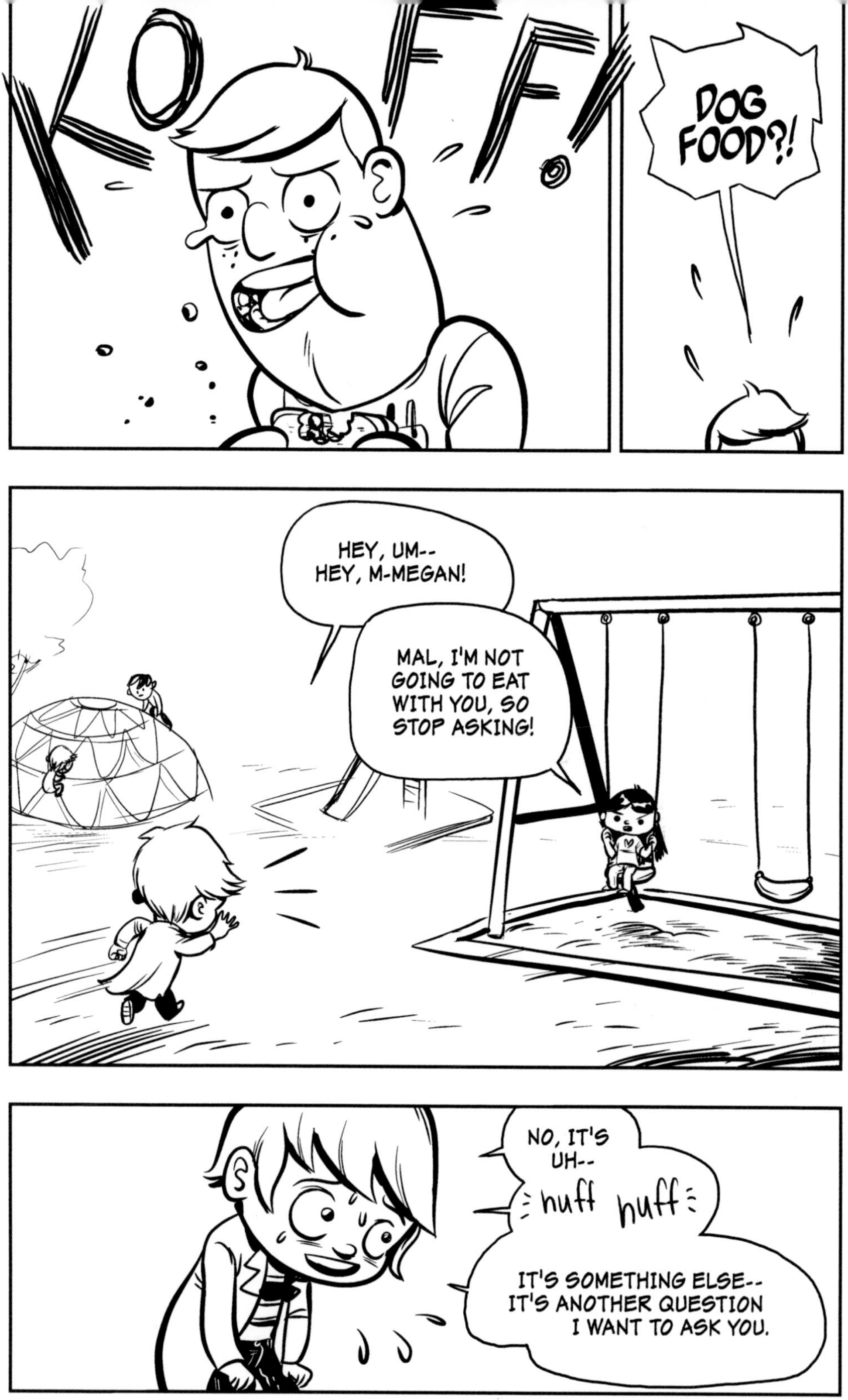
KOFF!
DOG FOOD?!
HEY, UM-- HEY, M-MEGAN!
MAL, I'M NOT GOING TO EAT WITH YOU, SO STOP ASKING!
NO, IT'S UH--
huff huff
IT'S SOMETHING ELSE-- IT'S ANOTHER QUESTION I WANT TO ASK YOU.

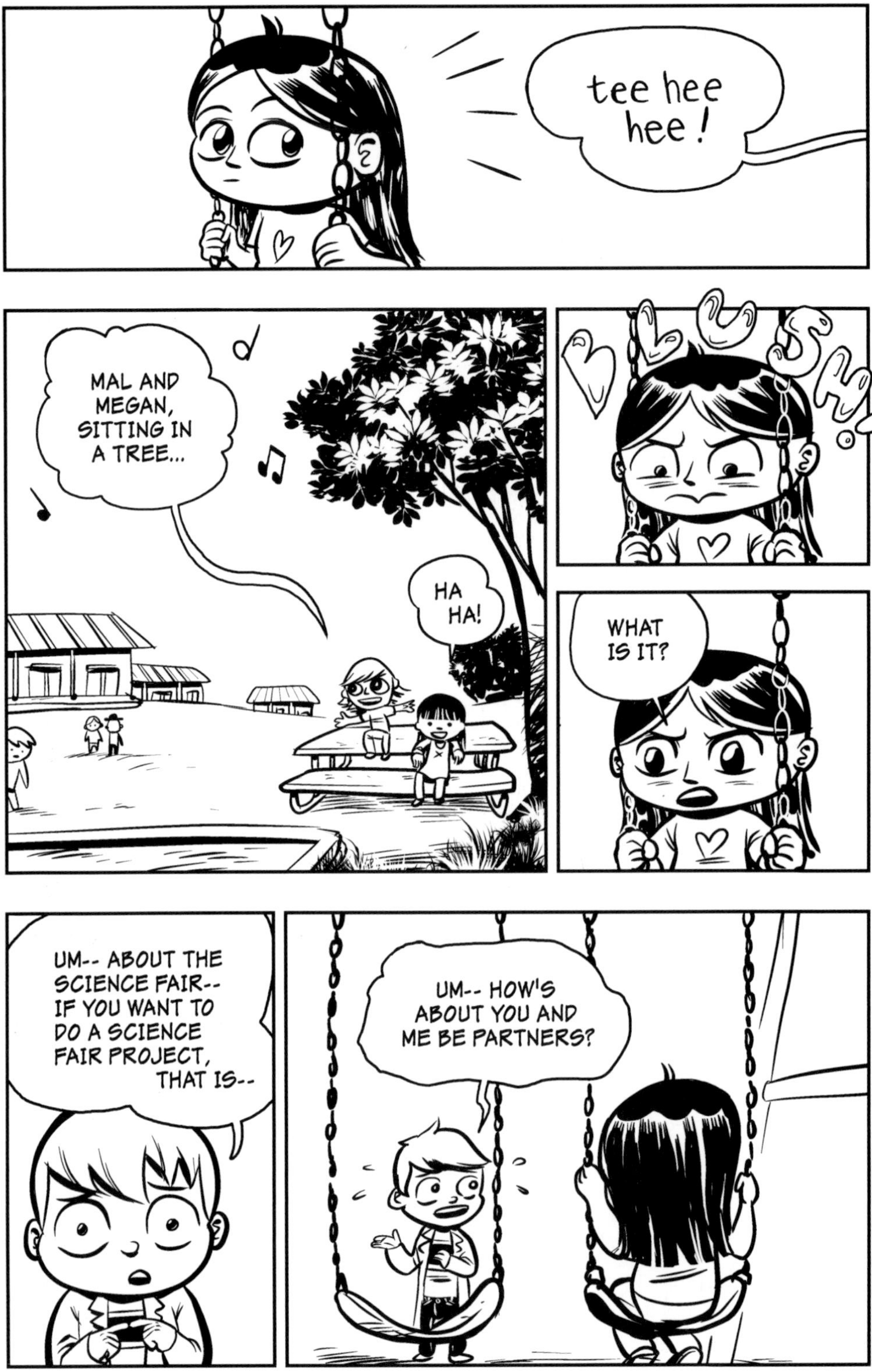
tee hee hee!
MAL AND MEGAN, SITTING IN A TREE...
HA HA!
BLUSH!
WHAT IS IT?
UM-- ABOUT THE SCIENCE FAIR-- IF YOU WANT TO DO A SCIENCE FAIR PROJECT, THAT IS--
UM-- HOW'S ABOUT YOU AND ME BE PARTNERS?

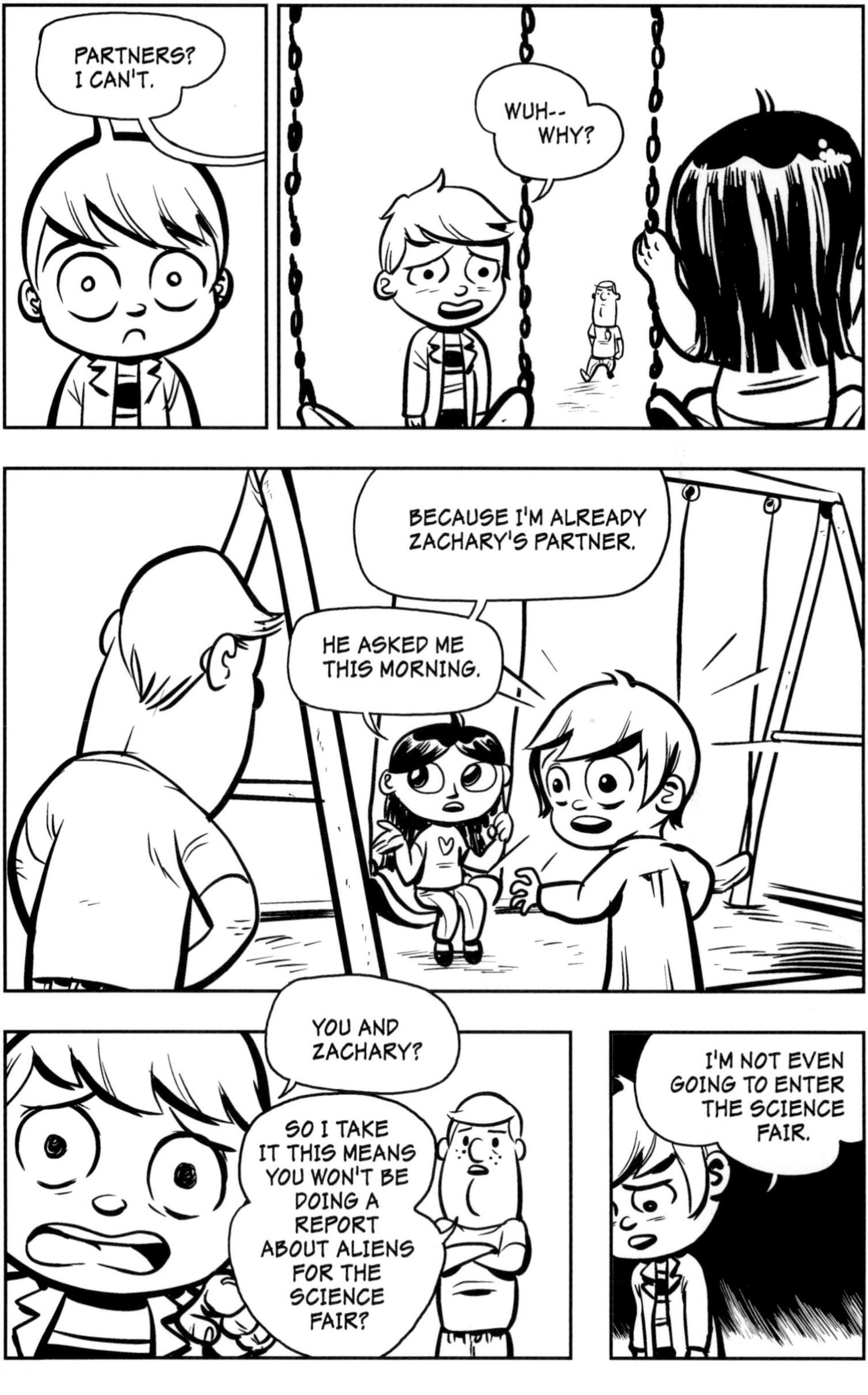
PARTNERS? I CAN'T.
WUH-- WHY?
BECAUSE I'M ALREADY ZACHARY'S PARTNER.
HE ASKED ME THIS MORNING.
YOU AND ZACHARY?
SO I TAKE IT THIS MEANS YOU WON'T BE DOING A REPORT ABOUT ALIENS FOR THE SCIENCE FAIR?
I'M NOT EVEN GOING TO ENTER THE SCIENCE FAIR.

THAT IS ONE WEIRD KID... DO YOU KNOW WHAT HE BROUGHT FOR LUNCH TODAY?

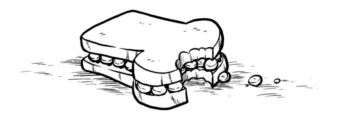

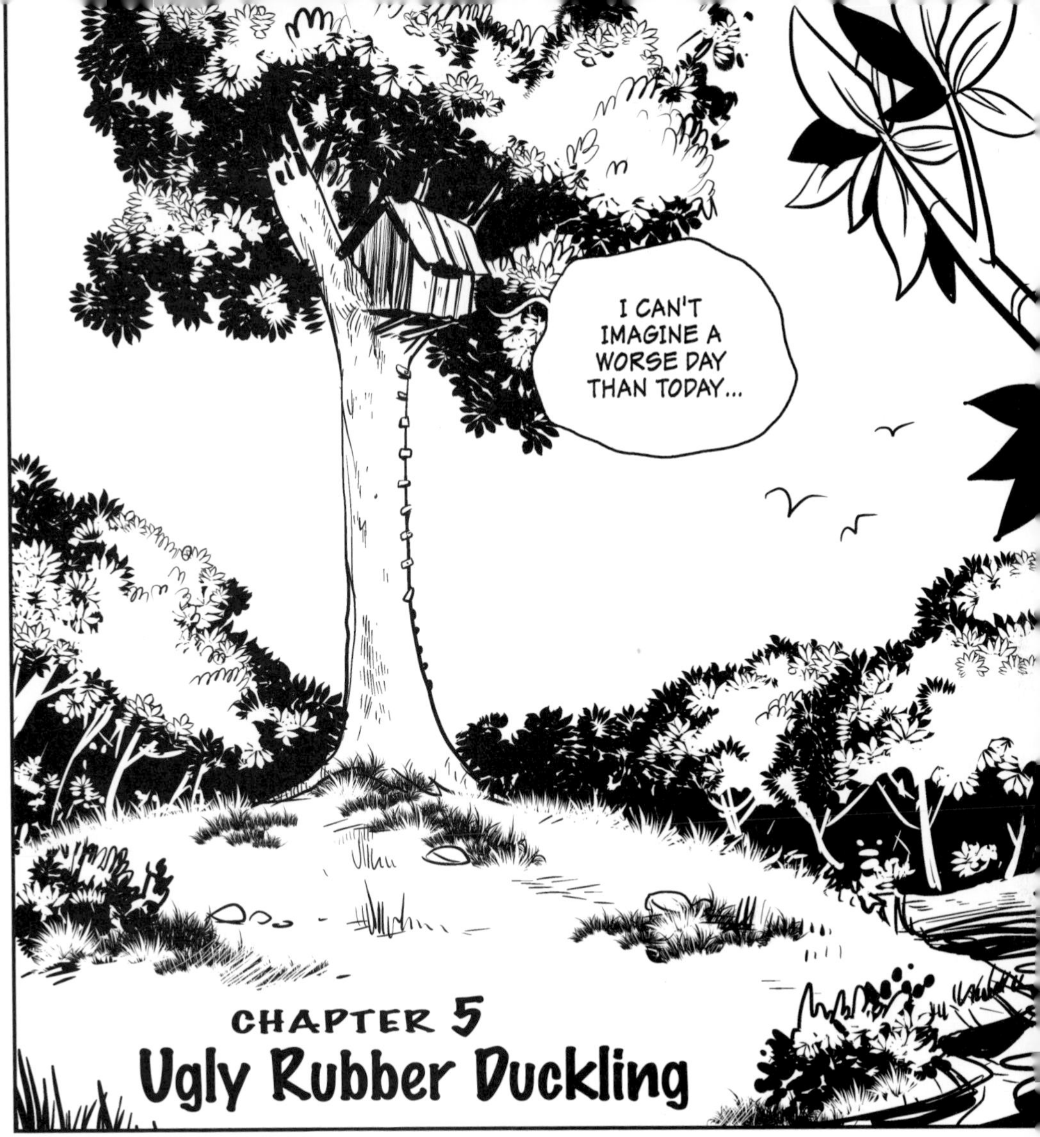
I CAN'T IMAGINE A WORSE DAY THAN TODAY...
CHAPTER 5
Ugly Rubber Duckling

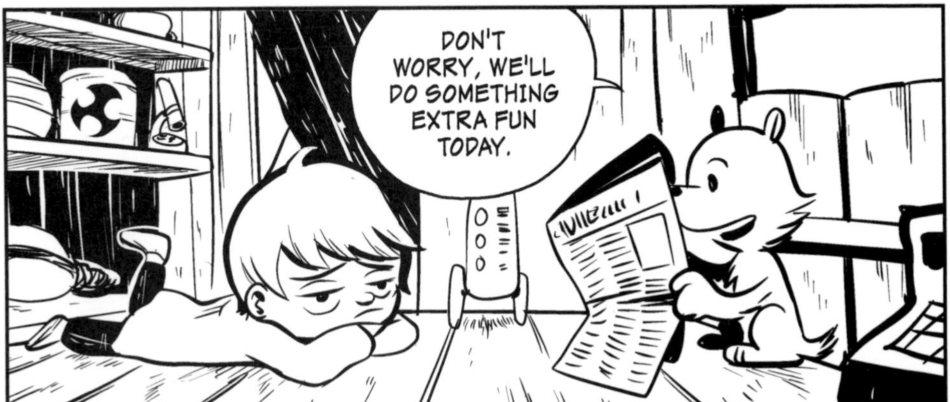
DON'T WORRY, WE'LL DO SOMETHING EXTRA FUN TODAY.

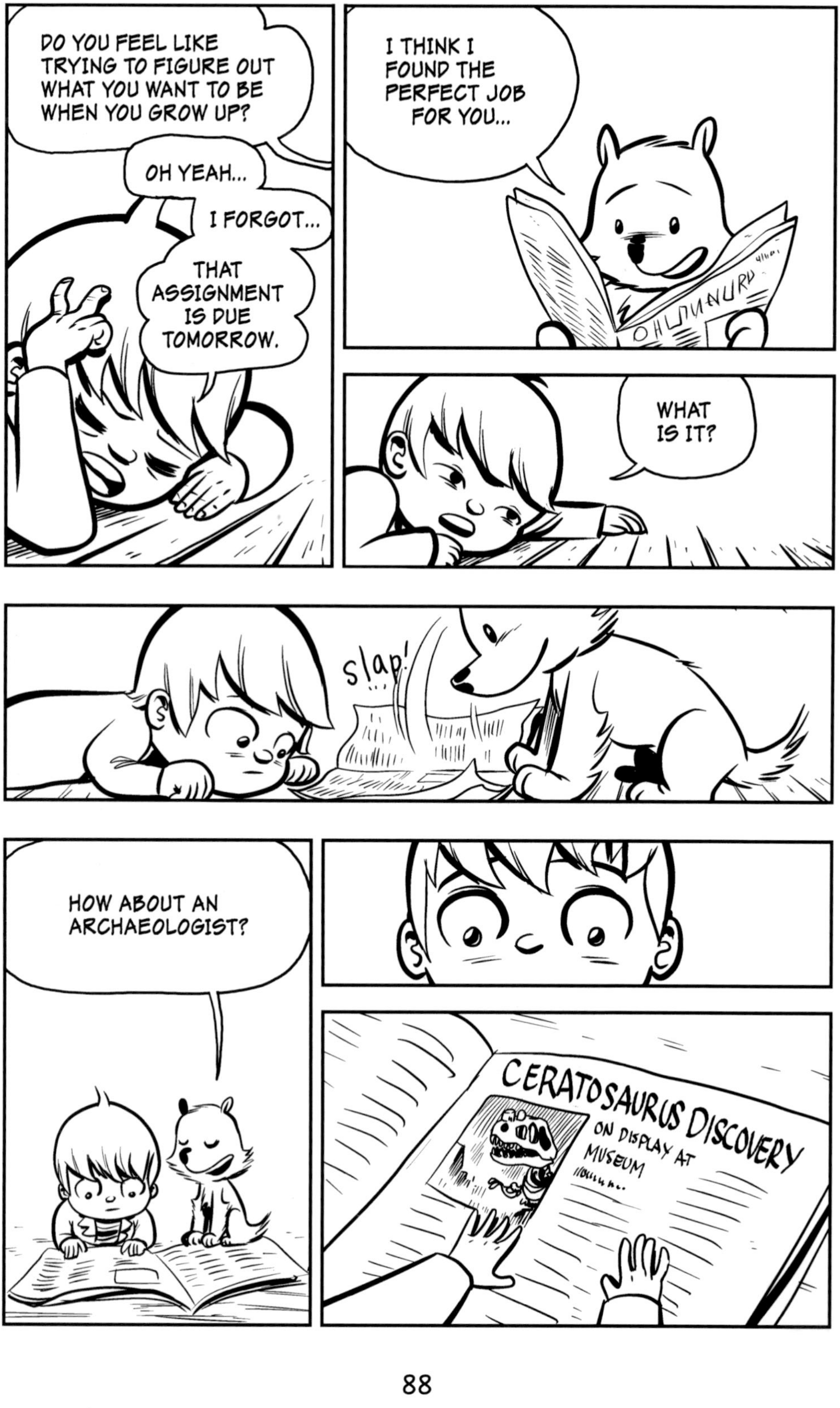
DO YOU FEEL LIKE TRYING TO FIGURE OUT WHAT YOU WANT TO BE WHEN YOU GROW UP?
OH YEAH...
I FORGOT...
THAT ASSIGNMENT IS DUE TOMORROW.
I THINK I FOUND THE PERFECT JOB FOR YOU...
WHAT IS IT?
slap!
HOW ABOUT AN ARCHAEOLOGIST?
CERATOSAURUS DISCOVERY
ON DISPLAY AT MUSEUM

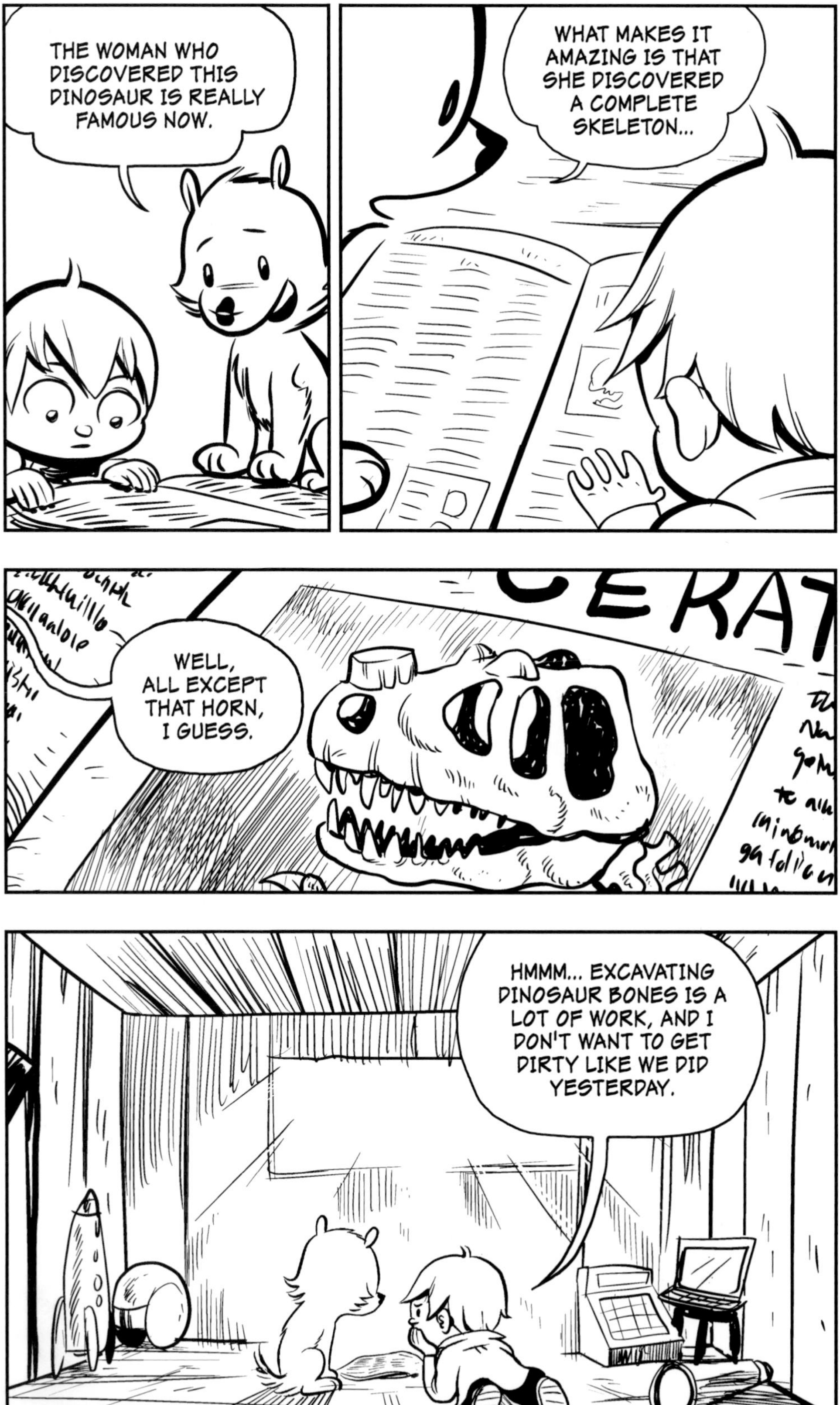
THE WOMAN WHO DISCOVERED THIS DINOSAUR IS REALLY FAMOUS NOW.
WHAT MAKES IT AMAZING IS THAT SHE DISCOVERED A COMPLETE SKELETON...
CERAT
WELL, ALL EXCEPT THAT HORN, I GUESS.
HMMM... EXCAVATING DINOSAUR BONES IS A LOT OF WORK, AND I DON'T WANT TO GET DIRTY LIKE WE DID YESTERDAY.

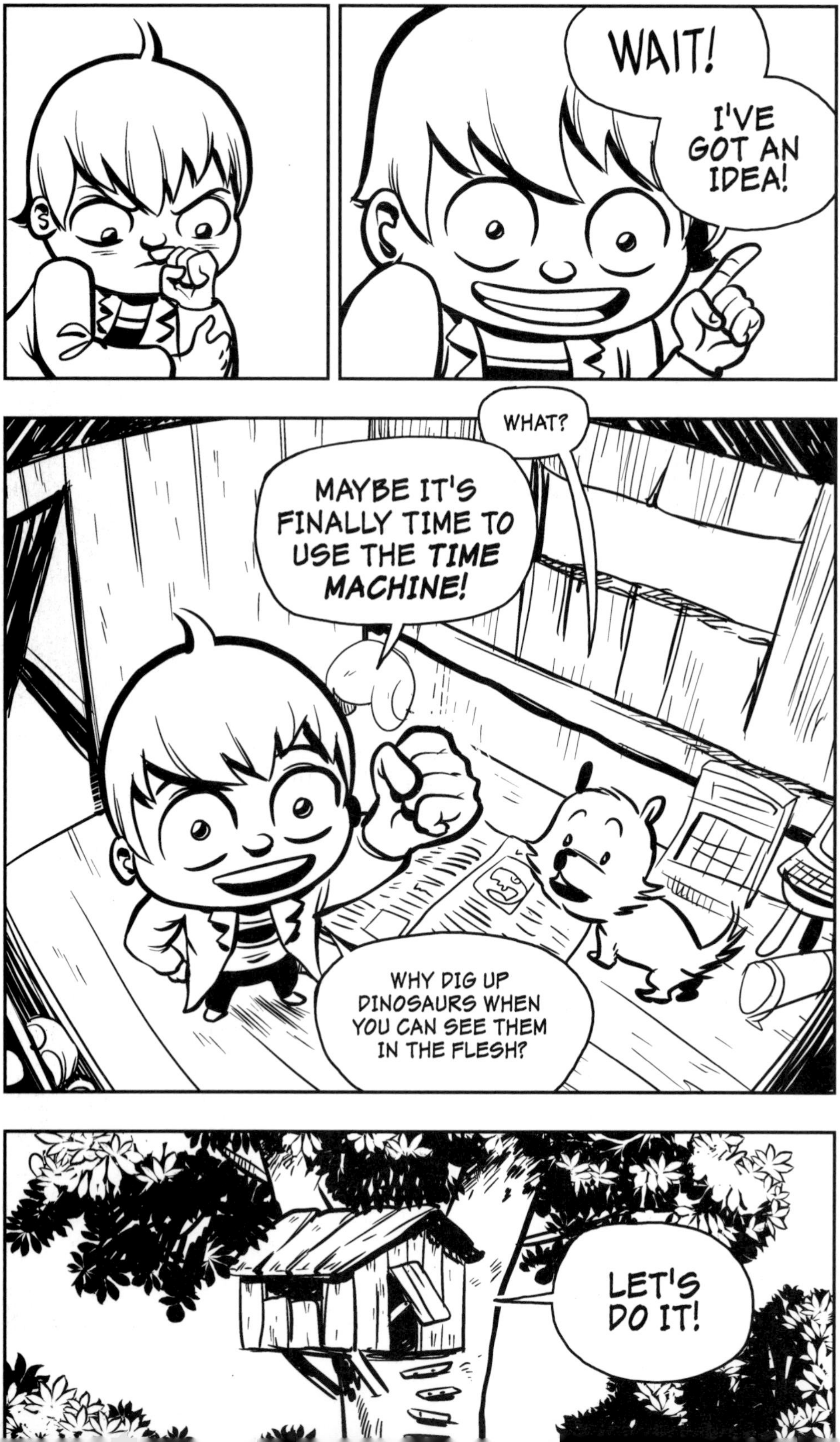
WAIT!
I'VE GOT AN IDEA!
WHAT?
MAYBE IT'S FINALLY TIME TO USE THE TIME MACHINE!
WHY DIG UP DINOSAURS WHEN YOU CAN SEE THEM IN THE FLESH?
LET'S DO IT!

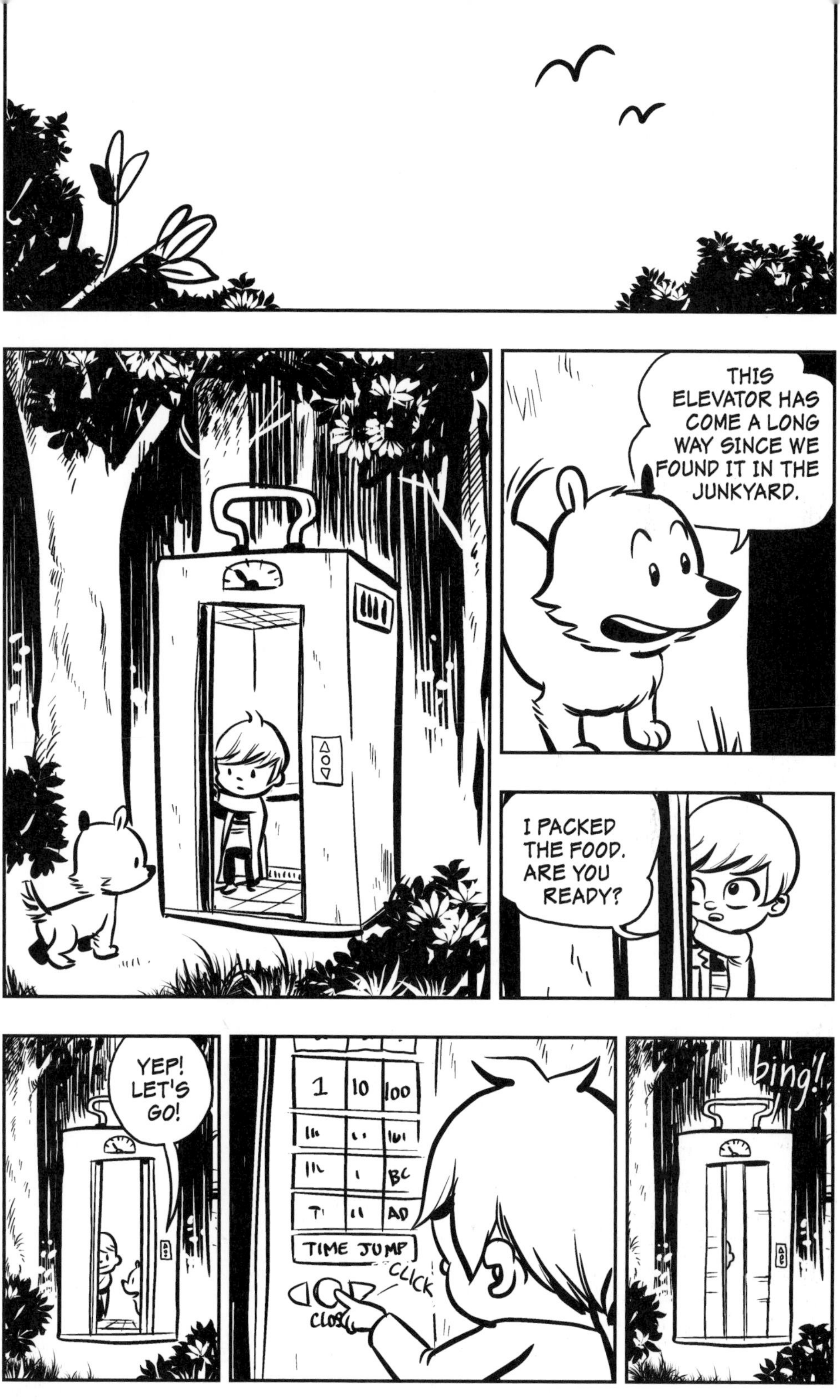
THIS ELEVATOR HAS COME A LONG WAY SINCE WE FOUND IT IN THE JUNKYARD.
I PACKED THE FOOD. ARE YOU READY?
YEP! LET'S GO!
TIME JUMP
CLICK
bing!

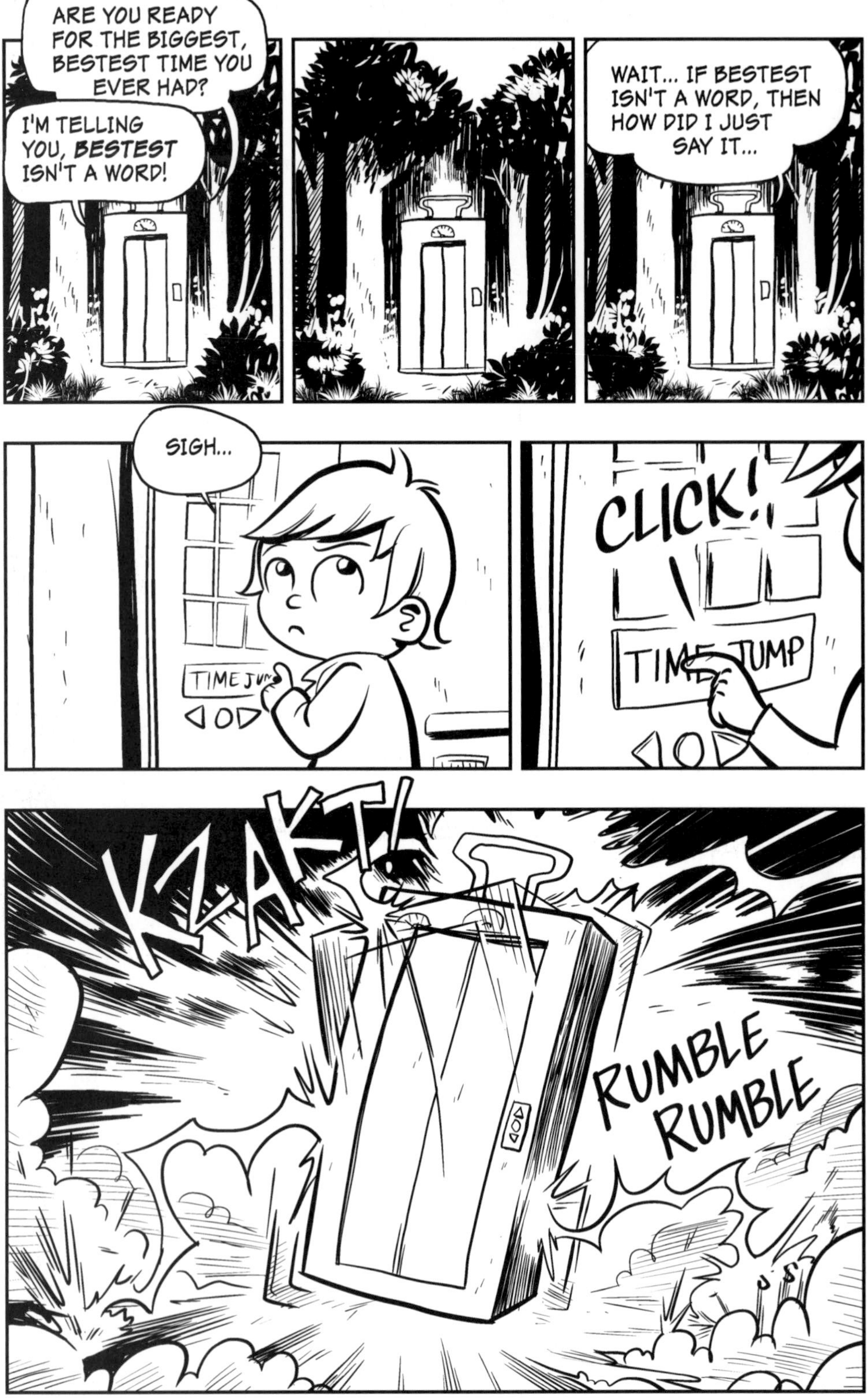
ARE YOU READY FOR THE BIGGEST, BESTEST TIME YOU EVER HAD?
I'M TELLING YOU, BESTEST ISN'T A WORD!
WAIT... IF BESTEST ISN'T A WORD, THEN HOW DID I JUST SAY IT...
SIGH...
TIME JU
CLICK!
TIME JUMP
KZAKT!
RUMBLE RUMBLE

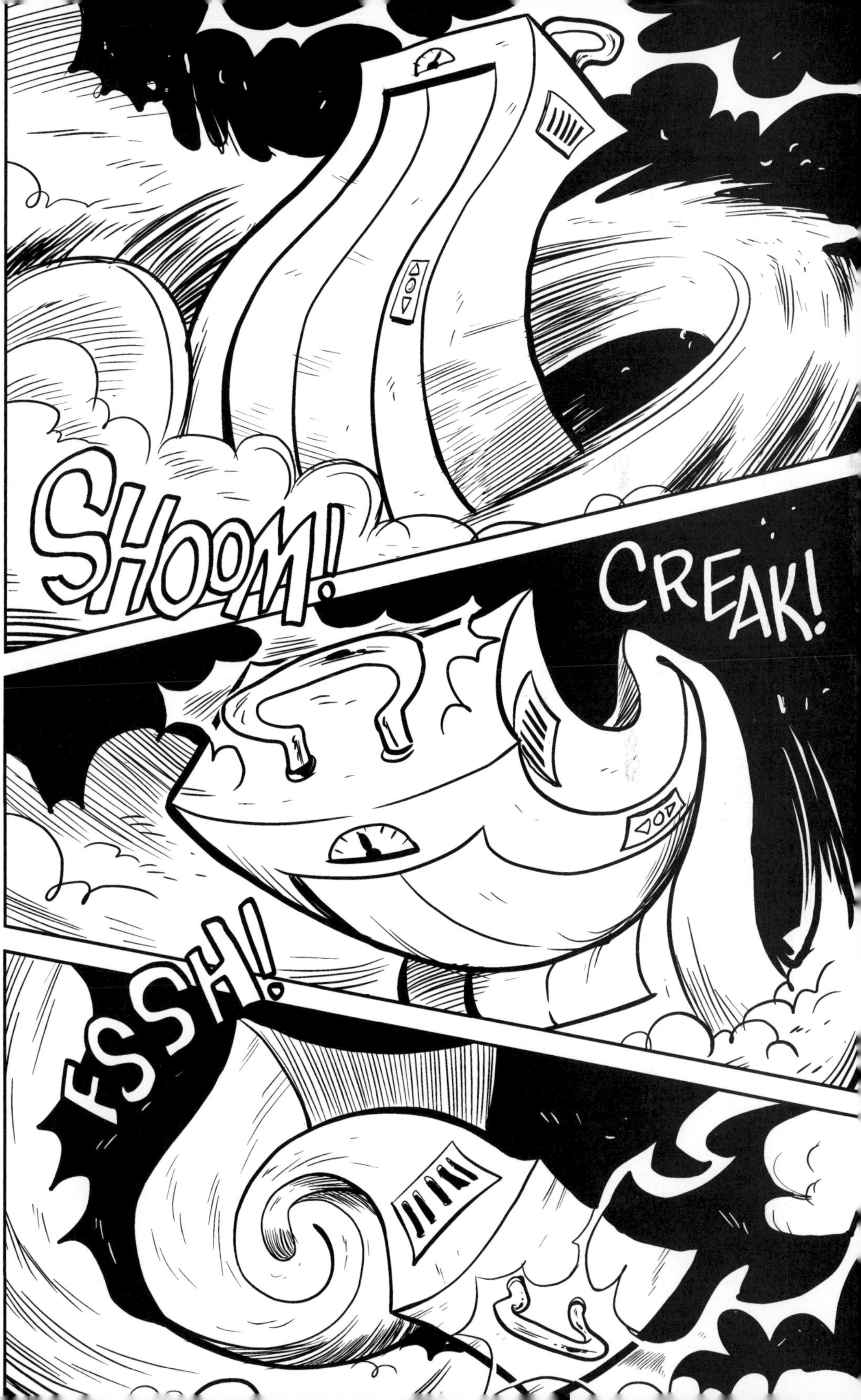
SHOOM!
CREAK!
FSSH!

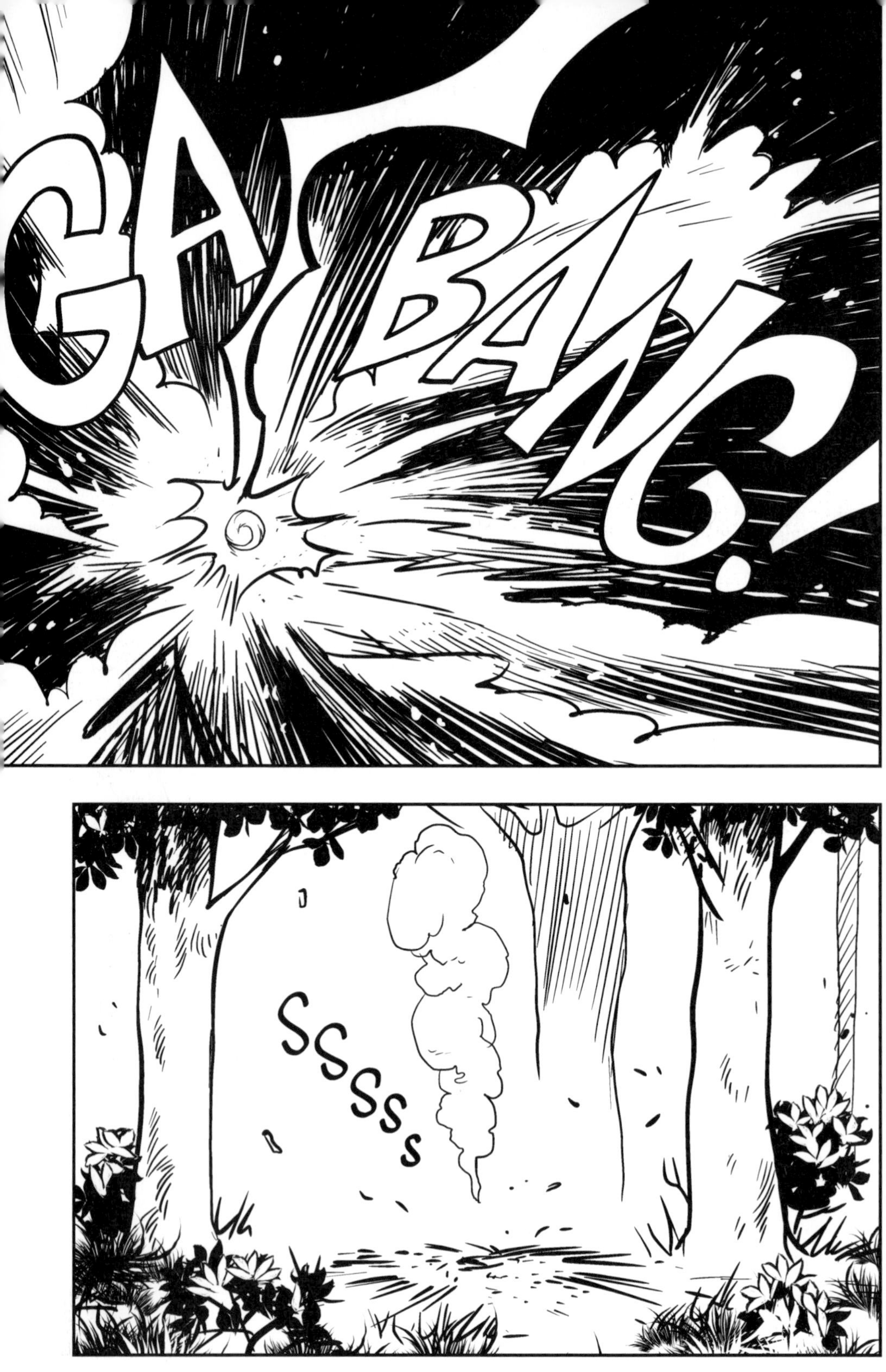
GABANG!
SSSSSs

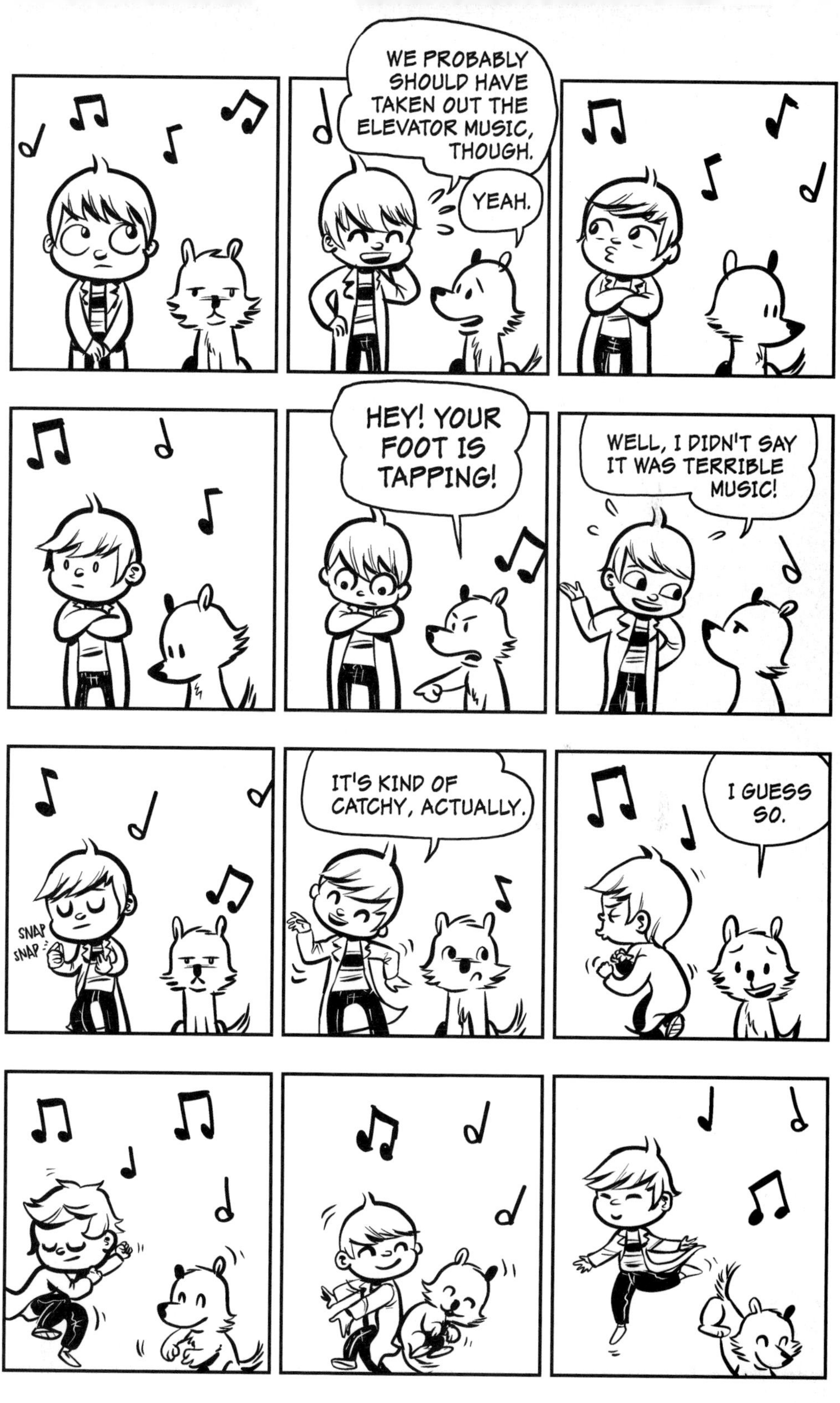
WE PROBABLY SHOULD HAVE TAKEN OUT THE ELEVATOR MUSIC, THOUGH.
YEAH.
HEY! YOUR FOOT IS TAPPING!
WELL, I DIDN'T SAY IT WAS TERRIBLE MUSIC!
SNAP SNAP
IT'S KIND OF CATCHY, ACTUALLY.
I GUESS SO.

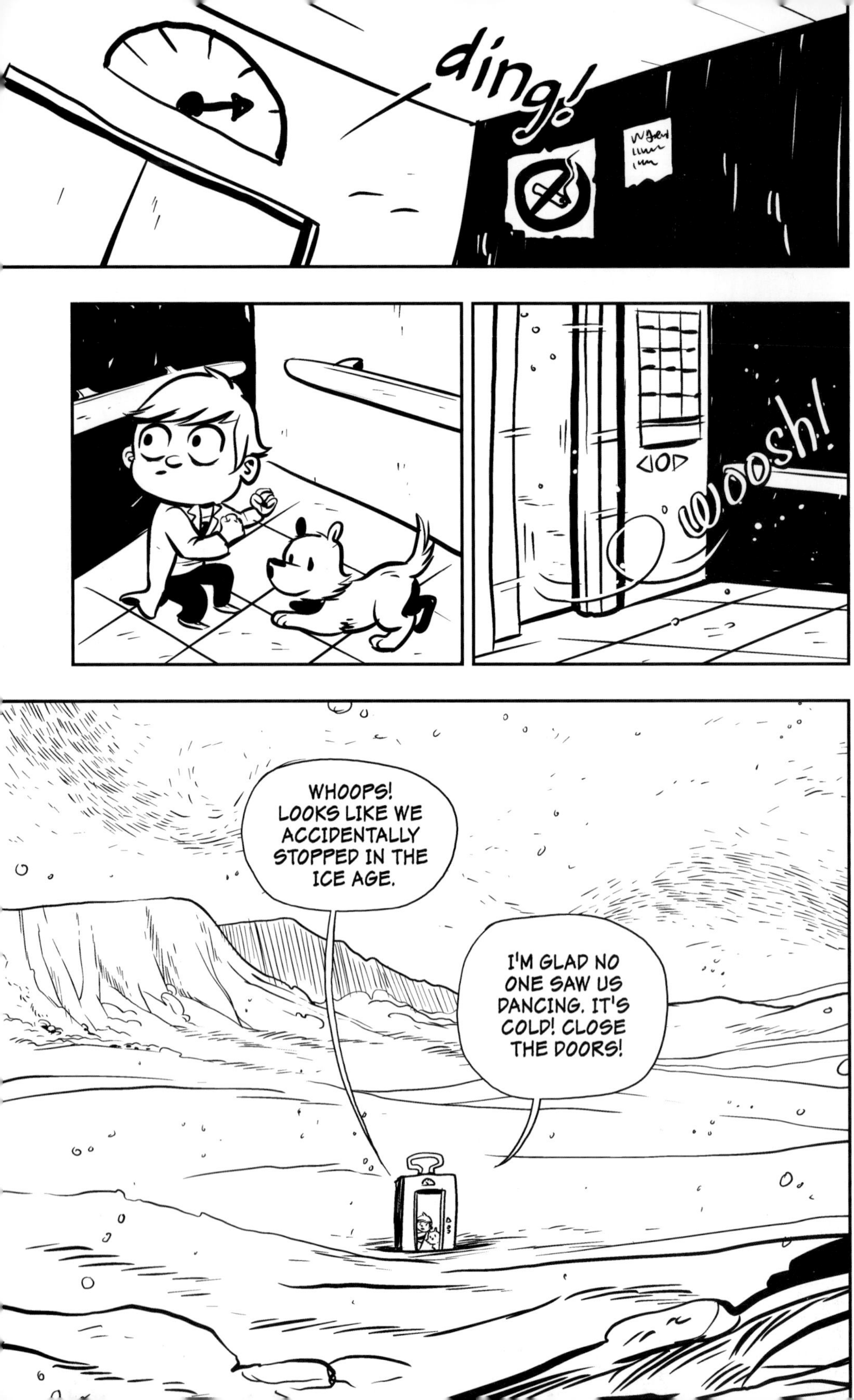
ding!
WOOSH!
WHOOPS! LOOKS LIKE WE ACCIDENTALLY STOPPED IN THE ICE AGE.
I'M GLAD NO ONE SAW US DANCING. IT'S COLD! CLOSE THE DOORS!

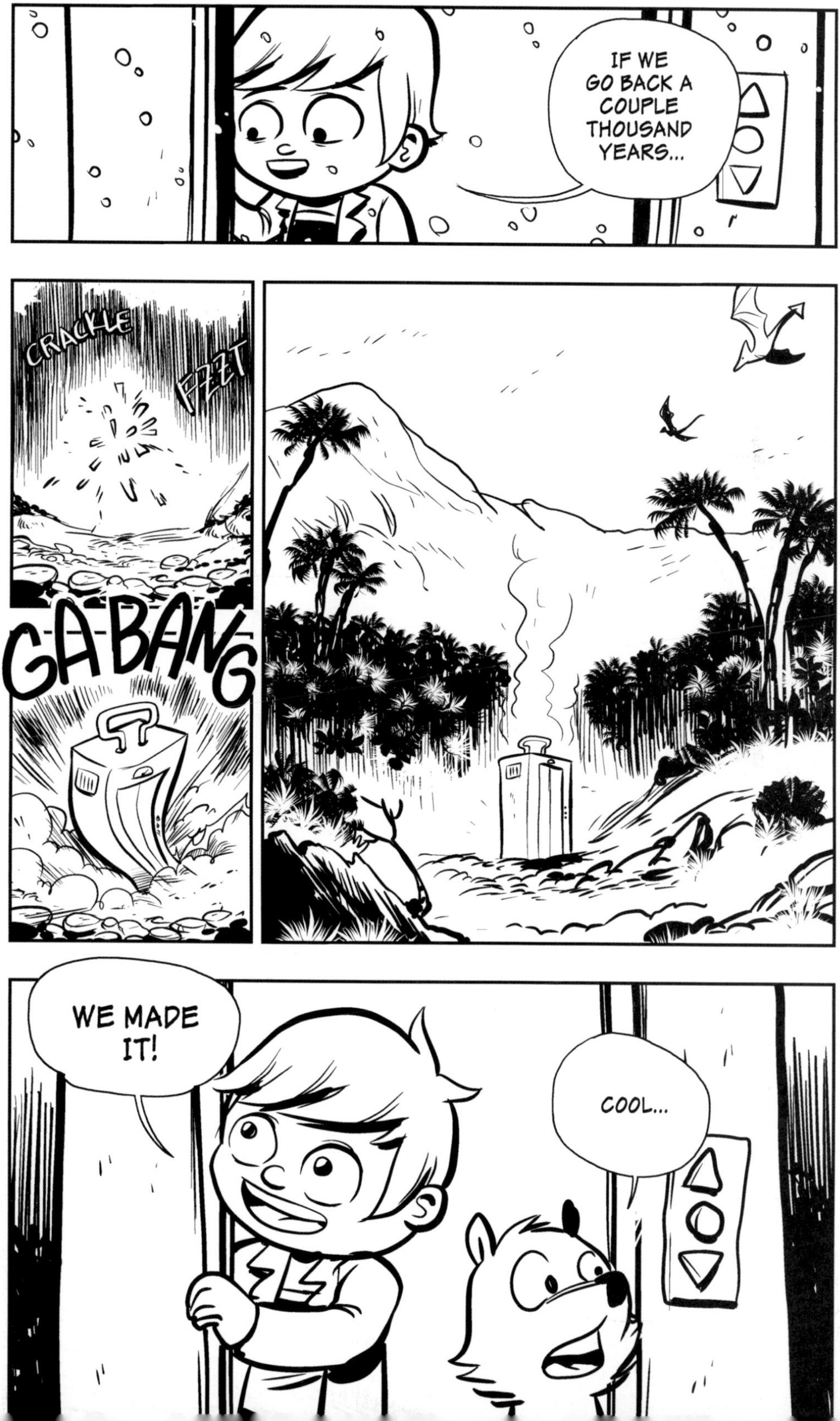
IF WE GO BACK A COUPLE THOUSAND YEARS...
CRACKLE
FZZT
GA BANG
WE MADE IT!
COOL...

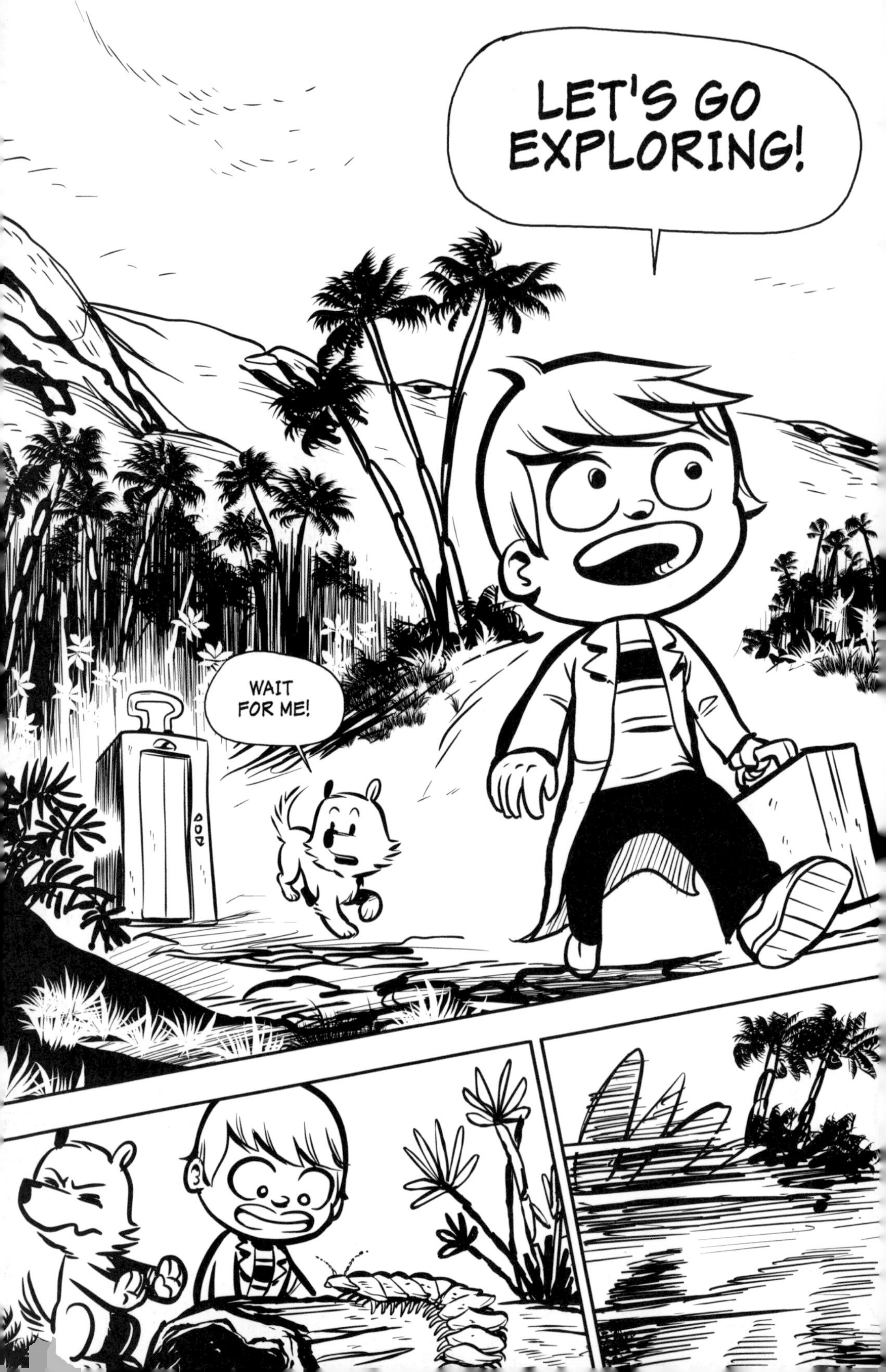
LET'S GO EXPLORING!
WAIT FOR ME!

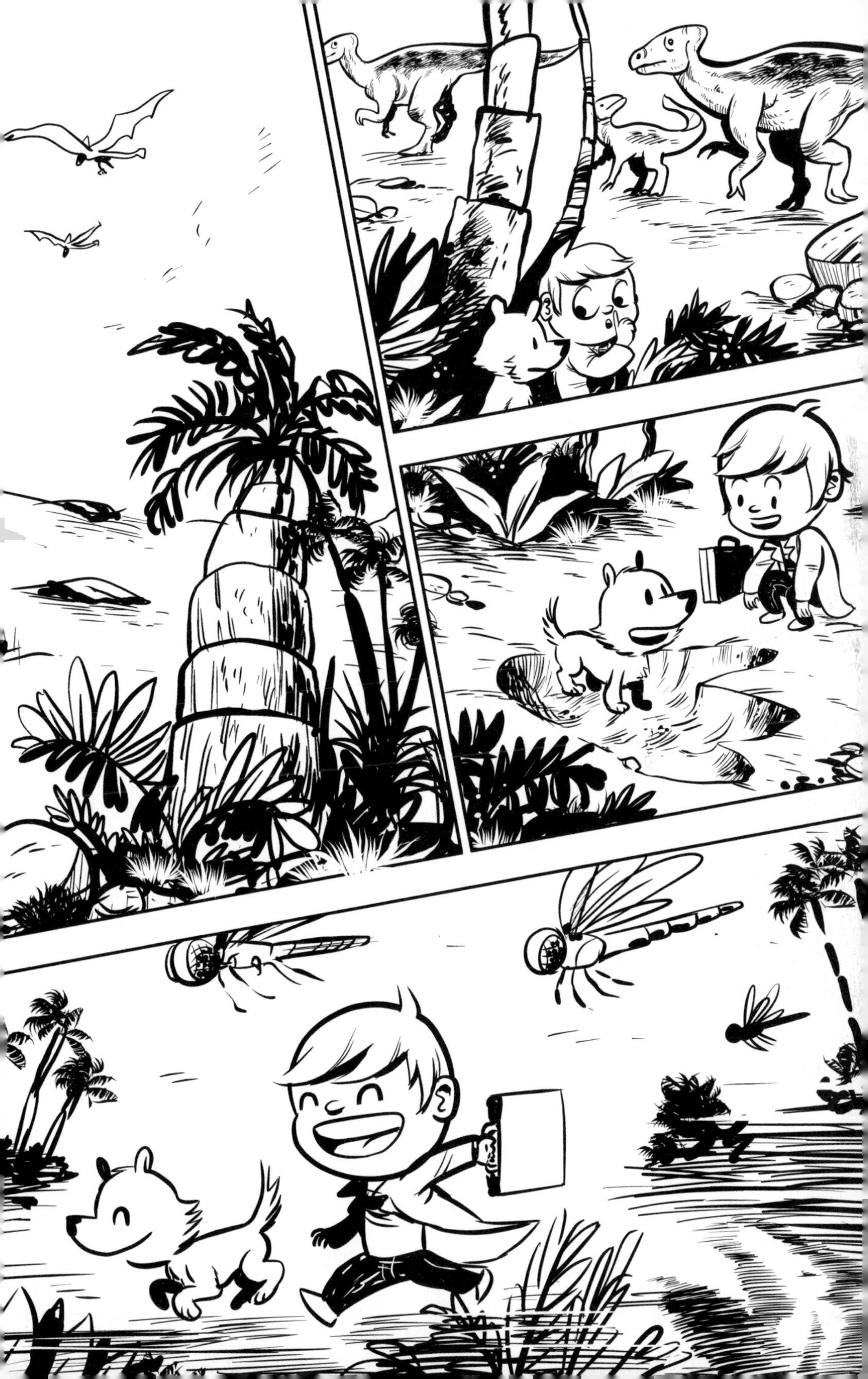

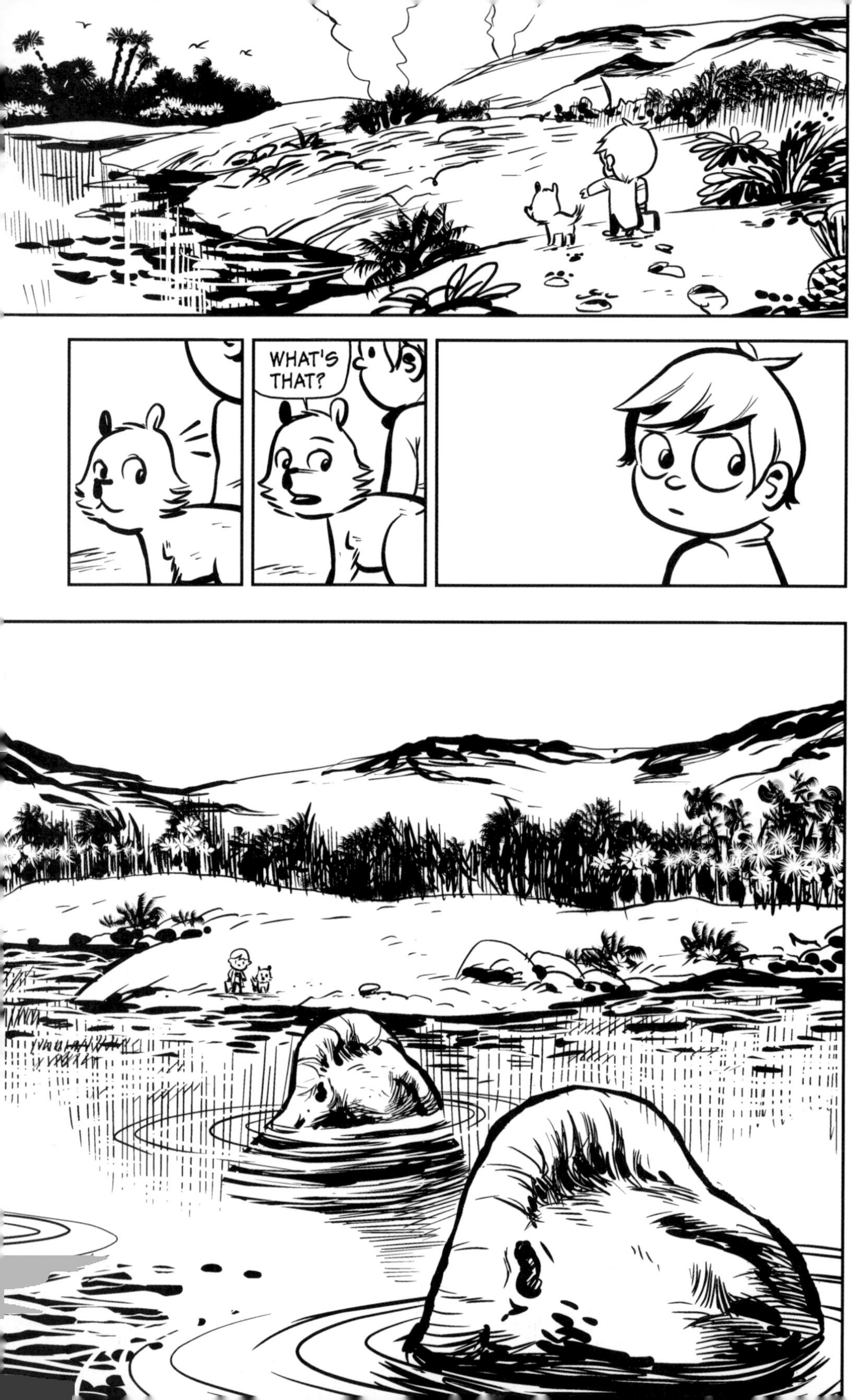
WHAT'S THAT?

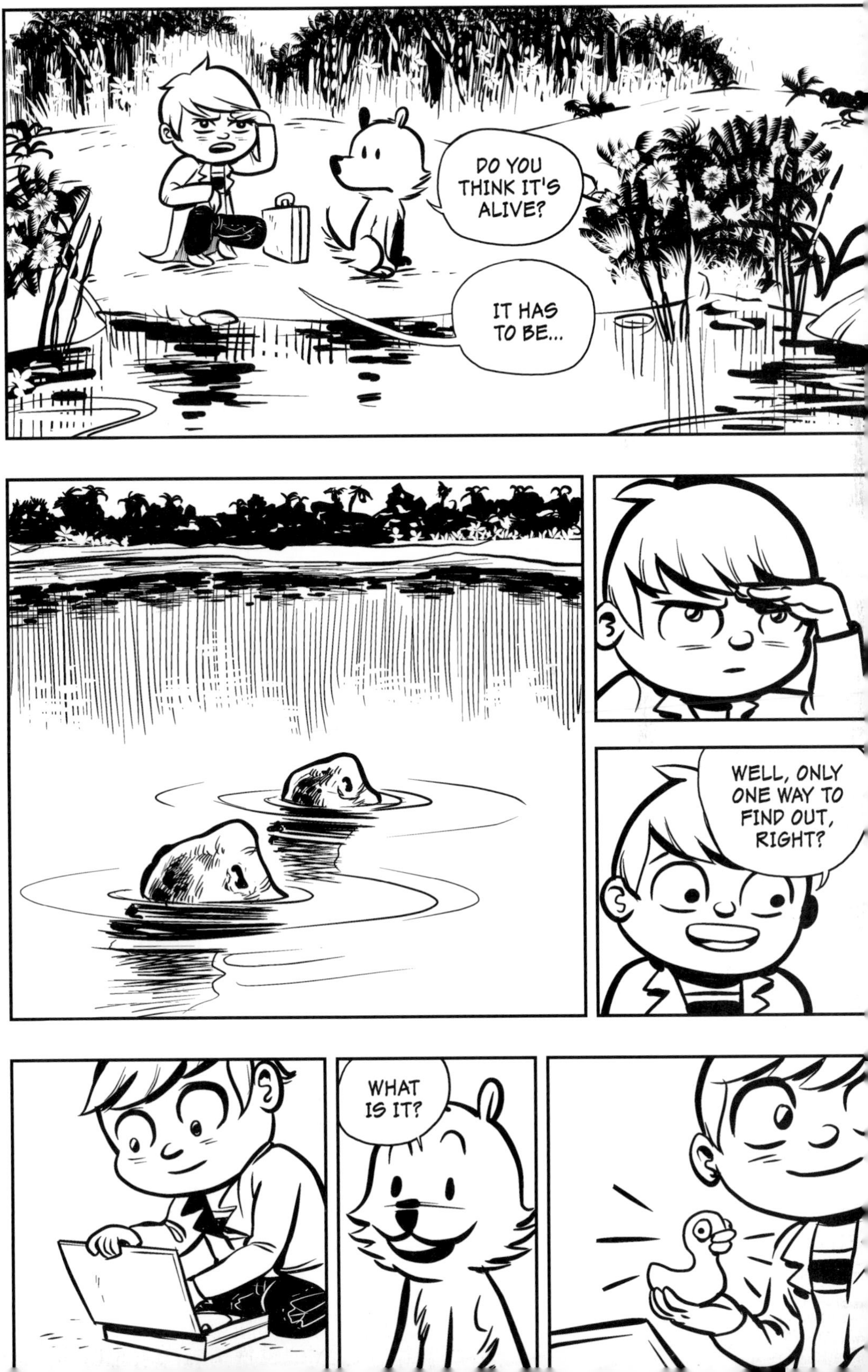
DO YOU THINK IT'S ALIVE?
IT HAS TO BE...
WELL, ONLY ONE WAY TO FIND OUT, RIGHT?
WHAT IS IT?

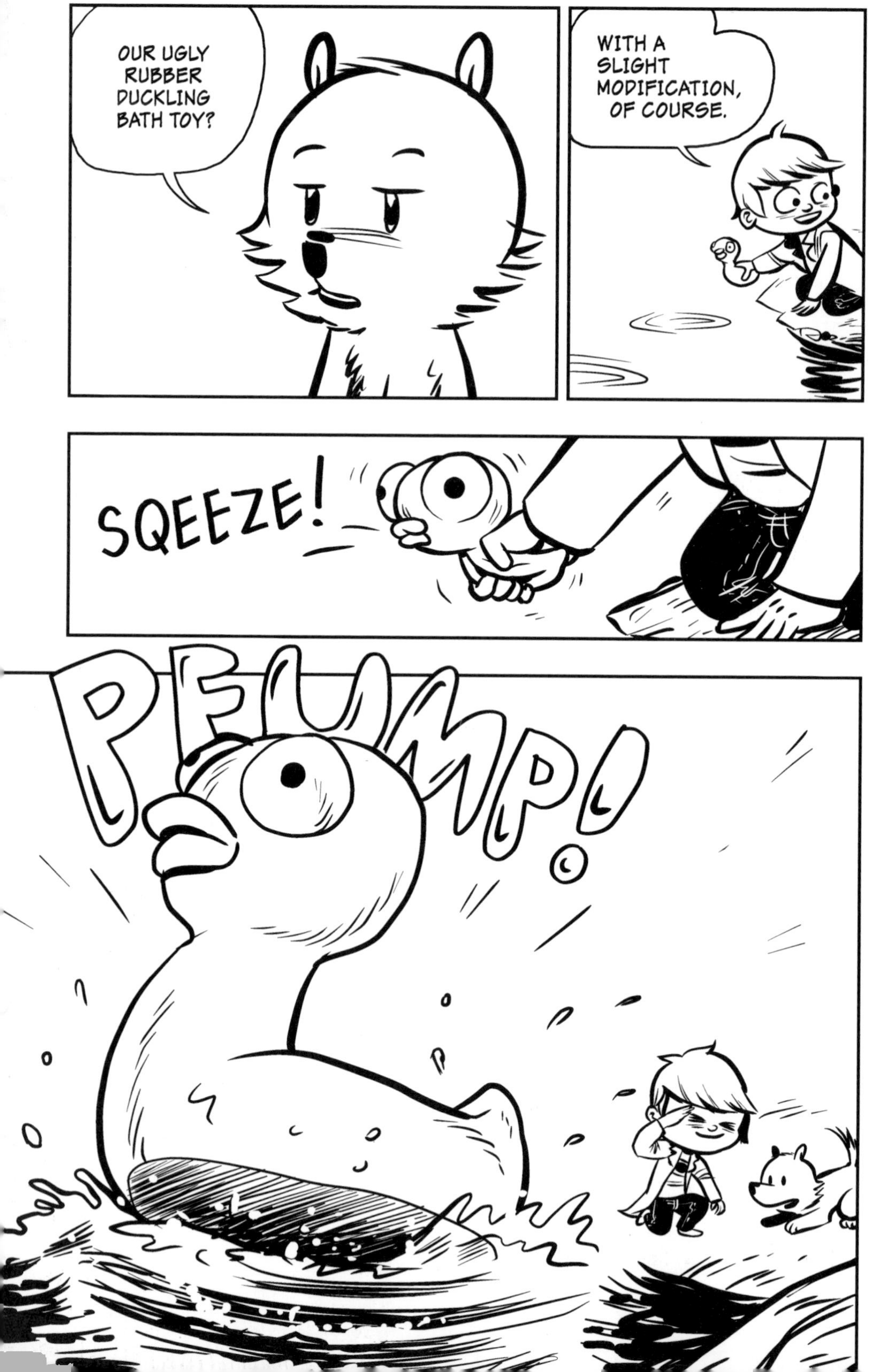
OUR UGLY RUBBER DUCKLING BATH TOY?
WITH A SLIGHT MODIFICATION, OF COURSE.
SQEEZE!
PFUMP!

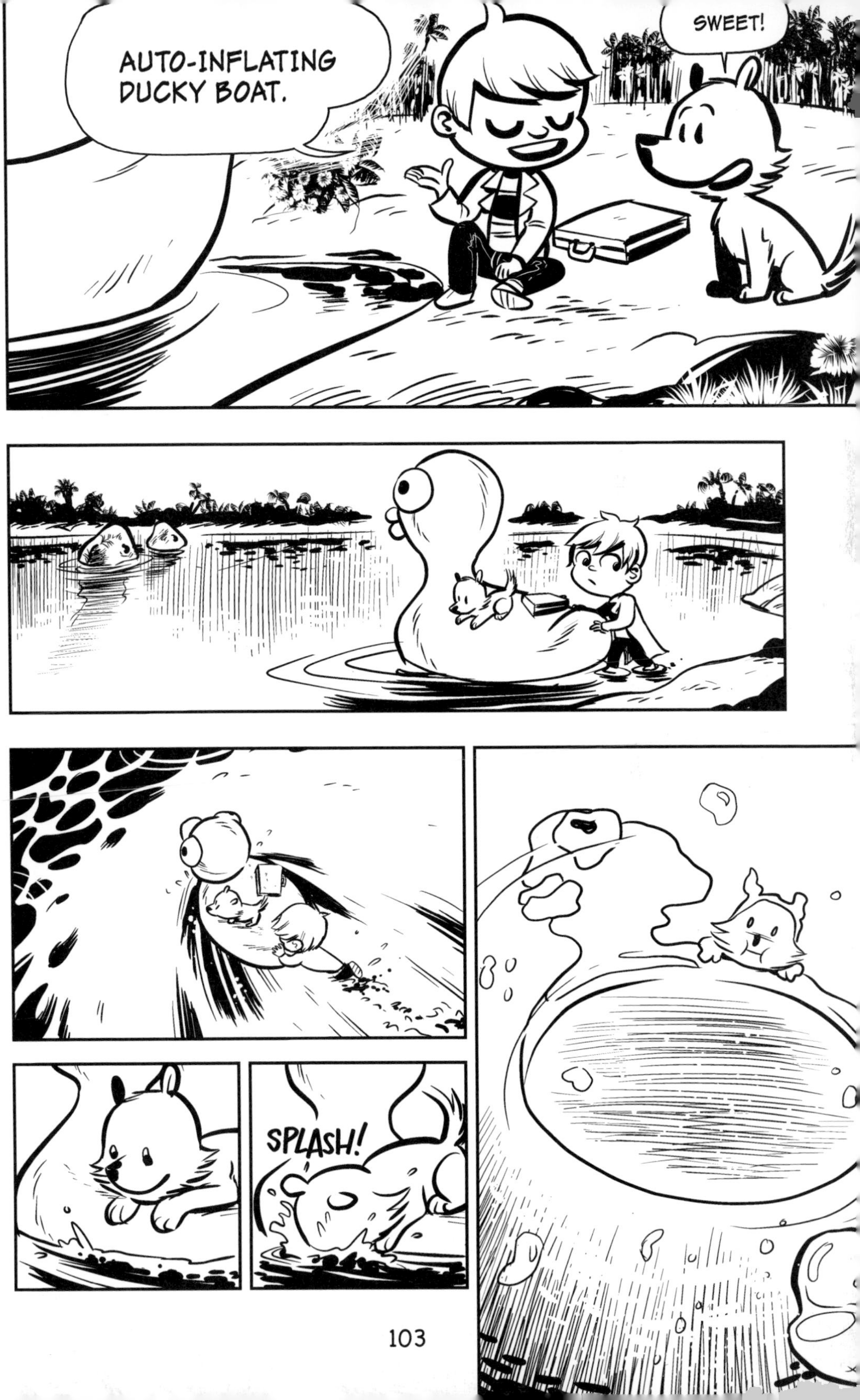
AUTO-INFLATING DUCKY BOAT.
SWEET!
SPLASH!

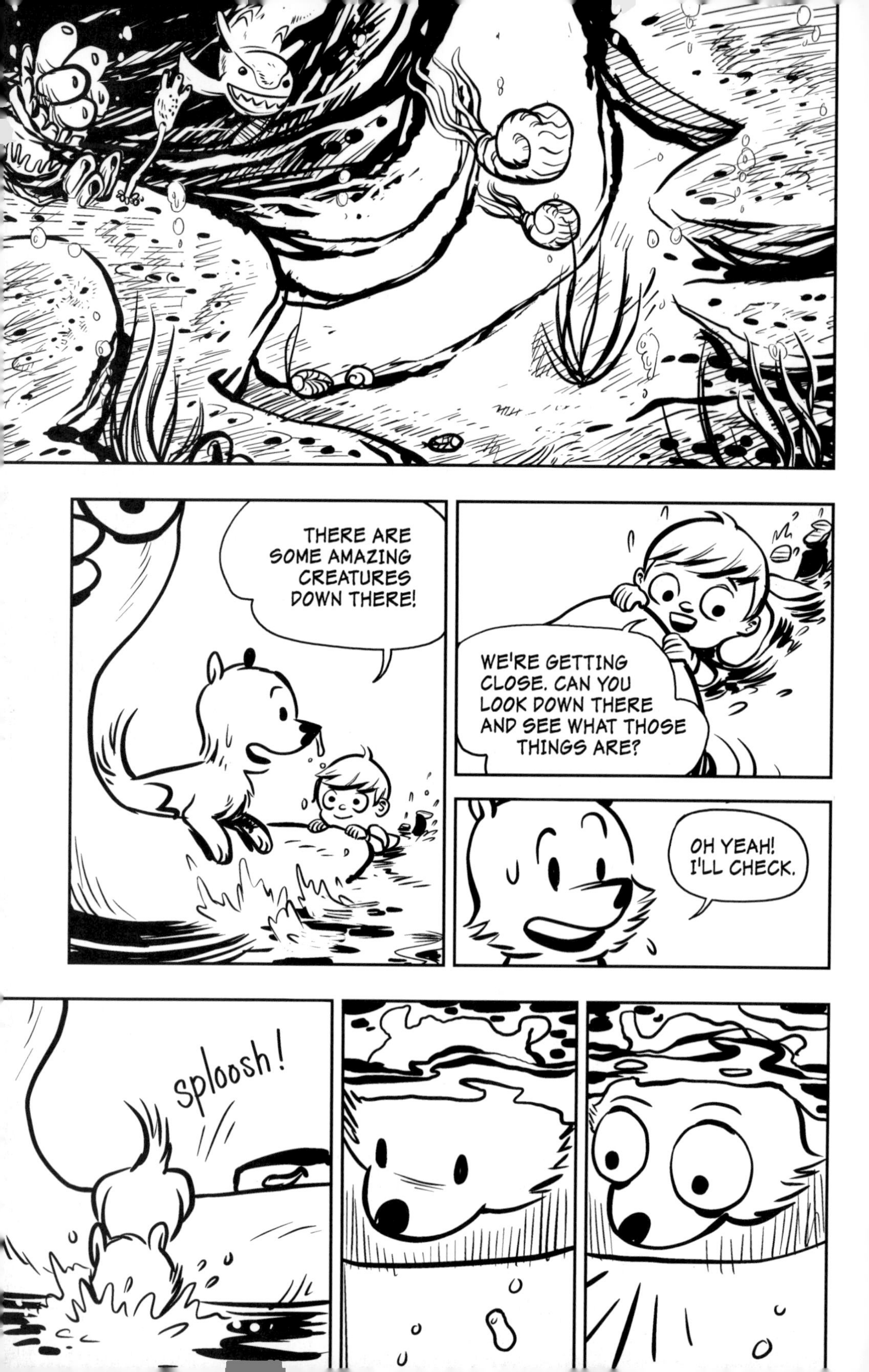
THERE ARE SOME AMAZING CREATURES DOWN THERE!
WE'RE GETTING CLOSE. CAN YOU LOOK DOWN THERE AND SEE WHAT THOSE THINGS ARE?
OH YEAH! I'LL CHECK.
sploosh!

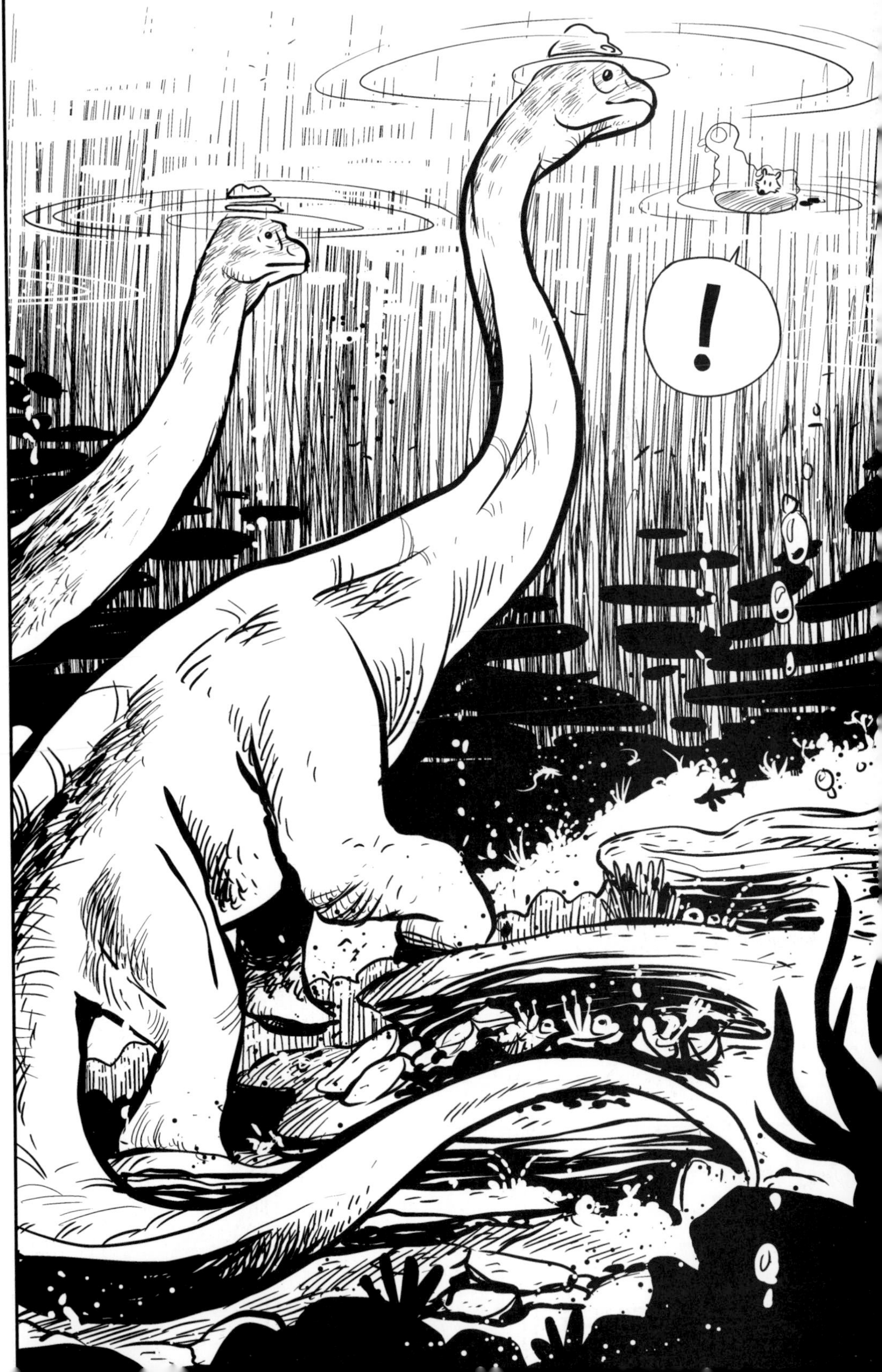
!

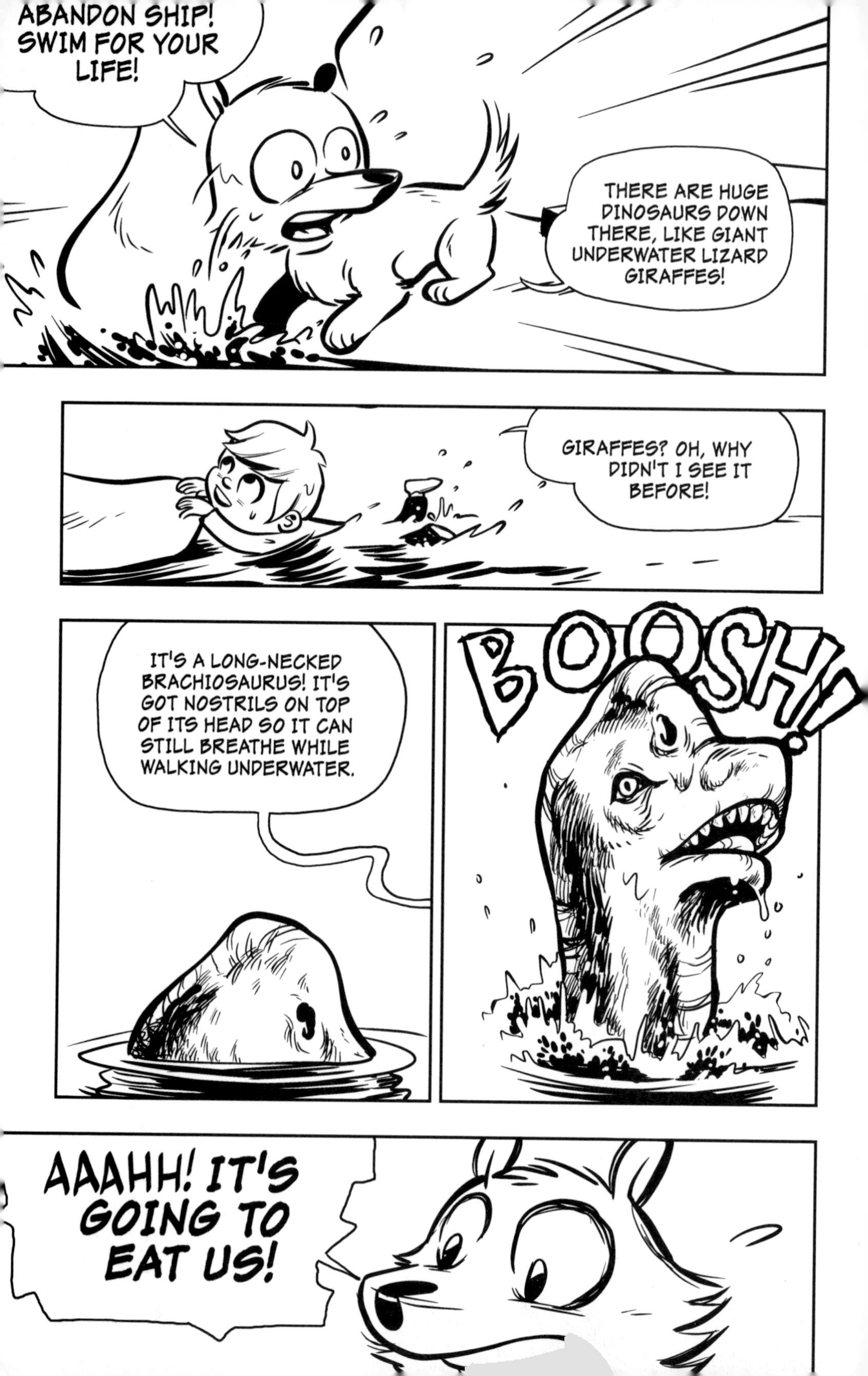
ABANDON SHIP! SWIM FOR YOUR LIFE!
THERE ARE HUGE DINOSAURS DOWN THERE, LIKE GIANT UNDERWATER LIZARD GIRAFFES!
GIRAFFES? OH, WHY DIDN'T I SEE IT BEFORE!
IT'S A LONG-NECKED BRACHIOSAURUS! IT'S GOT NOSTRILS ON TOP OF ITS HEAD SO IT CAN STILL BREATHE WHILE WALKING UNDERWATER.
BOOSH!!
AAAHH! IT'S GOING TO EAT US!

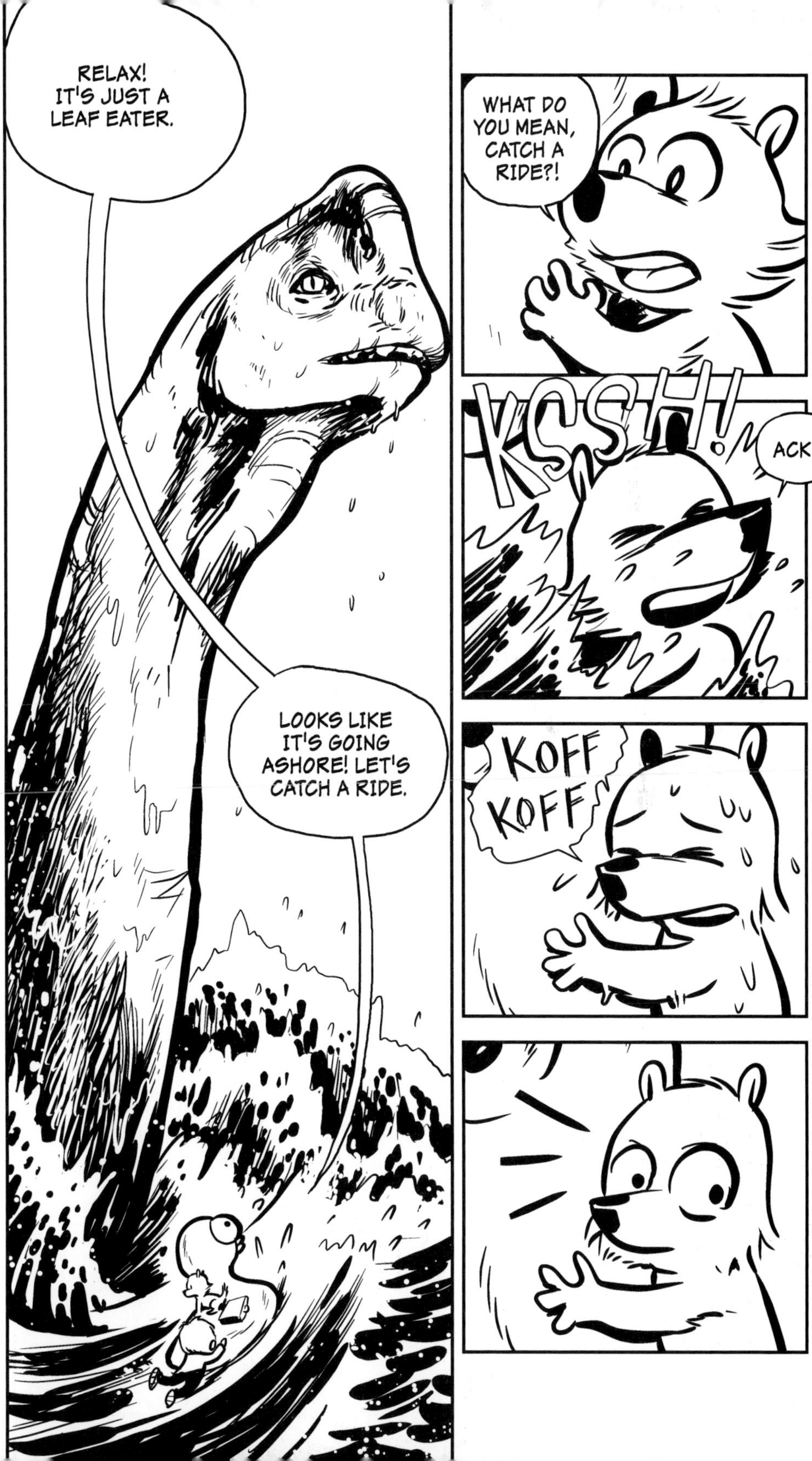
RELAX! IT'S JUST A LEAF EATER.
LOOKS LIKE IT'S GOING ASHORE! LET'S CATCH A RIDE.
WHAT DO YOU MEAN, CATCH A RIDE?!
KSSH!
ACK!
KOFF KOFF

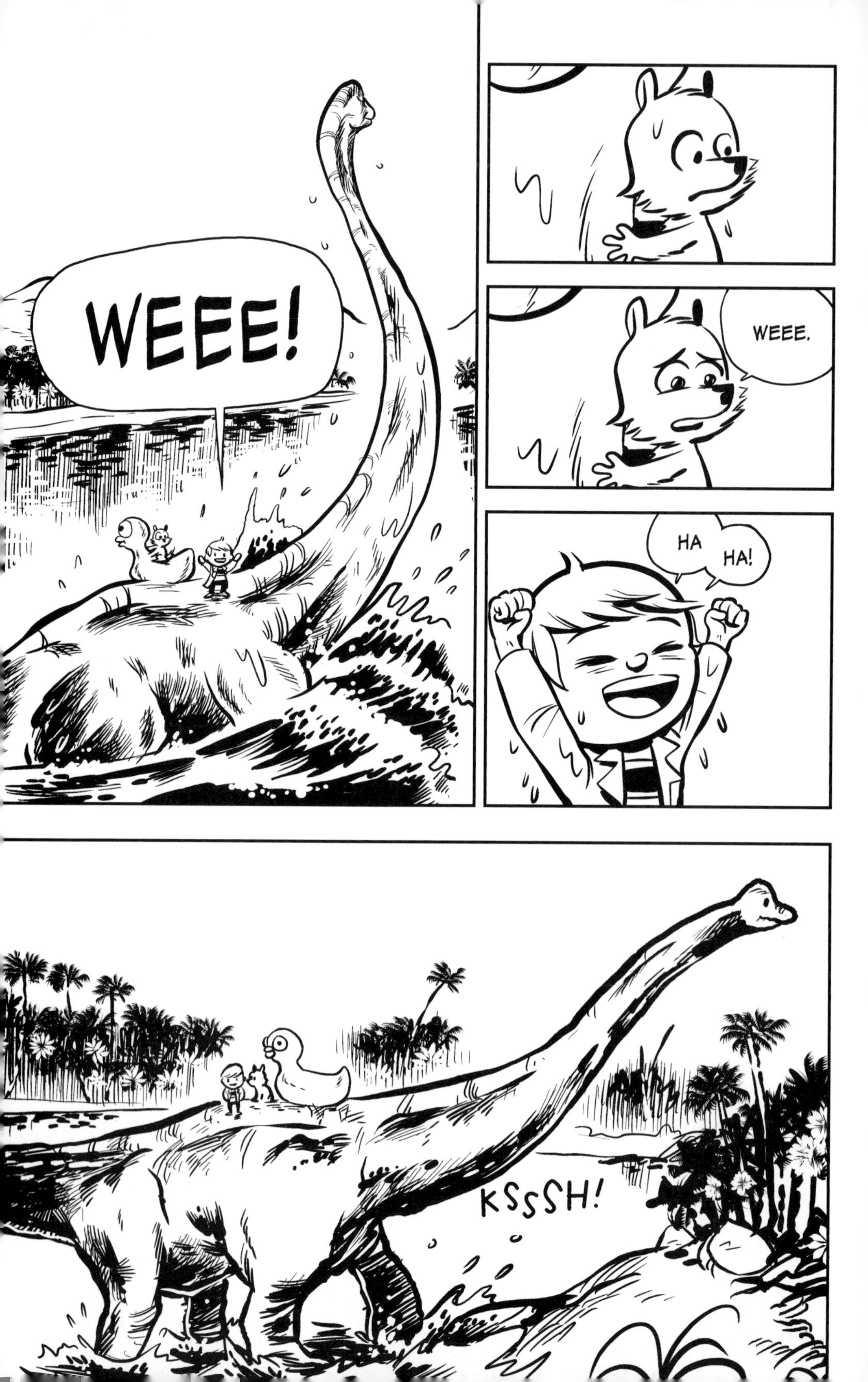
WEEE!
WEEE.
HA
HA!
KSSSH!

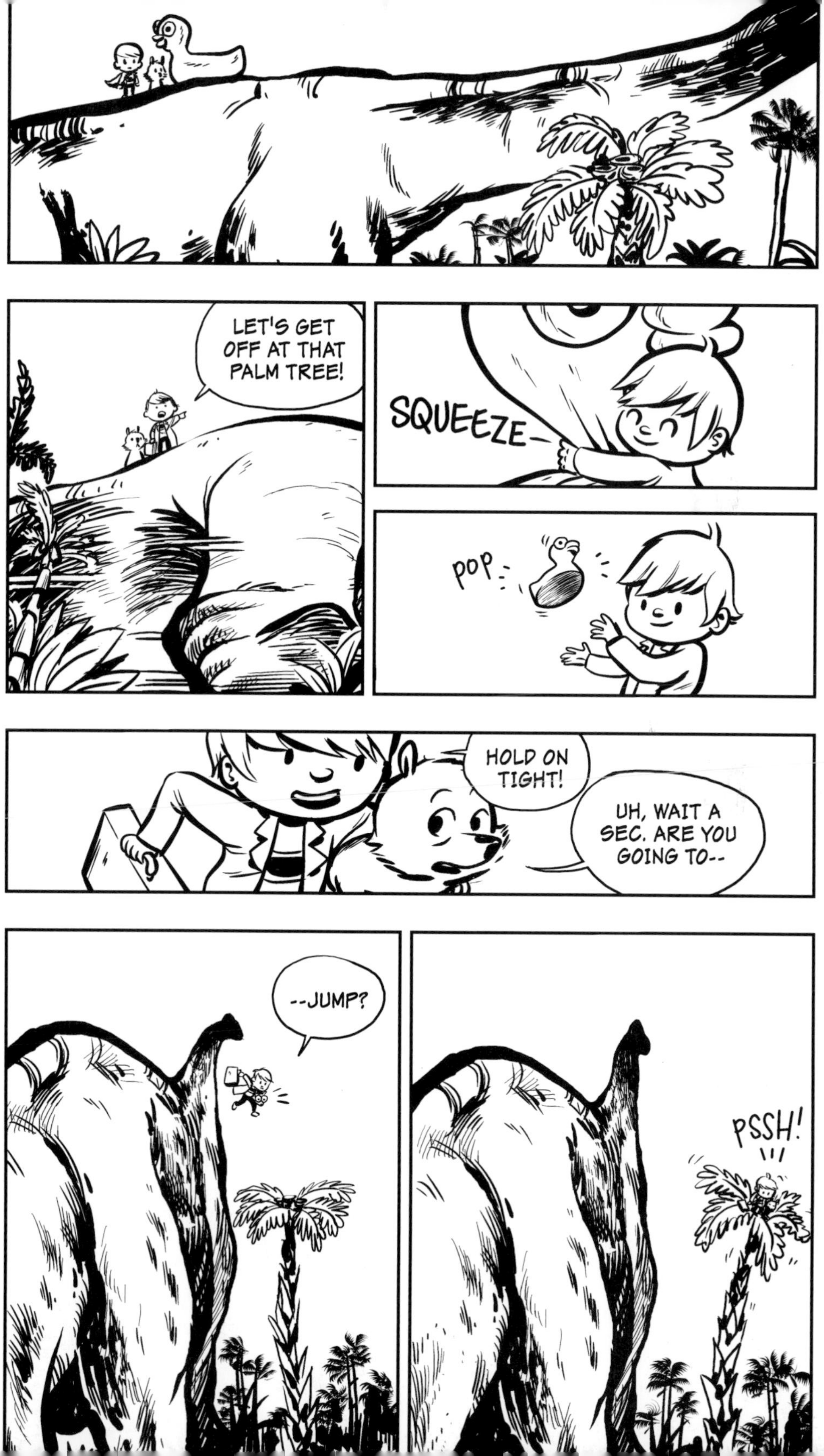
LET'S GET OFF AT THAT PALM TREE!
SQUEEZE
pop
HOLD ON TIGHT!
UH, WAIT A SEC. ARE YOU GOING TO--
--JUMP?
PSSH!

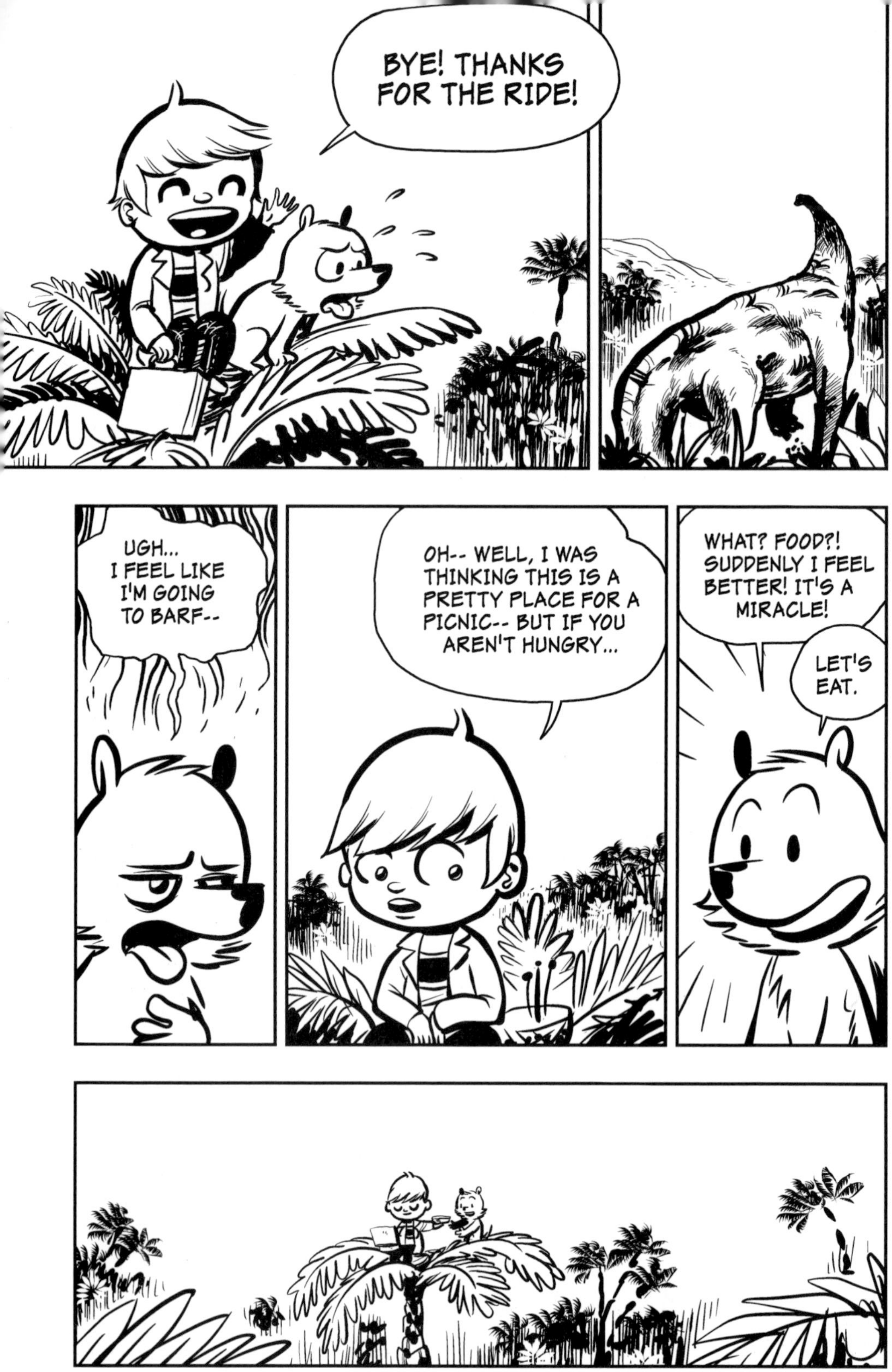
BYE! THANKS FOR THE RIDE!
UGH... I FEEL LIKE I'M GOING TO BARF--
OH-- WELL, I WAS THINKING THIS IS A PRETTY PLACE FOR A PICNIC-- BUT IF YOU AREN'T HUNGRY...
WHAT? FOOD?! SUDDENLY I FEEL BETTER! IT'S A MIRACLE!
LET'S EAT.

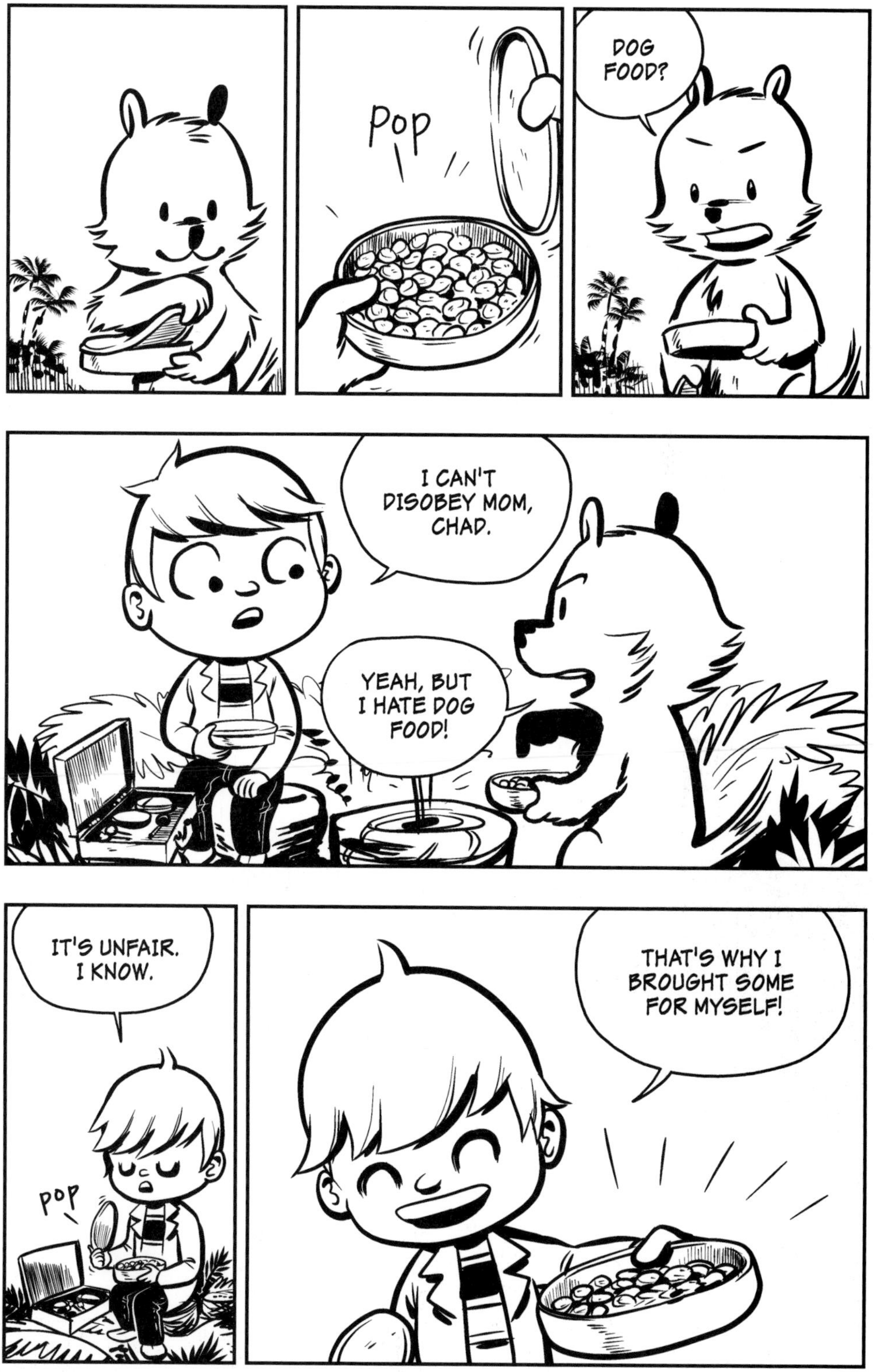
POP
DOG FOOD?
I CAN'T DISOBEY MOM, CHAD.
YEAH, BUT I HATE DOG FOOD!
IT'S UNFAIR. I KNOW.
POP
THAT'S WHY I BROUGHT SOME FOR MYSELF!

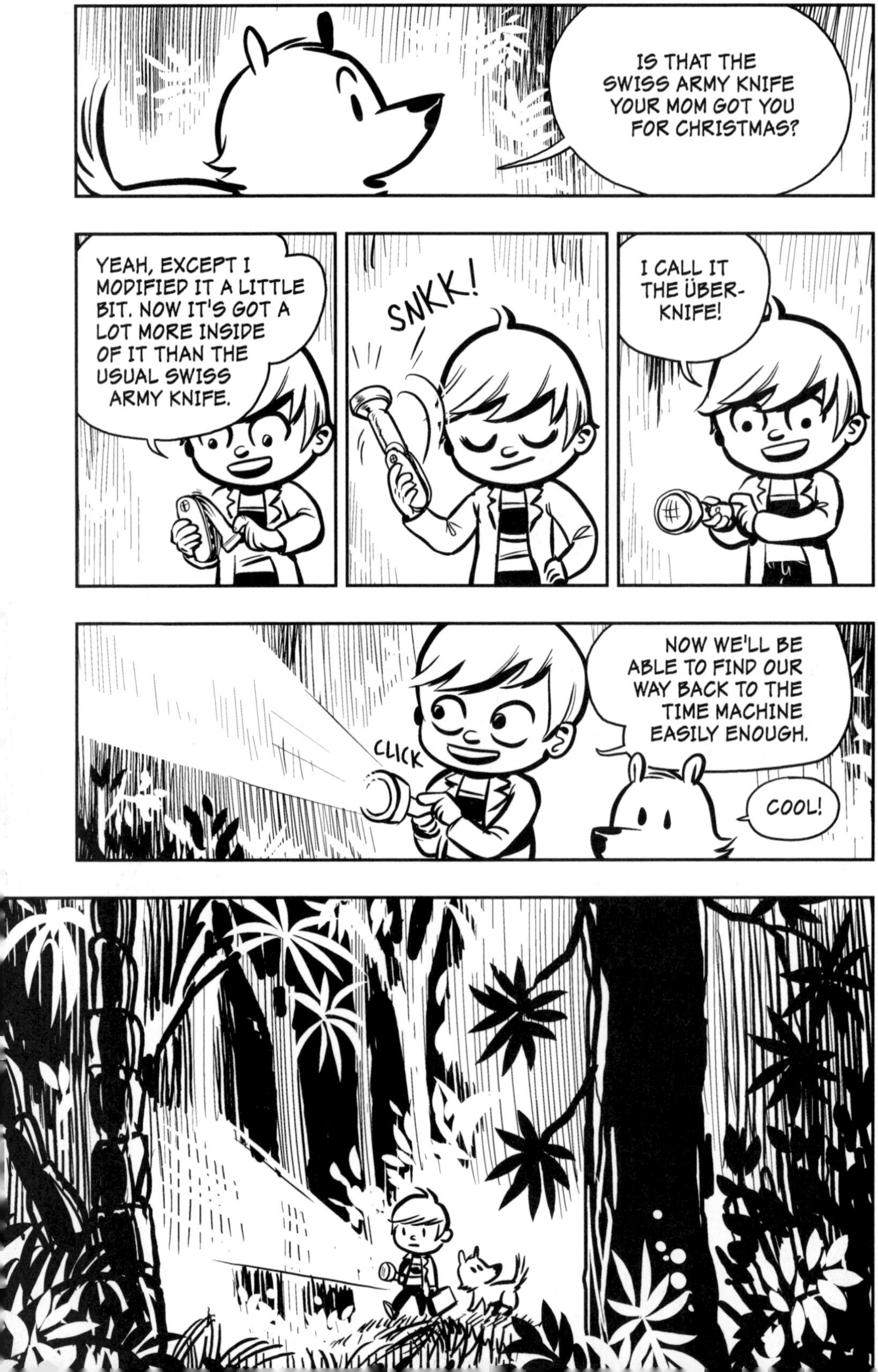
IS THAT THE SWISS ARMY KNIFE YOUR MOM GOT YOU FOR CHRISTMAS?
YEAH, EXCEPT I MODIFIED IT A LITTLE BIT. NOW IT'S GOT A LOT MORE INSIDE OF IT THAN THE USUAL SWISS ARMY KNIFE.
SNKK!
I CALL IT THE ÜBER-KNIFE!
CLICK
NOW WE'LL BE ABLE TO FIND OUR WAY BACK TO THE TIME MACHINE EASILY ENOUGH.
COOL!

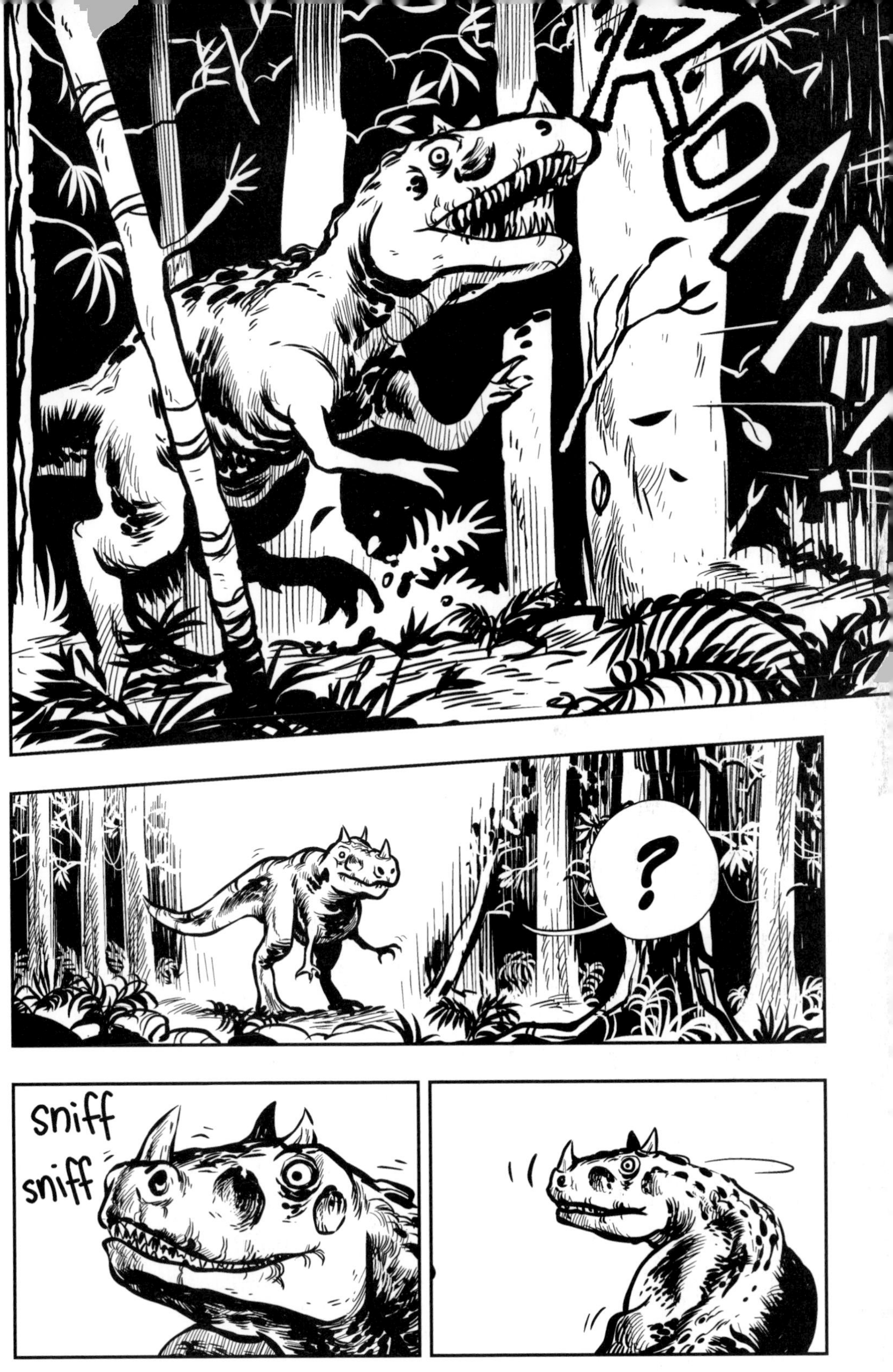
ROAA
?
sniff
sniff

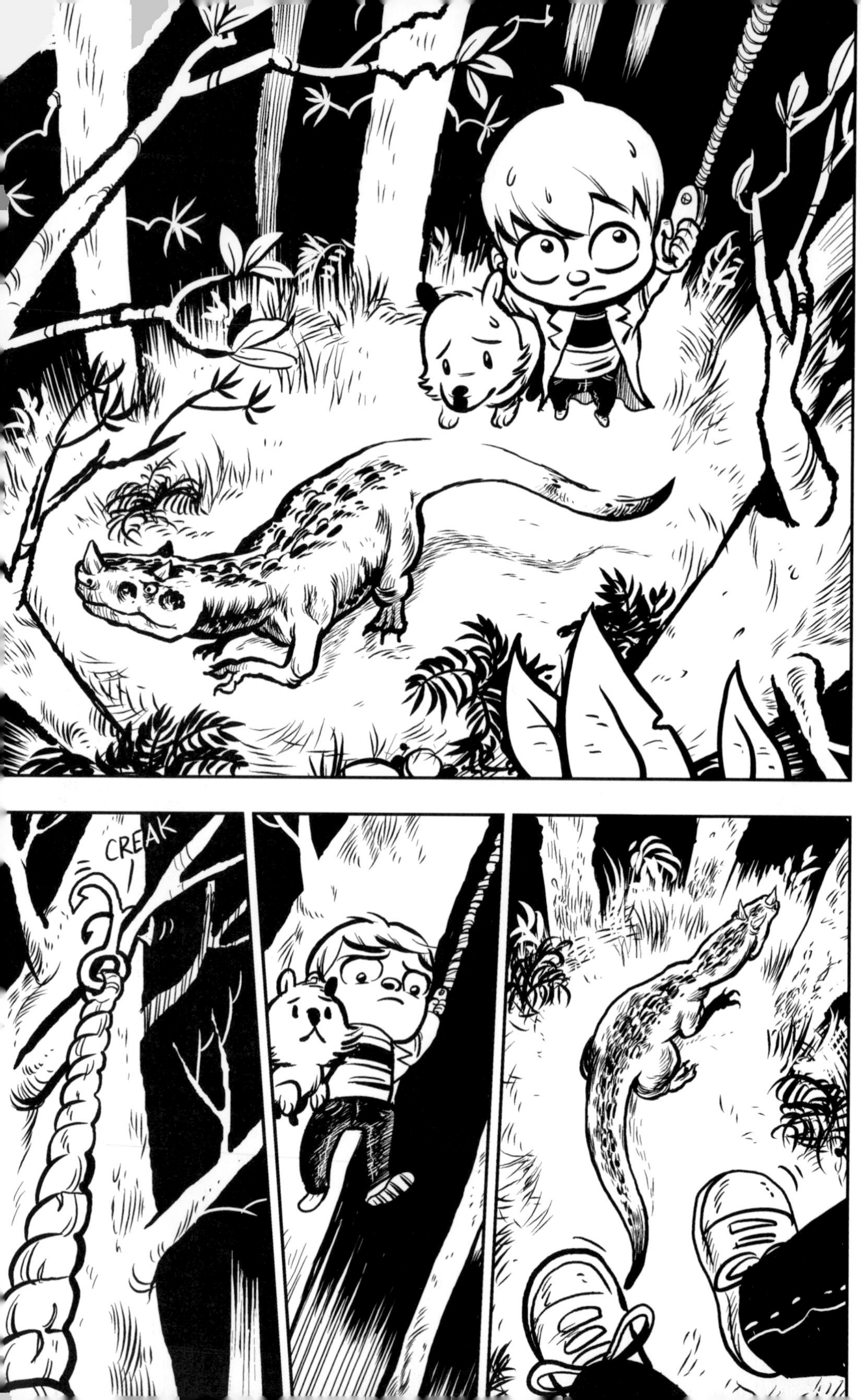
CREAK

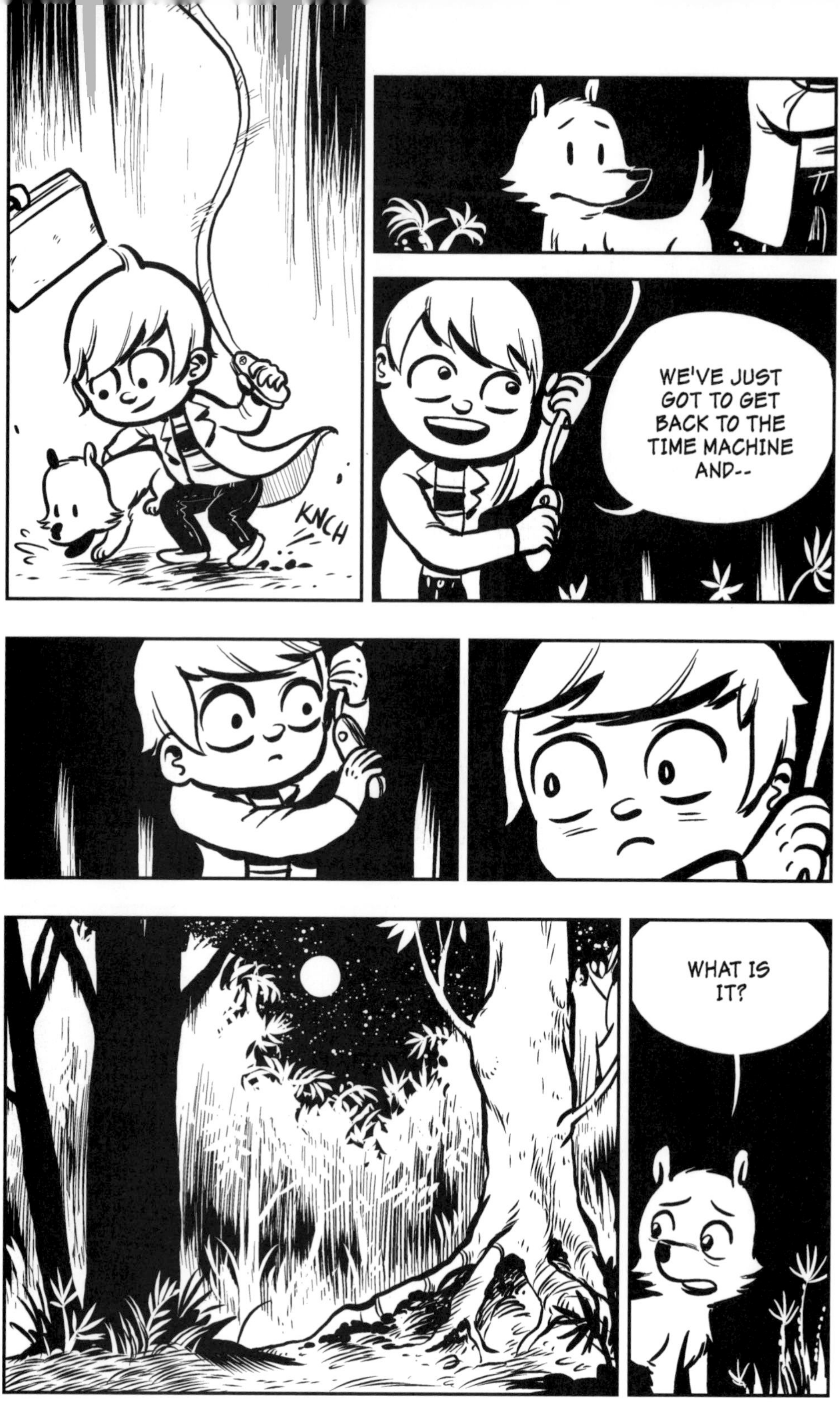
KNCH
WE'VE JUST GOT TO GET BACK TO THE TIME MACHINE AND--
WHAT IS IT?

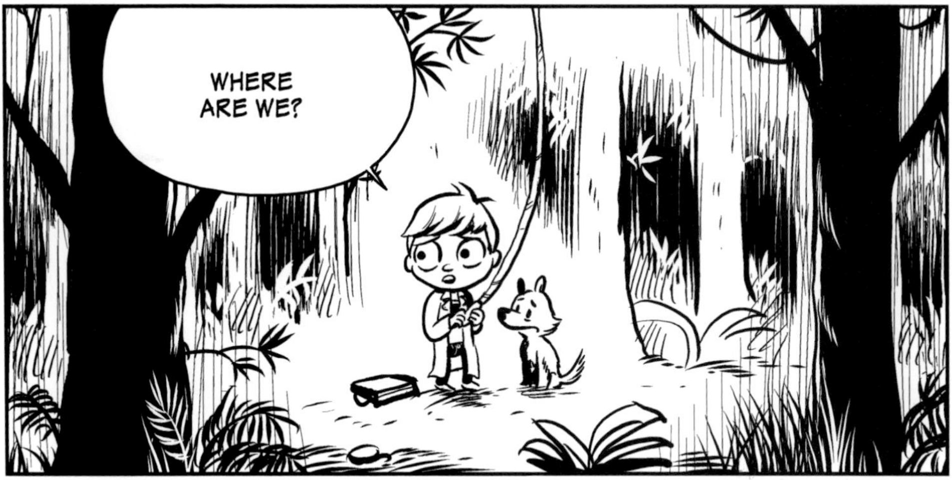
WHERE ARE WE?

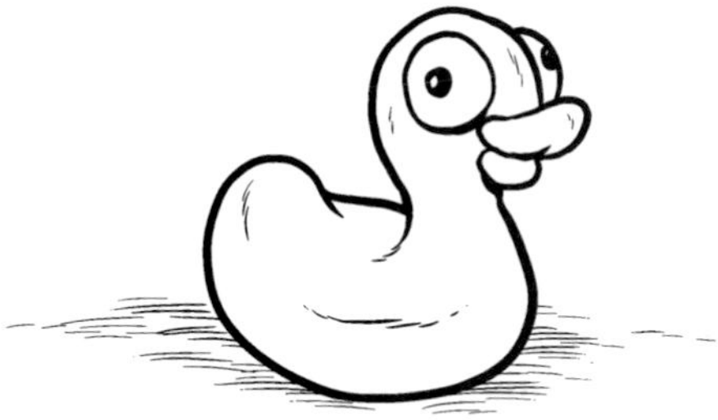

CHAPTER 6
But Mal, Think of the Omelets!

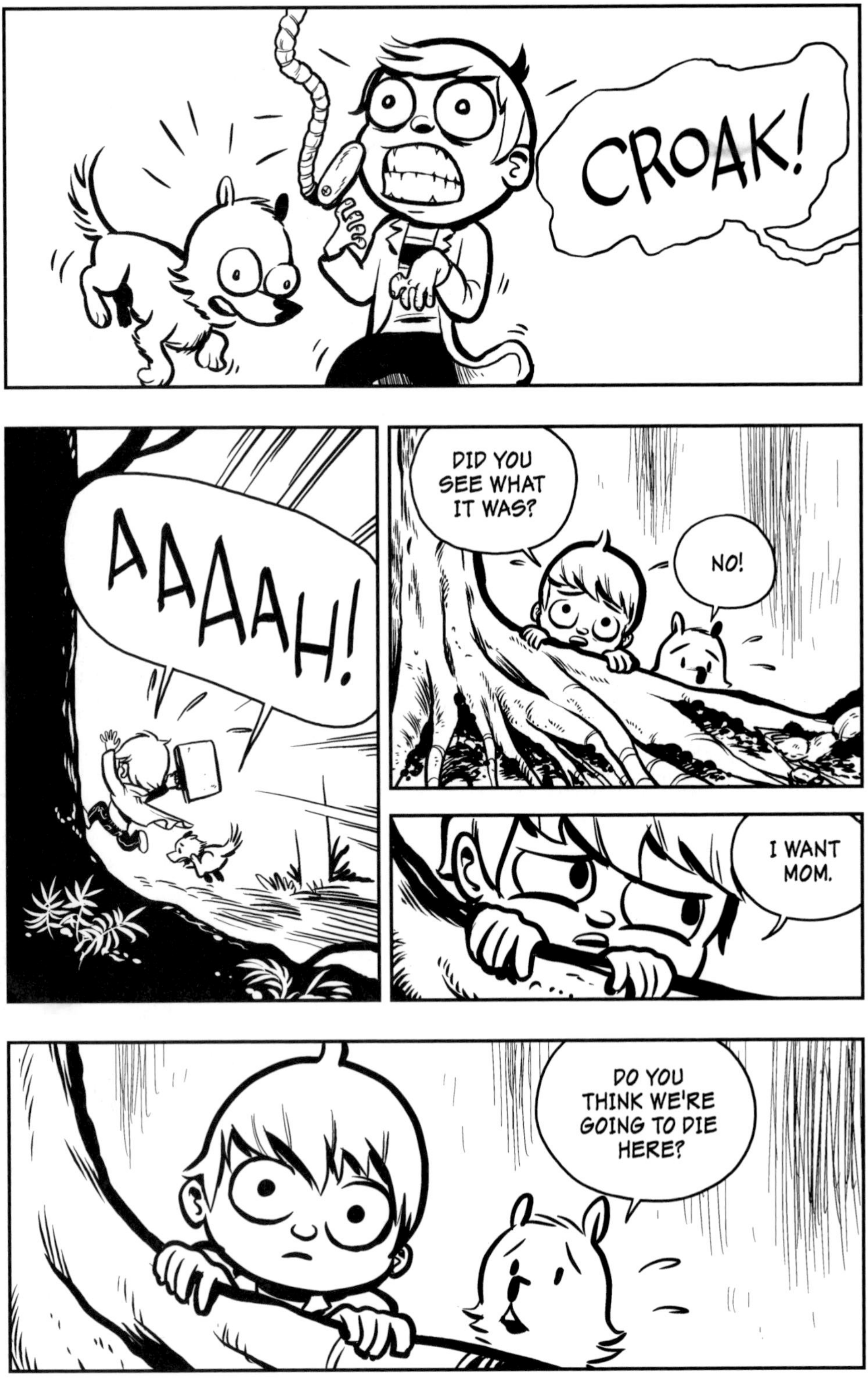
CROAK!
AAAAH!
DID YOU SEE WHAT IT WAS?
NO!
I WANT MOM.
DO YOU THINK WE'RE GOING TO DIE HERE?

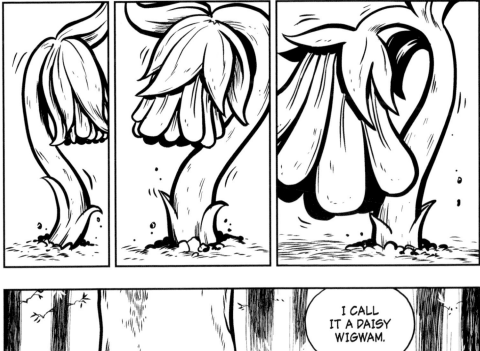

I CALL IT A DAISY WIGWAM.

QUICK, GET INSIDE! I THINK I JUST FELT A RAINDROP!

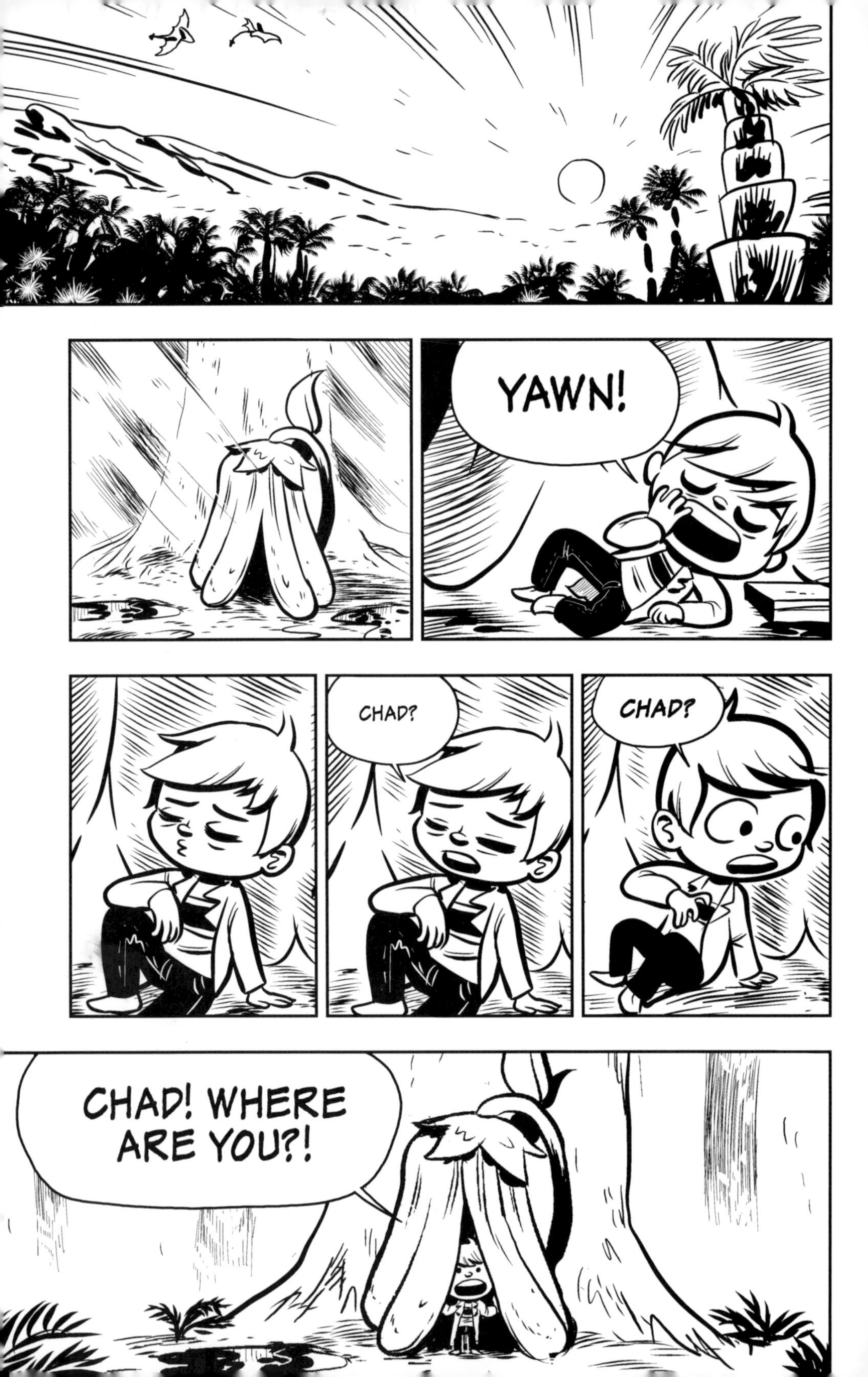
YAWN!
CHAD?
CHAD?
CHAD! WHERE ARE YOU?!

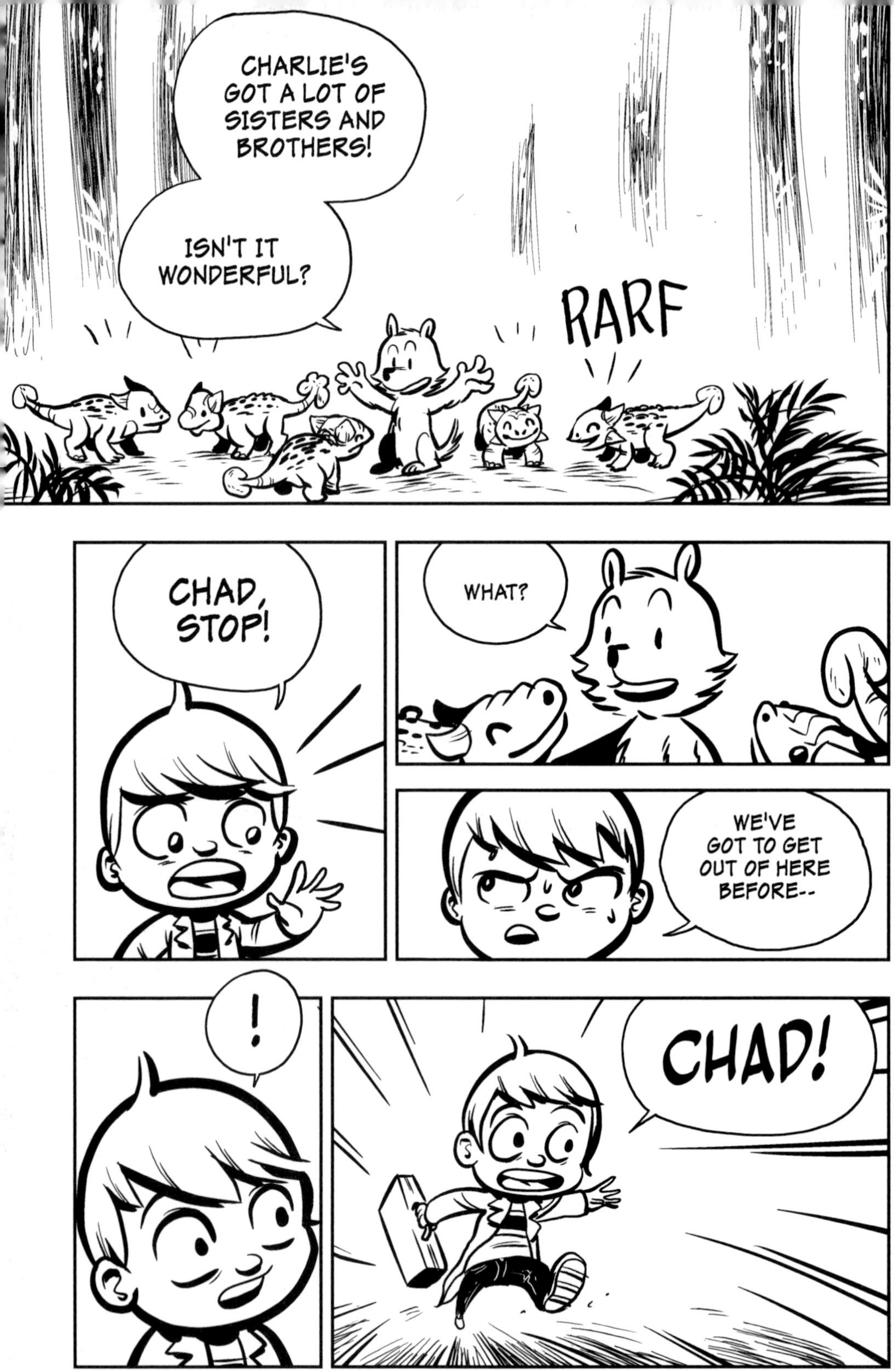
CHARLIE'S GOT A LOT OF SISTERS AND BROTHERS!
ISN'T IT WONDERFUL?
RARF
CHAD, STOP!
WHAT?
WE'VE GOT TO GET OUT OF HERE BEFORE--
!
CHAD!

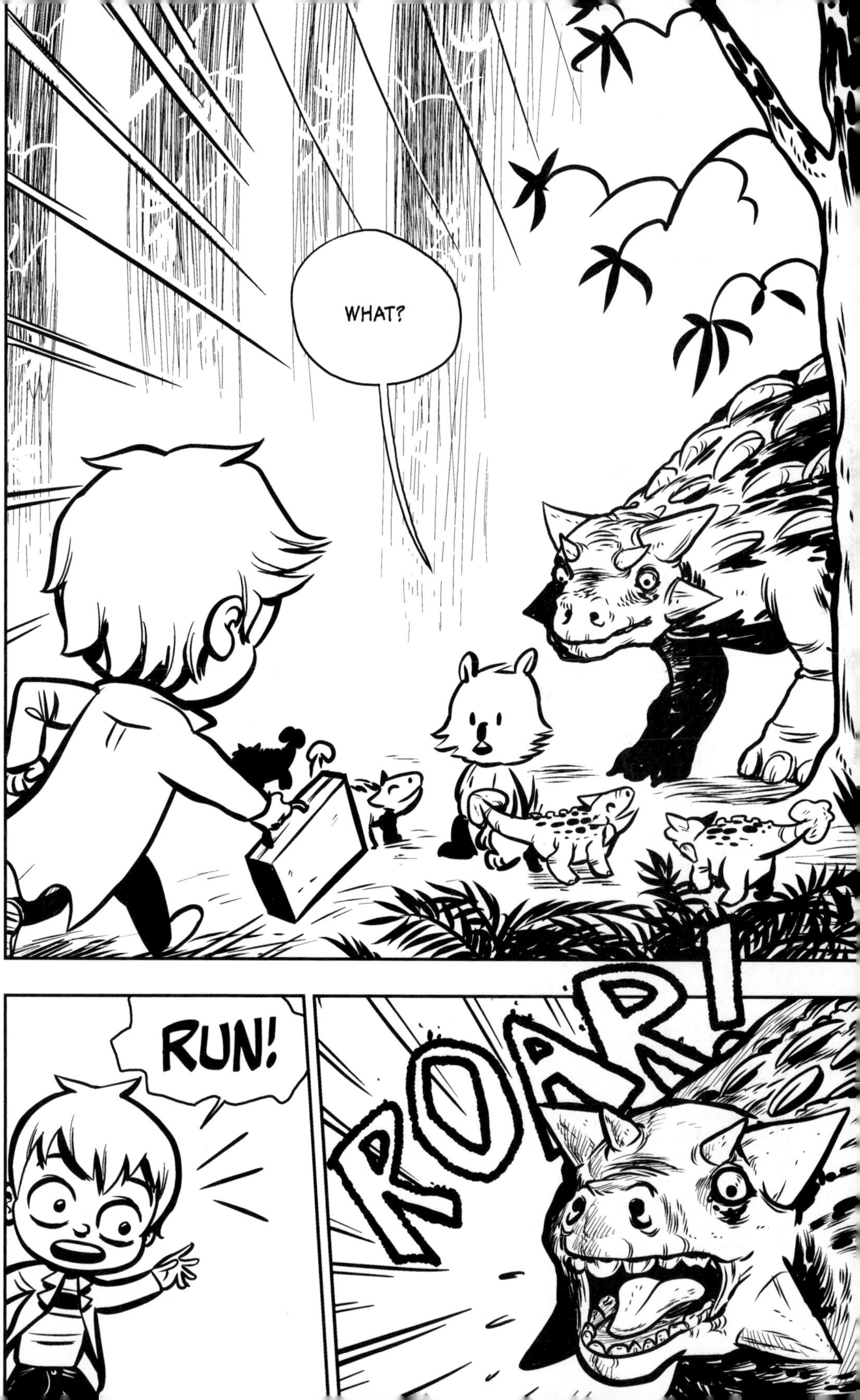
WHAT?
RUN!
ROAR!

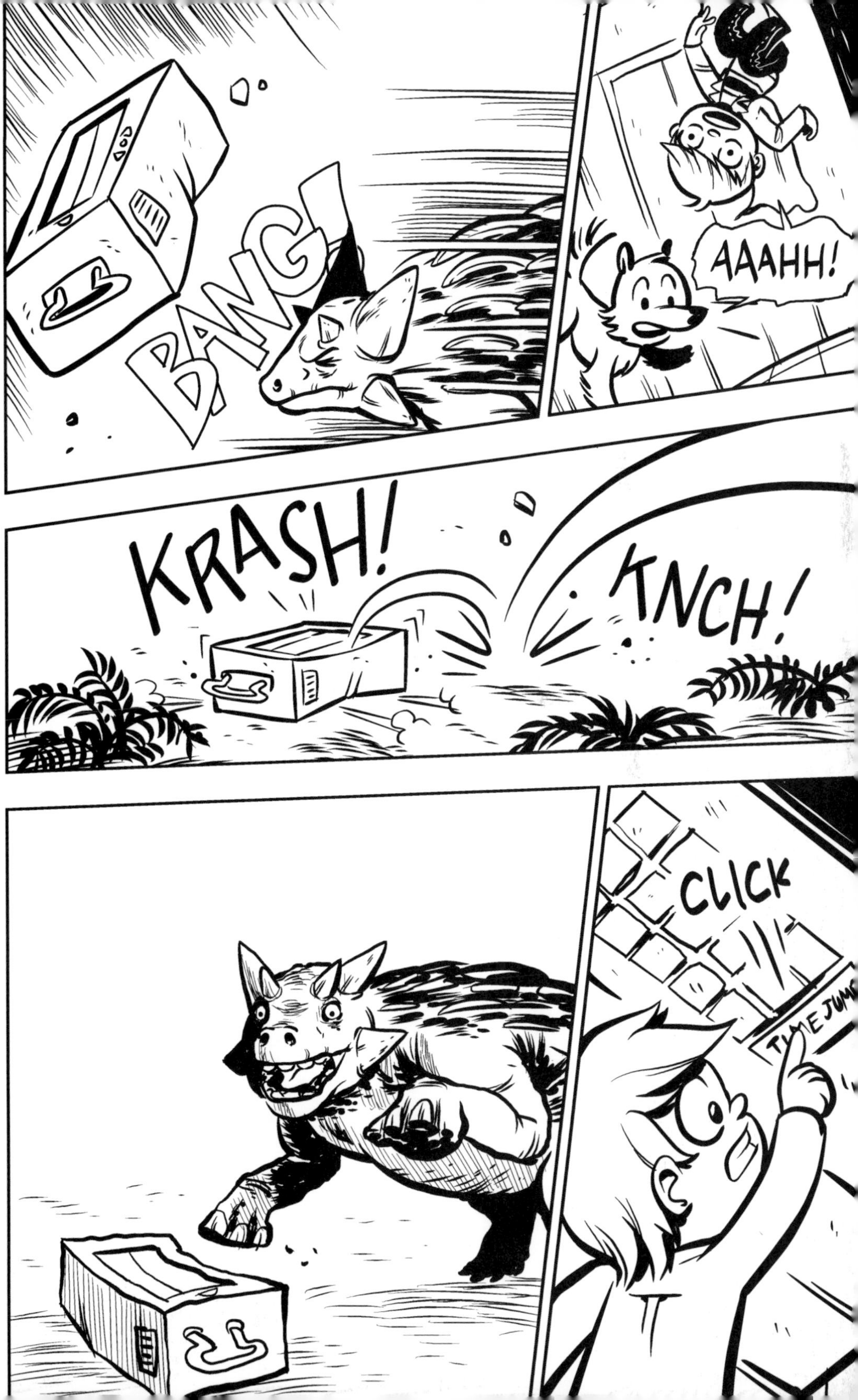
BANG!
AAAHH!
KRASH!
KNCH!
CLICK

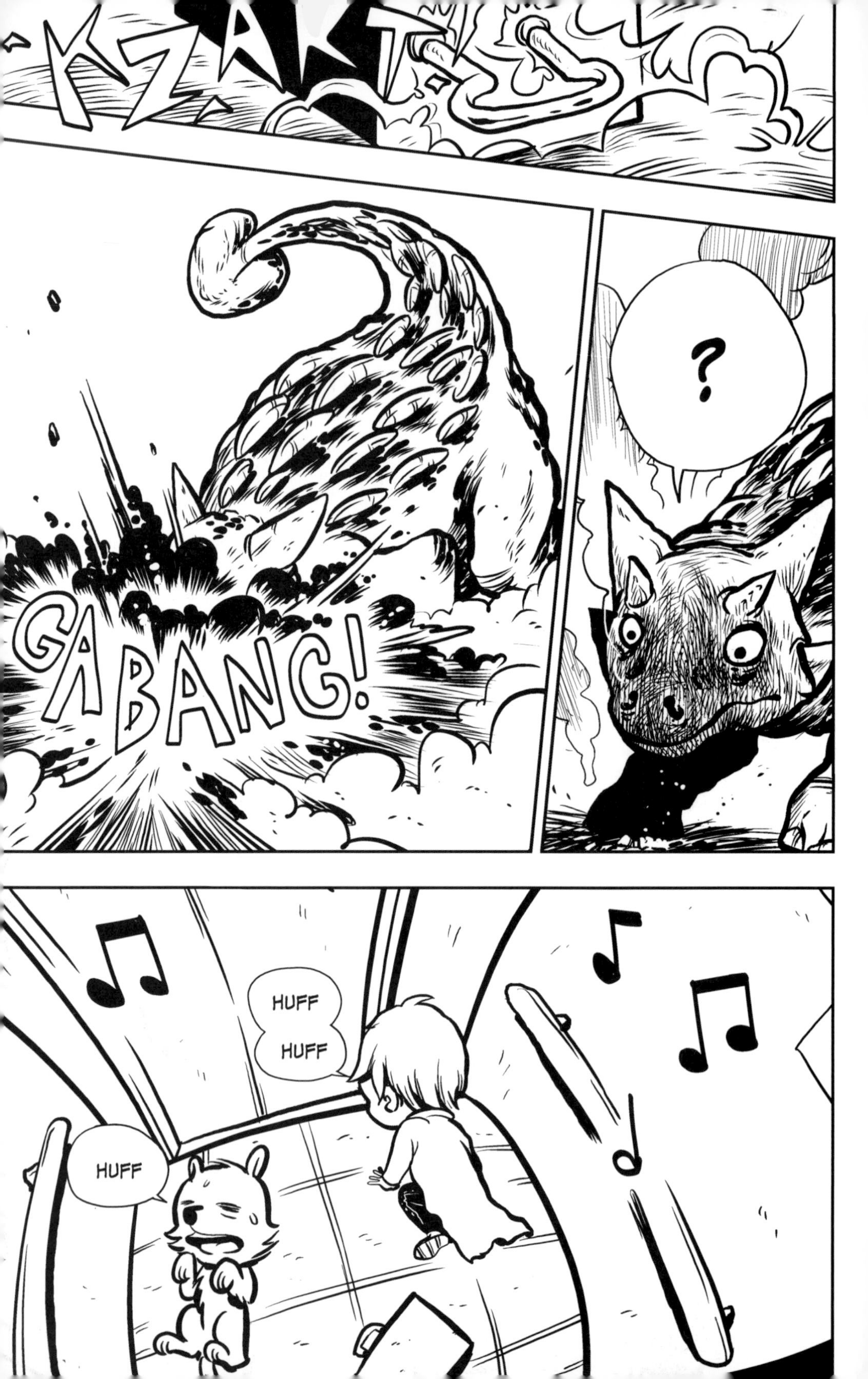
KZAKT
GABANG!
?
HUFF
HUFF
HUFF

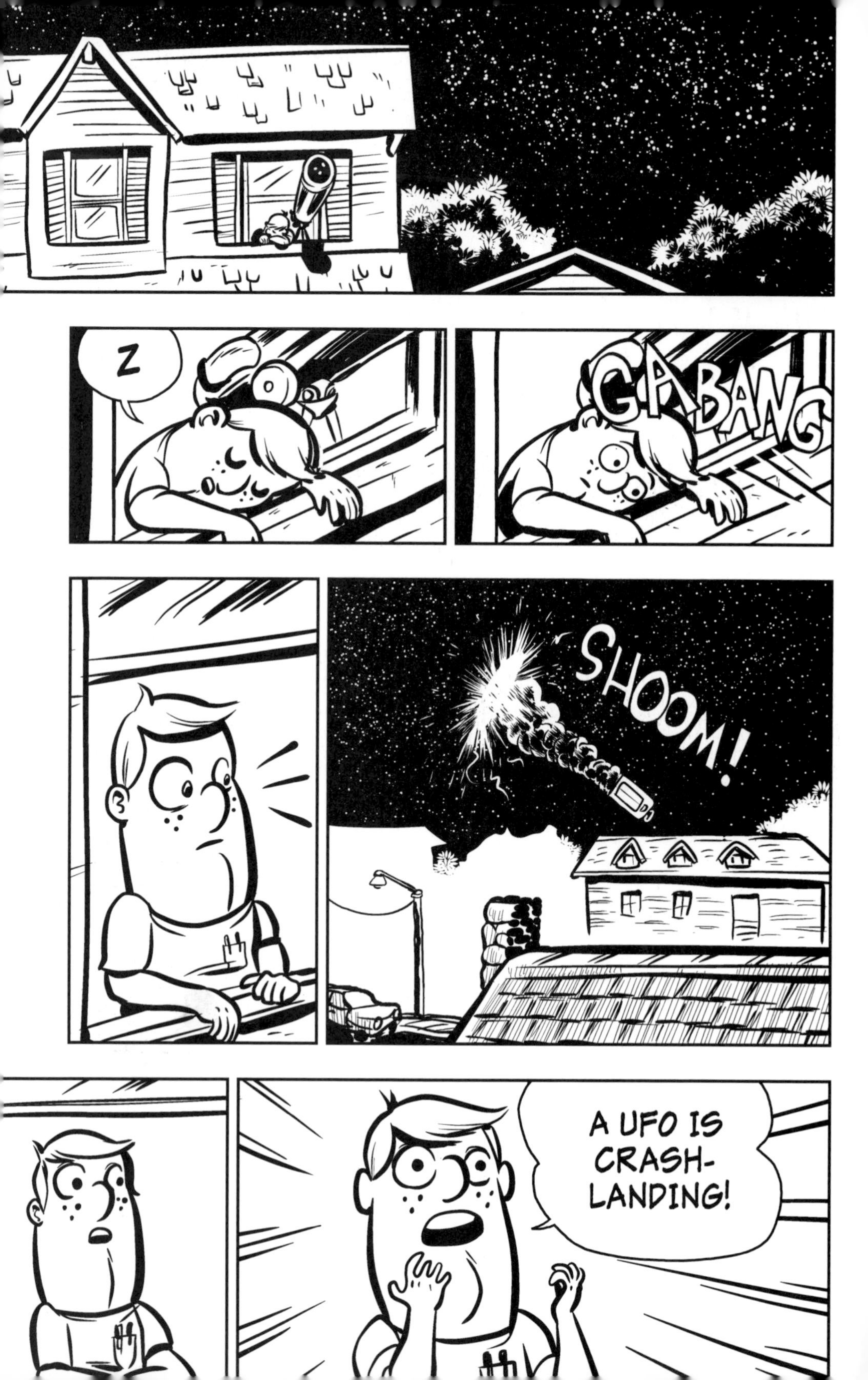
Z
GABANG
SHOOM!
A UFO IS CRASH-LANDING!

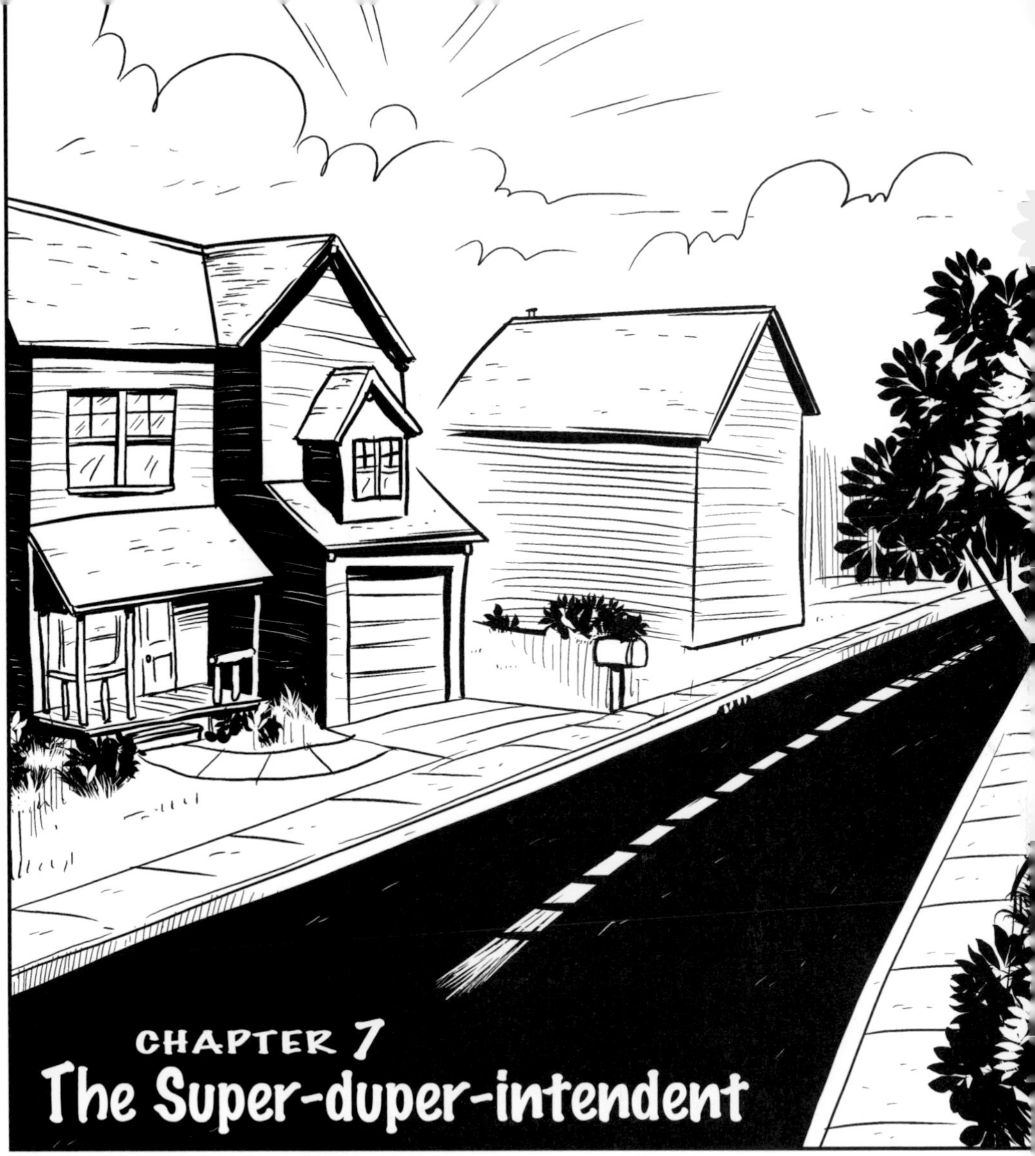
CHAPTER 7
The Super-duper-intendent

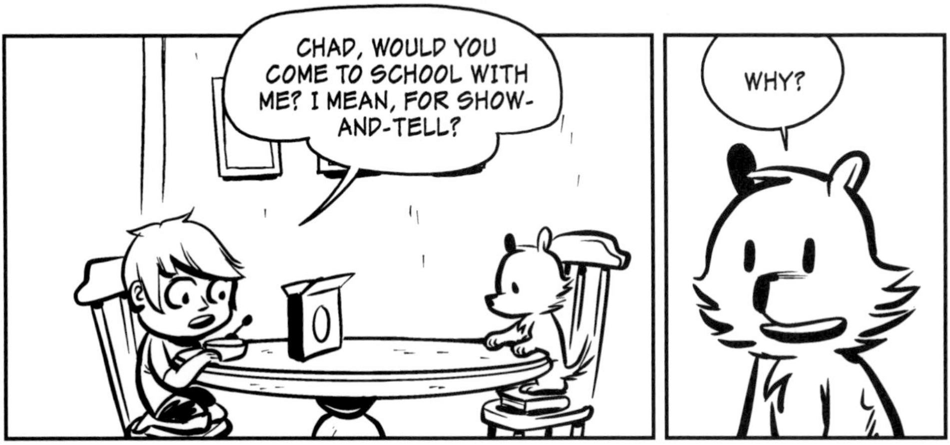
CHAD, WOULD YOU COME TO SCHOOL WITH ME? I MEAN, FOR SHOW-AND-TELL?
WHY?

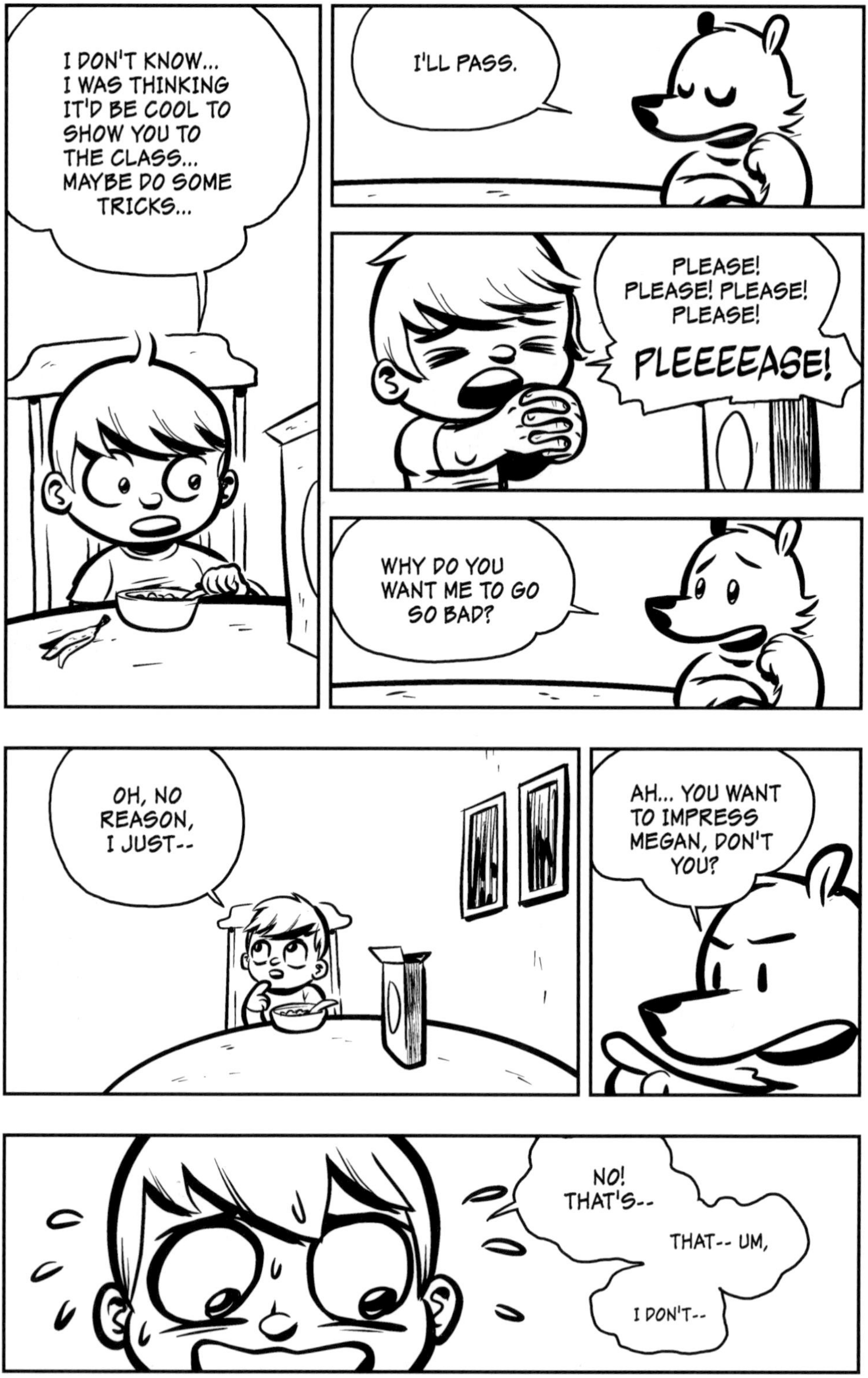
I DON'T KNOW... I WAS THINKING IT'D BE COOL TO SHOW YOU TO THE CLASS... MAYBE DO SOME TRICKS...
I'LL PASS.
PLEASE! PLEASE! PLEASE! PLEASE!
PLEEEEASE!
WHY DO YOU WANT ME TO GO SO BAD?
OH, NO REASON, I JUST--
AH... YOU WANT TO IMPRESS MEGAN, DON'T YOU?
NO! THAT'S--
THAT-- UM,
I DON'T--

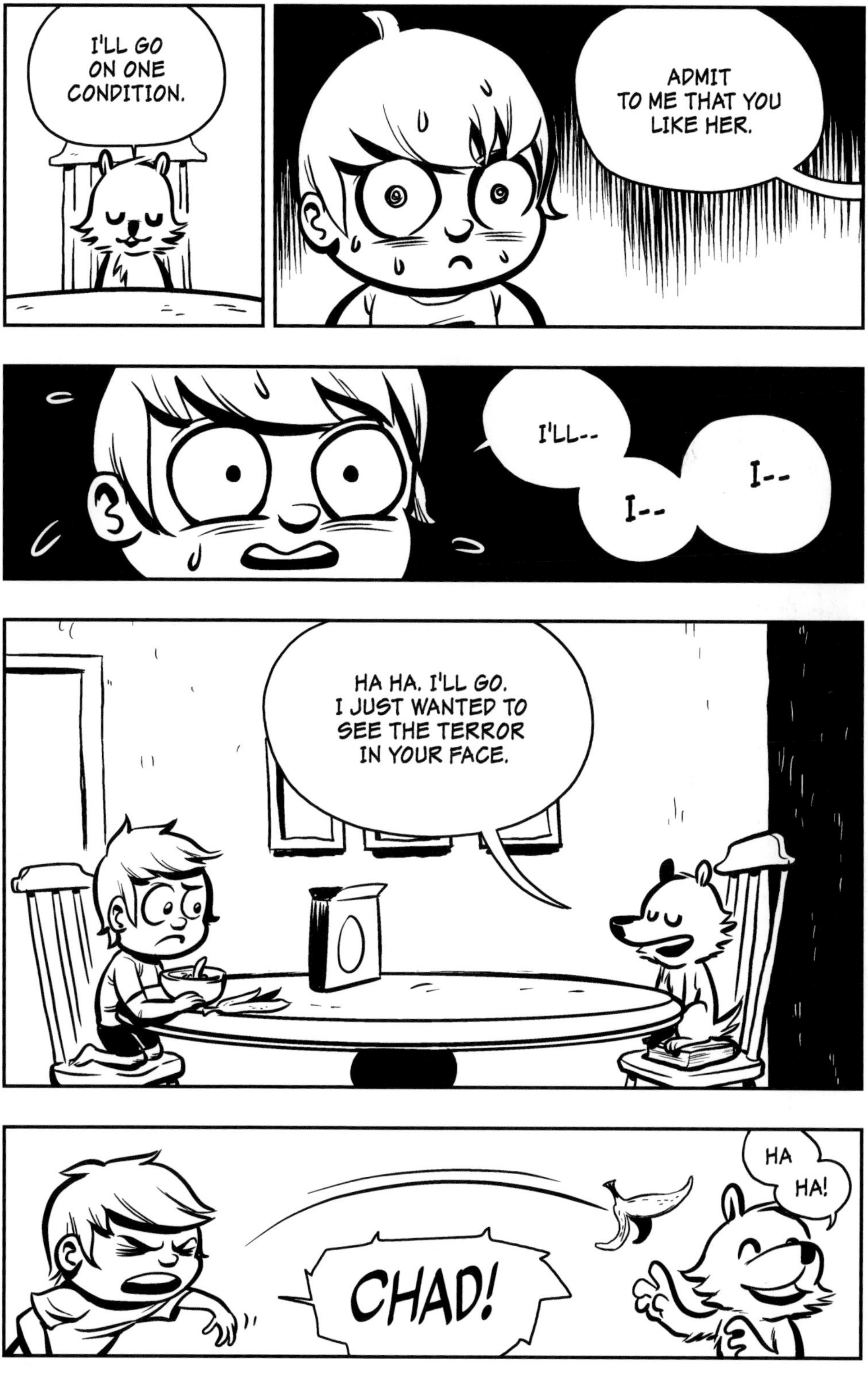
I'LL GO
ON ONE
CONDITION.
ADMIT
TO ME THAT YOU
LIKE HER.
I'LL--
I--
I--
HA HA. I'LL GO.
I JUST WANTED TO
SEE THE TERROR
IN YOUR FACE.
CHAD!
HA
HA!

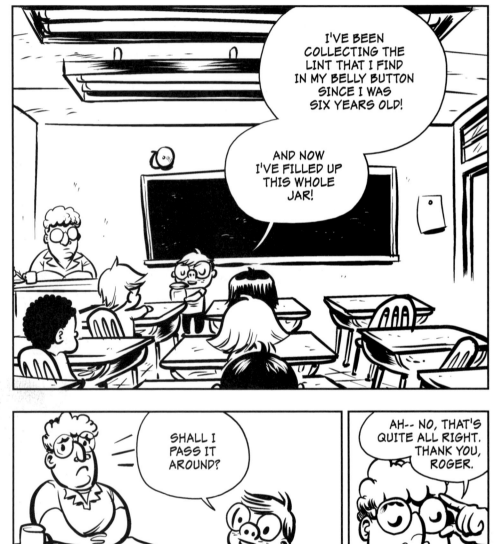

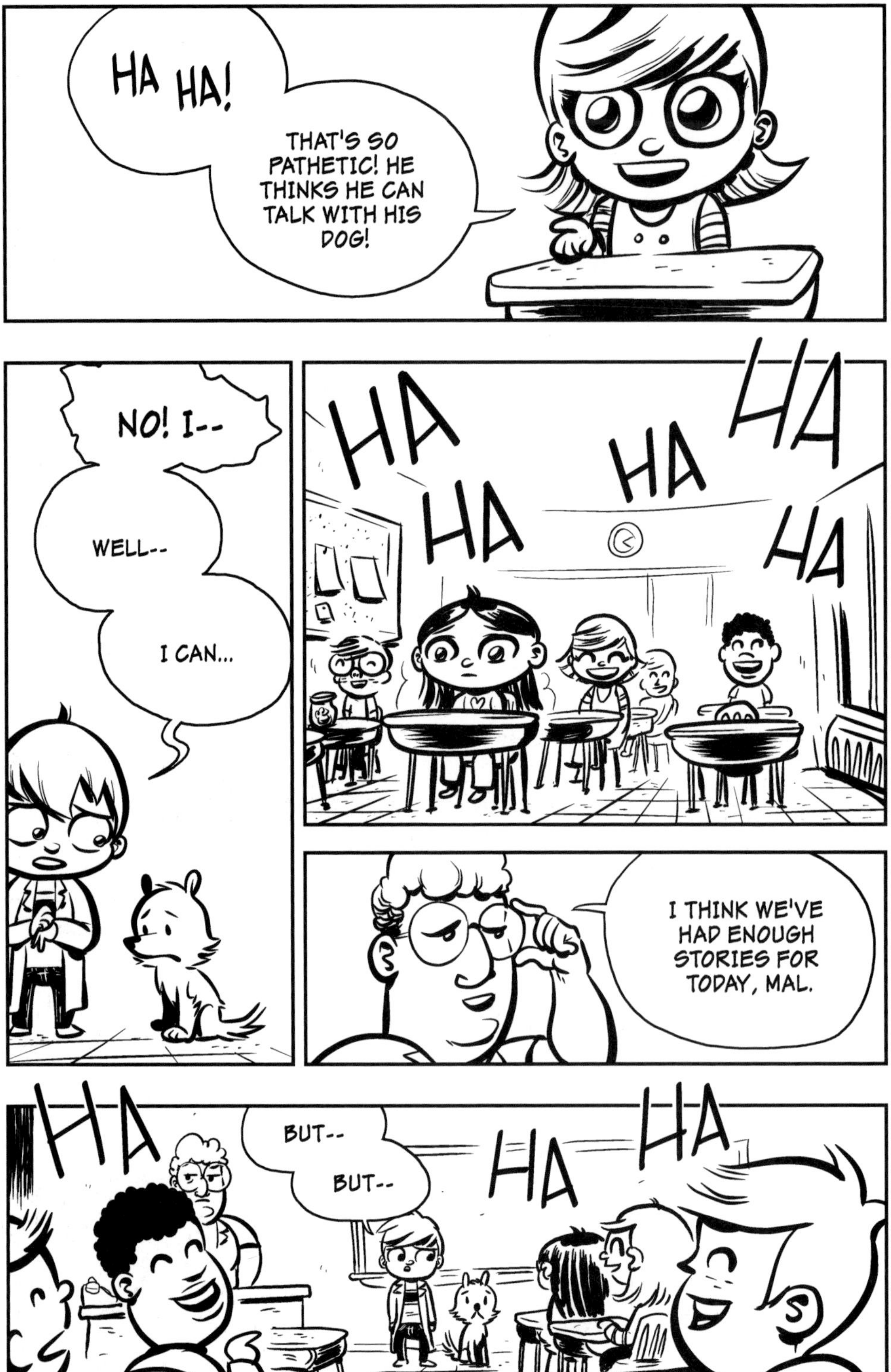
HA HA!
THAT'S SO PATHETIC! HE THINKS HE CAN TALK WITH HIS DOG!
NO! I--
WELL--
I CAN...
HA HA HA HA HA HA
I THINK WE'VE HAD ENOUGH STORIES FOR TODAY, MAL.
HA
BUT--
BUT--
HA HA

167

169

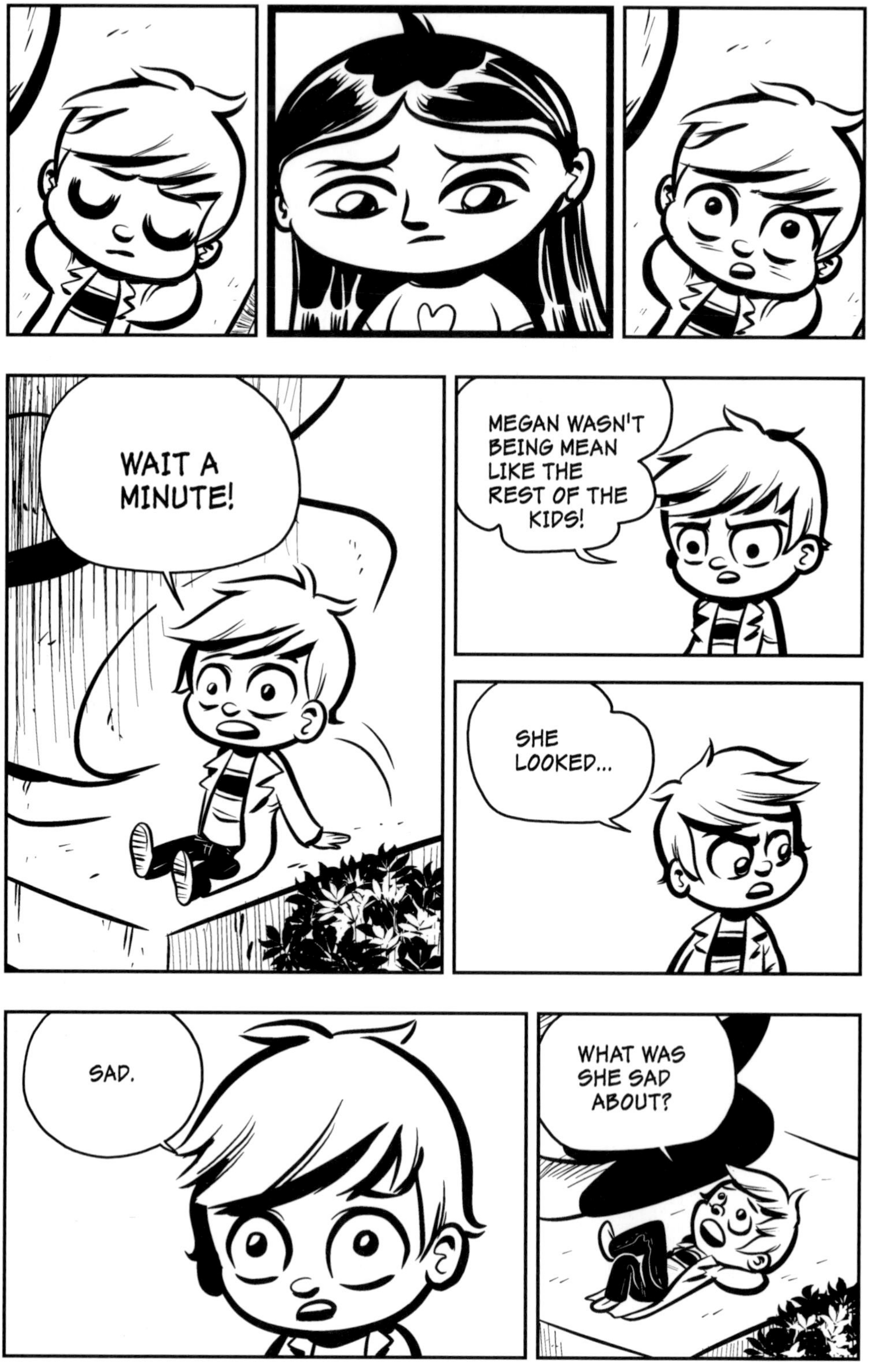
WAIT A MINUTE!
MEGAN WASN'T BEING MEAN LIKE THE REST OF THE KIDS!
SHE LOOKED...
SAD.
WHAT WAS SHE SAD ABOUT?

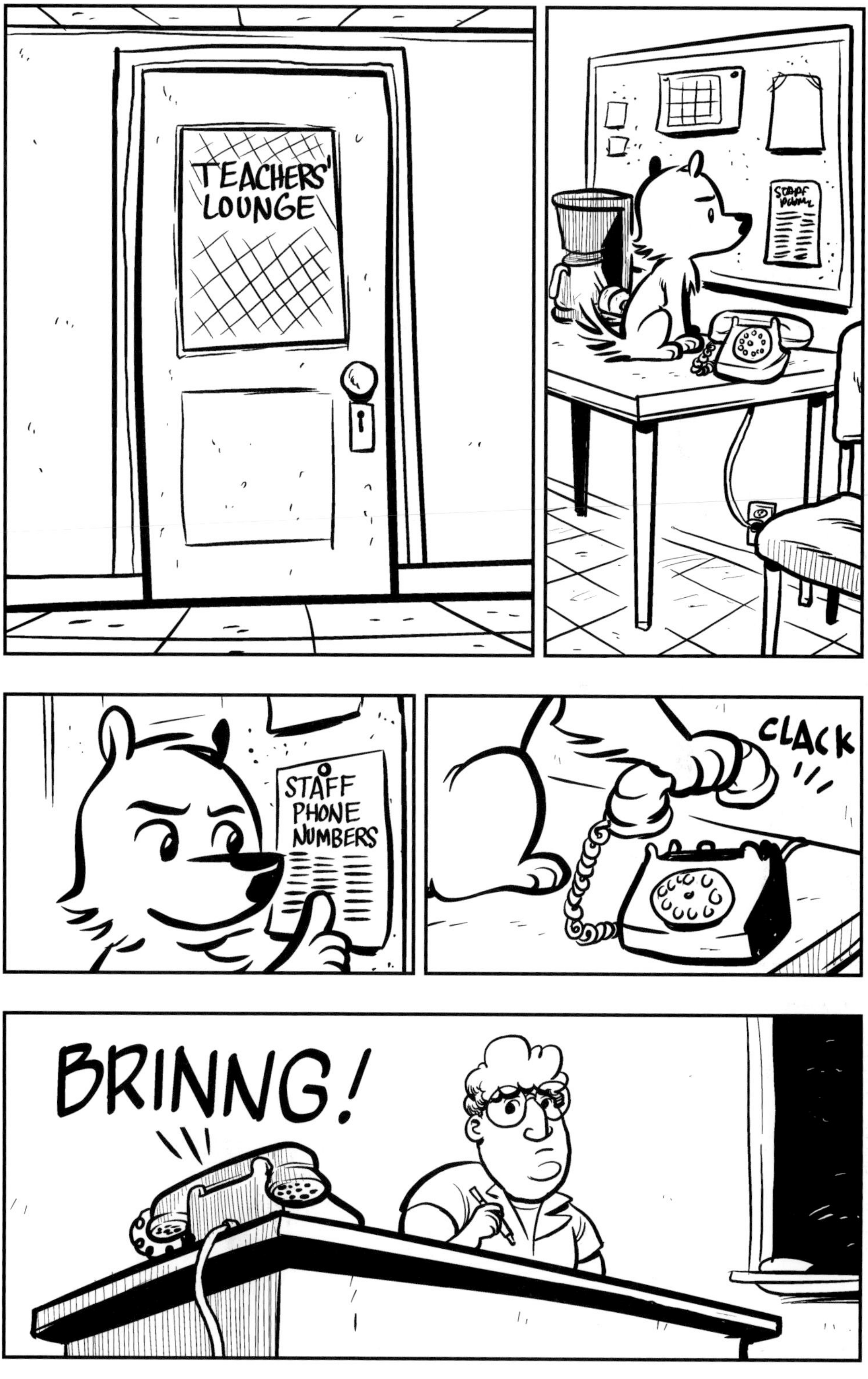
TEACHERS'
LOUNGE
STAFF
PHONE
NUMBERS
CLACK
BRINNG!

175

CHAPTER 8
Peekabooasaurus

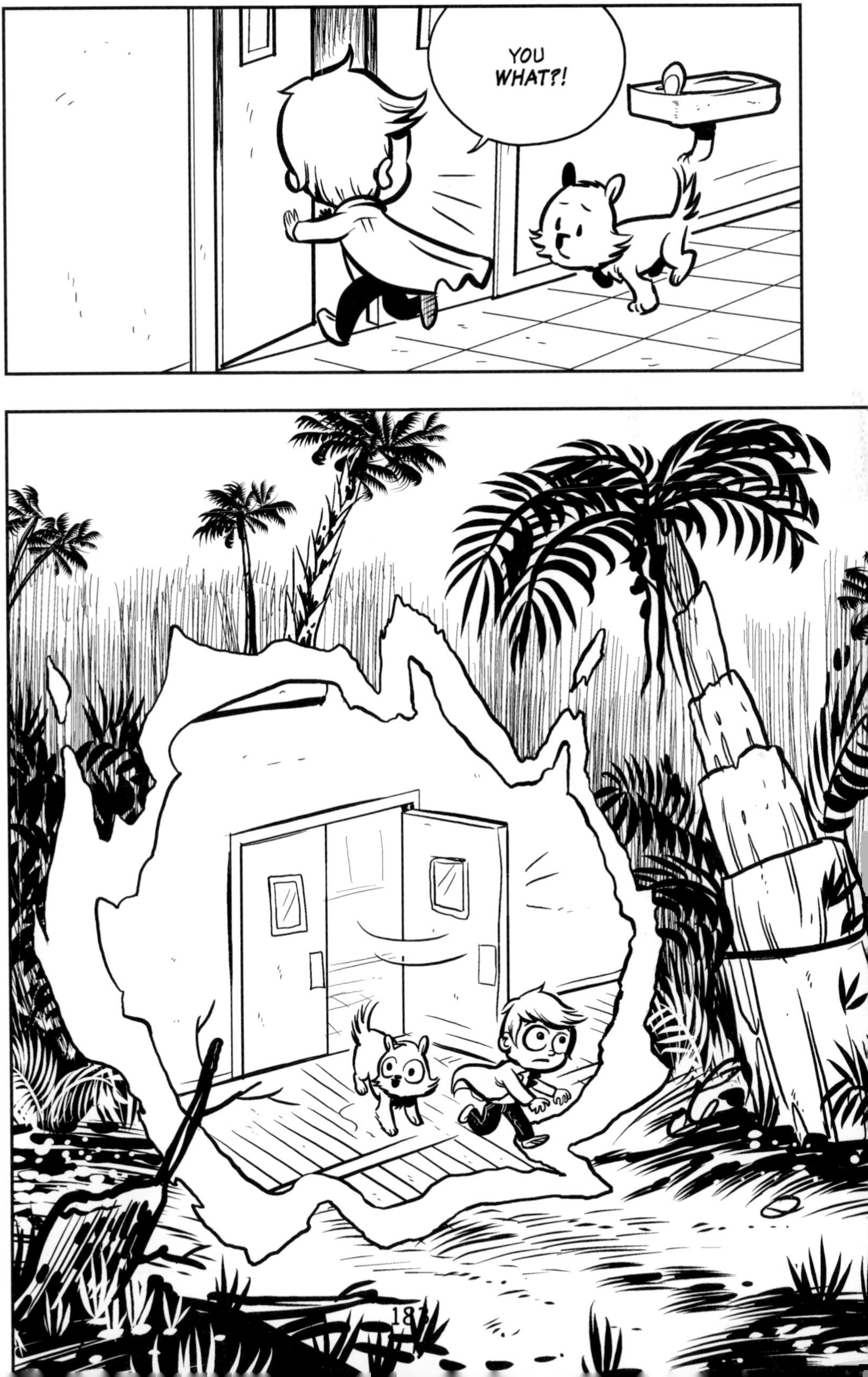
YOU WHAT?!

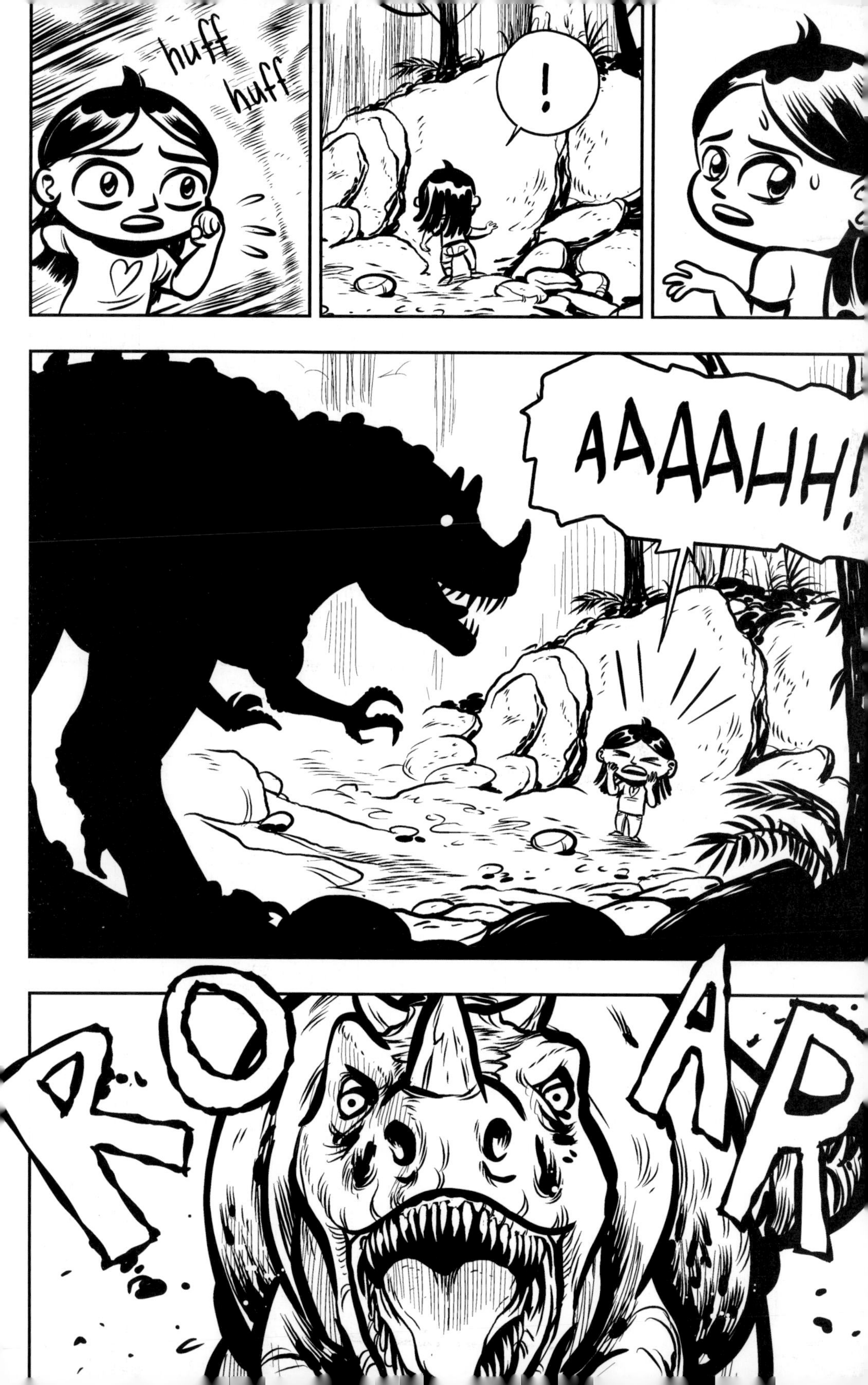
huff
huff
!
AAAAHH!
ROAR

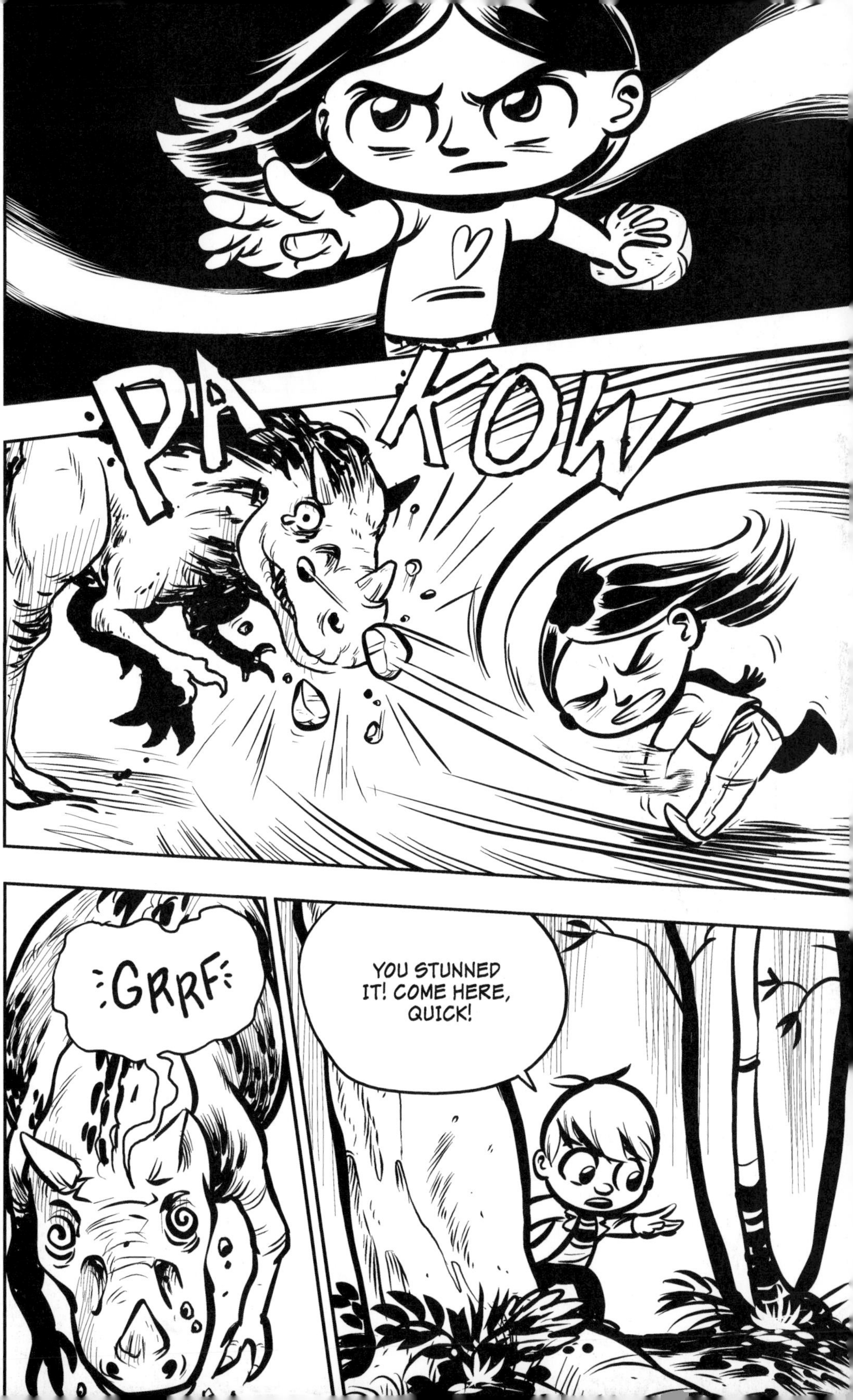
PA KOW
GRRF
YOU STUNNED IT! COME HERE, QUICK!

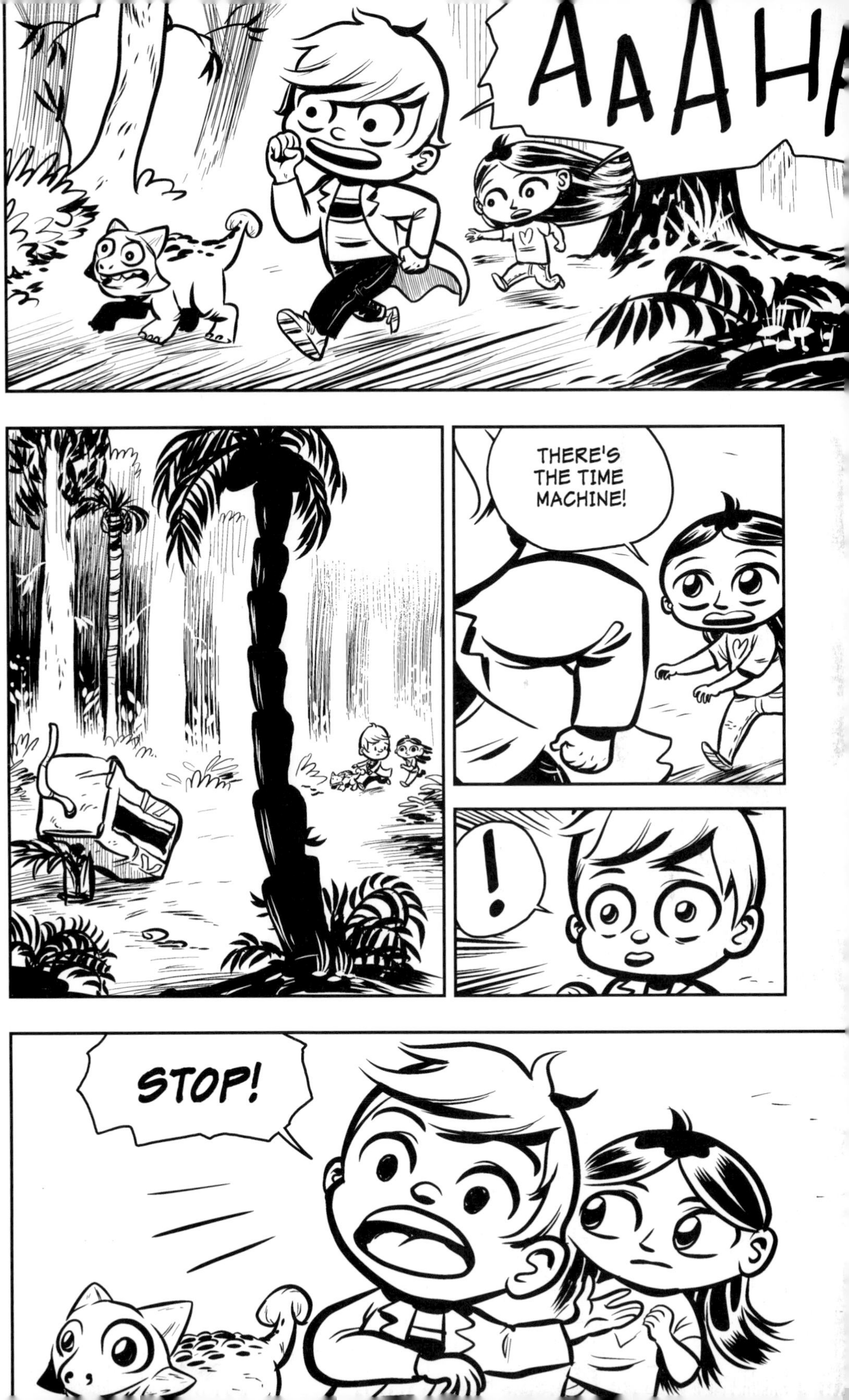
AAAHH
THERE'S THE TIME MACHINE!
!
STOP!

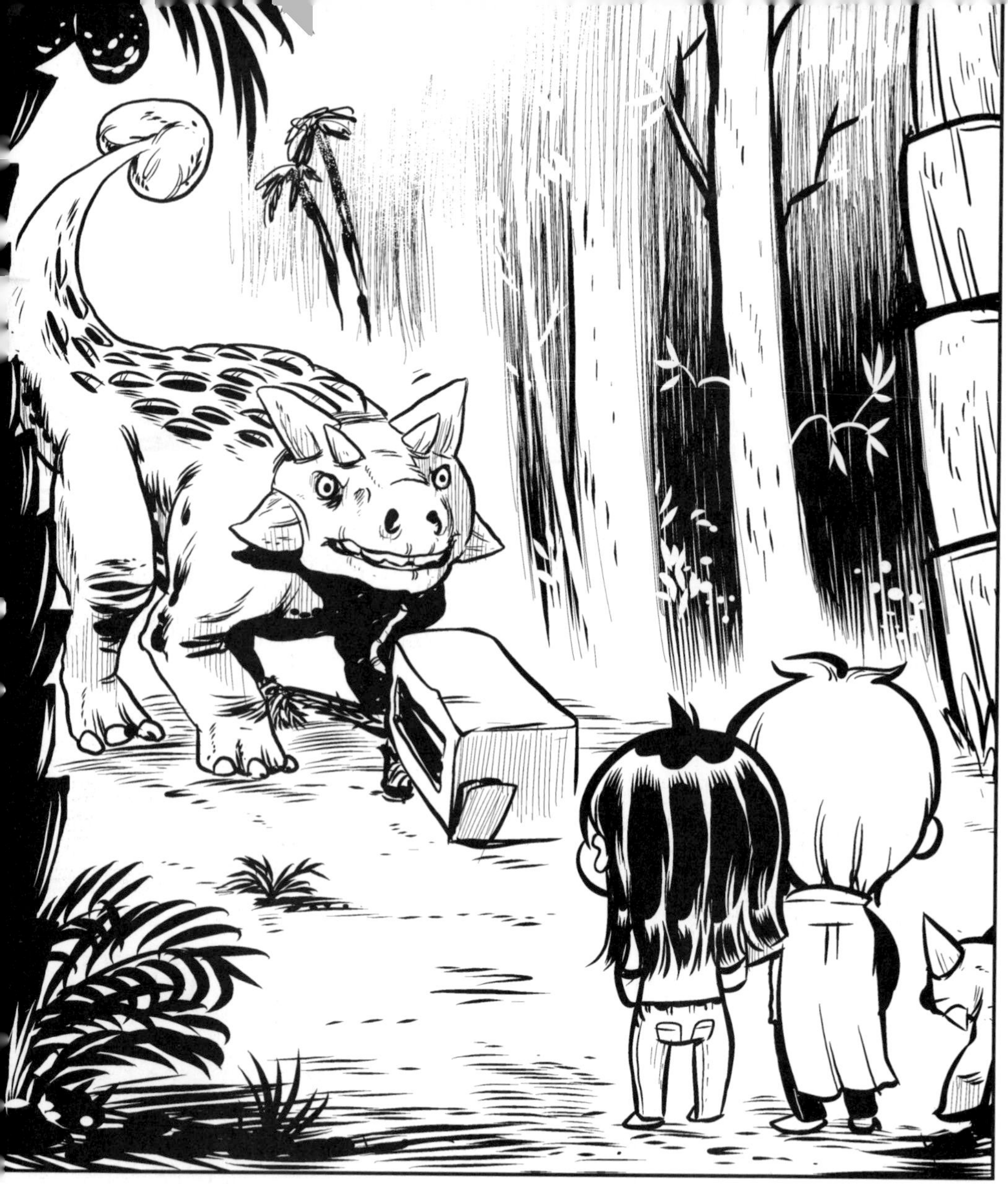

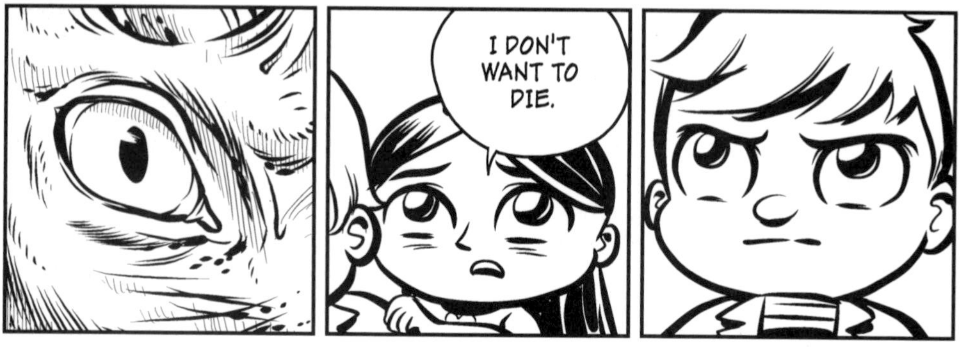
I DON'T
WANT TO
DIE.

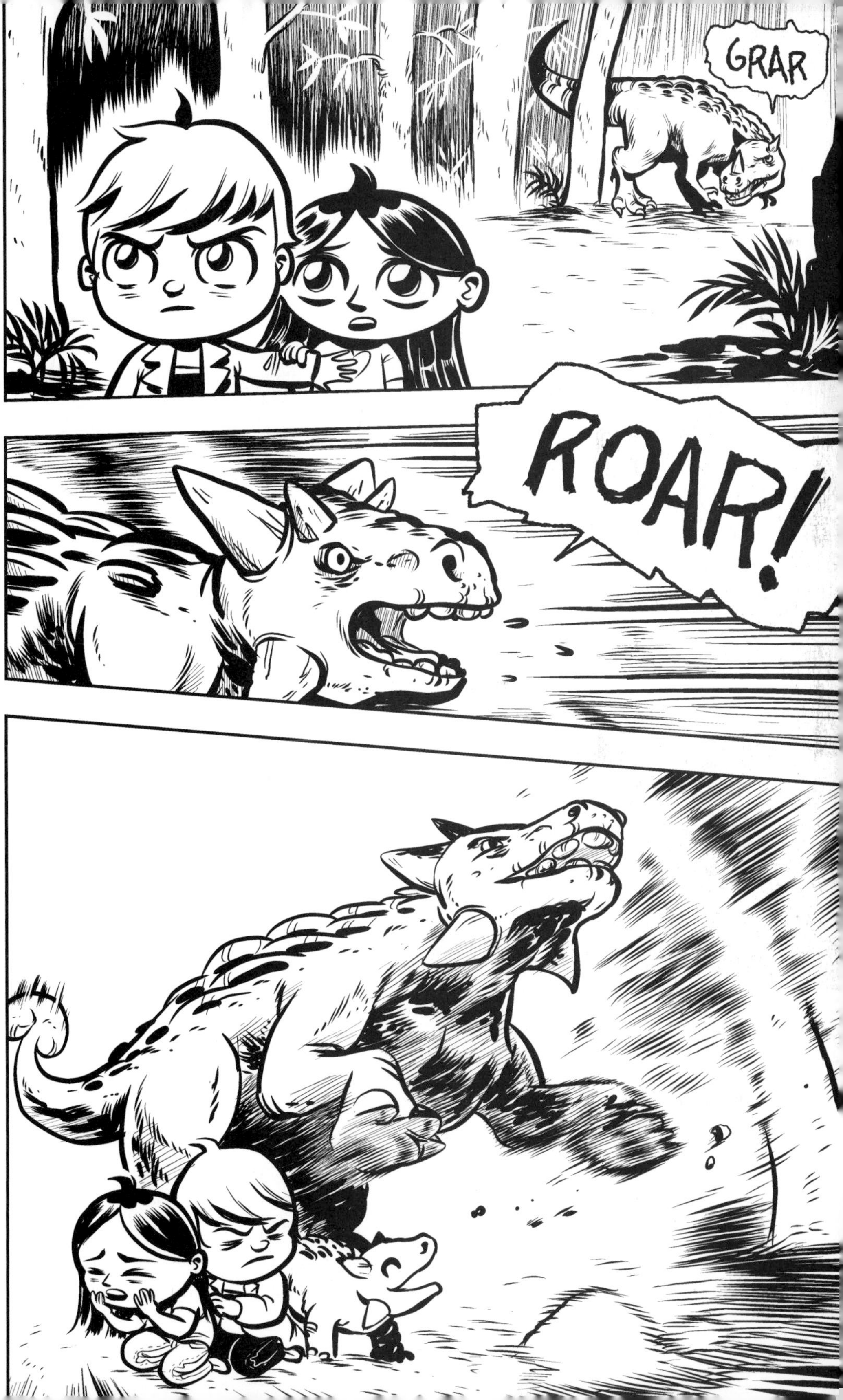
GRAR
ROAR!

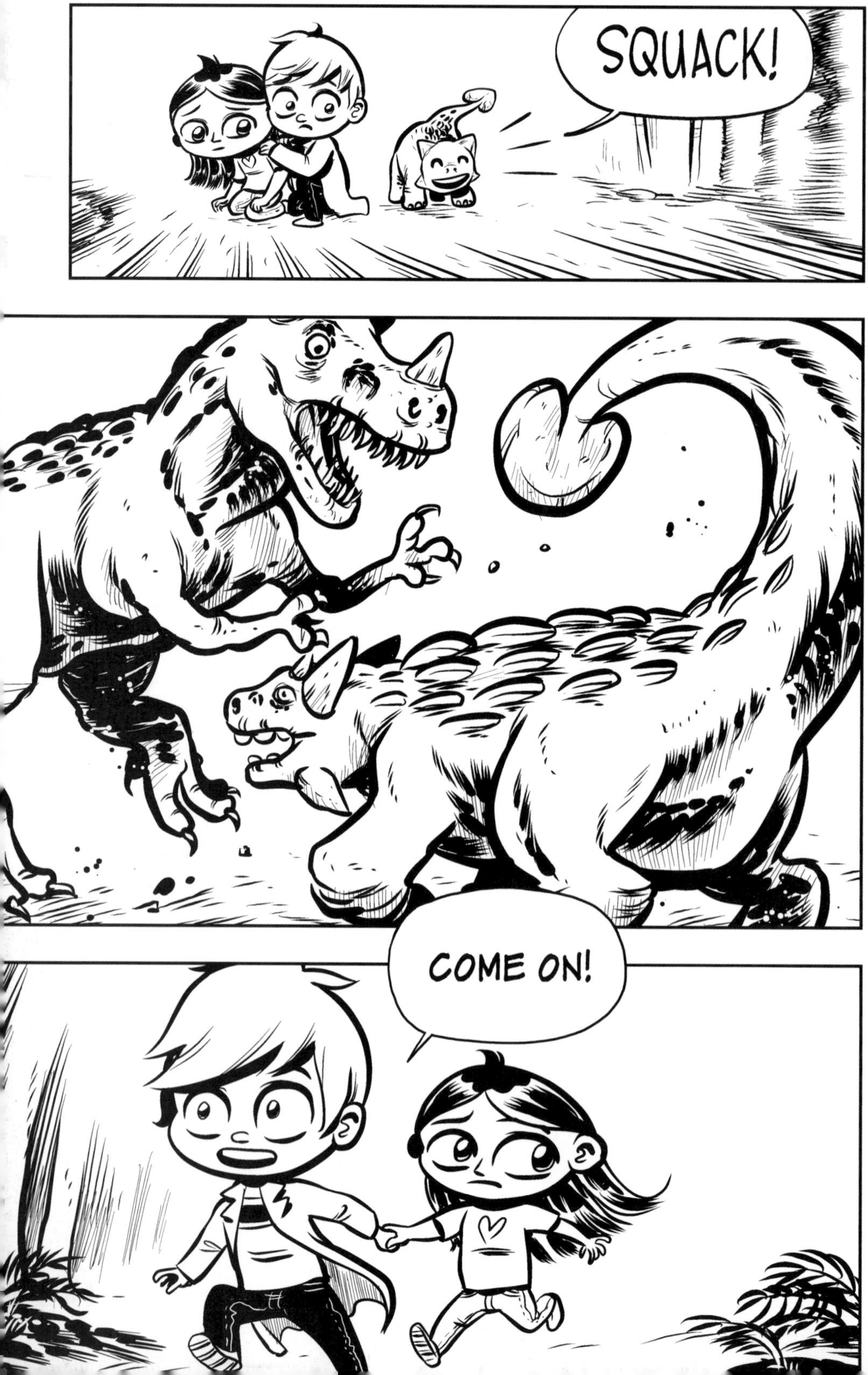
SQUACK!
COME ON!

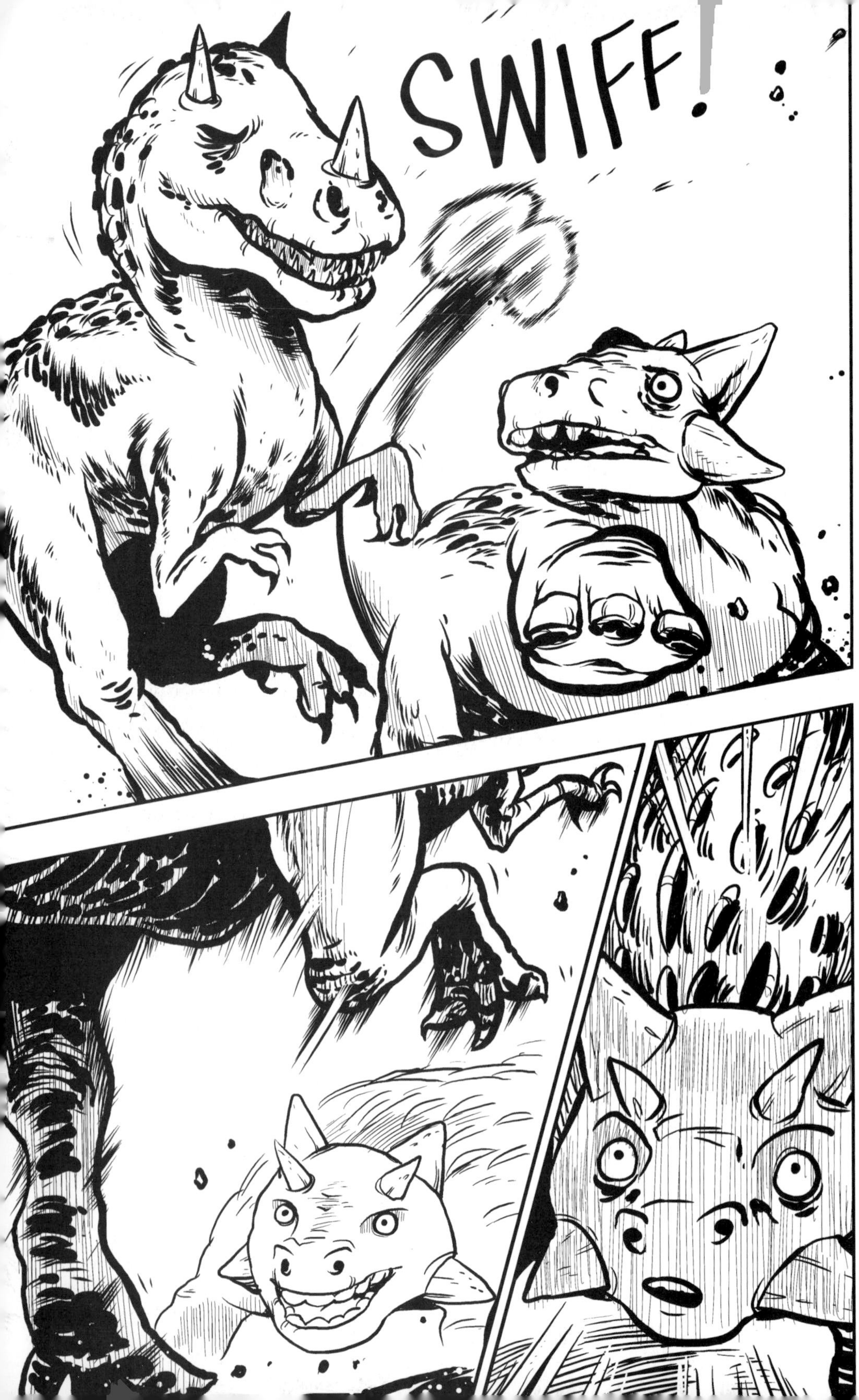
SWIFF!

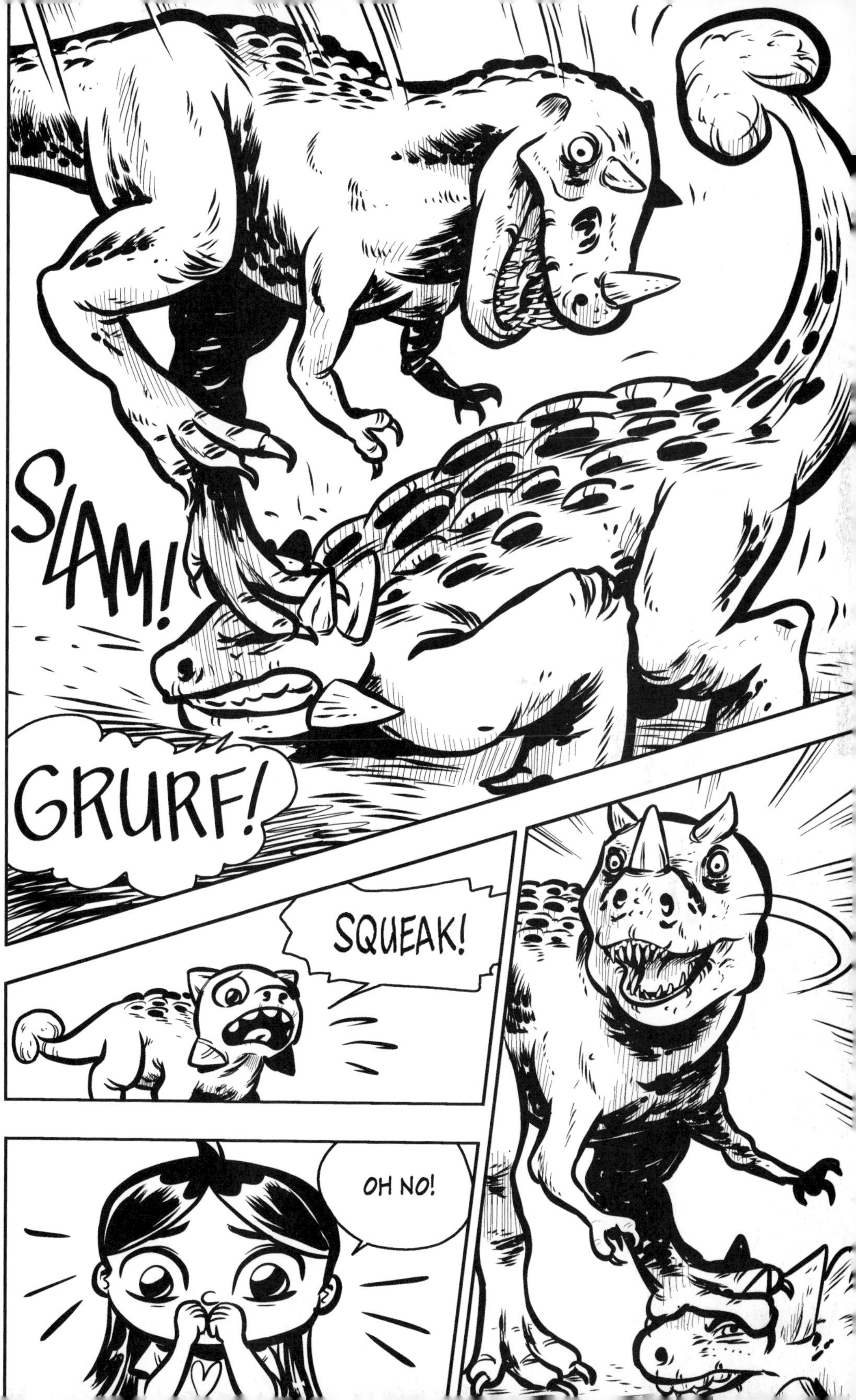
SLAM!
GRURF!
SQUEAK!
OH NO!

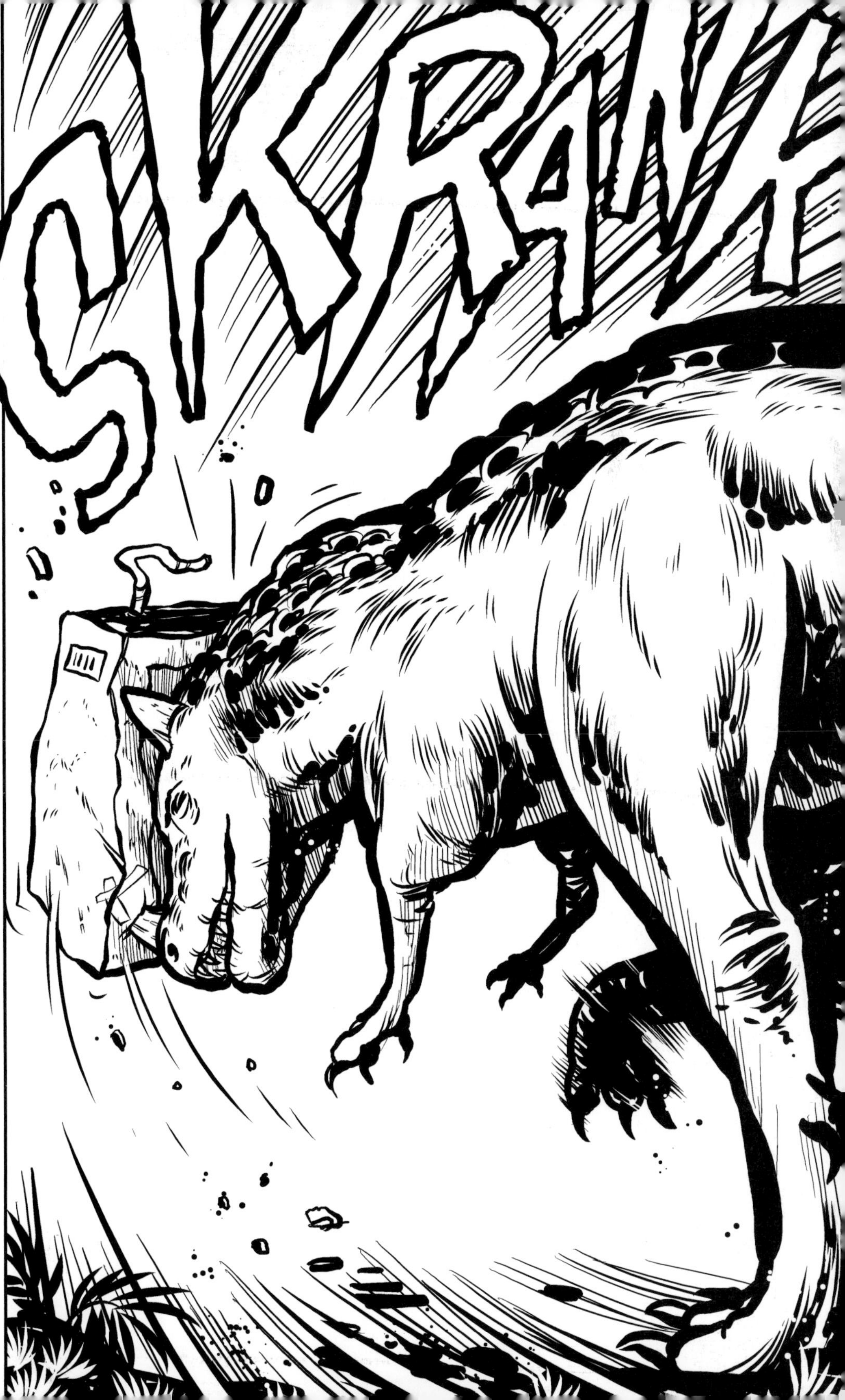
SKRAN

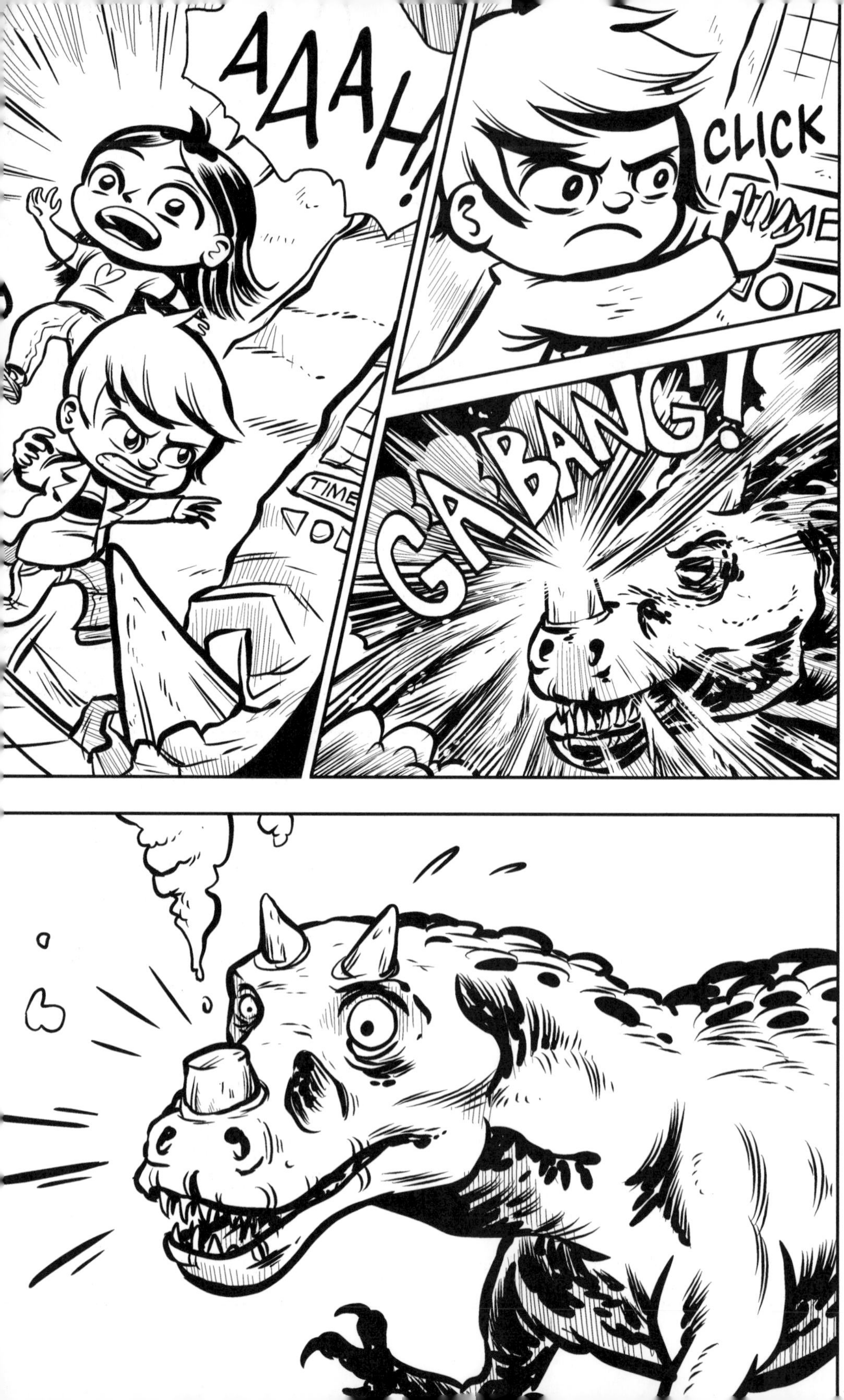
AAAH!
TIME
CLICK
GABANG!

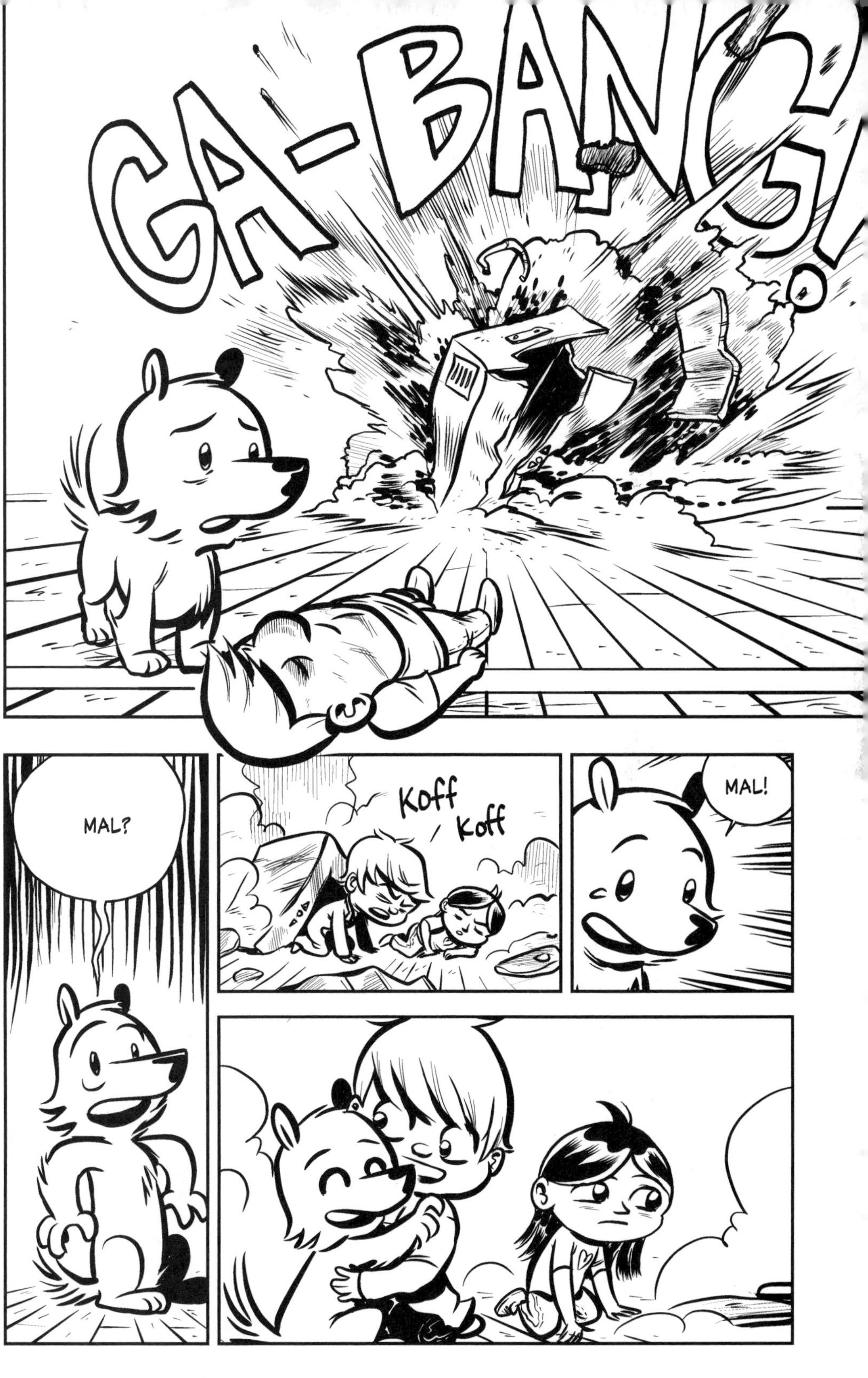
GA-BANG!
MAL?
Koff
Koff
MAL!

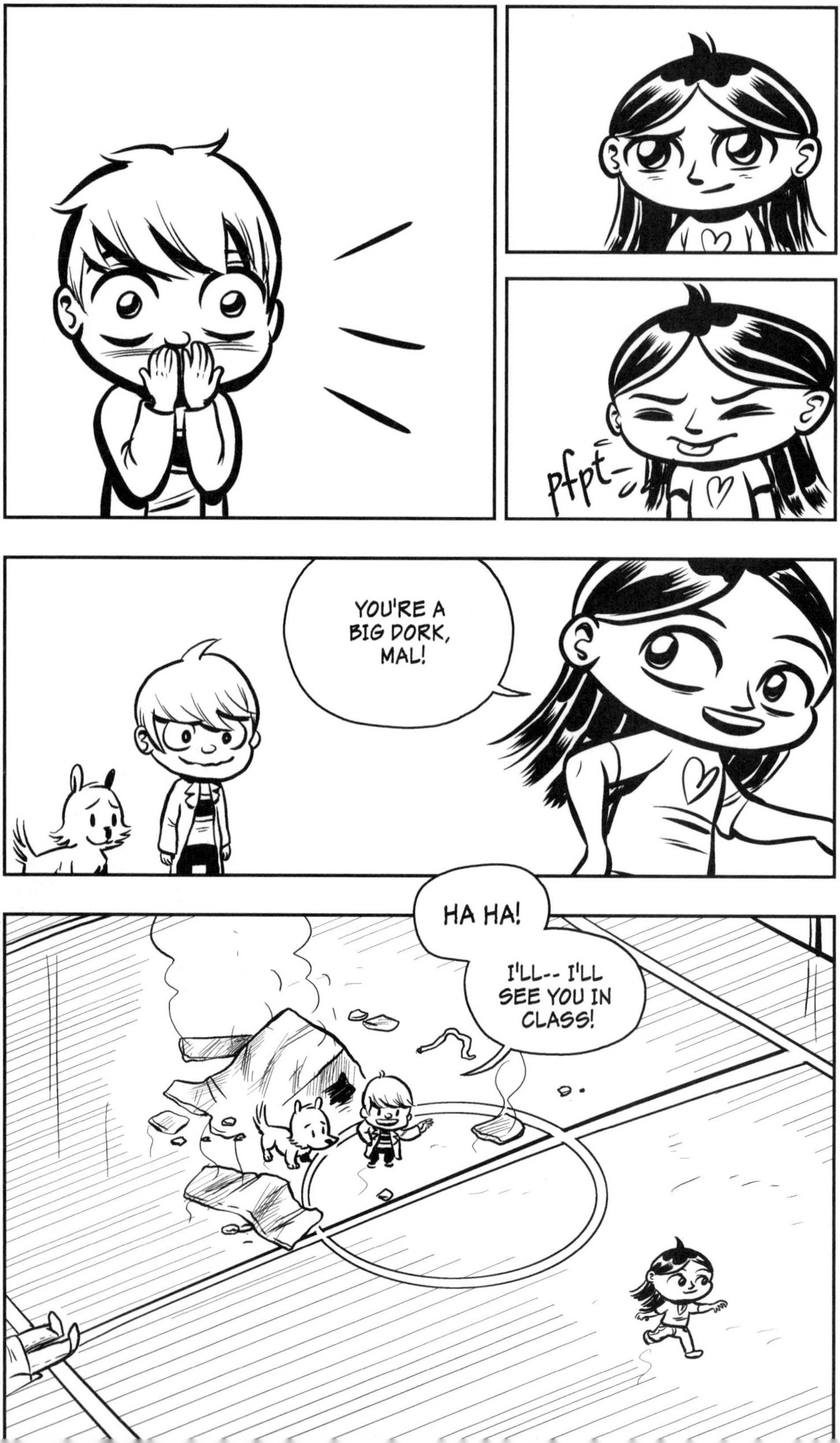
pfpt
YOU'RE A BIG DORK, MAL!
HA HA!
I'LL-- I'LL SEE YOU IN CLASS!

CHAPTER 9
The Biggest, Bestest Day

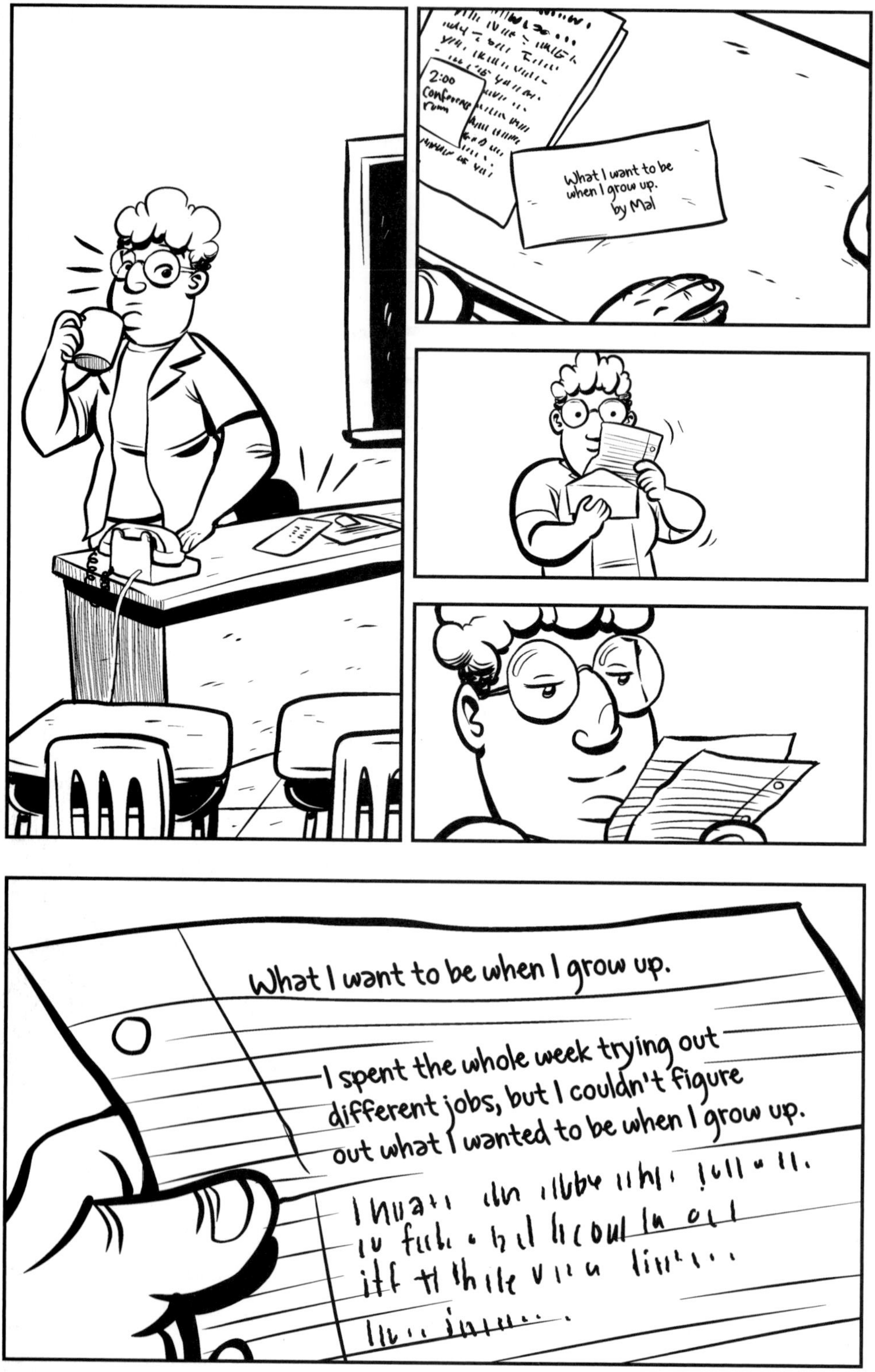

2:00
What I want to be when I grow up. by Mal
What I want to be when I grow up.
I spent the whole week trying out different jobs, but I couldn't figure out what I wanted to be when I grow up.

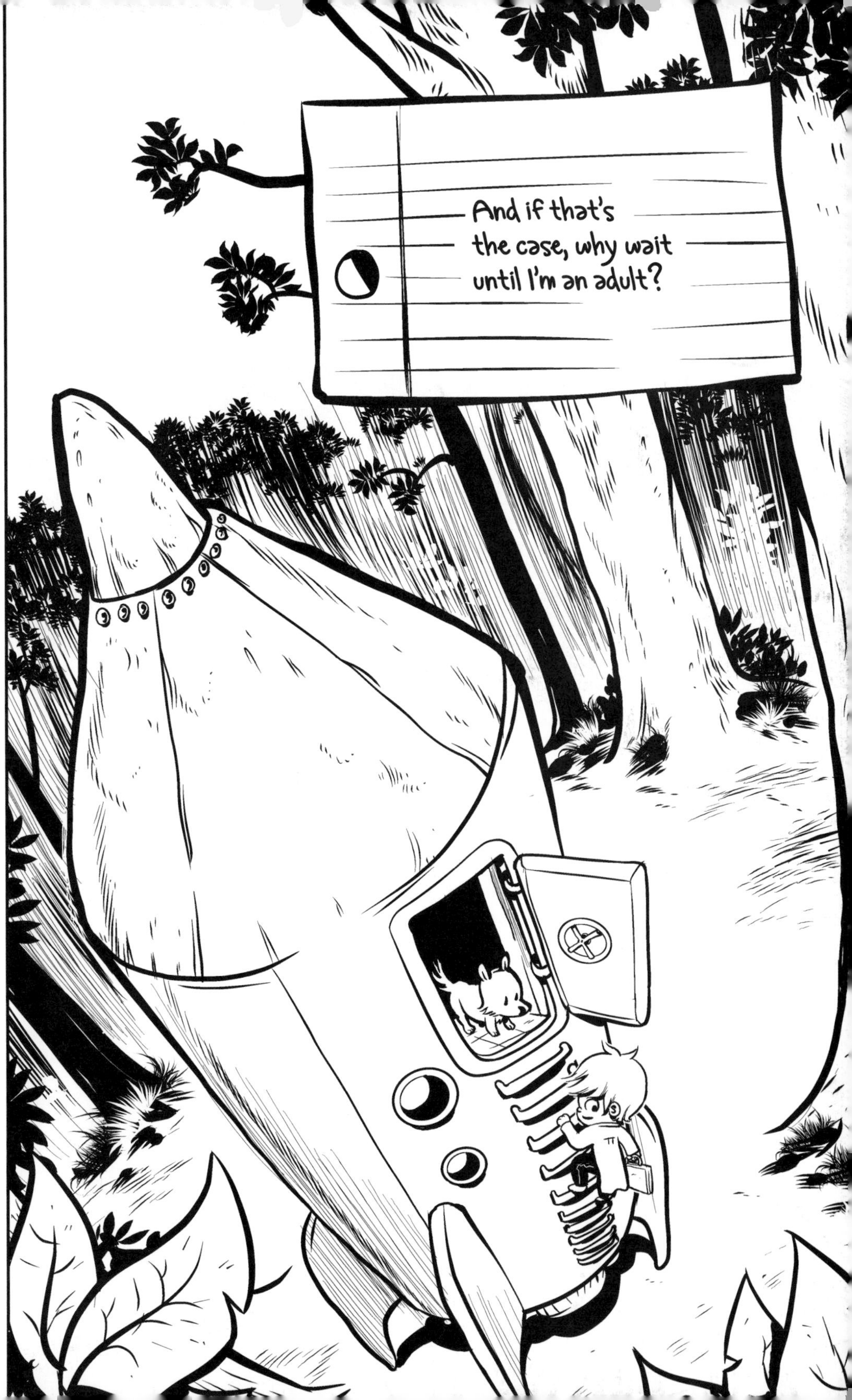
And if that's the case, why wait until I'm an adult?

the
end

For more fun, visit MalandChad.com,
and be on the lookout
for their next all-new book!

Stephen McCranie resides in New Mexico, working out of his apartment bedroom. He has been drawing comics since before he knew how to write, and the volume of Mal and Chad you are currently holding is his first published book. Stephen originally created Mal and Chad as a comic strip for his college newspaper. You can read this strip in its entirety, as well as find other fun stuff, at www.malandchad.com.